SEASON OF HOPE

Also by Anne Schroeder

Central Coast Series

Maria Inés

The Caballero's Son

Palomita: Dove of the Gabilans

Cholama Moon

SEASON OF HOPE
FIELD OF PROMISE
BOOK II

ANNE SCHROEDER

Season of Hope
Paperback Edition
Copyright © 2024 Anne Schroeder

CKN Christian Publishing
An Imprint of Wolfpack Publishing
701 S. Howard Ave. 106-324
Tampa, Florida 33609

cknchristianpublishing.com

Paperback ISBN 978-1-63977-492-0
eBook ISBN 978-1-63977-491-3
LCCN 2023951026

SEASON OF HOPE

Chapter One

Jacob Ruth kept his eyes fixed on the familiar path he walked across his brother's farm, trying to ignore the ache in his belly. Not jealousy, he assured himself. Envy was a sin that must be confessed at service on Sunday and John was entitled to the family farm—firstborn, like the Bible instructed. The pain consuming him today was of another kind. Across his brother's field, a huge maple-shaded Amanda Miller's white clapboard house, its squat door and two windows grinning like the carved jack-o'-lantern displayed in Good's Mercantile window each October.

Jacob glanced around the yard for signs of activity, a habit he'd worked to shake since the time he returned from a winter's work in Florida. He'd ridden home from Sarasota with the other Amish fellows at the end of March to find his Englischer neighbor's house empty. Memories of her fine laughing eyes and her ready smile lived behind the simple framed windows, memories to make a Plain boy doubt his decision to remain in the community.

With a shrug of disgust, he turned to his horses and took up the reins. *Some fine Pennsylvania Dutchman I make, pining for something that must be put aside. It is hard labor I need. Hard labor and a disciplined mind.*

Ahead of him, his father's trusty Belgians strained under the weight of the cultivator's load. "Step up, Fiddler, Deacon." The big draft horses started forward; their creaking leather harnesses as familiar as his mamm's shushing at Sunday service. *Hot business, but necessary. John expects a good harvest when he returns.* At the end of the row, he called a halt, shaking numbness from his fingers as he groped for the mason jar that held his mother's lemonade.

The dinner bell rang as he made the turn. *Time and enough for a meal.* He unharnessed the horses and let them drink before sloshing his neck and armpits to rid himself of the morning's work. He toweled himself off and started toward the house, careful to stomp his boots on the coil mat before entering the back door. He made it to the table in time for his father's blessing. The morning's work had taken its toll. His stomach rumbled loudly as he bowed his head in silent prayer. His younger *bruder,* Samuel, looked up and grinned as their *daed* declared, "Amen."

When the chicken and egg dumplings reached him, Jacob heaped his plate and passed the platter down the table. By the time it reached the younger children, the dumplings were almost gone. He winked at Samuel and teased, "Don't get bent out of shape. Workers eat first here on the Ruth farm. That's the way of it."

They ate in silence until their father swirled the last of his bread across the plate to sop up the gravy, gave a loud belch and looked up. When the sound of clicking forks stilled, Mamm carried in a pie topped with fresh cream from yesterday's milking. The scent of citrus and butter caught him in a sudden, unbidden memory that forced his eyes shut in pain. *Key lime.* His throat closed in protest while his mind raced to forget. "Where did you find the makings for this, Mamm?" he asked. "Seems more fit for a wedding than for us poor field folk."

"Mamm says we can plant a lime tree," Samuel volunteered. "But it needs to stay in the kitchen all winter against the frost."

The first bite lodged in his throat as he recalled the Englischer girl who had spent the year living alone in the Miller house down the road. She had made him this pie, served it in a skimpy dress that caught the candle glow, her teasing words and soft smiles trapping him like a deer in the lantern light, nearly lost. He shook his head and shifted his thoughts to the image of Katie Melvin, the girl from his community he'd begun courting after Amanda left. When the effort of forgetting failed, he set his fork down and pushed his chair back. "Best get myself back to the task before Fiddler gets restless."

By the end of the day, his straw hat was soaked in sweat, his hands blistered, and his back strained from the tug of the cultivator through the stubborn water hemp and pigweed grown to the underbelly of his draft horses. He fought the deep roots until sweat carved a channel down the back of his homemade shirt, and his lungs wheezed with pollen dust. But his mind was clear —at least until he glanced over at the neighboring house again, hoping for a familiar lamp in the upstairs bedroom.

On his way into the kitchen with a bucket of milk for household use, he kept his head down to stave off a lecture for some imagined sin his father would point out if he didn't keep his thoughts hidden. He set the bucket on the counter and chucked his mother under the chin. "Meatloaf sandwiches and applesauce for supper again?" he teased.

His mother shrugged him off with feigned impatience, but the smile on her lips betrayed her. "Be grateful you don't be eating with the hogs," she returned. "Cores and peels for you, instead. It's a grateful man who gives thanks when he's well off, son. Now wash your hands and have a grateful heart."

After supper, he gave into Samuel's pestering for a game of softball with their youngest brother, Young Levi. He swung and tapped a ball into the vegetable patch. As he waited for his brothers to find it, the shifting dusk caught his attention and he looked around, capturing the neat farmyard as a tenuous thing, apt to fly from his recollection like fireflies released from a jar. Through the open window, lamplight lit the living room while his father read from *The Ohio Farmer* and smoked his pipe. Mamm sat at her rocking chair, darning woolen socks as was her wont. Nothing out of the ordinary, but an image for tucking away.

He turned back, his heart filled. "Toss the ball, bruder. I don't get any younger, waiting on you!"

❦

On Sunday, the first preacher recited a passage he'd memorized from the tattered Bible that the *Ordnung* required. The quaint, old-German language used in the

Bible was losing favor as fewer and fewer among them knew to read the words. Some preferred an English version at home, but the rule was set. Only the quaint old German allowed in church.

Later, the third preacher spoke from the heart without using notes while the men nodded in agreement. "Labor is necessary to our people. This is what Gott requires. Work is our path through errant judgment and sinful deeds." Jacob stifled a yawn and looked down at his shoes. The preacher continued. "Hard labor is a right-good solution to lustful thoughts that plague our young men and women at night when the house is quiet and fathers snore in the beds."

The congregation snickered, and Jacob gave a quick glance at his father. Nothing new, the same warning repeated every time. Only the preacher was new, a fellow chosen from among them by lot to fill out the number. Jacob had been among the congregation when the new preacher was chosen. Three men reluctantly set their Bibles in a row on the table. Someone placed a slip of paper into one, and the books were mixed up to allow Gott's will the choosing. A moment later, Bruder Miller's smile turned to a dark scowl when he opened his Bible and found the slip of paper. Miller wasn't so good at public speaking. He only repeated words he'd heard some other preacher say, sometimes under his breath as though he wasn't sure. Now he would serve until his dying day. *No getting out of that one.*

The long service dragged this morning. Jacob mouthed a hymn without enthusiasm, his mind captured by the image of the Englischer girl he'd brought to the service the previous year. Amanda Miller—would her name ever fade from his memory?

When the service ended, he was careful to keep his jokes hearty and his teasing impersonal, lest one of the unmarried girls take his smiles to heart. When it was time for the bachelors to take their seats at the table, after the oldsters had finished, he filled his plate with fried apple fritters, ham, scalloped potatoes and the fixings from two-dozen bowls and jars, some holding pickles and red beets. He scanned the table crowded with custard, pumpkin, shoofly, and apple pies, and chose a half-moon pie and a slice of apple-filled schnitz. A lilting voice behind him caused him to turn.

"Jacob, are you still wearing that store-bought aftershave? Time you were letting your beard grow like a decent married fellow."

He looked up to find one of the married girls he'd known since they were both *kinder,* too young for school. Across the yard, her husband Johnny approached with his plate overflowing.

Jacob grinned. "Regina Byler. You baked the schnitz pie?"

She nodded and slipped into a seat next to him, with a quick glance to see that no one had overheard. "Jacob Ruth, when do you settle into baptism and join us? I remember when we began our rumspringa. You and Johnny, the others and me, we run around like hooligans every weekend while our folks slept. But most of us decided it was just plain stupid, all that beer we drink. Only to wake up sick and *stomack-sour* the next morning and not able to remember what we did the night before." She patted his hand and leaned in closer while her toddler clambered to be let up. She pulled the little boy into her arms without breaking her train. "It's time you accept the Believer's baptism, Jacob. Johnny and me, we already have the two little ones." She smiled at the boy who reached for the ribbon of her *kapp* before she glanced down at the desserts piled on Jacob's plate. "If you announce your wedding, I will bake a schnitz pie for your *Eck* table. Just for you."

He looked past her to her husband and scowled. "Your wife delivers the message, ja?" He turned back to her and shrugged. "Who knows? Maybe you save some dried apples this season, just in case!"

She attempted to curb her son's fidgeting. When she looked up again, she had a gleam in her eyes. "Oh, Jacob, such good news! I tell no one. But my heart is happy for your mother's sake. She worries for you."

He picked up a slice of bread and slathered it with butter as she made her way to where another young mother washed plates and forks for the hungry women and children who waited their turn to eat. She whispered something to her friend, and they both turned toward him.

So much for secrets. He took a bite. A moment later, his eyes slammed shut in appreciation. A slab of fresh-baked pie and a cup of coffee in the company of his friends was welcome compensation for the three hours he'd just spent on a hard, backless church bench.

On Monday, he was reminded of the preacher's words as he retraced his steps to the fields. His brother was still away, his time spent with his new wife's people. It wouldn't be long before John returned to take over the farm.

Jacob made a mental list of the tasks that he had already finished, but he was hard-pressed to add to it. The buildings had gotten their coat of whitewash even before it was his family's turn to host the Sunday service next month. Fresh-picked cucumbers filled bushel baskets for Mamm's busy hands. Still, his body burned with restless energy. The preacher claimed hard labor was the solution. If his aunts would not think it odd, he might even take a turn with the sad irons they used to press the bed sheets flat.

His mother kept a tight eye on him this morning. Perhaps she had heard some gossip from Regina Byler, because she followed him to the porch and quietly fussed with a bushel basket of green beans that needed stringing. Her back was giving her problems this morning; pain pursed her lips together even as she ran a light hand over her spine in a poor attempt to dismiss her discomfort.

"Bad today, Mamm?"

"Oh shoosh! Not so much. A sacrifice to give back to the Lord is all."

He grinned. "You think the Lord wants your bad back?"

Her eyes shone with joy, even as her face twitched when a muscle spasm hit. "Enough talk of my infirmities. What has the Lord in store for my Jacob is what I pray about. So much goodness in that sweet face. Such strength in those hands. It wonders me. Surely the Lord has great things planned for you. Plans for you ta prosper and not ta harm you, plans ta give you a hope and a future."

Jacob dawdled over the door latch and weighed his words. "Ja, but what talents? Surely not my love of art, my camera or the photographs of nature. That is all behind me now."

She looked relieved. "I'm thankful for that, Jacob. I have enjoyed these months without your brother John about. Often, he seems to breathe the air for both of you." She glanced back into the noisy kitchen and continued. "It has been good to share coffee after supper, on the porch with you, even with the mosquitoes and the chiggers."

He understood the lesson in her words. And he was of the same mind. In her gentle, calm manner, freed from her husband's correction, she'd recalled moments from her girlhood with him. Always before, it was his father and brother John who dominated the table talk after the supper dishes were cleared and the coffee drained. Alone, with his father inside reading the paper, his mother blossomed in a garden of insight and wisdom.

He glanced into the house before he spoke. He would miss talking with her like this. Not too many opportunities for heart-to-heart talk once he took the baptism and married. Probably none at all. Too soon he would be expected to talk with only the men, and work would be all they shared.

"Mamm? Do you take all the bishop's words to heart? Do you ever feel the doubt like I do?"

She glanced inside, where her husband was still reading. "Hush. You want us all under the *Bann*? You know better than to raise doubts. We must obey the Ordnung. No excuse to shirk our duty there."

He let the matter drop. "Tomorrow, the off-week. No Sunday service. I will enjoy a day to myself."

"Can you take me with you?" Samuel waited eagerly at the door.

Jacob grinned and reached to tousle his bruder's hair, quick to recoil with a dramatic grimace of faked pain when his brother boxed his arm. "And in two years, when you have your own buggy, will you haul me around on your free Sunday?"

Samuel shook his head. "Nee, I will visit girls and find a wife. And I will have a farm like our bruder John."

"Well see then, I am justified. But I take you to the feedstore when next I go, ja?"

❦

On Monday, Jacob staggered down the stairs and repressed a yawn. His mother frowned as she served him a heaped plate of ham, eggs, biscuits, grits, and gravy. "Jacob, I will surely be glad ta see your marriage date set. The bachelors, they try to fit too many hours into their free day." She set the skillet on the table. "Even the long drive home from your hoedown in the dark brings dangers from Englischer drivers."

His scowl gave credence to his sour mood.

"Our ways have taken hold. Let the boy be," Levi cautioned. "At his bruder's wedding, he went to the table with the other eligible young men. One day soon, he will make the Believer's baptism and choose a wife. Better ta get the work from him while he is still under our roof, as the Lord provides."

No secrets among this community. Jacob ducked his head while his bruders smirked at his embarrassment.

Levi Ruth returned to his newspaper. "I read news that the state court in Kentucky does not budge. But the Swartzentruber congregation, down in Graves County, stand firm. The leaders are set that the orange reflectors on the back of the buggies violate their beliefs."

"What's the problem? We use them," Jacob grumbled.

"Our community has prayed over this. Each ta their own conscience. If Gott protects them on the public roads, then there is no need for the State of Kentucky to interfere."

"What will happen?"

"What happens to us all? Jail, fines, trouble from the outside authorities. Those believers will weather this trial the same as every other. To suffer the pangs of persecution is good for our souls."

"And if they lose?" Samuel listened with wide eyes.

Levi shifted his newspaper. "They will leave Kentucky. As some left Pennsylvania, years back. It is our lot ta be persecuted. Makes us fit for the Kingdom."

"They could use gray reflective tape and hanging lanterns, the same as others do," Jacob mumbled.

"We do not question a man's convictions. That is for the bishop to decide." His father's stern look brooked no interference. Jacob rose, pulled his hat from the hook and started to the door.

"Can I come with you?" Samuel asked.

"Nee. You have school. Your time to put in long hours will come soon enough." Jacob strode out past the yard and pulled a manure fork from the rack near the huge double doors of the new barn. Since the day his father's barn burned to the ground, two other neighborhood barns had burned as well. One was Amish, one belonged to an English farmer, but The Ruth family had helped with the rebuilding of both. Gott did not ask for a man to love only his friends, but to love strangers as well. The preachers were clear on this.

Jacob forked dirty straw into the back of his father's

farm wagon to curb the tangle of thoughts that occupied him today. Conformity seemed to be more important than conscience. Some of his friends argued that works had taken the place of faith. Maybe they were right. Was a man forbidden to love an outsider? His grave sin, an Englischer girl who wreaked havoc on the mind when a fellow's thoughts strayed to her? In the quietness of the barn he repeated his vow once more. He would bow to the rein for the sake of conformity. He would not love Amanda Miller.

His mind was still tangled in thought while he drove into town later that day to pick up a late shipment of seed that had arrived at the farm supply. At a bend in the road where thick trees shaded a patch of poison ivy, a car narrowed the distance behind him and raced its engine in impatience. He reined hard to the right and felt the buggy lurch as the horse carried the buggy off the road. In the next instant, the car's taillights froze and the car spun in a half circle onto the shoulder.

"What now?" Jacob bore on the reins and fought for control as his horse dragged the buggy into a patch of green on the side of the road. When the buggy came to a stop, he jumped down and made his way to the front to run his hands over Yankee's forelegs. Satisfied, he turned to the high school-aged boy who had jumped from his car, and a girlfriend clad in skimpy shorts and a tank top, both looking around as though they expected him to remedy their foolishness. He slapped his hat against his leg to ease the harsh words that threatened his better judgment.

"Are you okay?"

"Yeah, we good. Sorry about that." The driver looked over with a grin. "Gnarly, dude!"

"Ja, *gnarly*. So I pay the price for your recklessness," Jacob mumbled under his breath.

He led his horse through a tangle of blackberries and poison ivy, across a drainage ditch, and back onto the road where he could check for wheel damage. When he straightened, the strangers had already climbed back into their vehicle. The girl gave a flutter wave as the car fishtailed in the deep ruts on its way onto the paved road. Jacob wiped away a splatter of mud before he climbed back into his buggy.

By the time he arrived home, tiny blisters had formed on his wrists and ankles where his trousers had ridden up in the poison ivy. He shook his head in disgust. It seemed that no part of him would escape the itching in store for him tomorrow. His mother was next door with Grossmummi Sarah who was ill with a summer cold. She had taken supplies with her; the VapoRub was absent from its place on the shelf, and the echinacea drops as well. He searched his mother's larder for a lemon and squeezed it into a small bowl before he added enough witch hazel to make a solution. He rubbed it on and muttered, "What is it the Englisch say, 'no good turn goes unpunished'?"

An old copy of the *Budget* lay on the table where someone had left it, probably intended for use on the dirty windows, later. He scanned the newspaper for news that he hadn't already heard from gossip. Ura Bylers from their community had welcomed a new son into the family. *Four boys already!* He and Ura shared a bench at the back of the service when they were kinders. They had begun their rumspringa together as rebellious sixteen-year-olds. He attended Ura's wedding to Esther Bontranger at her uncle's place, two years later. Now they had four, and the couple still young enough to have eight more kinder besides.

He ruffled through community reports that all sounded the same: tulips and crocus bloomed here, snow and ice still claimed winter in Missouri communities. Balmy sunshine in Belize. The correspondence was mostly written by women, with the names repeated so many times that it seemed like one big family. "*John Millers* attended a wedding and *Johns* stayed behind to visit her sister." He read the announcement through the eyes of Amanda Miller. What would an Englischer girl think, to be referred to as *Jacobs?* He stifled a smile as he considered her reaction. All of her efforts to graduate college for naught if she lived in the shadow of her husband. Not the Englischer way, for sure. She was probably well-rid of him.

His mood was no lighter the next morning, so he grabbed a cup of coffee without greeting his mother and started outside to start the milking. Daed's arthritis troubled him this morning, but even in pain he was outdoors. Jacob could ill afford to remain indoors, even though the milking and wash-up would be handled by the youngsters before they set off to school. Samuel was twelve now, already muscled and fit as a man. He had been washing down the teats and udders before each milking since the time he was five. Each day, he rushed home eager to do his part. As soon as he finished eighth grade, the boy would work full time on the farm.

A line of cows filed into the barn as his father approached. Limping from pain and aggravation, Levi latched a headstall and started toward the next. He muttered the same stale sermon as he banged the metal gates shut. In the early days, even his mother helped out with the milking, before her sons grew old enough to replace her.

Jacob's wool gathering came to a close when he heard his father's voice.

"Jacob, it is good you come to the common road. To make the Believer's baptism and set aside the wild oats!"

Jacob met his father's gaze over the back of a waiting cow. "Ja. Only one class meeting left. You and Mamm will be glad to see me stand the service." He straightened from his milking stool before he moved onto the last cow. A year ago, he would have reacted in anger. But he had thought hard about his future. Katie Melvin was a steady member of the community. They were secretly courting and she was in agreement to marriage. "We meet next Sunday—Arlis Miller's? I make sure to be there. Maybe I stand and make a little speech!" He hoped his words to his father sounded casual.

The milking done, his father rose and strode from the barn, satisfaction lifting his feet until he seemed to glide across the gravel, his limp gone. Jacob worked in silence, sorting the milk cans while his brothers cleaned the stalls. In the distance, the last cow disappeared into the pasture.

Outside, a white van pulled up, the driver's seat occupied by a corpulent, middle-aged man with sea-blue eyes that crinkled in a constant smile. The Mennonite driver tooted his horn and sat with the engine running while three women from their community chattered in the seats behind him, their laps filled with baskets.

Jacob waved on his way into the house. "Best get a

move on it, Mamm. You waste Bruder Eberly's morning," he teased. He carried his mother's woven basket to the van and handed it in, but not before he reached under the toweling and grabbed two fried donuts. The scent of cinnamon and sugar filled the air.

The driver accepted one with a nod. "*Wunderbaar gute.*"

Jacob nodded. His favorite were the raised donuts, made at Christmas with the windows clouded with steam, a fire in the hearth and family members who shared the kneading and shaping of dough before each was shaped and fried in lard, and the centers filled with rich creamy custard. Already, his mouth watered with anticipation.

From the door Jacob munched on a cinnamon donut as the gaggle of white caps inside the van pulled out into the road. No matter how much a man might envy such a fine automobile, a carload of chattering women was not to his taste. Women bound for a gathering of their friends, for quilting and singing hymns. His mother and grandmother were much loved members of the community. They would never know a life without sisters to console them in times of sorrow. For a moment he tried to imagine what it might be like to live among strangers. Good and bad. The chance to find his own course, but also the need to face mistakes alone. There seemed to be no right answer.

His gaze shifted to the lofty barn and silo looming over the farm. Above him, a layer of stippled clouds laced the sky like a barista's swirl on a cup of Englisch coffee he indulged in on rare trips to Medina.

"You intend to finish the field today?" Behind him,

his father poured himself a cup of coffee to settle his donut.

"Yep." Jacob waited for the complaint that would surely follow. But for once his father made an allowance. "You keep up the work for your brother, One day you may earn a farm like this one."

Earn, but not be given it like John. The thought gnawed at him like a worm. Not the firstborn—always a reminder that he was the second son, tasked to serve his family until John returned. Then he would be expected to leave and find a place in the world without harboring malice toward a favored brother was a tall order, but one that was expected of him. He understood, but discontent niggled at the back of his mind, a sin that must be confessed in front of the community. A glance at his father confirmed his suspicion that he had over-stepped their fragile peace.

"See that the horses get a good ration of oats when you finish with them. Good draft horses don't grow on trees."

"Ja. Don't get bent out of shape. I know to do this since I was a *kind*," Jacob mumbled as slipped his feet into a pair of rain boots and shut the door behind him.

On his way back from the field at the end of the day, he paused to give Yankee a handful of oats from the bag he fed the two big draft horses. His lanky buggy horse, a retired thoroughbred he'd picked up from a broker for its proud spirit and high tail, was the one treasure he owned: a beautiful work partner as well as friend. The two of them had learned what was expected of each other. They shared a bond.

In the house, his father suffered from nerve pain and gout that troubled his feet. Each night he grimaced as he pulled off his hard-soled shoes so that he could rub the sore feet and fallen arches. A ready sacrifice for a life spent farming with horses. Tonight, stiff-lipped irritation brought a wave of tension to his father's face, in spite of his attempt to hide his pain. His father had appealed to the Ordnung, but the community stood in agreement that no man should ease his pain with a pair of cushioned athletic shoes. "Better that a man endure for the sake of his mortal soul," someone had asserted, and the others stalwartly agreed. After dinner, Mamm rubbed her husband's feet. Their night table held an apothecary's trove of home remedies and tinctures that only partially alleviated the misery.

Another memory seeped into Jacob's brain, unbidden. The sleek night table in Amanda Miller's bedroom had held a collection of perfumed lotions and powders intended for beauty, not pain. Englischers didn't work as hard. They used their heads instead of their muscles —a character flaw in his father's mind. But he wasn't so sure. He glanced down at his own feet and gave a silent prayer of thanks that his time for suffering was still many years off.

Chapter Two

❧

A husband, a life mate. *If a girl is lucky enough to find both, she's to be envied.* The thought coming out of nowhere crumpled Amanda in the tractor seat as she gripped the steering wheel and drove blindly to the end of the row. The rubber band on one of her auburn pigtails slipped loose from the hasty braid she'd fastened that morning before she plopped on a limp, floppy hat that she'd worn since forever. With a backhanded flap, she swiped the hair from her face, but not quickly enough to avoid a near-miss with the greenhouse wall.

"Hey, watch what you're doing!"

Her father's warning jolted her from her reverie. Adrenaline shot through her while she carefully realigned the nozzle of the irrigation sprayer on the Kubota tractor. A fog of mist evaporated harmlessly into the air. A trio of hired laborers stared at her, their laughter and gestures accompanied by their Spanish remarks. She shook herself and took a white-knuckle grip on the steering wheel in time to save the gate, while the hum of the tractor's engine nearly obliterated her father's voice.

"You okay, sweetheart?"

She gave him a weak smile. He would accuse her of woolgathering, his favorite word for her daydreams. She took a deep breath and found her voice. "Depends. What's your definition of okay? Still got my legs and arms—so I guess so."

"What was that? I didn't hear you."

She shook her head. "Never mind." Today was not a good day. *Keep the bad stuff to yourself, girl. Just handle it.* No reason to dredge up the past.

"Peanut, shut the tractor down. I need to talk to you."

Her father slouched beside the equipment shed, clad in his worn red-plaid work shirt with two buttons missing. He wore his green trademark baseball cap emblazoned with the words *Miller Wholesale Nursery*, but underneath, his hair needed a trim. His eyebrows had taken on a life of their own; twin bushy tufts that sharpened his piercing-blue eyes and made furrows of the new frown lines etching his face. He'd aged in the past year. She studied him from the seat while the tractor vibrated with a familiar, comforting hum, pulling with it the memory of childhood. During her teen years she'd spent hours helping him with the chores while he kept a watchful eye for any "glitch in her hitch," as he liked to call her mistakes. *Nothing new there.* But when had he let himself go? She'd been so preoccupied with her own grief that she hadn't noticed.

She ignored his glare and backed the tractor into a slot among a jumble of implements and attachments. The shed was a money pit, filled with every gadget a commercial nurseryman could ever need. His nursery business had become a distraction. After her mother was injured, his lifeline.

She cut the engine and climbed down while he studied her with a penetrating look of concern. "School starts soon, hey, Peanut?"

"Two weeks. But don't worry. We'll be ready to ship, no problem." She picked at a loose thread on her leather glove and waited to hear what was on his mind.

"Sounds like you've got it calculated down to the minute." His hooded eyes posed a question.

She shrugged and managed a weak grin. "So much to think I might fool anybody, huh, Dad? I've been rehashing my life."

"Disappointments? Part of life's path. We get knocked down, we get back up again. You know that." He peeled off a pair of well-worn elk skin gloves and massaged his gnarled fingers. "Remember, what—"

"I know. What doesn't kill us makes us stronger." She gave him a gentle poke. "How many times have I heard that one?"

His wry grin softened the intensity of his face. "You have your mother's heart, Peanut. You're gonna be just fine."

Mention of her mother brought a familiar pain. "I miss her so much."

"I miss her, too. But I'm glad for her sake. You should be, too." He studied the horizon. "She's free now. No more wheelchairs. No paraplegia. No limitations."

She followed the direction of his gaze. "Dad, I never told you this...but when you finally hired a home health aide, I was relieved. It wasn't just us anymore. You took me to gymkhanas again. And every summer when Aunt Lydia came to visit..."

They walked together into the sunlight, her dad squinting until he straightened and his shoulders eased his tension. "Your mom's accident was a wrencher. But there was no reason to feel guilty. You were a little girl living under tough circumstances."

"I thought God would punish me for my evil thoughts." She was gratified by the understanding in his eyes.

"Your mom used to say she failed you, Peanut." His eyes held a sheen of dampness she hadn't seen since the day they buried her mother.

"Dad...she was dying when I left, wasn't she?"

"Oh, honey—"

"Tell me, Dad. I have the right to know."

"Doc said she had a few months." His answer was so strained she could barely hear it.

A few months? "Why didn't you tell me? I would've come home." And done what, reneged on Lydia's offer? Why had her aunt's Will put her in such an untenable position—that her niece must live in the house for twelve months or relinquish the inheritance? The answer brought a bolt of understanding. Because Lydia hadn't known either.

"Your mom didn't want you to worry. Her dignity was all she had to offer. Allowing you leave for Ohio gave her that."

"I thought I was taking care of her. But all that time she was the one who cared for me. I was so selfish."

Her dad grimaced. "I accused you of that when you left. And I'm sorry." His voice caught and he coughed, a short, sharp sound. "She held me to a promise. But I thought if I was rough on you, you'd stay without me having to betray her trust. Things turned out okay, though. I'd say you're right about where you should be."

She chose her words carefully. "It wasn't our fault, was it, Dad?"

Her father's look of perception unnerved her. "I wasn't sure you knew that."

She managed a wry grimace, her best imitation of a smile she didn't feel. "I guess I did, on some level. I have to believe that good will come of this. I believe that."

"Come of this? You mean your mother's passing? Or that young man who broke your heart?"

"Both." She couldn't meet his eyes, but she knew what they held. *Pity*.

He nodded. "You'll get in that classroom and you'll be too busy to give heartbreak a second thought."

She clasped his hand in hers. "There was a time you would have said 'your mistakes.'"

"People change. Even your old dad." He tugged at her pigtail under her battered straw cowboy hat. "Come on. Let's get back to work."

She pulled on her gloves and tightened her mask. "Dad, have you ever thought about growing organic?"

"Hey, don't push your luck." He winked. "When you take over the business you can make all the changes you want."

All the changes she wanted? She was drowning in change. On that day, only a month ago, she'd watched from her window as Jacob drove past her farmhouse without stopping to say goodbye. She'd seen his face, filled with anticipation of spending the winter months in Florida earning money and having fun. The following day she'd filled a rental truck with her aunt

Lydia's things, at least the stuff that would fit, especially the furniture Jacob had built for her. She'd left the big horsehair sofa and bed frames behind, and Lydia's canned peaches. The rest, she'd donated to the Mennonite Relief Fund. She'd packed Lydia's Bible, a few family treasures, three pairs of candleholders and a battered set of deerskin gloves and tried not to think about what she'd regret leaving behind.

She'd stopped by her new best friend Carol's house, and they'd promised each other to maintain a long-distance friendship, even if they couldn't manage their weekly girls' night out. They'd laughed about sharing glasses of wine and shopping excursions to Cleveland and the Amish bakeries that added to their waistlines and made them crave another slice. Carol had confided that she and her boyfriend Rennie were serious. Amanda had listened, half jealous that her best friend would get married and she'd be an old maid. Carol had teased that Amanda was too young to be an old maid, maybe just a spinster.

"I'm not even twenty-five yet," Amanda had protested. And they'd suffered hysterics until they peed —but she wasn't sure whether they were laughing or crying. She'd said goodbye and driven away. Now she was home, determined to stuff the broken bits of her heart back where they belonged.

Her excuse for leaving Ohio depended on her mood, or who she was trying to convince. *My mother was ill and needed me to come home; she passed, you know. My aunt stipulated that I needed to stay for an entire year in order to inherit her house and my time was up. My contract came through to teach fourth grade; I'd be a fool to pass that offer up. My boyfriend and I broke up. Mutual consent. Time to move on.* The truth included all four, but sometimes it was hard to sort out her priorities. And harder yet to convince her heart.

"Ready to go back to work, Peanut?"

Her father's voice caused her to smile. What was it Levi Ruth, her neighbor back in Ohio, had told his grown son when Jacob helped her out on their first meeting? *Best I hire young John Yoder to do your work. It won't be much I'll be missing by hiring a ten-year-old in your stead.* An image of Jacob standing tall and strong in front of his barn caught in her brain as she aimed the tractor toward the next row of plants.

Enough about Jacob. He chose to leave.

Chapter Three

The tang of apples simmering on the stove caused Jacob's stomach to rumble with anticipation. Church had run overlong. Only a few more minutes and his future would be set. He tried to catch his Katie's eye, but she was intent on the men and women giving their *zeugnis,* their public confession in front of the congregation asking for everyone's forgiveness, a cornerstone of their faith. Each week Katie watched and listened intently, nodding as she forgave her friends for their failings. Her heart was in the right place; she would be a good wife.

He waited his turn while his palms itched with a bad case of nerves. He and Katie would be next. He had arranged that they stand together when it came time for him to speak. They had been careful not to spend too much time alone; some of the women already suspected news of their engagement. Neighbors who passed Katie's home saw their garden already crowded with rows of celery and the barnyard filled with chickens for roasting—telltale signs of their intentions that people pretended to ignore. He wanted his announcement today to be a surprise.

He squirmed as another man began his zeugnis—a trivial matter that surely the Almighty would not consider a sin. He suspected that some of the elders invented their shortcomings to show they sought a disciplined path, more a show of their righteousness than an examination of conscience.

Across the room, Grossmummi Sarah dozed in her rocker. The chair next to her stood empty today as it had been a year ago, on the day Amanda Miller joined them. Today her image filled the chair, a reminder of the day she'd sat through the long service, unable to understand a word of their language. He hadn't considered the oversight; everyone he knew spoke their Pennsylvania Dutch dialect. She had gamely traced the words in Grossmummi's hymnal, and the Bible in its old-fashioned German. He remembered the way she mouthed the words of the hymns, as awkwardly as a child just learned English.

Amanda Miller filled his thoughts at odd times, like today when he sat in church and closed his mind to any thought except the fact that he would soon be baptized. If he forgot, the itch of his new beard reminded him. It was good that she had returned to her father's house in Oregon; it would have been harder had she stayed. But he missed their serious talks. He thought it would be the same with Katie, but already he could see it would not be so. Different does not mean worse—or better—he reminded himself. In the month that the Miller house stood empty, he had climbed through an unlatched window and walked the house. When he stared at the claw-foot tub, he recalled the night of his family's barn fire when she had filled the tub with bubbles to his neck. After he had dressed in his clean clothes, he'd crept close enough to touch her. Had watched her sleeping body rise and fall with each breath until he thought he might explode. He had not been honest when he told her he merely stood at the door.

His thoughts rebounded to the present, and he glanced across the room at Katie. She was a reminder that he and Amanda would have been unequally yoked. Englischers did not see their transgressions; for her, love included the right to find out whether they were physically suited to each other beforehand. It was good that they had halted when they did. So many times he'd struggled to set aside the passion he carried for Amanda, even before they had the right. But the sin had stuck. He would fight his memories for the rest of his life. With the Lord's help, he would apply himself to hard work and perhaps one day, when he was married to Katie and they had a family, he would forget the Englischer.

Only one more obstacle the elders required of him. Before he announced his engagement, he must give testimony of his 'sinfulness with the Englischer girl.' The thought soured his gut. He had postponed the moment until this last hour, trying to convince himself that he had truly sinned. Today, in a few minutes, he would tell the assembly that he had loved a woman who didn't share their faith. Katie already knew. *Since the time I meet her at John's wedding, I confess this. We are agreed—there should be no secrets between us. And no bundling in the darkness. That most of all.* They had made a vow to wait for marriage to be right between Gott and themselves. Sometimes it seemed as though he would break, so hard the waiting, but he had kept his promise.

He watched as his brother, John, transferred the baby to his father and stood. The fact that John felt the need of testimony surprised him. Perfect son John—what need did he have to stand and confess? Perhaps John had shined the brass on his buggy too pridefully. Or perhaps his apple trees had become unseemly with fruit this year. From the time he was a boy, everyone seemed to agree: it was the younger son, Jacob Ruth's, nature to act in ways that required forgiveness, but for John Ruth, goodness came as natural as rain.

He strained to hear his brother's words. "...it is my shame to confess this in front of my brothers and sisters, but I cannot do otherwise. When two years ago I spend the winter in Sarasota, I had no excuses. I was sure about Gott's will. I cannot say I lacked direction. But I meet a girl I knew from home. We find ourselves alone. We have each some marijuana that we buy from a man on the street, and we share a bottle of strong spirits. We try the drugs and we drink the spirits. In time I don't care that I have a girl back home in Spencerville who thinks I earn money for our wedding. My thinking is as randy as a goat's."

John straightened, but his head remained bowed. He continued in a low, monotone voice that caused everyone to lean forward to hear.

"Two times that day this girl and I, we do what is only the right of couples in their marriage bed. When we return home, twice more we do this act when we each are with someone else. It is as though we have no mind for anything but our pleasure. When I see the man she is to marry, I know the Lord has sent me a punishment. I have talked this over with my father, Levi Ruth, and he is in agreement. I must ask Gott's forgiveness...and yours...and the girl with whom I sinned..."

Surprise struck Jacob as he strained to hear his brother's words over the commotion from the women's side of the room. John looked around, but his gaze didn't include his own brother. In shock and shame for his brother, Jacob waited for John to finish. When his brother's forceful voice bellowed out his confession, the sin came unexpectedly.

"Who is soon to marry my brother, Jacob."

John and my Katie—together? Blood rushed up Jacob's neck and flooded his face. Fury blinded him until he could see no further than the sunlight that splayed through the open door. The women's side appeared in his peripheral vision. He watched his brother bow his head as the assembly anointed him with prayerful forgiveness. He watched Katie Melvin faint. Watched her father, and his, haul her out by the elbows, her heels scuffing the wooden floor and her black kapp flattened against her thick coiled hair.

John and my Katie? Fornicators. I have no forgiveness in my heart for them.

The entire fellowship shifted to watch him leave. A moment later they looked to their bishop to see how they should react. On the women's side, he saw a sea of pity and in some cases, anger and disdain, as though he deserved what he got. The same on the men's side. He saw individuals who had called him a black sheep.

Some watched impassively, already turned to console John. No one stood to stop him.

Shock rang in his ears. He fought to take a breath as he blindly made his way to his buggy and pulled up the heavy weight that tethered Yankee to the grass he grazed. The horse raised its head with a look of surprise and waited as Jacob led it in a circle to the edge of the empty lot. So many buggies, each one recognizable for the family it carried. His community. His family and friends for as long as he'd been alive. He knew each buggy blanket, the toys left behind on seats for the children to reclaim. He knew the scrapes and paint patches that told stories of collisions with Englischer automobiles and shopping carts.

He thought he knew the hearts of the men who drove the buggies, but from where he stood amid the circle of buggies and grazing horses, he felt as strange as Amanda Miller must have felt on the day she visited. With a last look at the horses, he climbed in and took up his horse's reins.

He was numb except for the roiling in his gut that sent him to the outhouse as soon as he reached his father's farm. He felt a bout of nausea and lost his breakfast. Afterward, he stared at the land as though he were a tourist visiting for the first time. The neat farmhouse, the cleanliness, the order; everything around him was an abomination. He unhitched his horse and scooped a measure of grain into a bucket. While the gelding rolled the ration of oats around in its mouth, he brushed its hide with quick, angry strokes that caused the horse to raise its head in confusion. He continued with a lighter touch, but the horse received no apology. Right-thinking and common sense dictated his actions.

He opened the gate to the paddock and slapped the gelding's flank. "*Redd up*, Yankee. You can't go with me." With a quick swipe at his blurred vision, he shifted toward the barn.

In the loft, he pulled his gunnysack from where he had hidden it on a rafter. Halfway down the ladder he let go and jumped without regard for his safety. Gott's will whether his sturdy boots would break his fall. But he was unlucky once again; he landed without mishap.

Inside the house, he paused at his mother's kitchen and glanced around at the pans and rolling pins, the worn wooden pie table, the wood-fired cookstove that had prepared their meals since he could remember. With a glance at the massive oak table that had nurtured generations of Ruths, he continued up the stairs to the room he had shared with John for twenty-three years. From his dresser he collected cash from his winter in Sarasota. He shoved it, along with his spare clothing, into the gunnysack alongside his camera and sketchpad. At the water basin he smeared shaving soap on his week-old beard and scraped it clean with a straight razor.

When he finished, he strode downstairs to where his winter hat hung. He picked it up and hung it back on the hook again. With his last remnants behind him, he opened the front door, the one his mamm saved for company. He would not use the back door with the worn threshold from decades of heavy boots that had skimmed off the finish as Ruth men came and went from work. He was no longer a family member; he would use the company door. With a last look at the farmyard, he started down the road to hitch a ride to the truck stop on Interstate 80.

Twenty minutes later, he no longer felt Amish, but he had no idea where he belonged. He paced the parking lot, unsure of his next move. When a sympathetic trucker in a battered cowboy hat asked if he wanted a ride, Jacob nodded and hopped in.

Chapter Four

❧❦❧

Amanda spent the last two weeks of October in a frenzy of craft projects and errands for her Halloween class party. Her students asked more of their teacher than Amish scholars did. Mrs. Zooks, the Amish teacher back in Ohio, with her one-room school, would have thrown up her hands at the demands thirty-four students made on one brand new teacher.

"Miss Miller? Can you tell us about your mother again? It's cool how she used a computer without any hands."

"Miss Miller! Merrilee isn't sitting down."

"Miss Miller—my mother says I'm not supposed to eat store-bought cookies unless they're on this list."

"Hey Miss Miller! B'nonce took my pencil."

"I did not. Lu Chin has it."

"Miss Miller, can we play Andy Over at recess? That game's cool. My dad won't let us play it at home 'cause of the roof peaks."

She realized she'd become a full-blown spinster one

afternoon at Target, when she bumped into one of the girls she'd gone to high school with.

"Hey, Amanda, is that you?" Her friend Melanie gave her drab maxi skirt a once-over and laughed. "Gosh, I hardly recognized you."

Amanda tried not to let her eyes linger on the tight, ripped jeans and tube top her friend wore. They might have been twins in high school, but their paths had clearly diverged since then. "Yep, it's me." She feigned a laugh. "Trying to update my wardrobe." She grabbed the first item she saw, a lime green cut-away top and tossed it in her basket. "Need some new shirts, I guess."

Melanie examined her from top to toe without easing her perfectly stenciled brows. "Amanda, what's going on with you? You don't have cancer, do you? Gosh, I'm so tactless. I hope..." She forced a laugh. "You used to be hot. What's going on? You hook up with somebody and he dumped you?"

"No one you'd know." Amanda laughed. "It's a long story. Anyway, I'm pretty busy. Teaching and all."

"How's your mom? She ever—?"

"She passed."

"Oh, sorry for your loss." Her friend looked chagrined. She backed her cart a few paces away and glanced around for an excuse. "Hey, there's my husband. I need to help him pick out a shirt—"

"Yeah, good seeing you. Maybe we should do this again sometime." Amanda waited for her to disappear around a corner before she released her breath. Social interaction had never really been her thing. Friends had visited her house, but they tended to make excuses after meeting her mother. She had some friends at school, and the inscriptions in her yearbook to prove it, but after a while it was easier to decline invitations to sleep-overs at other girls' houses and avoid the awkwardness. Melanie had tried to talk her into trying out for cheerleader in seventh grade, but she'd panicked at the idea of performing in front of the public. Instead, she'd talked her father into buying her a horse. *Napoleon.*

Spurred by curiosity and more than a little guilt, Amanda detoured on her drive home to visit her former horse. She parked alongside the road and saw the new owner racing barrels. Unless she was mistaken, the gelding was even faster than she remembered. *Napoleon's happy.* She ignored the fact that she'd nick-named her horse '*Jacob Amish*'. No more inside jokes with Jacob about our horses. She needed no more reminders of the Amishman she had lost her head over.

The next afternoon her principal, Mr. Benton, stopped by her classroom while she gathered homework to grade at home. He offered her a cheerful smile as he inspected her colorful bulletin boards and glanced at her lesson plan.

"Miss Miller, I wanted to see what you've done in here. Mrs. Sims, your master teacher, has high praise for your efforts. She claims you've incorporated some rather unorthodox methods for your students. Your...what do you call them? Your 'scholars'? A rather old-fashioned term, but it connotes an image of firmness." He extended his hand. "We're pleased to have you on staff."

Relief made her giddy. "Thank you."

"You're a natural teacher, Miss Miller. You'll do well."

She gripped her briefcase and walked beside him down the hallway while their shoes clicked staccato beats against the tile. A custodian looked up and gave a nod. A red-letter day. She reached the front door, waved to the principal and made her way to her car in the nearly deserted lot.

❧

The fall weather slipped into its final weeks and melancholy settled over the house like a well-used mop. Amanda stared out her father's living room window and watched winter stamp its mark on the fields and forests. Here and there, an evergreen tree stood sentry over the barren deciduous trees her father had planted for summer shade. Holly berries hung in red clumps along the driveway, a brilliant foil for the scarlet-colored satin ribbons she planned to hang on the front doors, once Thanksgiving was over.

Her neighbor's colts raced on the other side of the fence, tails arched, their high, graceful surges like another horse she'd watched pull an Amish buggy past a neat farm field. *Yankee.* The memory brought a surge of restlessness, but a walk down the lane seemed pointless; the ground was already patchy with ice, as the afternoon sun eased the thermometer into the low digits. In the coziness of the den, she fingered the stack of math worksheets feeding from her printer and decided she should grade the week's assignments and have an empty file for once. Another Sunday afternoon wasted; how different from the day, only a year ago, when the rain had held off long enough for a ride in an Amish buggy.

She played with her hair, twisting it into a coil that reminded her of an Amish girl's under a black Sunday kapp. As the sun dropped behind the trees, she recalled the landscape of an Ohio day while a fire crackled in Lydia's fireplace and a young farmer sat across the room in her sofa. She allowed her mind to recall Jacob in a hundred different ways.

It was November already—the season for weddings. She pictured Jacob at the reception, eating and drinking with his friends while his new wife pressed her toes against his, under the table, while they waited for their guests to leave. He would keep an eager eye on the departing guests and another on his lovely bride—if he had bothered to curb his carnal desires until after the wedding. Maybe he had forgotten his vow of celibacy and decided that his requirement for a chaste bride was negotiable.

With a sigh, Amanda shook herself out of her dark mood and resumed her grading.

⬥⬥⬥

January seemed bleaker than she remembered. Spring was still months away, too far distant to dissolve her melancholy. She attempted to watch TV, but the movie was a romantic comedy she'd already seen, and she lacked the energy for anything more intense. She clicked off the remote and made her way down the hall.

In her mother's bedroom, the hospital bed had been replaced by a queen-sized with a pretty tapestry coverlet and matching shams purchased at a brick-and-mortar close-out. She ran her fingers along the fold marks on the coverlet that no one had ever used. The room still retained the scent of baby powder. With her eyes closed, she lay on the bed and imagined the sound of her mother's agitated breathing and the hum of the respirator. The room seemed filled with her mother's presence. For a moment she was a girl again, intimidated by the machinery and desperate to have her mother's attention. Today, she clutched a decorator pillow to her cheek and imagined her mother as she typed words onto a computer screen with the aid of a laser headband that encircled her forehead.

READYTOTALK?

She didn't need to ask *About What?* Instead, she nodded.

HEHURTYOU.

She started to nod, then shook her head. "It wasn't his fault. It just happened."

TELL

She managed to choke out a few words; "I thought I could change him. That he would change for me. But he couldn't. Maybe one or two small behaviors. But not his entire world."

HEPROPOSE?

She shook her head. "N...no. He married someone else."

WHATWOULDYOUHAVESA
ID?

The image blurred in front of her. She blinked and tried to clear her voice. "I'd have told him 'no,'" she lied. "I couldn't stay. Not on his terms."

She imagined her mother's electric wheelchair

whirring across the hardwood floor and halting beside her. She remembered how it felt to brush her arm against her mother's. With eyes closed, she saw her mother's tears as she telegraphed her pity. Her mother had been an expert at analyzing life's unfairness, but for all the years she'd suffered in her frozen world, her eyes had never held the sorrow that Amanda imagined today.

She tried to speak, but the sound emerged as a sob.

She wiped her tears with the back of her hand. "It's January, Mom. He's already married." She sniffed and looked around for a tissue. "Knowing him, he signed up for the first open date they had. The first Thursday in November. That's already passed." She opened her arms and imagined her mother's thin shoulders against the breathing apparatus trying to respond. She nodded. "Yes, much better. Thank you, Mom."

In her mind, her mother's eyes darted toward a plaque that hung on the wall. "Yeah, Mom. I've read it before." In her mind, her mother frowned. "Okay, I'll read it again." Her mother's eyes pleaded. "Okay, aloud."

"Love is patient; love is kind; love is not envious or boastful or arrogant or rude. It does not insist on its own way." She paused to swallow. *"Love does not brood over injuries. Does not rejoice in wrongdoing, but rejoices in the truth. Love never ends."*

In her imagination, her mother's tears streamed down her cheeks—until she realized they were her own. She lay on the edge with just enough room to wrap her arms around her mother's imaginary form. She had always taken care to avoid the tubing, so caution today was second nature. She wondered how many hours she had spent in that position, absorbing her mother's love—not silent at all, but clear and sure and strong.

When chill drove her back into the living room, she settled in her favorite chair, in front of the fire, and pulled a soft throw over herself. A copy of Jane Kirkpatrick's latest novel about a historical Oregon heroine lay unopened on the coffee table. She picked it up, but the words blurred together. Suddenly she understood what her mother had tried to teach her about letting go. She remembered the nighttime prayer they had prayed together when she was a child, and she said the words aloud; "*Thank you, Lord, for blessings big and small. For obstacles that make me tall. For friends and family, one and all. Amen.*"

A noise in the yard broke her concentration. She set the book aside and grabbed a jacket to see what her father was up to. He was on the tractor as usual, moving pallets around to get ready for a shipment early the next morning.

"Peanut?"

With a start, she realized he was calling her name. He shut off the tractor and jumped down, tugging off his gloves as he strode toward her. She'd watched him do the same motion a thousand times, but today he seemed agitated. He began before he reached her, in a tone he usually saved for late shippers and tardy yard foremen. "Your heart isn't in this business, is it, Peanut? I had hoped when you came home last summer, everything would be settled. But it's not, is it?"

She shook her head, afraid of what was to come.

"This was a good business for your mother and me. I'd hoped it would be for you, and someday your husband."

A sudden image of Jacob on her father's tractor brought a clench of pain. A moment later she recoiled, afraid of what her father was saying. "Dad, you're not sick are you?" He shook his head. "Then what—?"

"I've got a buyer for this place," he blurted. He turned and squinted to see how she was taking his news before he added, "All of it. Lock, stock, and barrel."

"Even the house?" Her eyes felt like they were the size of saucers—she couldn't help herself. "When? How? Where would we go?" Her voice was scarcely a whisper. Her knees wanted to buckle, but she leaned against a tire and tried to act nonchalant.

"Look at it this way, Peanut. I'm not getting any younger. Your mother and I talked about this. She wanted me to see the country—all the places she and I couldn't travel to. Buy a motorhome and hit the road. Get a boat. Spend some time in seasonal RV parks. Maybe go down and visit the Keys. I can get a mail-forwarding service and a smartphone like the kids have today. Maybe even find myself a special gal. I've talked to one or two of them online. They seem nice enough." He paused. "Maybe revisit my old stomping grounds in Oregon."

"You mean Ohio?"

He smiled. "Maybe I'll meet those Ruths you think so highly of."

She hesitated. "Dad, you went to school with Levi Ruth. You remember, don't you?" Her heart slumped at the strange, uncertain expression on his face.

"Well, of course I remember." His tone seemed slightly accusative as if she were treating him like a child.

"Dad, I didn't mean anything. I just—"

Her phone buzzed. She dug it from her back pocket in time to see the caller ID. Spencerville. "Hello, Mr. Wright. How's everything back there?"

"So it's 'Mr. Wright,' is it?" The voice on the other end sounded upbeat. "What happened to calling me 'Clem'?"

"I just can't. You're my attorney."

"If your aunt Lydia had taken the plunge, I would have been your uncle. I wanted to; Lord knows." His tone shifted. "The peaches you left in the cellar were the sweetest I ever tasted. Every bite reminded me of her. I should have pressed her for an answer when I proposed."

Amanda laughed. "How's my house?"

"It misses you. Tenants keep it up okay, but they've given notice. They won't be renewing when the lease expires. The market is hot right now. They plan to buy while the market's down."

"Thanks for the warning."

After a few minutes of small talk, he came to the purpose of his call. "Amanda, I wasn't sure if you'd heard. Jacob Ruth is gone. He left home without a word. A week before he was to be married."

Her throat constricted. She swallowed with the hope that her voice didn't betray her. "Where did he go?"

"No one knows. His father and mother moved into the grandparent house after his brother arrived with the new wife and took over the farm. Appears his grandmother moved to Sarasota Springs for the winter with a sister and some of the other oldsters. But Jacob's in the wind."

She hung up as quickly as she could and shifted her

attention to where the neighbor's colts frolicked in the pasture. From the corner of her eye, she saw her father watching and her brave veneer crumbled. "He's not there, Dad. He's gone."

He gave her a pitying look, and a clumsy pat on her shoulder with his thick gloves. "Life can fool a person, Amanda. The thing is to keep the faith. If he separated from his people, you may find he's like a dry sponge, eager for change. Some of them soak up new ideas pretty quickly. He could surprise you."

She nodded. "I need to go for a jog. To clear my head."

"Sure. Just watch out for the ice. Pasture can be slick."

She stuffed her phone into her pocket and faced him. "Dad, don't do anything rash, okay? Let's think this selling idea through."

He looked surprised. "Who said anything about selling?"

She caught herself before she blurted out her surprise. Was he having a senior moment?

On her way out the door, she rang the first number on her speed dial. "Carol, you busy? I need a shoulder right now. You available? Good. Hey, I have some news. My attorney, Mr. Wright, just called."

Carol's voice filled the phone. "Uncle Clem. He's my fiancé's uncle. Did you ever consider, if he'd married your aunt Lydia, he'd be your uncle? Instead, if Rennie ever pops the question, he'll be mine. By marriage at least. That means we're related in a weird way." Her peal of laughter ended in a snort.

"Hey, I'll take it, weird or not." She joined Carol in

a bout of hilarity until she almost forgot why she'd called. "Carol, you'll never guess what happened."

"The news about Jacob? Yeah, I wasn't sure you'd want to know. He left his horse and buggy behind. I saw his brother driving it today."

"Maybe he's in Florida."

"I don't think so. Someone gave him a ride to the Interstate. I think he's gone." Amanda let the silence drag, her speech stuck behind the clog in her throat until Carol began to speak again. "How's the rest going? Meet the cute coach at the high school yet? Maybe he's single. Anybody worth stalking?"

"No. No, nobody at all." In a few minutes she made an excuse to hang up and spent the rest of the day trying to process her thoughts.

Chapter Five

✿

"Where you headed, son?" The truck driver who picked up Jacob had a congenial Southern drawl.

"Makes no mind. I am grateful for the ride."

"Amish, huh? You have an argument with your hardheaded father and decide to run away? Don't seem the type to hook a freighter west for the thrill of it."

Yacob ignored the driver's curiosity. It was the word "west" that caught his ear. The idea soothed his fury better than a dose of his mother's *zunly druppa* when he had the croup. He squinted into the setting sun and nursed his anger. Amanda had loved the West. He would see what her world offered.

The trucker continued, "I'm headed to Wyoming, son. That work for you?"

"Ja. Right as rain."

"I'm headed to Cheyenne. You can hitch a ride that far. We'll get you fixed up with another connection, you don't see yourself headed home by then. What's your name?"

"Jacob Ruth." He pronounced it the way the Englis-chers did, instead of *Yacub*. The sound was strange, but he didn't correct himself. "You can call me Jake."

The next question was harder to answer.

"You Amish?"

He heard the hum of tires against the pavement, felt a blast of warm air from the heater. Outside, the wiper blades clicked with a crisp, regular rhythm that made him fight to keep his eyes open. If he were home, he would be wrapped in his buggy blanket, fretting lest Yankee slip on the ice. "I don't know what I am. Best ask me tomorrow."

He was no surer two days later, when the driver woke him after a short nap to say, "Up ahead is the Wyoming state line. Got a while before I drop my load. You can stay on for the return trip, or you can try to hook another ride. Either way's all right by me. This place has hot showers and a pretty good chicken-fried steak. Anyway, I'll get you fixed up with a hot and a cot and see if I can set you up with one of my buddies headed to California. Unless you've seen enough?"

"No." His throat was scratchy from disuse. He coughed and tried again, this time his tone not as sharp. "No. I get off at the next stop."

"Any idea where you're headed?"

"I'll need to find work."

"Bet you know horses, huh Amish? What else you do?"

"I can work an honest day."

"Well you'll be welcome out here. But I'm not sure you'll find work. It's coming up on snow season. Might find pickings a little lean until spring."

"I'll manage."

"There's a fellow up ahead, Calvin Baker, might need a wrench monkey. Regular guy walked off when the first rains came. Whatya think?"

"I've done mechanic work, some."

"We're talking engines here, not buggies."

"I've worked on engines. In Florida."

"Well, you won't be too talkative. He'll like that. His wife might try to open you up. Watch out for her. She'll likely get you in trouble with her husband, same as the last guy."

When Jacob followed the address to a modest house set alongside a commercial garage on the outskirts of town, he discovered that the truck driver was right about Ruby Baker. He didn't want to believe bad about anyone, but something about Mrs. Baker set a caution that he should take care. Like the way she liked to call him Brad Pitt every time he pulled off his cap and the first time, tousled his blond hair like she had a right. He resolved to spend as little time as possible in her home. Her familiarity hinted that she knew a secret about him he did not yet understand—a joke at his expense.

She tapped on his door the first night. "Jake, hon, you want some supper? I kept a plate warm for you."

Jacob heard his boss in the living room. "Hey—what about me?"

"You too, Calvin. But I always keep yours warm. I was telling Jake so's he'd know that I'll keep a plate hot every night for him."

"Yeah. I'll bet you will. Boy's got more sense than that."

Jacob tried to block the argument. Never had he heard such harsh words spoken between a man and his wife. "The food makes for enough, Mrs. Baker. I eat it in my room."

"You'll do no such thing. Calvin, let Jake have your seat. He looks hungry."

"It makes no matter. I don't wish to be a bother."

"Believe me—you're no bother. Besides, I like your company. Look! Calvin's fallen asleep in front of the TV again. You act like you don't care about the 'boob tube' one way or the other. That's what I like about you, hon. What do you do in that room of yours every evening? Ever need company? Lordie, that blush looks good on you. I didn't think there was a man alive who could still blush. You're a good-looker, you know that? You plan on cowboyin' come spring? Calvin says you're a natural mechanic. What else you got instincts for, Jake? I was cleaning up your room today, noticed your sketchbook. You got something going with that gal you're drawing? She don't look 'Aimish'. You saving yourself for her? That why you're so shy around me? A woman can always tell. Hey, don't rush off—the night's still young. You're welcome for the meal anytime. Way to a man's heart is through his stomach, my mother used to say. 'Course she meant booze, but food works. That's something we agree on, right?"

On his second Friday, Ruby interrupted him on his way through the living room to collect his stuff. "Hey, Jake, darlin'. Calvin says you gave notice. Hell, it's only been two weeks. You barely made it to payday. Hope it wasn't nothing I said. I like you, kid. Gets real lonely down here in the wintertime."

⁂

The wind swept across Johnson County, Wyoming, wilder than anything Jacob had ever experienced; drifts as high as the rooftops piled in lazy froth like the cotton candy Bruder Mast sold in his mercantile back home. Jacob climbed from the flatbed truck he'd hitched a ride in, waved to the driver and hunched his back against the wind while cold burned through the fabric of his coat. The whistle of wind drove pins into his brain, carrying with it a fear that he would die before he found safety. He thought to reconsider, but the taillights of the truck were already disappearing in the darkness.

Hunger gripped his belly, giving him something to concentrate on besides fear. The hunger was new. Ahead, the lights of a motel cut through the blizzard with the promise of a warm room and a hot shower. He stood undecided on the sidewalk, pitched against the blowing snow. He still had a few dollars left in his pocket, but none of it was intended for a warm room in a motel. When a sudden gust nearly blew him off his feet, he pushed open the door and stood uncertainly in the lobby.

A dark-skinned clerk interrupted her duties at the registration desk to inquire, "Son, you look like you've walked clean from Sheridan on your knees. Need a room, do you?" Jacob was too tired to do more than nod. The clerk looked a little closer when she saw his gunnysack. "I was only kidding about you walking. Where's your car? You got one out there, don't you?" Jacob shook his head. "You got any money?"

Jacob felt his small bundle of cash hidden in his gunnysack, but he remained silent.

"We don't rent without a credit card. You got one of those?"

"N...no." He tried not to think about the snow outside, two feet and piling deeper with each blast of wind. The storm gates at the end of town were closed; the town was locked in for the blizzard.

"Sorry, no credit card, no lodging. That's corporate policy. Keeps out vagrants." Jacob wasn't sure what a vagrant was, but he must be one. The woman looked as though she could have a grandson his age. When he lifted his sack and started for the door, she motioned him back. "There's coffee over there in the lobby. Help yourself. Here's a map I'll loan you." She lowered her voice and waited until the other clerk answered the phone. "Open it up. If it takes you a couple of hours to decide where you're going...no business of mine, I expect. Might happen, you doze off in the middle of studying the map and that won't be my business, either." She walked him to a chair in the empty lobby and leaned close to whisper. "How's a man find himself out here in the bowels of Johnson County, in a blizzard, with no more on his back than what you're wearing? Them fancy pants—not even a pocket to hold your money. Them's broadfall britches with a placket. My brother wore those in the Navy. Buttons, 'steada zippers. Where you from, son?"

"Ohio."

"Ohio? Wait a minute. You're one a' them Aimish folks, ain't you? Well do tell! I seen some of your kind in Missouri. Some of them had a tractor. Seemed strange to me, but the land there is pretty poor. Your people got it harder than ranchers 'round here. You got a job for the winter, son?"

"Nope. I just...I'm looking."

"Take a load off your feet and I'll think of something. Go on now before my friend there gets off the phone."

After his second cup of coffee, Jacob must have dozed off. He woke with a start when the woman tapped his shoulder. "Come on, son. You got to get now. We're locking the lobby for the night." She directed her attention to the other night clerk. "I'll lock up the vending room. Louise. You got it last night, and it's blessed cold out there."

Jacob followed her into the dark, surprised by the frigid air. Back home, he would have worried that the water trough would freeze over. Here, he wondered how he was going to survive the night.

"Here, kid. Help me with this roll-away. I need to get it into storage before it gets soaked—and the bedding right along with it. Here, let's just shove it into the vending room for the night. We've had some trouble with vandals in there. Have to lock it at night, now. Say, you wouldn't care to keep an eye on it? Wouldn't take much. I'll just store this bed in there overnight. Don't trip over it. Here. I'll leave a couple of blankets, just for storage. Appreciate the favor. And in the morning, if you hear Maria cleaning the room next door, ask her to let you use the shower before she starts the room. Most people leave a clean towel or two behind, and the soap gets tossed out anyhow. There's a coffee shop across the road, opens before sunrise. Might be some rancher over there could spare a bed for a few days in exchange for work. Check it out. 'Night now. God bless you, son."

Jacob heard the door shut behind him. The room contained a furnace and a half-dozen snack machines. He counted the coins in his sack and found three-quarters and a dime, enough to buy a bag of chips, the first food he'd eaten in hours. They tasted better than his mother's cracklings. Then he dusted the crumbs from his shirt, removed his wet boots and collapsed on the bed.

The next morning, he discovered the clerk was right about Maria. When he emerged from the bathroom, showered and shaved, she was gone. He wasn't sure how to thank her, beyond getting out of her way so she didn't get caught. His skin tingled from the hot water, his skull from the electric hair dryer he'd used on his sodden hair before he covered it with a home-knit cap to maintain the heat. His legs hummed with new circulation clear to the tops of his now-dry boots. With a grateful prayer aimed at the dark and empty lobby, he started toward the café across the street where the windows glowed with steamy heat. He shuffled across the powdered snow drifts and opened the door, surprised to see a single customer hunched over a barstool, gnarled hands cupped around a mug of black coffee while he joked with the waitress.

The waitress led him to an empty table and whispered, "Don't mind him. Local rancher who likes early breakfasts and talking to strangers."

The old-timer grinned. "Got that right, Missy. Come on over, young man. I'll spell you a meal for the price of your company. Name's Tibbs Bell. Got caught in this gol-darn blizzard with my Rosie, when we drove our old truck into town to sign an insurance claim."

Jacob reluctantly took a stool and opened the menu the waitress placed before him, along with a mug of coffee that he hadn't yet requested.

"Give us both the sausage and eggs. Biscuits and gravy on the side." Tibbs winked and took a sip. "Good enough gravy to put hair on your chest." He studied Jacob across the table. "So what brings you out here in this soup?"

Jacob hesitated. "I wish I could give you a good answer for that, sir. Truth is, I wonder the same, myself."

"Got a job hereabouts?"

"N...no, sir. Had one, but it didn't work out."

The rancher gave him a hard look. "You got a streak of lazy under that bonnet of yours?"

"No, sir. I am a good worker. Nothing I'm not happy to learn." Jacob shifted and tried to control the heat creeping up his face. "But there are things I do not tolerate."

Tibbs slapped his hand on the table with a hoot. "Woman trouble. They'll get you every time!" He held out a gnarled hand. "I got a job for you at my place. Whatya say? A cot and three hots. Wife's a good cook and she'll darn your socks as a favor. You can have my son's room." His eyes darkened. "He's got no further need of it."

The door opened with a blast of frigid air and the old man looked up to smile at the sad, worn woman who walked toward them. She took a seat and set her old purse on her lap. Her white hair was wrapped in a loose bun that allowed a few unencumbered wisps to frame what had been a handsome face. Her eyes were still wide and intelligent but filled with sadness that hinted of recent loss.

"I been telling this boy we could use him out to the ranch. Waiting on his answer. What do you say, Rosie? Think you could throw another biscuit or two in the pan ever' morning?"

The old woman turned to study Jacob with a look of a woman drowning, until her warm brown eyes softened, and tears beaded the corners. Her lips trembled and she nodded.

Tibbs cleared his throat and reached for a sugar packet and ripped it open with his teeth. "Don't intend we should press you, son. But the blizzard gates'll be open in a couple of hours. You give us your answer by then?"

Jacob swallowed. "No need, sir. I'll take the job and be grateful."

"Dang, the horses got out through that busted gate again!"

On the way into the ranch, Mr. Bell eased the truck to a sliding halt and jumped out. Jacob followed, shivering with cold. One of the ranch geldings struggled with a length of barbed wire torn loose by the storm and looped around its pastern. The old rancher sidled up to the horse while he kept up a nonstop flow of chatter in a smooth, lolling tone that caused the gelding to cease its struggle. It cocked its head in the direction of the rancher's gloved hand and stilled. Tibbs attached a lead rope. The horse sniffed and backed up, but it kept its gaze trained on the battered glove that lifted to stroke its forelock.

Jacob backed slowly to the truck and reached for the wire cutters that Mrs. Bell pulled from the side panel. He gripped them in the spare gloves she handed him and crept back through the snow bank, trying not to make a bad situation worse by startling the animal. The rancher consoled the horse with child's talk and sweet soothings while Jacob located the spot where the wire lay half-submerged in the snow, the other end wrapped twice around the horse's leg. He grasped it tightly, snipped, and felt the wire tension ease. Gently, he drew the wire away from the injured foot and coiled it in a tight loop that he wrapped around the opposite fencepost—a project for another day. The horse's leg was cut to the bone and bleeding profusely.

The rancher limped across the snow, followed by the bleeding horse. By the time he was halfway to the house his limp had worsened to the point that every step seemed fresh agony. Jacob slipped the lead rope from his boss's trembling hand and started toward the barn.

Behind them, the pickup crept along with Rosie at the wheel. It paused at the gate long enough for Tibbs to open the barn door before Rosie disappeared into the house. By the time Jacob had the horse in a clean stable, she returned with a first aid kit and a bundle of bandages. Apparently doctoring was her domain because she shushed her husband away when he reached for it. He started to kneel in the frigid straw, but she swatted at his hand when he started to open the kit. "We've hired a helper. Let him work." She shot Jacob a warning look and thrust the kit into his hands.

Jacob ducked his head to hide his grin. *So like Grossmummi, the way women boss their husbands when they reach a certain age.* He found the supplies he needed to disinfect and stitch up the wound. When he was satisfied, he wrapped the leg while the old man chipped the ice from a bucket of water. When the horse lifted its head again, icicles clung to its whiskers, its fogged breath testimony to the frigid air in the barn.

Jacob had forgotten the cold in the panic of the moment, but he could no longer control his clacking teeth. He covered the horse with a worn blanket and wired the gate shut before he ran to the house.

Out of habit, he grabbed an armload of firewood and carried it inside. Rosie looked up from her coffee pot with a surprised glance and nodded toward the woodstove. He dropped in a log and stoked the coals while she poured three mugs and topped them off with thick, rich cream. Soon the smell of coffee filled the house with a familiar aroma that stung him to his core. So many reminders of home.

Warmed from the coffee and the loan of a Carhartt ranch jacket, he trotted to the truck for his gunnysack, glad for the excuse. His heart ached at what he'd seen so far of the sad couple. Surely they would have questions, but hopefully not tonight. To forestall the inevitable, he made a quick trip back to the barn to check on the horse. In the solitude, he released his pent-up breath in a burst that caused the horse to jerk in surprise before it resumed its meal from the feedbag the rancher had hung on a post. Cold ate through his thin clothes while he considered the miracle that had occurred this day. It had taken all of his skill and more than a few quiet prayers, but the horse was stitched and medicated. *A day's work done*; he could almost hear his father's voice. *Nothing about my skill or patience—never a compliment*. He shut the door behind him and strode from the barn, old resentments fading with each stride until he stamped the last of them on the mat outside the farmhouse door.

"You know your way around horses, that's for sure, Jake," Mrs. Bell said as she poured him a cup of coffee and waited for him to take a seat.

Jacob pulled a wet glove from his half-frozen hand and massaged his fingers to increase the circulation. "Once, my father's Belgian, it gets caught in the fence. We have this salve to doctor it with. I watch my mother sew the flesh closed with her sewing needle. We—the Amish—don't waste our money on animal doctors. Most of our tending we do ourselves."

"Well, wasn't any way the Doc could make it out here today. We might have lost it, you hadn't come along. Got the gift of healing, that's for sure."

Jacob nodded. *Gott's gift. Nothing of my own doing.*

He found a set of long underwear folded on the bed, welcome heat after a warm bath. The next morning he pulled on a pair of denim jeans someone set out for him during the night. He fumbled through the pocket of a secondhand wool shirt and found a tube of sunscreen. He read the instructions and applied some to his face, experimentally, before he pulled on a battered brim hat that he found beside a pair of worn deerskin gloves. A peek in the full-length mirror on his bedroom door brought heat to his cheeks at his changed appearance before he eased into the hallway and shut the door behind him. In the kitchen, Mrs. Bell thumped pans and lids. With no desire to sit to breakfast yet, he slipped out to check on the horse.

For the next week, he followed the same routine, a pre-dawn rising to start the fire before the older couple began their day. He mucked out the stalls, trimmed hooves and tacked fence boards while the sun rose over the eastern rim. Most days, Tibbs insisted on keeping up, despite his wife's scolding.

After two weeks of trying to keep up, Tibbs drew off his wet gloves and tossed them into the pile of clean straw next to the barn door that Jacob had jacked up to correct the sagging hinges. "You work harder than any two men I've ever seen. But let's knock off for the day before you kill me off complete!" On the way to the house, he paused to take a breath. "Hope you hang around 'till spring, son. Anyway, you have Mother's Christmas dinner to look forward to. It'll settle you to rights. Fill your belly. Expect we'll have a neighbor or two over for the holidays. Can't imagine her fixing all that food for just the two of us. Once the snow melts and we can find our fence posts, might see what you can do with 'em."

Jacob paused before he extinguished the lantern and started to the house. A dozen mended harnesses hung from hooks, along with hoes and axes, knife-edged and handles freshly oiled. One hook held an ancient varmint rifle he'd blued the barrel on, and sanded down the burled walnut stock until the seventy years spent inside a sad-sack saddle sling were scarcely noticeable. Afterward, he hung it back over the mantel. When he finished outside, the barn floor gleamed like an Amish woman's kitchen.

At night he planned his tasks in the warmth of his bed. Within the month he'd have the ancient toilet in the ranch house repaired and the dry-rot subfloor replaced. The work was easy; the hard part was having to hear the old man and his wife thank him a dozen times a day. He wanted to protest that it was Gott who gave him his talent and his energy, that he only gave fair measure for his board and room, but he watched their faces and saw their need for gratitude. It was their way.

"Thank you again for tending that horse out there or we'd a blowed our savings on a vet visit out from town."

Mrs. Bell hadn't heard her husband just tell him the same. Jacob hid his smile behind a feigned cough. So little they had in the way of fortune, their son dead and his belongings hung in the bedroom he now used. The son's clothing on his own back.

"You're welcome, Mrs. Bell. This dinner is a fair trade. It makes no wonder Mr. Bell is so healthy. He will live to be a hundred with your good cooking." Once spoken, the words ceased to be blasphemy in his mind. Surely the Lord provided the food, but this old woman cooked it up, and served it, and washed the dishes with birdlike arms that seemed incapable of lifting even a single plate. But her joy was a beacon of light for any man. Learning to thank them had been the hardest part, almost as hard as watching their faces when he spoke of leaving in the spring.

"You're more than welcome. But you best call us 'Tibbs and Rosie.' We don't stand on ceremony."

He studied his plate and nodded. He'd remember to mind their customs. Easier all around.

"Tibbs and I will be married fifty years, come May. Surely you'll stick around for the celebration."

Jacob grinned, but he stopped short of a promise. He would stay until the thaw and leave when the fences were fixed. At the rate Mr. Bell thought of projects, if he didn't stay firm to his plan, he might still be here in another ten years. Yesterday, the old man had decided the sheds that hadn't seen paint in thirty years suddenly needed whitewash. In this weather, the paint would freeze in the sprayer. But he stopped short of complaint, even in his mind. He'd been led to this little family. That first night he'd stretched full-length in the narrow bed that had been their son Steve's before he left to ride in the rodeo in Red Bluff, California. The next morning, he inquired about their son while he attacked a stack of pancakes and bacon. "I've never seen a rodeo. But I gather they're dangerous?" He noticed the look the two exchanged, and he wondered if he should attend to his meal in silence.

"It wasn't the rodeo that killed our boy, but a speeding pickup, a drunk driver and a tight curve in the road," Mr. Bell explained.

Jacob glanced up to see resolve steeled behind their dry, emotionless eyes. Killed by outsiders, just like the Amish, their buggies and their lives destroyed by drunk drivers and reckless speeders. The son's photo hung above a Bible on the bureau in his bedroom, a dark, green-eyed cowboy in his bundling years. He finished his meal in a rush, and gulped the last of his coffee before he picked up his work gloves.

Rosie looked disappointed. Her husband noticed and hooked a thumb in the direction of the wood stove. "What's the hurry, son? Work'll wait. Sit yerself down and settle yer stomach."

Rosie returned to the kitchen and ran the dish water while she warbled an ancient hymn in a voice that resonated under the low ceiling of the yellow kitchen he had painted for her.

That night, Jacob's thoughts settled heavy on Amanda Miller. She had been right. If he had married Katie, their talks would have come down to discussing the price of seed grain. Already he had forgotten the scent of Katie's skin, or the trapped look in her eyes when she heard his brother, John, confess their truth. He'd spent many such hours thinking about Katie, but her memory always included his brother and the betrayal of their fornication. After only a few months, he'd forgotten the attraction he once felt for the girl. At night, Amanda was his every-night girl; the memory of her in a light blue dress was hard company for a lonely man in a snow-bound ranch house.

Maybe she had been right when she encouraged his talents. He'd filled his sketchbook with images that didn't seem wrong, only curious. His camera captured dozens of images. He spoke with a neighbor of Tibbs's who promised to show him how to develop his own prints in a darkroom. Gott had plans for him, even if his own people did not. He closed his eyes and visualized that last day at the preaching. The day he fled. Had anyone given him the benefit of the doubt? They would put him on the Bann in his absence. Tonight, he realized it didn't matter. For the first time in months, he could bring his family to mind without pain.

He pulled the Bible from the bureau and opened it to Psalms, the same words as the preachers back home quoted to the congregation from memory. None of them had read the words for themselves, not even the preachers, for the High German Bibles they used were filled with archaic phrases and strange-to-understand words, centuries old. He'd heard that the Reformed churches used English Bibles like the one in his hand— a book worn out from use.

He found the twenty-third Psalm and read it for the first time in English, hearing the cadence of the poetry and the images that made memorization easy: Verdant pastures, still waters, rods and staffs, mercy and goodness. He marked the page and thumbed to the New Testament, and read words that resonated in his heart, but seemed strange in their English translation.

After a few minutes, he picked up a book that Mrs. Bell had recommended from the bookshelf in the hall. He intended to read them all before he left. Right now, a book on veterinary medicine lay on his night table alongside books about ranching, bookkeeping, and electricity, and a paperback volume of poetry by Robert Service. He'd opened the book, curious about the poetry of an outdoorsman like himself. Afterward, he wrote a poem, satisfied with the way his thoughts flowed onto paper.

In the evenings, he'd taken up the habit of studying a repair manual for the Dodge pickup. Tonight, Mrs. Bell noticed and suggested he start classes at the community college. "They got welding, mathematics, and drafting. Even an English class." Her grin was filled with impish humor.

"So I will no longer feel like a *dummkopp* when I hear people discuss topics I know nothing about?" he teased.

"You do well enough. Don't get hard on yourself. Hold yer head up and soak it all in. You'll get there soon enough," she said, the smile gone, her eyes gentle and soft like his own mother's.

Mr. Bell had taught him about anger—when it helped and when it wasn't worth the effort. The Bells were good people. They discussed ideas around the table after supper, and sometimes he surprised himself with new ideas he had read in their books. But he promised himself that when he had read all the books in the bookcase, it would be time for him to leave.

The next morning he woke to blinding sun on the snowy landscape and made a plan to dig out the fence line. He'd start work on the posts as soon as the ground thawed. By late April, or June at the latest, the snowline might have receded. Once the earth warmed, the work would go easy.

In the kitchen, the radio was tuned to the country station. The Bells liked it on, so the house didn't seem so lonely. Mrs. Bell had told him that her son had been a content boy, just like him. At first he had thought she was making a joke at his expense, but he thought back on the weeks since he had arrived. He'd stopped brooding in their presence, after she told him about her son. It seemed the least he could do if his laughter pleased them.

"Steve was a miracle baby," Rosie explained from her rocking chair, while flames crackled in the stove. "Like Sarah, I was, praying over my barrenness 'till he arrived. I was over forty when he was born. Never a more welcome baby in the country, I expect." Her eyes captured the light while her cheeks glowed with strange red heat. "We were blessed for a season. That's all."

Chapter Six

✖❧✖

"Jake...you seen Rosie?"

Jacob looked up, surprised at the fear in Tibbs's voice. "Nah. I only just come out for breakfast. It makes surprising she don't have even the coffee ready this morning, ya?"

"She never said nothing about going outside. Something's not right." Tibbs led the way out the path that Jacob intended to clear after breakfast. A set of small, faint footprints lay in the fresh snow, their imprint barely visible without a clear idea of her direction.

"Where would she go first thing this morning?"

Jacob ignored the question as he wrestled with a pile of lumber that had been knocked down onto a stack of boxes at the southern edge of the house. He knew why she had ventured out; only last night he had mentioned craving his mother's apricot coffeecake. He gritted his teeth and set one box on top of another. At the bottom of the slope, near the door to her fruit cellar where she kept her canned apricots, a small foot lay exposed on the snow.

"Rosie? Can you hear me, Rosie?" Tibbs reached past Jacob with shaking hands to feel his wife's skin. "She's still warm. Cold, but still warm." He didn't use the word, *alive*.

Jacob pulled the dislodged snow from around a bright blue shawl that partially covered her. One of Rosie's gloves was missing. Already a bruise darkened her forehead. "Before I lift her, let me feel for broken bones." He choked back panic and added, "I've seen this done many times. I will be gentle." He felt her legs while the old man knelt at her side and rubbed her wrists with a corner of her woolen scarf. "I don't feel a break, Mr. Bell. Her hips don't seem at odd angles. That's the fear when a woman falls on hard ground. Maybe we will be lucky today. Let's get her inside." Her lack of weight nearly set Jacob off balance as he lifted her from the snow and found his feet. She lacked the sturdiness of any Amish woman he had ever seen. Small-boned and frail, she had the structure of a child.

Inside, Tibbs heated water for tea while Jacob laid her on her bed. By the time he arranged the pillows, Tibbs was back, fretting like a mother hen, and Rosie had stirred.

"I caught the corner of the roof with that cussed rake I drag across the ice, and it brought down that corner of the shed on me," Rosie confessed. "I felt myself falling. But wasn't much I could do. Thought you boys would never get there." She laughed and rubbed her chilled fingers together. "Fortunate those boxes sheltered me 'till the scouts arrived or I'd be a goner."

Her husband engulfed her in a clumsy embrace. "Lucky, Jacob here caught sight of your footprint or we'd a been looking down at the barn, thinking you was milking Bessie."

Rosie looked up at her husband and her eyes darkened with love. She caught Jacob's stare and gave an embarrassed cough. "I'm sure sorry about that coffee cake, Jacob. Maybe tomorrow?"

Jacob shook his head, too overcome for words. When he brought his gaze up from the floor, he found the two of them studying each other again with soft expressions of gratitude.

❧

Tibbs caught the corner of the door as Jacob carried the milk pail into the kitchen. "Jake, how's about you drive us into town tonight? Take a break? They're having a barn dance at the Community Center and Mother's hankering to go."

Jacob grinned. He tried to picture either of the Bells dancing. He failed, but the idea of driving the battered old '87 Dodge pickup into town wasn't a bad idea. "Sure. I can drive you."

"We'll go early and cash our social security checks. Mother needs some supplies. She isn't used to cooking for a big eater like you." Tibbs winked and his craggy face broke into a grin. "Likes it, though."

Jacob tried to ignore the latest hint to stay. He planned to leave in a couple of weeks, but the picture of the two of them rode in his head. A family needed more than one son. A son needed a family. An image of him standing on his father's manure pile while the two of them argued reminded him that he had not always honored his own father as he should have.

At the Community Hall, a trio of musicians tuned up their instruments. In the past four months, listening to Rosie's radio, he'd learned the difference between rockabilly and classic western. Now it looked as if he would learn to line dance. He checked the snaps on his new shirt, part of his earnings for a winter's work. He had plans for the rest of his money; he wanted to buy the Bells' old pickup and take it to Oregon.

"One, two, three, four, turn. Back, two, three, clap and turn." The caller's words moved faster than his feet while he concentrated on the other dancers. He tried to anticipate the next move, but his feet were clay pots. Even the children danced better. His enjoyment was in the freedom. He pivoted and spun under the bright lights reflected on the shiny pair of tan western boots Rosie had pulled out of her son's closet and polished until they shone.

He recognized a cowgirl on his left. Before the dance, he had stopped at a barbershop. She had teased him about looking like Brad Pitt, and leaned close as she trimmed his hair and massaged his scalp until his nerves quivered. He walked out twenty minutes later, with a short haircut, an opinion about the Broncos' passing game, and her phone number on a card in his pocket. Tonight she looked as though she needed a partner.

"Pretty Boy," she teased. "I hoped you'd be here."

"I am new to this. At home we dance...differently," he stammered.

"Nah, no excuses. Nothing says the Texas Two-Step can't be done by Ohio boys with two left feet."

He felt his face heat. "Maybe I do better to sit this one out."

"I can sit it out with you." She leaned close enough

to comment on his clear blue eyes. "You mean to tell me you don't have a gal somewhere?"

Jacob winced. Many of the English ways were good, but this girl's manner seemed rough as a man's. He remembered his manners. "I don't...my girl doesn't live around here."

She frowned an exaggerated pout and gave his shoulder a playful shake. "Too bad for her. Look what she's missing." Her breath on his cheek was warm and smelled of alcohol. "Let's take it outside, cowboy. I got a bottle in the truck says we're partying tonight!"

He looked around for a reason to decline and saw Tibbs wink. The old man would make sport of him on the way home if he didn't enjoy himself. He shrugged into his jacket and followed her into the dark.

The whiskey burned his throat while her kisses burned him everywhere else. By the time he remembered he was driving home, he was hot from his belly to his boots. "You're not a country girl." He spoke the first thought that came to mind.

"Says who?"

"You don't smell like a country girl." He heard his words and winced. He wished he could talk to her like Amanda; she had never led him into such a dead-end canyon.

"Says who? You an expert on cowgirls?"

"Maybe." He knew Amish girls. He wasn't some city boy that just rode in on a buggy. The thought caused him to pause. When had he started to think like a cowboy? Like the English, he corrected himself. "I know country girls."

"I'd like to know you better, cowboy. I got pretty

personal with your hair today. Now I'd like to meet the rest of you."

Her honesty caused a surge of heat. He knew what she asked and his body wasn't objecting. He watched her eyes widen in pleasure when he pressed her against the back of her pickup seat and found her lips. The effect was fire in a blacksmith's forge. He couldn't remember her name, but it didn't matter. He had gone this far over the fence—maybe he would go the rest of the way tonight.

She began to unbutton her blouse.

He saw her fancy underclothing, like the night he had seen Amanda Miller in her living room with lamp light on her shoulders. Another picture flashed past; Amanda in the rocking chair at church. And months later, Katie Melvin as she heard the churchgoers make their zeugnis without a thought to her own transgressions. Suddenly he knew what sin lived in her mind. She had learned to crave the thrill without feeling shame. This girl was like Katie. And he was another of the same. Disgust flooded his brain while pleasure made stopping unbearable.

An image of John coupled in bed with Katie chilled his desire. His brother would live always with the memory of his forbidden pleasure. And in the years ahead, he would crave more. "Stop!" Jacob heard himself protest. "You're not my Saturday-night girl."

The girl looked up, flushed, disheveled and impatient. "Whatcha talkin' about? Come back here, cowboy!"

"I don't be asking you to be my Saturday-night girl. And you shouldn't let me. Have a care about yourself." He opened the door of her steamy cab and jumped to the ground. On his way back to the dance, he heard her empty bottle hit the weeds.

Jacob started the pickup's rattling heater and waited for the cab to heat up, wrapped in his own thoughts. The Bells had so many new stories to share that they didn't notice when he ground the old Dodge pickup into second gear and began the slow drive home. The heater cranked a continual blast of hot air that forced him to roll his window down for a breath of clear night air. Stars filled the sky, cupping the valleys in a blanket of light while the lulling dance of the empty road swept the rhythm of the balky radio in sweeps and dips through the canyons. When the radio signal was lost to static, they rode in companionable silence.

In the darkness of the cab, Tibbs thrust an envelope toward Jacob that Rosie had extracted from her purse. "Go on, take it. You worked hard. We owe you more than that." His arm trembled as he held up an envelope from which he pulled the title to the truck. His eyes glittered in the light of the dim dome light that Jacob switched on. "Dang heater dried out my eyes," he grumbled. "Here, take it. The missus, she'll be all over me, you don't."

"The insurance check came. We bought a new pickup with heated seats," Rosie explained. "Our Steve, he'd be proud to have his money used for a new truck to keep us safe."

"There's nothing wrong with this one, but we want one of those new Chevy diesels we seen for sale in Sheridan. I want to be able to set it in four-wheel drive without a struggle. Mother, she wants a CD player so she can listen to Travis Tritt without straining her hearing aid."

When Tibbs fell asleep, his head against the passenger window, Jacob finally spoke. "Mrs. Bell? Rosie? Would you show me how to find someone in Oregon?"

"Of course, dear. We'll check down to the library. You'll be needing those computer skills, sooner or later."

"I'll have to check a map. She lives somewhere in the Willamette Valley, I recall."

Rosie was laughing at him; Jacob heard it in her voice. "The librarian in town will show you how to locate that gal of yours." The heater seemed to have affected Rosie's eyes as well, judging from her rapid blinks.

"What makes you think I have a gal waiting?" Jacob pressed the accelerator and heard the engine wheeze.

"Pshaw! I'm not that old I can't recognize the signs. You marry her and fetch her back here for the honeymoon. You hear?"

"Yeah. I hear you, right as rain."

In the morning, he finished his oatmeal and helped clear away the table before they left for town. The library opened at ten. He followed an older couple in and used Rosie's library card to claim a spot at the bank of computers. The librarian introduced herself as *Mavis* before she showed him how to put in the search name. When his research revealed five other Amanda Millers, he added her middle name, Rose, like the flower she loved.

"Your young lady has a pretty name," Mavis teased as they waited for the slow connection.

"Old-fashioned. I'll bet it fits," Rosie chimed in from across the aisle where she browsed for a large-print copy of a Craig Johnston novel she hadn't already read.

Jacob glanced over and tried not to blush. "Amanda has some peculiar notions. But she's not so worldly as other English girls I've seen. She suits."

Rosie smirked. "She suits? Lad, you'll need to be more romantic than that if you think to woo her."

"Do you love her?" Mavis exchanged a knowing glance with Rosie and winked.

Jacob felt his face flame. Love was not a word to bandy around, but tenderness that grew between a couple after they married. He was spared a reply when the search site appeared on the monitor.

"Looks like you got a match. See here, *Amanda Rose Miller*. We can learn more if you want to pay for a search service. County says we have to pass the cost on to our patrons." Mavis waited with her hand over the mouse and her mouth screwed in concentration below her owlish trifocals, like she protected the county's investment.

"How much?" Habit made him ask. But no matter the cost, he was so close, the money would be well spent.

When he pulled the dollars from his pocket and handed it to the cashier, Mavis called out the search result in a voice that boomed across the room. "Your Amanda Miller is twenty-three. She lives near Portland. Place called Silverton. Farming and orchard land—hazelnuts."

Rosie moved closer to squint at the screen. "We took the train to Portland once. Made the drive down the coast highway to Brookings. You'll find yourself in a real pretty area, you intend to stay there, son."

He wasn't sure if he intended to stay. He wasn't sure Amanda would want him to. But he knew one thing; he intended to ask her.

"There's more. Where she went to college, her net worth and all. Here, I'll show you how to print it out." Mavis reached to hit the "Print" button. "While you finish, you might as well play a computer game or two 'till someone else needs the space." She squinted over her glasses and added, "Help get you used to this contraption. You're too young to be without the skills. It's the computer age. Our patrons value their ability to use the internet."

He spent hours on the computer, learning to research, to type a letter and send it out. On mornings after the cow was milked and the horses fed, he drove back into town to make a spreadsheet and to search for answers. Soon Rosie was asking questions about how a computer worked. When the electricity went out in a late storm, he paced the house until Rosie insisted he head back into town so he didn't waste the day.

She handed him a sandwich to eat on the way. "Doesn't take long to get used to convenience, does it?"

He took a bite and shook his head. "I can easily see the way sin comes into it."

"Huh! Sin follows the sinner. Always been that way."

The next morning, he waited until the Bells stepped out to check on their horses before he used their phone. "Hello, Mr. Miller? This is a friend of Amanda's. Does she make...is she home? Yes, I'm from Ohio. Maybe she won't want to see me, after so long. You think so? Well that gives me hope. Yah, I do that in a couple of months. Early March is pretty cold where I live. Not the time for travel. Let me get a pen and piece of paper, okay? Yah, I have it written down, just so. No, don't tell her I called. Don't worry—I won't lose my nerve. I hope to meet you soon, too. Thank you for your trouble. You have been a fine help, Mr. Miller. Goodbye."

Chapter Seven

Amanda poured a quick glass of orange juice and glanced at the clock. "Who was that, Dad?"

Bob Miller hung up the phone and looked up without meeting her gaze. "Just an old friend. He had a question that needed an answer. Nothing to bother yourself about."

Amanda noticed the strange smile on her father's face. If she didn't know him better, she'd suspect he'd swallowed the cat's cream. "Okay. I thought maybe it was someone with an offer for this place. You give any more thought to selling?"

"Who said anything about selling?" His voice sounded carefree. He picked up his mug of coffee and added a teaspoon of sugar like it was the most interesting thing in the world.

She heard the humor in his voice, welcome after so many months of grief. "I'll pick up a roasted chicken after school. We need anything else?"

He shrugged. "That's your department. I'm not fussy. Just glad to have you in the house."

She hurried out to the car and slipped her key in the ignition. The sun had scarcely risen over the far horizon, but it was her day to serve as door monitor when the students arrived. She climbed inside and smoothed her skirt, smiling at her mousy hairdo and the sedate length of her hem. The skirt was one she'd pulled from Lydia's closet before she'd given the rest to the thrift store. She looked like a spinster schoolteacher, but her clothes were practical. Besides, nobody noticed what she wore anyway. With a wave at her dad, who watched from the window, she pulled the car into the roadway.

Her amusement lasted through a challenging school day. Maybe it was her imagination, but she felt Lydia's influence as she met with angry parents and negotiated a potential landmine in the faculty lounge when one of the tenured science teachers made a bid for the grant money she'd counted on to fund a field trip to the *End of the Oregon Trail Interpretive Center* in Oregon City.

After school, she pushed a grocery cart down the canned goods aisle until she bumped into a guy she knew from her senior year in high school, Charlie Rivers. A cowboy with an eye for the ladies. He made a respectful grab at the brim of his western hat and grinned. *Same old Charlie. A mouthful of dazzling teeth and a bucketload of charm.* He hooked a thumb over his belt, where a shiny new trophy buckle boasted his latest rodeo win and gave her a quick once-over. He flashed a second glance and his eyes widened in surprise.

"Hey, Amanda, darlin'—haven't seen you around! You look good! You been doing any rodeoing? Used to take home the day money with that horse of yours. That gelding was cut proud! But it's been a while. You plan to go down to Red Bluff next month?"

She glanced down at her scuffed boots, released her messy bun and gave her skirt a swish before she realized she was flirting. "Gosh. Maybe. I'm not sure what I'm doing the day after tomorrow. Dad needs me on the farm, but I'll see if I can get away."

He grinned. "Still checking in with your old man? Too bad about your horse. I seen it around. New owner rides the cloverleaf pretty regular. How come you sold it?"

She gave a short laugh. "Long story. Anyway, I've been pretty busy. I teach fourth grade now. Lots of preparation every night. Seems like that's all I have time for these days."

He leaned closer and gave an exasperated shake of his head. "That's a lame excuse, sweetheart! Everybody has bills to pay. I'm talking about the good stuff."

"Yeah, maybe you're right. I should get out more." She backed up a step. "Let's say I lost interest in horses and leave it at that."

"Not sure I believe you. But hey, wanna get together? Bunch of us are goin' to Bronco's this Friday. Some of your high school girlfriends will be there, like to see you."

"I'd like to, really, but—"

"Hell's bells. Tie on your wild rag and have yourself some fun!"

"I haven't danced in...like...forever," she blustered. "Not sure I still remember how."

"I don't believe that! After all, I was at our high school prom." He gave her a wink. "A little *do-si-do* will do you good. Work the kinks out, you know?"

She laughed and felt the heat in her cheeks. "Bronco's? Maybe I'll see you there." When he gave her what he liked to call his shit-kicker grin, she realized he didn't believe her.

At ten o'clock on Friday night, she pulled into the crowded parking lot and watched a couple emerge from a steamed-up pickup, all smiles as they tucked their rumpled shirts back into their Sunday-best denims. Two guys in the parking lot traded swings over a girl who watched from the door. Amanda picked her way through the clutch of stragglers smoking outside and pushed the door open.

Charlie was leaning against the bar, deep in conversation with another of their former classmates, Jim Scoville. He'd sat behind her in English and pressed her for answers to every homework assignment, in a hurry to graduate so he could start cowboying. He was looking pretty full of himself. So was the girl with him, a short brunette quick on her feet when they slid onto the dance floor for a Texas Two-Step.

Amanda brushed her palms across her jeans and looked around to see who else she knew. Most of the crowd were strangers. She spent a few minutes catching up with Cindy, her best friend, Sophomore year. But when Cindy started dating one of the football players, they lost touch. She'd married the guy right out of high school, but they were divorced now. She was working on husband number two.

After Cindy talked her into joining the line dance, she kicked and swirled through an entire song, surprised at how much she'd missed it. When the music ended, she felt a hand on her shoulder. Charlie stood looking down, grinning, his words lost in the hoots and laughter of the room. Before she could decide if she wanted to pair off, he had already guided her to a table and disappeared toward the bar to place an order for two beers. Back at the table again, he crooked his finger toward the dance floor and reached for her hand.

The Two-Step was familiar. *Like riding a bicycle.* The simile made her wince. *I sound like a schoolteacher.* By the time the music ended, she was ready for her beer.

Charlie followed her into the booth and made room for Jim and his girlfriend. Jim grinned and saluted her with a happy, buzzed tilt of his bottle. "Where you been hiding yourself, 'Manda?"

"Ohio." She managed to share some of her story over the bar clamor, enough to make her life sound interesting, without mentioning the Amish. Someone suggested whiskey chasers with the next round. Suddenly they were all back out on the floor, having too much fun dancing a raucous line dance on the crowded dance floor. When the music ended, she made her way back to the table. "Whew! That was fun!" She took a sip of her drink and grimaced. "No wonder I'm dizzy. What's in this?"

Jim winked. "Sloe gin. Party brew! Lay you out stiffer than a mother in a morgue!"

She glanced down to hide her shock. Charlie's elbow dug into his friend's side and Jim looked up, chagrined. "I forgot about your mom. Sorry. Sorry."

She saw his face, twisted in drunken remorse and she made herself smile. "It's okay. People never know what to say. I'm used to it."

Jim nodded. "I remember, you missed a lot of good times. You stuck pretty close to home in high school.

We used to wonder if your old man wanted to send you to a convent."

"Sorry, no convent. Just helping out my dad." She managed to act like she thought the joke was funny, even as she glanced for a way to escape. "I didn't mind. Mom was totally worth it. I had a great childhood. Really." Everyone stared at her like she was a freak. She felt claustrophobic in the crush of sweaty bodies all embarrassed for her. Fifth grade all over again. "Hey, I need... sorry. Just...need...to go. I'm sorry." She fled before anyone could think to follow.

On the way home, she braked to a stop and cut her engine at a spot where she could see the twinkling lights of the Willamette Valley. In the darkness, the river cut a swath across land that her ancestors had homesteaded a hundred and fifty years earlier. She heard herself say the word out loud, "Home." But where was home? She didn't know where she belonged anymore. Or where she might be in another few months. "I can't tell Dad, but I feel like I'm just marking time," she whispered. "Oh, Jacob, I miss you so much."

By Friday, she decided to take Charlie up on his offer. The drive to Red Bluff, after school, was worth the trouble to watch her old horse compete. She prepared herself for the moment when she would see the new owner race out of the gate, complete a lightning figure-eight, plow down the center toward the next barrel and emerge with a triumphant fist raised in the air. *Pride. That's what I'll feel. A rush of pride. No sorrow.* Napoleon loved to win. He was having fun. Her new life was less complicated without a horse. Simpler. *But why can't my head convince my heart?*

The fairgrounds were crowded with competitors,

some of whom she recognized. She made her way around the back lot, where four bull riders had pulled off their competition trousers and were skinned down to their stretchy black bicycle shorts. They pulled on tennis shoes and baggy shorts for the long, all-night drive to the next competition. A fifth guy hobbled back from the first aid station, sporting a fresh bandage on his head.

His friend looked up and grinned. "Way to go, Bonny. One for your collection."

He chortled, the laughter free and unconcerned, despite his obvious pain. "Hell, they say the only reason we ride those monsters is to meet nurses."

"Darn straight. Was she perty?"

"Nah, too much hair on his chest."

One of them looked over and grinned before he stuffed his gear into his duffle and tossed it in the trunk of a dusty pickup. She watched, thinking of the families they left at home, the winnings they needed for the next leg of their journey. Some of them would be on the road all season, desperate to make enough to tide them through the lean months. One or two would never see their families again. She recalled a previous year, when the announcer had asked for a moment of silence for a competitor from Wyoming who had been killed by a drunk driver on the way down. She wondered about his family.

She'd agreed to share a room with Cindy, at a motel that catered to the rodeo crowd. On her way to her room she saw Charlie in the parking lot, trading sips from a bottle of Jack Daniel with a buckle bunny—as Charlie liked to call his groupies. The girl looked about seventeen, with her sexy legs squeezed into tight jeans cinched with a silver buckle beneath a mane of long blond hair and a skimpy top. They sat on his tailgate, making out like they meant business. Amanda recalled a similar outfit she'd worn on her arrival in Spencerville, Ohio. No wonder Jacob had blushed like a ripe cherry when he saw her.

She looked down at her bootcut dress jeans and worn boots, paired with a lacy long-sleeve top she'd picked up on sale at the Grange. More demure, but still not up to Amish standards. She shook off the thought while she fumbled with her room card. This was rodeo weekend, but she was exhausted from the classroom and the long drive. Still, there was no point in trying to sleep; the drinking and partying would go on into the early hours. Worse, she heard her roommate inside, and by the sound of it, Cindy wasn't alone. Reluctantly, she grabbed her valise and stowed it back in her trunk.

She gave Charlie a wave on her way to the bar, where the noise of a western band filled the night. A few minutes later she joined a line dance forming on the dance floor. The rest of the night was a blur. She remembered dancing, and accepting beers offered by a half-dozen cowboys, until she had the presence of mind to slip out the door and make her way back to her motel. Alone.

On Sunday morning, she started home, badly in need of sleep. Her roommate had paired off with a bronc rider and was headed down south with him. They'd spent half the night locked in the room while she tried to catch a few winks in her car. When the two strolled arm in arm to the bar, she moved into the room and claimed the second bed. She'd propped a chair under the doorknob and stuffed a pair of earbuds into her ears so she wouldn't hear them pound on the door while she got a few hours of sleep.

She was exhausted by the time she pulled into her driveway. She set her phone alarm to give her just enough time to shower and wash her hair before work. The next morning, she managed to pin her hair in a messy bun before she slipped into a long skirt rescued from Lydia's cast-offs, tucked her tee shirt into the band, and topped it with a western belt before she donned her scuffed boots. With a quick glance in the mirror, she headed out the door, yawning and clasping a mug of strong coffee.

Chapter Eight

❧

Jacob ran his hand through his short hair as he drove across the sweeping turns of the Wyoming countryside. *Amanda will be waiting when I climb out of the next canyon.* To the right, a smattering of May wildflowers, yellow, white, and blue, resembled spilled buttons on a green quilt, while patches of snow on the hillsides still carpeted the shadows. At Greybull, by the Bighorn River, a trio of horses frisked in the fragile spring morning after months of being penned up. He pulled over and and joined them for a quick sprint along the fenceline, wind whipping his cheeks and cold driving the sleep from his head while the smell of fresh meadow grass and ozone filled his nostrils. His muscles burned by the time he returned to his pickup and pulled back onto the empty road, alert again.

Sunshine penetrated the chill and warmed the cab as the road climbed the Rockies. In four hours he would be over the Continental Divide, traveling west. *Best I find a place to pull over and get some honest sleep. The nights are still cold enough I'll need the blanket Rosie sent along.* She had set a loaf of her banana nut bread still warm from the oven on the torn vinyl seat next to him. He was tempted to tell her to save it for their own breakfast, but he caught himself when the look in her face reminded him that it wasn't only Amish women who sent their loved ones off with home cooking. *Loved ones.* That was the word she'd used when she told him not to be a stranger. The word didn't embarrass him like it had at first, one of many ideas that had changed in the past months.

His mistrust of the English had died in the Bells' kitchen. They'd taught him soft lessons about love and belonging, when he'd wanted to spend the cold months brooding. Their lessons had begun with the gift of their son's clothes and bedroom, followed by the gift of an apricot coffeecake that nearly cost a life. He recalled the way Rosie rumpled his hair when she teased him about his good looks. He'd watched them cope without sons or daughters to care for them, only their trust in Gott's will. They weren't so different from his own family in that.

With an impatient twist of his neck, he put aside thoughts of his family and squinted into the sunlight. The pickup sputtered and Jacob remembered to check the gas gauge. It was a new responsibility, remembering to feed the truck. A horse didn't need such a reminder. A road sign indicated he was still fifteen miles from the Oregon border. He pulled his new wallet from his pocket, extracted three twenty-dollar bills, and set them on the dashboard where he would remember.

Rosie had suggested he apply for a credit card, just for emergencies, but he'd fought the suggestion at first. A credit could mix a fellow up for sure. Of all the ideas he'd adapted from the English in the past four months, pockets were the most useful. But pockets meant money, and a comb, and a few coins, and a driver's license. And that meant a wallet and a social security card. It had been some task to establish his identity. He carried his wallet in his denim jeans for safekeeping and formed the habit of patting the pocket a dozen times a day.

His father had been right; one thing led to another with the Englischers. If he were still living Plain, he wouldn't need a driver's license. Or an insurance card. The Englisch seemed to stack one responsibility on top of another—layers of government and expense—until a person got caught up trying to earn enough money to cover his expenses. But Rosie Bell had been adamant about having insurance.

When he came to a small town, he eyed a motel across the street, saw the advertised price and decided to keep driving. He'd pull over when he needed to sleep. The people he'd met on the road had surprised him. In each town where he stopped for gas or a meal, someone gave him a kind word or a tip for his travel. Since the day he made the call to Amanda's father, he felt like a horse running back to the barn. Her father promised not to tell Amanda of his call, but what if he'd changed his mind? What if Amanda had changed hers?

In his memory, she'd taken his breakup in silence. Maybe she hadn't cared that he planned to marry someone else. Her silence had made it easy for him to leave, but now he wondered what she might have said, had he listened. He hadn't cared about her plans that night. Only his own. She was right about one thing— more than one. Every time they had disagreed, he'd acted like his path was the only right path. The past months had taught him that hardheadedness wasn't inherited from a father. It grew inside a man when his pride wouldn't allow for new ideas. The world had enough to occupy a man for a lifetime. The problem, and the temptation, was to sit and listen so the noise didn't block the voice of Gott. It wasn't ideas that led the Englischers astray, it was greed and lust and pride— the same as with the Amish. Maybe John would suffer. Maybe he wouldn't consider that he'd sinned against his brother. Maybe he would be satisfied that the church had forgiven him, but a brother would know the truth. Conformity couldn't keep sin at bay. It was there where brothers lived. And there was more than one kind of sin. Refusal to yield was one. Hardheaded, he was no longer. Maybe Amanda would see that—if she let him explain.

The headlights of an oncoming car jerked him from his thoughts. With a surprised glance at his new watch, he realized he had been driving for eleven hours. A blast of noise from behind shocked him into wakefulness as a rider on a low-slung motorcycle whipped around him at eighty miles an hour. The rider stood up on the pegs and wove his bike in a friendly zig-zag salute before he pulled back into the lane and disappeared. At the crest of the hill, he saw the rider fade into the distance. *One day I want to feel such freedom. No more conformity for this fellow.*

For the first time in months, he felt pity for his

brother. More so for Katie Melvin, who was probably destined to be married off to a stern, older Amishman who would agree to overlook her sin, and who would maintain a firm hand while she struggled against the wanderlust that must be racking her insides. The stern husband would fill her with babies until she was too tired to dream, and everyone would pronounce her "cured." Maybe she would turn truly to the Lord, and babies would be enough for her.

He'd found no satisfaction in leaving home with anger in his heart. He could find a church and a new family, but his old family was dead to him. Maybe Amanda would see that he had changed. But if he was too late and she had found someone else in Oregon, then that would be Gott's will. But to give up without knowing was a coward's way—the way of a man who doubted the power of forgiveness. Not that it would be easy. Amanda had her own ways. They would have furrows in their path, that was for certain, but maybe this was the path that the Lord had chosen for them.

The front of the brick school building filled a city block. Jacob waited at the curb while children pressed against the plate-glass doors and rushed laughing and crowding down the stairs. A woman on the sidewalk blew a whistle at two older boys who jostled each other in their rush to escape and Jacob saw himself back in his own school days. He kept his eyes fixed on the heavy glass door until the first crush of scholars cleared the stairs. Each time a teacher emerged, his heart thundered until he realized it wasn't Amanda.

A dozen cars waited at the curb, picked up students and swept back into the stream of traffic. The woman with the whistle knocked on his window. "Can I help you?"

"I wait for someone."

"Well, you can't park here. This is a school zone. Are you a parent?"

"Nah. I wait for a teacher."

"Who would that be?" The woman's tone was suspicious. She fiddled with the two-way radio in her hand.

"Miss Amanda Miller."

"Is she expecting you? Let me have her paged."

"No. That is, it's a surprise."

The yard attendant's voice went tight with panic. "You need to leave now! Before I call the police." She raised her radio and spoke to someone in a sharp, authoritative voice.

The door opened and a young teacher with a tight coil of auburn hair emerged. Her dark skirt and white shirt moved with her slender body as she made her way down the steps, one at a time, without looking up. A tendril of hair escaped and she pulled it back. She looked studious, familiar—almost Amish. Jacob's heart raced as he waited beside his pickup. He felt his forehead, sweaty under his western hat and reached up to remove it.

☙❧

Amanda glanced in the direction the yard-duty teacher pointed. Framed by the afternoon sun, a man leaned against an old pickup, his face shadowed from the glare.

The breeze ruffled a strand of his blond hair and for a moment her heart lurched. He looked so much like— she squelched the thought as quickly as it occurred. A passerby who had no business parking near the school. He looked harmless enough, probably a working cowboy on his way to the rodeo. Too good-looking for his own good, he stood with the confidence of a man used to having his own way. Without thinking, she glanced at his long legs, clad in bootcut denims, his feet in worn boots with rounded tips. A working cowboy, she would give him that. Not the drugstore variety that didn't know the business end of a horse from a mule's.

At the end of the walkway, she pivoted onto the sidewalk and caught a glimpse of the cowboy from the corner of her eye, slumped against his pickup, preening like he owned the spot. His truck was just washed, a point in his favor. Sometimes cowboys waited so long that the seed grain from their hay bales sprouted in the dirt on the back bumper and grew into a carpet of grass. The afternoon sun slipped behind a cloud, and she no longer needed to squint. The cowboy shifted so she could see his face.

She slowed. Someone bumped into her and hurried off in another direction, but she scarcely noticed. The man's blond hair cradled like a halo of light. Ruddy cheeks lifted in a smile that nearly brought her to her knees—and that was before he spoke. With his first words, she felt herself tremble. Ten feet away, she lost her grip on the folder of papers she carried home to grade. He swept his hat off and stood grinning like a blond hero in a popcorn romance. *Legends of the Fall.*

"Watch yourself, *Englisch.* You must think the side-walk makes the place to do your reading."

"Yacob?" The pronunciation came without conscious thought. "Yacob?"

Jacob pushed away from the truck and stood on the sidewalk above the bundle of fallen papers. "Jay-cub," he said. "It's Jacob."

Chapter Nine

❧

The sun had already set in the west, where rolling emerald knolls of grain were rimmed by aspen, fir, and oaks. Amanda reached to unfasten her messy bun, shook it loose, and raked her fingers through the thick tresses while Jacob gave an undisguised grin. She slipped her hand into his and started toward her hidden place along the Yamhill River, a narrow tributary that rippled its way to the Willamette River. Jacob's easy laughter sounded hushed in the canopy of dense trees. At a spot where kayakers had left a firepit, she found a seat on a fallen log and waited.

After a long look at the river, Jacob slipped down beside her. He was nervous, too; she saw his uncertainty in the way he rubbed his palm against his denims. After a moment, he brought his mouth to hers in a slow, velvet motion that caused her heart to race.

"I have waited for this, Amanda," his voice low-pitched and satisfied.

Their first kiss was an exploration, but the ones that

followed seared her insides. On the drive, she'd promised herself that she would practice restraint if the situation escalated to fever-pitch, but faced with the reality of his presence, she held on by sheer will. She needed answers. *Still, one more kiss couldn't hurt. Could it?* She closed her eyes. Her body tingled with a million goose bumps as she inhaled Jacob's rich, musky scent and felt the gentle scrape of his facial hair on her cheek. Time eclipsed reason, her every sense heightened with awareness of his presence. When she opened her eyes again, the sky was painted in dusk, with the promise of a million stars. "I never thought I'd see you again, Jacob." she whispered. "I thought..." Her tongue thickened when his embrace stole her ability to think. She tried again. "We did the right thing, Jacob. I know we did. But you came back." She took a deep breath. "Why?"

His low, murmured words begrudged the interruption as he pressed his mouth against her skin. "I guess following the Ordnung wasn't my path."

"But why?"

He pressed his lips against hers and sighed. "I thought family and community were enough."

"But something happened."

He sighed and broke away. His eyes revealed his pain even before he spoke. "Enough to say that my community was spoiled for me." He stared at the creek as silence lengthened between them. When he began again, his low, cautious tone hinted of the pain it caused him to remember. When he finished, he gave a one-shouldered shrug. "I saw that what you'd said was true." *What she'd said? She'd said a thousand things, but he hadn't listened. Not then.* "I was betrayed by my brother. The people I loved best. After that, there was no way back," he whispered.

"All these months? Why didn't you call? Write?"

"At first I was lost. I was no good for you. I can't explain, but this I know—I was too raw." His voice sounded hoarse. "I went my own way. West. Into deep snow country. I stayed with an old couple for a few months who showed kindness in a way I could get my head around. Does this make sense?"

She remained still, with a prayer to understand. Everything had happened so quickly.

He shifted, his eyes troubled as the sky darkened to the color of the sea, gloomy and solid. He shifted as a voice inside her urged caution. *Not so fast, Manda-girl. We're not teenagers here. If this is a good idea, it'll be better tomorrow.* "Jacob, let's be sure this time."

He released his hold and nodded reluctantly. The glassy river's surface was interrupted as a fish shattered the surface. From a break in the tree line, farm lights twinkled across the valley. "I can see why you love this land," he murmured.

She nodded against his shoulder. "I want you to see my home. I want you to know everything about me."

Jacob's warm breath teased her neck. "I have found my home."

She felt her doubt ebb, maybe for the first time since they had broken up. So much had happened since then, and none of it mattered tonight. "I've dreamed of this. But after that last night, I never thought I'd see you again." She stopped as a single kayaker swept past toward the boat ramp. In seconds, he was out of range.

"You want for us to get to know each other again.

To court. I understand this about you, Amanda. I intend to show you my intentions are sincere."

She felt him close beside her, his arms strong from a lifetime of work, his scent earthy and raw, with a hint of store-bought soap that was new. His hair was different, too, the sides shorter and with a side part. "You went to a barber," she teased to curb her nervousness.

He ran his hand across her back and up her arm while he nodded. "Only once. Usually Rosie cut it. It pleased her to trim mine like she did her son's. She said as much."

"You landed in a good place. With people who love you. How could they not? And they invited you to stay?"

He nodded. "Asked that I bring my bride back on the honeymoon." His face ripened and he added, "Not that I promised. You have reservations about me, and I don't blame you."

She fought the impulse of her body. *So much for taking things slow. Giving ourselves time.* She twisted the button on his jacket for a diversion. When his body responded, she retracted her hands.

"The old couple. I'm invited to visit anytime I want. We want." Jacob sounded as nervous as she felt.

"So what's next?" she heard herself whispering.

"I'll need a job." He glanced up, his eyes intent and serious. "I'll sleep in the truck tonight, find a place tomorrow."

She smiled at his intensity. "You think that's necessary?"

"Better believe I do. I must settle myself before the weather changes. I can feel a storm building. Maybe not tonight, but soon."

He brought his arms around her, and she had to remind herself to exhale. "We still talking about the weather?" She felt his smile against her ear.

"Right as rain."

A group of teenagers approached, their voices muted in the darkness. Amanda glanced at the fire ring. "I guess we're interrupting their party."

Jacob reluctantly straightened and shoved his hands into his pockets. She knew without needing to see, that his face was ablaze with frustration. She straightened to her feet as the group burst through the willows.

Back at the pickup, Jacob slipped his key into the ignition. "It will be improper to sleep in your house. What will your father think?"

"We won't do anything improper. He'll see to that." She hesitated. "Jacob, let's do this right."

❧

It was late when Amanda showed him the guest room. "Towels are in the cabinet. You can meet Dad tomorrow. He's down the hall." In her own room, she slid onto her bed and tried to quell the adrenaline pumping through her body. She managed to put in a call to the school district with a request for a personal day.

The next morning she set an extra plate for Jacob, who was already at the table when her father entered to take his usual chair.

He reached for the orange juice. "Who have we here?" He made a fatherly appraisal of Jacob and smiled. "So everything worked out, young man?"

"Yessir. Mr. Miller."

"Bob."

"Dad? You knew he was coming?"

Her father winked. "Peanut, two men can keep a secret better than a woman ever could."

She gave Jacob a playful elbow and demanded, "How did you get Dad's number?"

Jacob was fresh-showered, his hair still damp. He looked sunny and golden in the faint light streaming through the window behind him. She swallowed and tried to concentrate on the conversation.

"...googled it. Learned the computer while I was in Wyoming."

She set her spatula alongside the frying pan with more force than was necessary. "What other surprises have you two hatched?"

"That depends." Jacob sobered and the dimple in his chin disappeared. "I'll let you know when I figure it all out. You need to bear with me."

She thought to attend to the bacon in the skillet, but her eyes seemed to have a will of their own. She had no desire to look away as energy crackled between them— until the spell was broken by a cough.

Amanda's father cleared his throat. "Well, son. I can see you have feelings for my daughter. And it's no wonder. She's a spitfire." He indicated the platter of eggs and bacon she hastily set at the end of the table. "I suggest we eat those before they get cold."

Amanda filled Jacob's mug. "Not instant coffee this time around. Fresh ground."

Her father frowned. "You've had occasion to sample Amanda's breakfast coffee?"

Jacob colored, "Only once, Mr. Miller. The night of the fire. We were only..."

Bob grinned and aimed a playful tap at Jacob's

shoulder. "Only razzing you, young man. I trust my daughter. She'll take the straight road."

Amanda concentrated on her food while her father studied them from across the table. After an uncomfortable half-hour of interrogation and parrying, she felt the need to escape. "I'll soak the dishes, Jacob. Let's take a drive. I'll show you my town."

He nodded with obvious relief. "I need to get a cell phone. Is there a store in your town?"

"You want a smartphone?"

He carried his plate to the sink while he considered. "I live in the outside world now. I need to be able to do what they do. Not be thought a fool."

Her father interrupted. "You looking for work, you'll need to get the lay of the land."

Jacob nodded. "We can take my truck."

Amanda slid into the old leather bench seat and searched for the old-fashioned seat belt tucked behind the seat. The interior smelled of horse liniment and old hay. She picked up a pair of old leather gloves and feathered the worn fingers. "Yours?"

"Uh-huh. I did some fence-mending with those. Figured they still have some use left in them." He put the truck in gear. As the engine caught, he gripped the steering wheel and backed out. "I thought to get a cell phone. Probably ought to take care of that first."

"How romantic," she teased. At the stoplight, she leaned to meet his lips. Neither spoke as the pickup navigated the downtown tourist traffic, but the cab resonated with promise.

At the phone store, Jacob cut the engine and hopped out. "Let's get this over. A simple flip phone. No need for costly gizmos."

Inside, as a salesperson explained about the 5G capabilities of the Samsung Galaxy series, Jacob leaned closer to hear the camera's capabilities described. A few minutes later, he selected a password from the Amish dialect.

"Only need a flip phone, huh?" Amanda teased as they returned to the pickup. "Here, add my number. But teacher will take it away if you call me at school. And watch out for those chat rooms."

His chuckle belied the aggravation in his tone. "Amanda, cut me some slack, will you! I don't become an Englischer in a day. I hang onto my common sense until I see reason to change." He held the door for her then walked around to the driver's side. She noticed that he drove with his fingers curved over the steering wheel as if he held a set of reins. When he saw her watching, he grinned. "Old habits."

"I love it. Don't change a thing."

"Don't change? Is that even possible? I change every day. So much that I wonder my brain doesn't explode. But I promise you, I cling to my honor."

Amanda reached for his hand. "I think I must be dreaming. I'm so happy. And scared—all at the same time."

"Me, too. But certain." He braked to a stop and pulled her to him. When the kiss ended, they remained pressed together until a horn behind them blared. "Someone will see their teacher on her rumspringa," he teased.

"You never cut school?"

"With *my* daed?" He craned to study a wooden library building with colorful baskets of petunias hanging from the porch. "For a short time. When I was running around and I got in with a bad gang. What we call a group of friends. Nothing bad, just guy stuff." He nodded in the direction of the library. "I will make use of this place. One day I get my GED and then I start community college." He hesitated. "Some of the boys attended high school while they were in their rumspringa. They didn't do so bad. I thought about it, but I wasted my opportunity. Now maybe I make up for my lost time. You think?"

She smiled. "The empty cup will find its water."

His gaze rested on hers. "Amanda, truly, I am filled." He shifted into drive and eased into the traffic lane. "No more libraries and phone stores today. We will make time for us."

❧

The Oregon Coast was clear, with gentle waves that lapped the coarse sand below an empty parking lot. Amanda found an old woolen blanket under the seat and led the way down the blackberry-lined ramp to a rocky beach. In the distance, a couple walked their miniature Australian Shepherd on a leash, but otherwise the beach was deserted.

She spread the blanket and tossed her sandals on the sand. After a moment, Jacob tugged off his boots and added them to the pile. "Come on," she urged, "let's hit the water." She sprinted ahead and turned a cartwheel on the hard-packed crust at the water's edge until he followed her into the surf, and yelped in shock when he felt the cold water. A wave undercut the sand shelf he stood on. When a second wave doused him to the knees, he backed up like a kid.

"Have you ever done this before?" she asked.

"In Florida, but we didn't go to the beach much. It was frowned on, the swimsuits and all." He grinned. "I did some body surfing down there, but I didn't make a habit of it. Me and my friends got away when we could. Locals claimed the water was too cold, but we didn't mind too much."

"Colder than ours?"

He laughed. "Not even close. This is brutal. But I'm hearty. Trust me."

He found an abandoned sea shack washed apart in high tide and began to fit whorled, polished limbs into a rough lean-to while she ran off in search of driftwood. She managed to drag a log from the end of the beach and dump it at his feet. "This one's mine. Mitts off!"

"We see about that. Quiet now. This fella is working. A man builds a home for those he cares about." He picked up a stout branch and slowly fit it to form a rough roof while she locked the verticals together with smaller driftwood branches.

When the last piece was fitted, Jacob captured their whimsical sea shack on his camera while Amanda crawled onto it to watch the sunset. Inside, Jacob's first kiss tasted of salt. "I could get used to this," he whispered. The breeze ruffled his hair as he kneeled in the golden-orange orbs of the setting sun, painting his skin like a Greek statue as he studied the horizon. When he turned again, she felt her body flush and she realized she'd been holding her breath.

"Me too."

His look melted her insides. "Amanda, I do not leave again."

"I know."

"My home will be where you are. Where my children are." He faced her unflinchingly as the red flames of sunset painted his face. He moved slightly and his skin seemed to be on fire. "Amanda, I'm here to marry you."

She wanted to breathe, but her life no longer depended on oxygen.

He tilted her face to glimpse her eyes. "Then yes?"

"Yes."

"I have plans to buy you an engagement ring, but I will need your help." He grinned. "It makes my first such purchase." He brought his lips to hers again.

They huddled in the driftwood shack with the blanket draped over their shoulders, watching the moon's reflection on the water while Amanda traced her name on the dry sand, tempted to add his last name after hers, but she refrained. They spent hours talking, lulled by waves slapping the rocks. In the distance a foghorn blasted. Night-birds scurried away and a car horn honked on the neighborhood street behind them.

"I want this for my life. With you." Jacob filled his lungs with the tang of saltwater, his eyes closed. His fingers tightened against hers. She caught his scent as she leaned against him, so close that her hair fanned across his arm. He brought his free hand up to brush her shoulder, so slowly that his stroke replicated her pulse. He caught a lock of her hair and brought it to his lips. "You smell of oranges, Amanda. Just like the first time in the buggy. Oranges and honey. I wanted to kiss you then, but all I could think of was the reasons I should not. Now I have only the reasons why I must."

From the parking lot, a beam of light swept across the sand. Amanda bolted up at the sound of a car door.

"Shhh, stay still. We're not supposed to be here after dark." She crouched down in the sand beside him. The beam swept the darkness while she held her breath. Jacob's low chuckle sounded loud over the crunch of boots on the sand.

Before the flashlight reached their shack, a dispatcher's voice crackled on the radio. The bearer of the flashlight halted, muttered something into the radio and turned to retreat back across the sand. A moment later, the light disappeared up the ramp, a car door slammed and the vehicle roared out of the parking lot with its lights flashing.

Amanda giggled with relief. "That was close."

Jacob nuzzled her with breath that reminded her of milk cows and alfalfa hay. Sexy milk cows. "I can just see the headlines. *Oregon teacher arrested for public loitering,*" he teased.

A faint layer of fog obscured the moon before it wisped away, leaving gaps of starlight through which Orion and the Big Dipper danced before yielding the sky to the Morning Star in the east, just before sunrise. They woke, wrapped in a blanket, as the first rays of morning filled the gaps between the driftwood. Amanda opened her eyes to the squawk of cormorants and murres searching for food.

A pair of joggers spoiled the ambience for Jacob. "They have the right idea. This fresh air makes an appetite."

"Only the fresh air?" She ran her fingers along his muscled forearm, where his farmer's tan was still visible. "You deserve to starve," she teased. "You made me miss dinner."

He grinned. "You are not wrong in this. It takes

energy to resist you. Come, let's find something to fill the belly." He pulled her to her feet and leaned to kiss her. "Then we set to work. We plan a wedding before this fellow is lost."

※

Jacob's arrival revitalized her father. He seemed calmer, sharing ideas about the nursery and the plants. Amanda stood at the stove scrambling eggs while the two forged a bond. Even now he talked as though Jacob were a longtime employee.

"Today, we prune the bushy varieties. Get them ready for shipping. You'll ride along on a delivery. See the operation start to finish."

Jacob looked down at his hands before he answered. "Ja. Maybe I trade horses for greenhouse farming. We see."

"Someday, you and my daughter will run this place. Take my word."

Jacob glanced over at Amanda, his eyes warm. "Gott does the planning for us."

Bob laughed. "You sound just like your father. I remember Levi as a boy. We rode that big yellow bus fifteen miles every morning. First day, we were both scared enough, thought I'd wet my pants. Big journey for two little farm boys."

"Levi Ruth rode the bus to school?" Amanda paused with a pancake to study the two men. Jacob looked happy and relaxed. Her father seemed younger than usual as he relived the memories of his childhood in Ohio.

Bob nodded. "Had to. Was the law at the time.

States were required to consolidate their school districts so all kids got the same education. Everyone was bused to the larger schools. Didn't matter, their parents pitched a fit at the school board meetings, the law was the law."

Jacob nodded, his forehead furrowed in thought. "Daed said the community voted against that. We had the small school. Our teacher, Mrs. Zooks."

Bob continued as though he hadn't been interrupted. "None of the Amish wanted it. They argued for their rights. Got themselves a lawyer and took it all the way to the Supreme Court. Took twenty years, but they prevailed. I remember it well. Wisconsin vs. Yoder. The High Court agreed with the locals. Maintained that parents had the right to educate their kids as they saw fit. After that, no more consolidated school districts unless people agreed."

"That's when you went to the one-room schoolhouse with Jacob's father, Levi?" Amanda asked.

"Through eighth grade. Then he stayed on the farm and I went over to high school. Never saw much of him after his rumspringa. The family kept him busy."

She plated the bacon and eggs and started toward the table. "And you met Mama?"

"Later. In the military. Met her on leave, traveling through Oregon on my way back to Ft. Lewis from San Francisco. She handled the counter at a Greyhound Depot. Bus stopped. Went inside and bought myself a Baby Ruth candy bar. Stood there with that candy bar, making sweet talk while she ignored me. And perteee! I'd say so."

Amanda grinned. "Dad, you never told me that story."

He looked down at his fingers, his front teeth worrying a scab on his bottom lip. "Guess that story belonged to me. All fresh hopes and strong beginnings, you know?" He looked up. "Later, those memories were all we had. We kept them to ourselves."

Jacob glanced from father to daughter, unsure that he should be hearing such a personal conversation, until Amanda crossed the room to place her hand over his and it felt as though he was already a part of this small family. She leaned to give her father a kiss on his forehead, an act he had never seen a daughter do. Handshakes, even hugs, but in his family—never a kiss for a father.

Bob patted her hand and teased, "We going to eat those hotcakes or nail them to the wall?"

Jacob took a sip of the pasteurized milk that came in a plastic jug. "Maybe I get myself a cow. I would raise pigs with this store-bought stuff."

Amanda smiled. "Store-bought is pasteurized. Safer for us. The bacteria is treated."

"Ja, sure. But I prefer raw milk straight from the udder."

"Okay, but you do the milking. Not me."

Jacob placed the empty carton in a bin filled with cardboard, tin cans and plastic containers. "Better to grow from the garden and cook from scratch." He thrust a thumb at the trash bin. "Where do you send this waste?"

"Landfills. Buried. I dunno. Maybe burned. Someone takes care of it." Amanda glanced at her father and saw that he too was embarrassed. "A cow sounds like a great idea. I can get a bread maker. The county ordinance doesn't allow us to have pigs."

Jacob hesitated. "We find a middle path. Some of your ways, some of mine. But good milk is for certain. We will need it to make strong babies."

Amanda laughed. "Babies? We better get married first."

He stood behind her with his arms encircling her. "Since you ask, I will consider the proposal."

Her father looked from one of them to the other and scowled. "Finish up your grub and let's take a tour of the place. See if it's what you want for a future. You two should think about getting married."

Amanda looked up to see if her father was joking. When they had arrived home from the coast, she'd shared her engagement news with him. He seemed to have forgotten. She pushed her chair back. "No school today. Let's make the most of it."

The tour began at the stables, away from the greenhouses and the nursery business with its loud trucks and busy forklift. "My mother used to love to sit at her window and watch the trucks," she explained. "But this was my favorite place to be." Jacob inhaled the scent of oats and molasses, old hay and leather. He plucked a halter off its hook with a faraway expression. "Stalls are empty now. I had to sell Napoleon—Jacob Amish—to pay for the repairs on my aunt's house. I had him fostered with a friend, but I had to let him go."

"So many losses—your mother, your aunt, your horse. This was a hard year for you." Jacob's eyes were dark with compassion. *And I left, too.* He didn't say the words, but she saw regret as she led the way to the sliding doors and slid one open. A blast of sunlight hit her face. The nursery crew was hard at work loading evergreen shrubs and holiday bushes into two delivery trucks. She introduced Jacob to the office manager.

"Doris, this is Jacob Ruth. You'll be seeing a lot of him." The older woman gave Jacob an appraising glance and she smiled. In the yard, Amanda waited for the forklift to pass before she led him into a greenhouse filled with seedlings. "We sterilize the tools after each use. Plant our starts in fresh potting soil. Keep the humidity and temperature regulated. Dad will give you the details. A lot of this is automated. Less work than when we started out."

"Just you and your daed?" When she nodded, he added, "We call it apprenticeship."

"Apprenticeship? Out here in Oregon, some of our neighbors called it child abuse."

Jacob's eyes softened with understanding; clearly he'd experienced the odd looks and gossip by strangers who thought children should spend their time in recreation. "My people went to court to defend their beliefs against child-labor laws. The Ordnung makes an argument for apprenticeship. Good for the body and mind, they believe. And the soul."

He said little for the remainder of the tour. Instead, he watched silently as workers carried, stacked, and loaded pallets while the foreman noted their progress on a clipboard. She led the way back to the house and made BLTs on sourdough bread from a neighborhood bakery. The cookie jar held a few molasses cookies from the same source. She opened a jar of applesauce and set it on the table next to fresh glasses of iced tea.

"We have a lady who comes in three days a week to clean and cook for Dad while I'm at work, but she's off today," Amanda explained.

Jacob swallowed and looked down at his food, none of it prepared from scratch. She felt her face heat with embarrassment when she realized the train of his thought. At his home, neighbors would probably drop by to help a widower who needed help. Englischers hired the Amish to clean and cook. They traveled in the winter and needed someone to keep their big houses clean while they were gone. Maybe he thought she was lazy. But she'd show him she wasn't lazy, just busy with a job that prevented proper meals and cleanly-maintained houses. He needed to understand that about her when they married.

Chapter Ten

A day later, Bob Miller surprised Jacob with a question. "So you two've set a date? Will you invite your family, young man?"

Jacob sat on the sofa next to Amanda, with a log blazing in the fireplace. Her father sat in his favorite chair with his newspaper, with three rescue dogs sprawled at his feet.

Jacob wrinkled his nose at the musty throw rug, and the dozen dirty chew toys strewn about the room. Amanda claimed that her father had always been faithful about keeping his Labs bathed when they needed it, but the house smelled like a kennel. He hesitated. "I will ask Mr. and Mrs. Bell, but it will be hard for them to travel from Wyoming. 'Your bride is welcome here for the honeymoon,' they told me, and I agreed." He winked at Amanda and saw her father grin.

"Okay. How about we elope?" Amanda asked.

He blinked, surprised that she would even consider such a proposal. "No. You will have a proper wedding.

With everyone you know as witnesses. And a proper ring. You will regret it otherwise."

She bit her pencil as she composed her invitation list. She nudged him playfully, her eyes happy. "You're right. I'll ask Lucy Knowles, my mother's health aide. She and Mom bonded after I left for Ohio. Maybe Mom talked to her about her hopes for me."

⚜

"I'd love to help!" Across the phone, Lucy Knowles's enthusiasm kindled Amanda's memories of cheerful prattle down the hall when her mother was alive. "With no children of my own, dear, I will consider it a joy to help. Let's meet for coffee on Saturday, at that cute little diner your mother loved. She used to have me sneak a cinnamon bun from now and again. Her guilty pleasure."

Amanda blinked back tears. "She was so fond of you!"

"Likewise. For me, she was an angel in disguise. I miss her terribly."

On Saturday, Lucy arrived with a tablet of ideas. "First of all, what is your color scheme? We can coordinate the bridesmaids' dresses so everyone looks and feels lovely."

"I've decided on turquoise and brown. Jacob says my eyes are turquoise in the right light."

Lucy's eyes crinkled at the corners. "He's a romantic. Good for him. Turquoise is a rich, horsey color. And brown is earthy." She studied Amanda's features like an artist with a model. "You're so lovely, dear. That hair. And that body. Not to mention your beautiful skin.

What I wouldn't have given at your age. You're what we call a *natural beauty*."

Amanda's gratitude swelled with the unexpected compliment. "Mom used to say the same, but she was biased."

Lucy smiled sadly. "That's what makes you so special, dear. You don't even know how lovely you are. Beautiful inside and out."

Amanda wasn't sure where to look. "Jacob says the Amish don't concern themselves with how a girl looks, only with her character."

Lucy laughed. "Oh, posh. If you believe that, I have some oceanfront property in Arizona I'd be happy to sell you." She blew a raspberry and grinned. "Men fall in love with their eyes. And that boy didn't know what hit him when he saw you." She patted a strand of imitation pearls at her own neck and smoothed her short bubble haircut.

When Amanda squinted, she could almost see her mother's face, flushed with excitement. *For a stranger to get to sit in her mother's place? It isn't fair. But Lucy wasn't just Mom's health aide, she was her best friend. They laughed and cried together. They had the same tastes. Sisters.* She blinked and realized Lucy was still talking.

"...I know a great winery. I can get you a deal on the facilities. Of course they cater. Shouldn't cost your father more than a new car." Her laughter reminded Amanda of her mother.

Amanda shook her head. "Let me discuss this with Jacob. He may have some other options." She bit her lip to contain her tears. "Mom should be here."

Lucy nodded and quietly gripped her hand. When

she left a few minutes later, she held Amanda against her in silence.

❧

Jacob's reaction came as no surprise, even if Amanda's heart fell when she heard it. "Twelve thousand dollars? For a wedding? How can this be?" His voice softened and he waited for her to admit that she was only joking.

Amanda flicked a glance at the pile of bridal magazines piled on the coffee table for support, but the glossy photos of models in tiaras *did* seem indulgent. "There's a lot to consider. The dress. Reception hall, flowers, invitations, rehearsal dinner, reception, planner, makeup, shoes, gifts for my bridesmaids, a band, photographer. It all adds up. Weddings aren't cheap." She heard herself parrot the argument a consultant had used at her consultation.

"Twelve thousand dollars?" His voice rose in disbelief. "Amanda, this is not who we are. You and I...we cannot spend this. It is prideful. Sinful. The money should be put to better uses." His tone was firm, even as his eyes pleaded for understanding. "Do you not agree?"

She closed her eyes and saw the simple dresses and the homemade food at the Amish wedding she had attended. *Almost attended.* In truth, she'd stood in the corner until she could deliver her gift to Jacob's brother. On second thought, technically she'd crashed the family event. But she saw Jacob's point. "Jacob, you're right. What about a buffet reception at the church hall? We can have a caterer serve it, supply the cake and clean up afterward. I'll find a dress on sale. We can do it for a lot less if we're clever." Another thought occurred. "I'll fire the wedding planner. We'll figure it out ourselves."

"A wedding planner? Nei! It doesn't matter if we make mistakes. It will be our day until we are too old to remember."

The next day, the caterer phoned to schedule a meeting as Amanda walked out of her classroom. A few minutes later, the bakery promised a taste test for Monday afternoon. She took a rain check on the first call, with the excuse that she would need to revise her budget. She ordered a carrot cake from the bakery that would serve sixty guests.

That evening, Lucy Knowles listened while she explained her reasons for a revised celebration. Her advice sounded like something Amanda's mother might have agreed with. "Whatever you decide, it will be lovely. People say it's about the marriage, not the wedding, but I say it's about the dress. You need to go to Portland. Next week. You know that TV show? Find a dress that will do you proud."

"Lucy! I'm not saying 'yes to the dress.' I promise to try some on, but this is Jacob's day, too.

"He's the groom. Forget him! This is your day! Take your bridesmaids. Make a party of it. Have some fun."

Amanda nodded into the phone. "I need to think about this. Don't worry. We'll figure it out."

Her next call was to Carol. The two-hour time difference in Ohio made it almost nine there. *Carol's probably off work at the cafe by now. Maybe hyped up on coffee while she studies for a college exam, but this is important.* "Hi, Carol. You'll never guess. Jacob's here. We're getting married."

"Jacob?" On the other end, silence finished the sentence. "So that's where he disappeared to! I should have known. You two are crazy for each other. Wow! Just wow!"

"He's different now. He's—"

On the other end of the line, Carol sighed. "He's yours. Amanda. I guess you can't argue with fate." Her tone lifted. "How can I help?"

Amanda felt her eyes tear up. "I don't have a maid of honor."

Carol laughed. "Matron of honor. Renny and I tied the knot. Surprise! We wanted to jump-start the honeymoon, and our minister wanted us to get legit before we...you get the picture, right? 'No hanky-panky until the ink is pink.'" She laughed. "We're moving into your house this weekend. Uncle Clem offered us a deal we couldn't refuse. You'll be our new landlady."

"Does Timberly go with the deal?" Amanda pictured Aunt Lydia's cat in the warm spot beneath the porch.

"Of course. Clem's no fool! The lease agreement is for three tenants, including one large Maine Coon cat. But he said he'd waive the pet deposit."

Amanda laughed. "He should pay you!"

"Yeah, probably. He's intimidated by that monster cat. But Renny loves her."

"Carol, does that mean you'll be my matron of honor?"

"*Absolushly*! I'll fly out early. Stay a week and help you with the pre-nuptial nerves. Got your dress yet? Fishtail, strapless, or all three?"

Amanda laughed. "Carol, are you drunk?"

Carol giggled. "Just celebrating your engagement."

She smiled at the sound of Rennie's congratulations in the background. "I found a few dresses I like. I had the clerk at the bridal shop take some shots. Can I get your opinion?"

"Heck yeah. Let's do this!" They chatted while the photos came through. Carol clicked through the four photos. "I like the first one. You look absolutely gorgeous. The second one is nice. Hello! What is this? Amanda, you nailed it on the third one! Jacob will trip out on it. Number three it is. I love the back, too. Love the spaghetti straps. Rose-pink. Makes your skin glow. And look what it does for your red hair." Carol paused to take a breath. "Hey, I forgot to ask, which one do you like?"

Amanda laughed. "Auburn. And number three's my favorite, too."

"Absolutely. You'll knock Jacob's socks off. A nip at the waist. Otherwise it's perfect. Get some heels you can dance in."

"So true. I want to be able to celebrate."

Carol's grin filled the screen. "Speaking of...do you have any celebratory bubbly in your refrigerator? Let's make a virtual toast to the occasion. I'll do the same." She returned in two minutes with bubbles fizzing from a champagne flute. "To my best friend and my only bottle of Stella Rosa Black. May your bubbles flow forever."

Amanda lifted her glass. "To my best friend Carol, whose marriage I did not attend because she didn't invite me. May she forever rue her loss."

"Hey, no honeymoon. We didn't leave the hotel room. We'll fly out there and vacation on your dad's dime. We can afford cheap seats on a red-eye."

"Deal. Come for the week."

"We can honeymoon together on the Oregon Coast."

Amanda laughed. "Take your own honeymoon. I'll loan you my car."

When they hung up, Lucy called. "The minister's wife has a dozen good ideas for the reception at the church hall."

⚜

Jacob agreed to accompany Amanda to a bridal shop for a fitting. He wandered around the men's section and studied a rack of starched shirts the colors of little Amish girls' dresses. When the clerk made a suggestion, he carried the suit into the fitting room and shut the door. When he emerged, ignoring the shiny shoes the clerk laid out, clad in his stocking feet, he stood in front of Amanda clad in a blue suit with a matching cummerbund, stiff with the effort of maintaining a straight face. When the clerk disappeared to assist another customer, he whispered, "Amanda, truly, is this what men wear on their wedding day?" He glanced over to see that the clerk was still engaged. "Would I have to wear this to church every Sunday, after we are married?"

"You don't like it?" she asked innocently as she reached to kiss his face that blazed with embarrassment.

The clerk returned and Jacob made an effort to appear serious. "Yeah. I think we pass on this."

Amanda pulled a black tux from a hanger and held it up. "What about this?"

He made his mind up in the time it took to shake his head. "My mother already sewed my coat. I wore it to

John's wedding. It is serviceable and well made. It suits me."

Amanda laughed weakly. "So I guess we got that covered. No tux." She met his blue eyes, heightened by his five-o'clock shadow, and her smile vanished. *This man of mine is sooo hot!* "Jacob, you'll look great. I'll be proud to stand beside you in your beautiful Amish coat."

He returned to the fitting room, grateful for the familiar feel of his work clothes. They were barely out of the store before they collapsed in laughter as Jacob painted a visual picture of the cummerbund he'd mistaken for a tie and tried to wrap around his neck. He mimicked how it felt to try to button the tiny buttons on his wrists. "Now I know what it feels like to wear a clown's outfit. But no one pays me to scare children on my wedding day," he gasped.

Amanda convoluted in laughter. "Oh, Jacob, you looked like you hated every minute of it. And that clerk. And those shiny black pumps."

"Pumps? Is that what those shoes are called?" he chuckled as he opened the door of his pickup and helped her in. "A pump is a machine you folks use to do your work for you."

He turned his pickup toward home, but her laughter broke his concentration until he pulled over in a burst of laughter. Amanda pointed out her favorite ice cream shop. "Remember the day we met? You had an ice cream cone...in the rain." She considered a moment. "Now I crave ice cream. Let's go get some. To celebrate the most embarrassing day of your life."

On her way home from work, Amanda stopped by the bridal shop to try on a white sheath-gown with modest three-quarter sleeves she'd noticed in the mark-down section. The clerk explained that the fabric was bias-cut, with the sheerest modesty panel underneath, a slam-dunk with her skin tone and eyes. The modest cut of the bodice would please Jacob. She studied her hair and her apricot skin in the muted lighting of the mirror and made her decision. The dress would look perfect against Jacob's wool coat.

One of her father's former business associates texted with an offer of bulk flowers. One of her teacher friends had just opened a catering business on the side and called to offer her a discounted rate in exchange for an endorsement. She visited Costco and picked out a carrot cake with plain white icing. Almost as an afterthought, she arranged for a substitute teacher to cover her classroom.

A week before the wedding, Amanda's teacher friends, Ruth and Madilyn, threw a bachelorette party. Lucy Knowles arrived with Carol in tow. Someone had alerted her friends and Amanda spent the evening with a dozen friends from high school rodeo, grad school and former coworkers. The party was planned at the Spirit Mountain Casino. She played the roulette table, and a slot machine that Carol nicknamed *Salome* for its temptress manner. And drank margaritas until she was woozy.

Cindy arrived with two of their friends from high school and an apology. She caught Amanda alone. "I don't drink any more. I was so ashamed of how I treated you. You were always so quiet. I thought you had totally missed out on the fun. But you have it all, and I'm jealous. I want to be a better friend. Forgiven?"

Amanda gave her friend a hug. "Forgiven."

On the way home in the back of a cab, Carol murmured, "Thought you said you didn't have any friends."

As the car idled at a stoplight, Amanda sobered. "I thought so, too."

On the night before the wedding, Renny phoned at midnight to report that an impromptu stag party was in progress at Bronco's. "Amanda's cowboy friend, Charlie Rivers, and his friend Jim Scoville showed up, along with two of Jacob's new coworkers."

Amanda grabbed the phone. "Rennie, you better not bring him to the wedding hungover."

"He's happy and getting happier, but I promise to keep him safe until the ceremony."

Carol leaned in close to the phone. "You better, lover. Your neck's on the line here."

Rennie sounded happy. "Those cowboys are coming to the wedding. Charlie says no hard feelings. Tell Amanda he likes her guy. Wants to teach him to rope."

Amanda shook her head in disbelief. "Thanks, Rennie. Tell Jacob to have fun."

She spent the last night in her own bedroom, thinking of how much her mother would have enjoyed all the commotion. After a night's sleep, she woke to clear skies and slipped into her robe before she stole into the kitchen to make coffee before Carol filled the room with silliness. Mug in hand, she made her way into her mother's room and stood beneath the photograph of her parents, taken on the day they got married —so hopeful and in love.

"I miss you so much, Mom. And I wish you were here." A sound caused her to turn. Her father stood at the door watching silently, his eyes filled with wistful tears. They eyed each other in silence until she slipped into his arms. She felt his jagged breath and her heart broke for their loss. She started to speak and hesitated. He didn't need words to know how grateful she was to be his daughter. Words were too weak. But maybe he felt differently.

"Peanut, I guess this is it. I like your young man and he'll be good for you. I want you and Jacob to have your mother's room from now on. She'd want to share your happiness. Give her this."

"Dad? Are you sure? It's Mom's."

"Shucks, Peanut. We made it a shrine for too long. It'll be good to bring some life back into this house."

Her father's arm around her trembled, but his eyes shone as she slipped loose and started down the hall. At her door, she turned to acknowledge him.

When it was time to dress, Carol made sure Amanda's veil was attached with a borrowed hairpin, and that her garter contained the obligatory blue satin ribbon. She wore her mother's locket, filled with the sprig of hair she'd clipped from her head on the day of her funeral.

At the church, she waited until she was alone with her father before she whispered, "Mom's here. Can you feel her?"

He nodded, his eyes clouded with emotion. "She'd approve of your young man. He's sure the one for you."

"Dad, thank you for that. For everything. I don't

know how we got here, but I'm so grateful. Let's do this for Mom. And for Lydia."

Carol and Rennie headed the wedding party. The guests were scattered among the first few pews of the church, but their happiness reminded her that she should be grateful.

She tucked her arm in her father's, and they began a slow march down the aisle. When their minister asked, "Who gives this woman away?" he slipped and said, "Her mother and I do." No one objected.

❧

Jacob watched Amanda float down the aisle toward him through a veil of joyous tears, wearing a filmy white dress that moved with each sway of her hips. His fingers clenched and unclenched while his body burned with nerves. Never had he seen such a beautiful bride. Guests turned to look at her, in their eyes, every one of the same mind. When her father transferred Amanda into his care, her skin felt smooth and warm against his. His body trembled as their eyes met, and for that moment, no one else existed.

He was conscious that he stood out in the crowd of stylishly-dressed guests, dressed in his black wool coat, buttonless the way his mother had made it, but he prayed that he wore it with dignity. Amanda understood his reasons. The coat would not be their last compromise.

When it came time to say their vows, he made quiet assurance that he would love and protect her. He had written his vows with traditional Amish phrases to honor his past, and to celebrate what he knew about love and marriage. Her own vows carried the promises of a lifetime. She vowed to accept him as he was, first and always. Like him, she recited her vows with a combination of nerves and elation. His fingers trembled when he transferred the ring to her finger and felt his heart soar when she did the same.

Their kiss, made to erupting applause, lingered longer than he had planned. She pressed her fingers across his chest, and he felt his heart nearly explode with pride. Time stopped. A promise of forever behind her long dark lashes made his knees weak. She swayed and he reached to steady her.

The ceremony included customs that were strange to him. He was glad when the church erupted in applause and the minister indicated that they could leave. She eased her fingers through his and nudged him forward to face her friends and coworkers, and a growing number of people he could honestly call his own friends.

At the reception, Renny tapped on his wine glass and gave a nervous glance around the room. He fumbled with a folded piece of paper and began. "I want to introduce an Amish fellow who left the life he knew to follow his heart. He grew up secure in a large, hardworking family. He was loved. But he fell hard for an outsider, and he fought his community and his family over her. In the end, he left his home because his love for this girl sent him on a journey." Rennie gave a quick, nervous glance at the newlyweds. "He drove here and wooed her, and she said 'yes.' And we're all mighty glad she did." He met Amanda's gaze. "Because he's one of the finest men I've ever met. And from the community he came from, that says a lot."

When Rennie finished, Jacob saw Amanda's friends assess him with new respect. He whispered his thanks as Renny slumped back into his chair and wiped his brow with his pocket handkerchief.

Jacob waited for her before he loaded his plate with roast turkey and stuffing. Further down the table, he hesitated over a chafing dish and inhaled the familiar aroma of creamed celery. "How did you know?"

She leaned close, her breath warm against his ear. "Amish wedding food? Your mother told me about the tradition, so I looked up the recipe on an Amish blog. We added vinegar, brown sugar, lots of butter and evaporated milk, just like it called for." He inhaled the odor of celery with eyes closed. "I can see you now," she teased, "dawdling over your food in the corner Eck, laughing with your best friends. Old men ribbing you while we hold hands under the table like teenagers," She spooned a bite of creamed celery to him with a smile.

"You will make a good wife," he teased.

"You look Amish today in your wedding coat," she whispered. "Very handsome." She slipped her hand into his and he felt her gold ring.

For their first dance, he arranged for the band to play a George Strait wedding waltz, and he led her with steps he'd practiced until his footwork was as smooth as a cowboy's. His first steps were strange and stiff, conscious of people watching, until he felt the rhythm and guided her in a turn. From that point it was only the two of them on the dance floor. He bent his long legs and tossed his coat to someone while the crowd clapped and whistled. When the music ended, Amanda danced alone with her father. When it was over, she returned to Jacob with tears in her eyes. The floor filled. On their next dance, one of her friends cut in and Jacob reluctantly released her. "You're a good sport, Mr. Ruth," she whispered.

After two hours, Jacob tilted his head in the direction of the door, the signal they'd agreed on when it was time to make their farewells and slip out. Amanda gave her father a lingering hug before they dashed through a hail of birdseed and good wishes. Someone had decorated Jacob's old pickup with paint and tin cans. "Some things are the same in all cultures." He grinned as he tried to shield them from the birdseed. "Watch you don't slip."

On their way to the coast, he lifted his left hand to catch the reflection of the gold band in the streetlight. "I expect I'll get used to this." He gave her a quick look to see if his joke had offended her. They were still new to each other's ways. "I suppose it's better than having to wear a beard my life through. Cooler in the summer, for sure." He rotated his hand and examined his palms. "I shook hands with a lot of new friends tonight. They wish us well."

"Good wishes to last us a lifetime..." Amanda's voice trailed off when his kiss silenced her.

They spent the first night at a motel where the sound of the waves was white noise for their lovemaking. They emerged from their room in the morning, haggard from lack of sleep and starving. Afterward, they spent a lazy afternoon at a secluded lagoon with a basket of deli treats they'd picked up at Ray's Market. When her phone buzzed, Amanda glanced at the caller. "Carol sent us their itinerary if we want to join them. Crab Louie at an open café, lighthouse, and museum."

Jacob stilled before he asked, "What happens if we don't?"

Amanda shrugged. "Tomorrow they kayak the sea caves, visit tidepools in low tide, browse gift shops in Bandon."

"And the day after that?"

"Drive the Coast. Brookings. Hike the redwoods."

He slipped his hand across her thigh and whispered, "Turn off your phone, wife. The world can wait."

That night they walked down to the beach to watch the moon sandwiched between clear skies and a low fog bank. "Look!" Amanda pointed to a sea shack that stood empty in the moonlight. "That's ours. Or what's left of it. Someone's changed it."

He unfolded the blanket they'd brought and tucked it inside the driftwood structure, with Amanda lying beside him. Together they watched the moon slip in and out of clouds in a dream-like waltz across the sky.

"Those are the stars that guided the Vikings," Amanda whispered. "Do you think they gaze at us with the same awe?"

"Us? We are merely dust to the heavens."

"Dust?"

"But such beautiful dust, liebchen. I do not need the universe to find happiness with you."

"Liebchen? What is that?"

"Sweetheart. My name for you."

Chapter Eleven

Jacob tickled Amanda's lip with the tip of her hair. "Time to rise, liebchen. We can't be lazy forever. Even if I would wish to be."

"No. Too early."

"Every cat has its day, my mother used to say."

"I think it's 'every dog.' But cats need to be happy too." Amanda stretched and pointed a toe toward the edge of the bed. "What day is it?"

Jacob laughed. "It's Sunday. The day we must head home. You must face your scholars tomorrow and teach them to call you 'Mrs. Ruth.' No more spinster schoolteacher 'Miss Miller' for you. I saved you."

"You saved me? As if!" She reached to pull the covers from his naked shoulders, honed from a lifetime of hard work and good food, but he was too quick. He twisted in a half-roll that trapped her beneath him, giggling. When she recovered from a bruising kiss, she coiled his thick hair in her fingers and pressed it to her lips. "Remember the night you stayed at my place in Ohio? How much we wanted this?"

His pupils dilated with the memory. "A man does not forget such a moment, woman. Not ever."

"How we wanted to be sure of our feelings before any line was crossed?" She hesitated. "I felt guilty for a long time. I thought I'd ruined your life."

Jacob ran his hand along the curve of her breast. "You ruined nothing. People change. We find our purpose." He leaned to nibble her shoulder. "You are my purpose." To prove his point, he kissed her in earnest.

By the time they dressed and made their way to the dining room, his stomach rumbled. A handful of diners paused to stare at Jacob in his rumpled jacket and longish hair, and Amanda's smile betrayed them both. She felt strangers' eyes on her. Filled with pride, she glanced over and saw that Jacob felt the same.

"How could your father have called us unequally yoked?" she whispered.

Too late, she saw the brief flare in his eye, and then it was gone, his only concern the buffet of barely warm fried potatoes and omelets in front of them. He waited for her to pick up a plate and his eyes cleared, a thinly veiled attempt to seem unaffected by the break with his family. Clearly, he had felt their absence on his wedding day. *Too soon to think of reconciliation, but one day.*

When they arrived home in the late afternoon, her father waited in his living room, watching *Sunday Morning* on the television. "That Jane Pauley is a crackerjack," he quipped as he lowered the volume on the TV. "You kids have fun?"

Amanda wasn't sure where to look, as though she were a teenager faced with a curfew. She glanced down and noticed the half-eaten bowl of microwave popcorn on his lap. "Dad!" Three more empty bowls sat on the coffee table. "Is that all you ate while we were gone? And where is the new housekeeper we hired?"

"I let her go. Didn't need her. No point paying her to sit and watch her Spanish telenovelas on TV. I can do my own cooking, same as I always did."

Amanda halted, flabbergasted by the messy room, and the open refrigerator door in the kitchen. She dropped her suitcase and picked up a stack of dishes. On her way back from the kitchen she gathered old newspapers and set them on the kitchen counter. "How long have you been batching it?"

"Don't recall. It was a workday because I had that appointment with the state AG inspector."

"Dad, that's crazy. You need to call the woman back and apologize." She glanced at Jacob, who stood like a statue, uncertain of his role in the drama. "Jacob, let's go and choose closet space. Dad gave us the master suite. He said he doesn't need all that room and we're welcome to it."

The new housekeeper had apparently been there long enough to empty the bureau drawers and transfer her father's belongings into the guest bedroom he had claimed for his own. His shirts and pants were arranged neatly in the closet.

Jacob hung his clothing on a half-dozen hangers and filled two drawers from his suitcase. His dirty clothes found the hamper, his boots and dress shoes one of the shelves in the walk-in closet. He was unpacked before she finished making her plan.

He helped her carry a stack of trousers from her former bedroom. "So it's true what the funnies say about wives? You Englischers are like pack rats, always gathering more?"

She dropped her pile on the bed and plopped down beside it. "The funnies? Is that where you get your information about wives?"

He grinned. "Where else? I haven't had one to practice on until now. Soon I will write my own cartoon strip."

"Good decision. Now help me decide." She indicated three hat boxes piled in the corner. "How many western hats should I keep?"

He shook his head and lifted the top one. "You ask the wrong fellow. I don't want to put my foot in my mouth this early on." He pressed a quick kiss that lengthened into a suggestion. "Maybe we finish later? I want to check out the bed, to see if it suits."

Amanda dropped two pairs of western boots on the floor. In a swift motion, Jacob swept her up with her knees folded over his thick forearms. "What are you doing?" She giggled as he carried her into the hallway.

"I carry you over the threshold for good fortune." He retraced his steps and deposited her back onto the bed. "There. Now our lives are secure. No bad luck for us." His voice dropped as he pushed the door shut behind him.

Jacob described the cow he planned to buy. As they passed the barn on their walk, Amanda stopped in front of the stall and ran her hand across the top board where Napoleon had cribbed the wood.

"I miss my horse. Don't you?"

Jacob nodded distractedly, picking up a lead rope and hanging it on a nail. "Mine is a buggy horse. Big difference."

"Could you ride yours if you'd a mind to?"

"I rode as a boy. With my brother, John. An old, tame mare, took us to school or around the farm. Never on the roads with the cars."

"What happened to it?"

"For us the family buggy was used more often. Not so much room for cargo and passengers on the back of a horse."

"Your church made a rule about no horseback riding!"

Jacob's eyes shone with amusement. "Think a moment, liebchen. How would you mount and maintain modesty in a dress such as our women wear?" He studied her western hat and her Wranglers. "Look at your own clothing and tack. A horse is a matter of pride for you. Look at the movies you watch at night—John Wayne and Clint Eastman. They are always the lone man who needs no one, not even God. Only himself and a gun to survive. Man against nature, you would say. For us, no such thing exists. We do not think like that. For us, a horse like the English ride would be prideful, with a saddle and tack that would cost many months' earnings." He grinned. "But who notices a man in a plain buggy rig?"

"I did." She leaned toward him and placed her hand on his arm. "I saw you from down the street!"

He shook his craggy locks with a boyish grin that made her heart leap. "See, even then I did a poor job fitting in. They are probably glad to be rid of me."

"And you?"

With a look that said he was done talking, he brought her into his arms. "I make my choice. No question."

"What would you say to a couple of horses? We could ride together. Charlie says he'll show you how to team rope. It would be fun."

He hesitated. "Maybe. But soon we begin a family and I have responsibilities."

Amanda paled. "So soon? We already have a lot on our plate without more complications."

"Complications?"

"You know what I mean. We have no grandparents to watch the children. I need to work for a while. Build up a nice nest egg. We both know there will be complications."

Jacob stubbed his toe in the dirt. "Ja, this I do know. Every time I see you apply that lipstick I want to protest, but I hold off. Still, it rubs the wrong way that you paint yourself up. You need no such paint to be beautiful in my eyes."

Amanda turned to face him, her hands on her hips. "Seriously? You want me to toss my makeup?"

Jacob held out a hand in protest. "Don't be making me unreasonable. I only speak my mind."

"You never said anything before."

He smiled and reached for her hand. "You do what you must. I am not your conscience. That is not my job or I would have remained Amish. But I'm glad we don't use the birth control. We trust in Gott's plans for us." He smoothed her hair back for a kiss. "Enough talk. Now, wife, let's take a walk to see what our future holds."

They walked the pastures while Jacob studied the

combination of grasses. "Plenty here. A milk cow will be content in this pasture."

"When does she arrive?"

"We must wait for her to bear her calf. The breeder lets me know."

❦

Jacob sat at the breakfast table when a truck with a horse trailer pulled into the driveway. At the sound of the diesel engine, Amanda poured coffee for her father and glanced out the window. When the truck coasted to a halt, she sat the coffee pot on the stove, grabbed Jacob's hand and pushed him out of the door still holding a slice of toast.

"What's the rush?" he demanded.

She laughed and skipped ahead like a young girl. "Come see. It's your wedding present."

He gulped the last bite and licked the jam from his fingers. "Mine? I have no need of a gift. I have everything I need."

"Wait and see before you say that. You'll love it."

"A motorcycle?"

"Hardly."

They watched as the equine transport rig parked and the driver dismounted. After unlocking the back doors, he unclipped a lead rope and led a high-stepping race horse down the ramp. The horse lifted its head, moved its ears forward and looked around with a soft whinny when it caught sight of Jacob.

Jacob stared with a confused look. "Yankee?" He started and threw his arms around his horse's neck. When he looked up, his eyes were damp with gratitude.

"I have imagined this in my mind. Thank you, Amanda."

Amanda scratched a signature on the driver's device while he unloaded the tack and uneaten oats and hay. Afterward, he returned to his truck and drove off.

Jacob led his horse to its waiting stall already swept clean and laid with a fresh layer of straw. He watered and brushed the gelding before he released it to the pasture and watched as it broke into a run. When Yankee circled the field and came to a halt in front of them, Amanda shared the same joy she saw in Jacob's face.

"I cannot believe you did this. What was my father's reaction?"

"Mr. Wright arranged it." She hesitated. "Truth is, your father was glad to get rid of it. He'll sell your buggy at auction if you want him to."

Jacob nodded, his eyes thoughtful. "I have no further use of it."

Amanda watched the strange, defiant look fade from his eyes.

"Jacob, let's go dancing tonight. That western band we like is playing at Broncos. We don't need to stay late." She had waited until after supper, on a night when the house seemed quiet and stale. When he agreed, she set aside the bundle of homework papers she'd carried home.

The bar was packed with a dozen university undergrads, and townies hoping to pick up a date. Cindy wiggled her fingers and made the "I'll call you" gesture before she turned back to her date. Amanda took a sip of the beer Jacob carried over before he slipped in the booth beside her. "Music's great," she mouthed. He nodded at a couple making their way across the room. When they reached the booth, it was Charlie Rivers and his new girlfriend.

"You look happy, Amanda. Marriage agrees with you." Charlie winked and took a swig of his beer.

Amanda laughed. "No complaints here."

"Offer on the calf roping's still open, Jake. We meet at the arena Sunday mornings." Charlie's glance included Jacob. "Saw a Kentucky blueblood in your pasture. Yours?"

Jacob studied his glass, still half-full, and swallowed. "Yankee isn't suited for roping. I got my hands full with the nursery and the wife. No time to play cowboy."

Charlie's hoot of laughter caused the people in the next booth to stare. "Hell, we don't play. We're dead serious. Love cowboying as much as I love my dog—and maybe more than Bianca here." He nudged his date and got a begrudging smile for his efforts. "Guy needs a hobby to let off his steam. Come on over Sunday and I'll show you what I mean." He winked at Amanda and grinned. "I got a litter of pups from that Lab bitch you always liked. I saved a fat little female just for you. I'll bring her by as soon as she's weaned. You're gonna love her. Named her Princess. Guess you'll see why!"

Jacob drove home in injured silence. Amanda waited for him to bring up Charlie's attentiveness. Clearly the flirting had soured the evening for him, but he drove in silence. They were almost home before she gave voice to the issue. "Charlie was sure drunk tonight. I'm not sure what got into him."

"He's sore, that's what. He wants to make me look a fool so you'll realize you got the bad deal in our marriage."

"Jacob, he's a friend! He even came to your bachelor party. And our wedding."

"Ja, that he did." He scowled. "And now he's got you a present, yet."

Bypassing their driveway, Jacob headed toward the river. At a turnout overlooking the bank, he cut the head lights so the moon flickered on the slow-moving water. He drummed his fingers on the steering wheel and considered his next words. "Think what you will, Amanda, but I don't need to prove anything. Not to him." In the cab of his pickup, heat from the dancing and his frustration made his body a furnace. "If he can't see that, then he's blind—and a fool besides."

He pulled her into a tight, angry embrace. By the time the kiss ended, both of them were winded, and the windows were steamed. Amanda stared into the naked vee at the top of his western shirt where a band of chest hair peeked from the unfastened snap. He smelled musky and feral, a scent that belonged to him alone. Her heart thudded with mixed emotions, one minute racing, the next minute engaged in a battle of wills. "He wants to give me a puppy, not a gold necklace."

"Yeah." Jacob released her and turned. A moment later he ground the pickup into gear.

From the west, a motorcycle blasted by, its mufflers loud in the silence. Jacob watched through his rearview mirror until the rider disappeared around a curve. He returned his attention to the road with a thoughtful look.

Amanda scooted up against him. "You're crazy if you think someone will worm their way in between us, Jacob. I love you. But I want that puppy."

Chapter Twelve

‫❧‬

Amanda started down the driveway where one of her father's mongrel dogs had pulled something from the drainage ditch. Her dad had brought this latest mutt home from a trip to see a grower. It was a rescue dog with a torn ear; abandoned in the country by some townie who thought a farmer would take it in. He'd come across it and brought it home instead of taking it to the kennel. But now her father had four rescue dogs and he seemed to ignore them all. She retrieved a dried-up rabbit carcass from the dog's mouth before giving it a cautious pet. The mongrel had arrived with no distemper or rabies shots, no vet visit. Apparently that task would fall to her.

She clapped her hands to distract it. "Come on, pal. Let's see what's for supper."

She found her father inside the barn, standing on a patch of water-soaked cement with a tangle of electrical cord in his hands from a broken heat lamp. The other end of the cord was still attached to the socket.

"Dad, drop it!"

He glanced up with a look of determination. "I think I see the problem. Just need to reattach this little wire. If I can remember how."

"Dad, put it down!"

Electricity arched from the base. Her father jerked back and dropped the lamp. It crashed to the floor, shattering into a million pieces as he jumped to a safe section of flooring. Smoke swirled around the cord while he cupped his good hand over a small burn that was darkening his arm. His eyes cleared and he shook his head in confusion. "What happened?"

Amanda reached to unplug the cord with a wooden gnome she'd made in elementary school. "What are you doing?" His arm had swollen with an angry welt, and his fingers were slightly curled and still spazzing. He was lucky that she'd walked in when she did. "Let's get you inside."

She chatted nervously on the way to the house, but her mind raced with questions. He apparently didn't remember how he broke the lamp, or why he was attempting to repair it. Inside, mud-encrusted dogs wrestled on the kitchen floor still damp from her mop. She scooted them to the back porch and closed the door on them. "After supper, we can give them a bath, okay Dad? One of them smells a bit skunky."

He ran his hand across his forehead and admitted, "I left him out last night. Guess I meant to close the gate, but I forgot."

Forgot? "You've been doing a lot of that lately. Maybe we need to schedule an appointment with your doctor." Her heart froze as she recalled the time she found him on his tractor, the front wheels stuck in the drainage ditch. He'd put it in reverse and backed out, but the look in his eyes had indication panic and confusion. "I'll make an appointment tomorrow. Least I can do for my favorite dad." She watched as he picked up the newspaper as though he'd forgotten the whole episode.

After dinner, she combed matted fur from the dogs and gave them baths. She opened a can of the special wet dog food her father insisted they use and added it to a scoop of dry mix that he'd made a special trip to the pet store for, despite the fact that he already had three more bags stacked in the garage. As she groomed the dogs, she reviewed the mix-ups, miscalculations and annoyances in the months since her mother's passing. Her father seemed to be failing. Or maybe he was merely under the weather. The greenhouses were functioning well, thanks to a small group of loyal employees. Her father insisted on handling the shipping details. Maybe it was time to outsource more of the work.

"Dad, it's time for bed." She watched him check the doors and windows, a complicated routine he did every night. When he finished, he clicked off the hallway light and sauntered toward his bathroom. A moment later she heard the water run and the sound of singing in the shower. The familiarity made her question her fears. He seemed normal. Maybe it was just her imagination.

She paid attention for the next few days, but nothing seemed serious enough to jot onto a notepad for the doctor. Just his tendency to forget where he'd set his glasses, his hat, his wallet, his keys. Mornings became a game of hide-and-seek.

"Dad, you need to hire the housekeeper back.

Someone to keep you organized." She added the task to her list.

"We don't need a stranger nosing around in this house!" His tone was the inflexible voice of her childhood. But she was no longer a child.

"What did that woman do to upset you?"

He sat rigidly with his gaze fixed straight ahead until he admitted, "She tried to move the box."

Amanda felt her heart thud. "Oh, Dad. I'm so sorry. Where is it? Is it okay?"

He nodded. "I hid it. Now she can't find it."

"But you remember where it is, right?" Suspicion nagged at her. "Why don't we write the location on a sheet of paper and seal it in an envelope. Put it in the safe?"

He looked sheepish, and his voice dropped. "Not right now. I'm busy."

"Dad, you do remember where you put it, don't you?"

He stared dazedly at his feet; not an encouraging sign. But neither was it life threatening. She checked her watch and jumped to her feet. "I have to go, Dad. We'll talk more about this tonight."

After school, she hurried home with a phone number in her purse, a recommendation from the school secretary. Her head reeled with a mental "to-do" list: The Oregon State Assessment tests were scheduled for next month and she hadn't covered all the units yet. A poor OAKS rating would jeopardize her probation. One of her students had brought a note from a parent, demanding a parent-teacher conference. Amanda folded the slip of paper and added it to the pile already on her desk. She knew what the topic would be; the parent had already threatened to take her complaint to the school board. *Everyone wants their kid to get into Harvard. But the kid needs to hand in his homework before that will happen.*

Jacob's cow arrived, a sloe-eyed Guernsey with coffee-colored eyes and long black lashes. Twice a day, before breakfast and again before supper, he slipped out to the barn to milk it. By the second night, Amanda came home late from work to find three gallons of milk cooling in her refrigerator. She made arrangements to share the excess with one of the longtime employees in exchange for milking duties whenever Jacob wasn't available. The man's wife made a batch of *queso añejo* as a thank-you.

Jacob seemed happy to work in the shadow of his own house where he could pop into his kitchen for coffee twice a day. He returned each evening from the barn, whistling after spending his days learning the nursery business. But his mood was pensive when he mentioned to Amanda one evening, "Some of the lessons he teaches seems to change."

"Dad?"

Jacob nodded. "He gets upset if I question him."

The next afternoon she heard her father as she pulled into the yard. "Pay attention, Jacob. When I tell you that the C/N ratio in these plants decreases with the increase of potassium, you can take that to the bank. Don't contradict me when the nitrogen...the night...the rogen gets wrong. It's just wrong, okay?" Jacob listened with a look of confusion.

That evening she strained the latest bucket of fresh milk through a cheesecloth, poured herself a cup of coffee and took a seat at the supper table. Her father glared at Jacob as though he were a stranger, rapped his fork on the table and blurted, "This fellow's going to get hurt on that tractor. I've seen it before. No good can come of it. No good at all. He needs to get off the property." A moment later he asked for the peas as though nothing had happened.

Jacob waited until he was alone with Amanda before he explained. "Your father sometimes gets *stroovich*. Confused. He doesn't mean to speak ill, but his frustration grows. Maybe you take him to see the doctor. See if maybe there's a ready explanation."

Amanda waited for her fear to pass. "He has an appointment, tomorrow. I think we both know what Dr. Maffet will tell us." She slumped against him, careful to muffle her sobs. Her father had kept monsters from the door throughout her childhood. Had filled the house with off-tune shower songs and corny jokes. He'd been patient with her mother, and faithful, and generous. Now, instead of traveling around the country in a new RV, he would spend his retirement searching for lost memories.

"Jacob, he lost the box. He doesn't know where it is."

"What box?"

She waited until she could speak again. "Mom's ashes. He misplaced Mom's ashes."

The next morning, her father insisted on driving to his medical appointment. Without a valid reason to deny his request, Amanda reluctantly slid across the seat. She sat on the passenger side, braced to grab the steering wheel, but he drove carefully, only hesitating at the intersection. He correctly decided to turn right, and she gave a sigh of relief when he pulled into the parking lot and made a diagonal parking job that claimed two spaces. On the way inside, she took the keys and dropped them into her purse.

Dr. Maffet's battery of tests taxed her father's ability. He struggled to decipher a paper clock that clearly read 10:15, but he explained that he'd misread the long and short hands. He fumbled at the three words the doctor gave him to remember. Her heart sank as he struggled to recall: "Street, orange, letter? Silo, auto, lemon? house? I think mousetrap. Mousecrap?"

The doctor excused himself and looked down at his computer. "Bob, I've recommended an MRI to scan for hydrogen atoms in the brain. Don't worry, it won't hurt. We'll use magnetic fields and radio waves. You won't feel a thing."

"It's loud, isn't it?"

"I've got some earplugs here for you. And a sedative if you need it."

"When?"

"How about we do it right now? Get it out of the way, okay, Bob?"

Her father lay prone and silent while the machine clanged and pounded. When it was over, the technician assured them the doctor would phone with the results.

Amanda led the way to the car in silence, while her heart broke. Inside, she saw that his heart was broken, as well. "Dad, wanna stop at the DQ for a Blizzard? I know you love those colored sprinkles."

Inside the restaurant, she licked a soft-serve cone and tried to make small talk. But her father interrupted. "What's next for me, Peanut?"

She wiped vanilla ice cream from her cheek while she stalled. Her dad was a hero who had explained in grown-up words why her mother came home in an ambulance. Now it was her turn. She exhaled and tried to mask the weariness she felt. "We'll take it one day at a time, Dad. Isn't that what you used to tell me? Everything will be okay."

The report was as bad as she expected. Dr. Maffet took her aside to show her the vast areas in her father's brain that controlled his emotions and memories, an area that looked puffy and wan, with areas of yellow that reminded her of the balloons that the man in the park used to bend into weenie dogs and poodles on Sundays. "You'll need to make some changes. I've notified the DMV. Your father's driving privileges are revoked. He'll be issued a senior ID."

"What should I expect?"

The doctor raised an eyebrow and glanced down at his clipboard. "Don't get ahead of yourself. Take it one day at a time and remember to breathe. For now, concentrate on his physical comfort. Supervision will be essential. Consider child locks on your thermostat, door locks, range and stove controls. Chemicals. That sort of thing. Safety first, we advise."

"Will he be a danger to himself? To others?"

"Each patient reacts differently. Expect mood changes. Not everyone suffers volatility. It can vary. The important thing is to see the man inside the behavior. Be there for him. Love him." He patted her on the shoulder. "Just be his daughter, Amanda. That's what he needs."

The appointments clerk handed her a packet of information on the way out. One of the brochures was for an Alzheimer support group that met once a month, on Wednesday afternoons. She slipped the pamphlet into her purse and helped her father to the elevator. He used to refuse elevators. They were for wheelchairs, he used to say. But today he rode with a smile.

At home, she waited until Jacob came in before she fell apart in a splash of tears. "Jacob, hold me." She realized she was trembling. "We've only just begun our lives together. I want Dad to be a part of us."

Jacob stroked her cheek. "Shhh. He will be. He'll be a part of our lives. You'll see."

She slipped into her room and lay on the bed for a minute while dinner heated on the stove. Her thoughts tumbled back in time, to the day her mother had arrived home from the hospital in an ambulance—with the same fear and despair as she felt today. She remembered, too, the times her father held her and promised that everything would be okay. He was right. Jacob, too. They would get through this.

She roused herself back to the present when Jacob entered and lay down beside her. He slipped his hand under her shirt and began to rub her back with small, gentle strokes that eased her tension. In the background, house noises reminded her that her father watched TV, and the dishwasher ran with dirty dishes from the previous night. In her bed, she stayed in the moment, aware of Jacob's touch on her skin. When he shifted and withdrew his hand, she sighed. "Supper's probably ready," she sniffed. "Dad already ate. He wanted macaroni and cheese."

Jacob nuzzled her neck. "Sounds good."

She nuzzled him and smiled. "You were right, sweetie. The puppy is too much right now." She picked up her phone and turned so that Jacob could watch as she sent a text to Charlie Rivers. *Your puppy is a generous gift, but Princess needs to find another castle.*

She made a call to a friend who taught vocational skills at the community college. After explaining her needs, she got a recommendation for a young man from the nursing department to work part-time as a companion for her father. The young man, Rob, arrived a few days later, and managed to convince her father that he wanted to learn the nursery business. Her father was happily describing his early years in the business when she slipped out of the house to drive to work.

"I think that young man has a future," her father commented at supper.

The kid's a glorified babysitter. I lied to my own father. Amanda gave a guilty glance at Jacob. When he frowned and pressed his finger to his lip, she set her misgivings aside. "He seems eager. He can take you on errands. Until we find your driver's license. I'm sure it's here someplace." She pushed her vegetables around her plate, her stomach a bundle of nerves from the white lies that grew every day until she could hardly face her father.

"He doesn't deserve this," she whispered to Jacob that night while they lay in their bed. "I want my dad back. I hate this!"

"Then stop. Tell him the truth. You have your dad. He's safe and happy. Don't wish for more than that. Nothing is guaranteed, Amanda. Don't get cross with Gott because you feel sorry for yourself. It will only lead to dissatisfaction, and that is a sin."

"I know." She laughed. "I can hear your father say that to you."

His tone got serious. "Somethin' I been meaning to ask."

"Shoot."

"You know that crucifix you got in the living room?"

"The one with Jesus hanging on it?"

"How 'bouts we give it a new home for a while. The thing gives me concern."

"You know it's not an idol, right? I mean, it's a reminder that He died for us. Like a photo."

"Yeah, I guess. Still...I don't mind a lot of stuff, but that one gets me." He pecked at her neck and grinned. "So we find it another home, okay?"

"I'll hang it in Dad's room. After all, it's your house now, too."

On her way to the kitchen the next morning she found Jacob already pulling the crucifix down from where it hung.

⁂

She pulled up the home page for the local community calendar website on her phone and waved it in front of Jacob as he opened his eyes. "I have the perfect birthday present for you! You love country music, and Luke Combs is performing in Portland. I'll order tickets. You'll love him."

"Do I have a choice?" He rolled over to pin her beneath him in the sheets.

"In what?" She giggled. "No. This will be fun."

On the day of the concert, they joined the lines streaming into the auditorium dressed in new hats and old boots, short skirts and denim jeans with shirts rolled to the elbows in the humid heat of August. Jacob followed her to their seats and stretched his long legs under the seat in front of him. When she took out her phone and shot a selfie, he grinned into the camera. She pulled two beers out of her purse and poured them into an empty red cup she'd brought for the occasion.

"Happy Birthday!" She offered him the first sip and leaned to lick the foam from his lip.

"Who is this happy liebchen? I have not seen her in a few weeks!"

She laughed and waved her hat in a circle before she plopped it back. "We're newlyweds. Anyway, I'm too young to feel this damn old!"

When the music started, she sang along to the chorus. "Beer never broke my hearrrrt." Jacob quickly picked up the chorus and began to stomp his feet to "Hurricane." Later, after the break, he joined the crowd yelling for more.

"This one's for you," she whispered when the next set started. A moment later, the band began, "Better Together."

"Betterrrr together. We're better togetherrrr." Amanda's voice sounded slightly off-key. After her second beer, she kicked off her boots and wiggled her toes. When a really drunk guy barely missed her foot, she pulled the boots back on. She laughed so hard on the way out to the truck that she could hardly remember where they parked.

"You took a picture of the row number with your phone," Jacob reminded her. "A good trick I will remember."

"I'mmm mmmade forrr youuuu."

He laughed and pulled her closer.

"Lucky thing youu're not as drunk as me." She giggled.

He grinned and tightened his grip on her waist. "Not luck. I held back so you could unwind tonight."

"Did youuu know, 'luck' is a derivative of 'Luccc-cifer'? Someonnne told me tttthat. It's not true, ish it?"

"Luc's a Dutch word. Now shush."

She snuggled against him, trying to prolong the feeling. The ride home was precious and included a detour to a secluded spot along the river. They were still laughing when they hit the front door. "I'm on a date and it's high school and I'm out after curfew," she whispered.

"You ever do this back then?"

"Nooope. But there's always a first time." She giggled again.

"I'm glad it's with me," he whispered. "Weeee're betterrrr togetherrrr."

Chapter Thirteen

"Jacob, I have a doctor appointment this morning."

"Doctor? Are you sick, liebchen?"

"Not me. It's Dad. But I *am* a little tired. It's probably just the strain of work on top of Dad's issues. I'll stop off at the pharmacy and see what they recommend for exhaustion. See you after school."

The doctor made suggestions as he gave her some samples of new drugs for unspecified dementia. "Not a cure, but it might slow the progression." She blinked and tried to concentrate on the doctor's next words, but everything was a blur. When the visit was over, she followed her father to the car and waited for him to put on his safety belt. Afterward, she picked up a bag of burgers and drove to the lake so they could eat while they watched the ducks swim. She pointed out the teals and mallards.

He fumbled with the bag and rummaged through it. "No french fries?"

She opened a packet and set it on the picnic table. "Here. And extra ketchup. The way you like them."

"I don't like ketchup. Never did."

"Since when?"

On the way home, she stopped at the pharmacy to pick up a prescription for her father. She was ready to pay before she remembered her promise to Jacob. "What's good for iron poor blood?" she asked. "I'm exhausted."

The pharmacist, a middle-aged woman, looked up with a smile. "Haven't heard that expression since the old Geritol days. Maybe you just need a glass of wine with your dinner."

"No, that sounds disgusting. I've been off alcohol for a few weeks. Doesn't agree with me."

The pharmacist glanced up to inspect Amanda's coloring. She reached for a narrow box and handed it to her. "You might want to start here. Rule out the obvious."

Amanda looked down at the pregnancy test the woman held and laughed. "I don't think so. It couldn't be. We've only been married a few months."

The woman gave a brief wag of her fingers and returned to her post. "Be sure to let me know, one way or the other."

At home again, Amanda dropped her stack of math notebooks on the counter along with her purse and locked the bathroom door. She read the instructions twice before she performed the test, drumming her fingers on the sink while she kept track of the passing seconds. *I'm in a movie. I'm Uma Thurman waiting in a hotel room to find out that my life's about to change. I'm terrified.* She knew the answer before she picked up the stick. The plus sign reminded her of the addition factor she taught her students. *I guess Jacob got his wish. But what about mine? So much for tenure and a savings account and waiting until Jacob earns his A.A. degree at the community college. This is happening!*

She waited until her father finished eating and settled himself in his favorite chair to watch a rerun of *Mayberry R.F.D.*, to make her announcement. Jacob was still at the table, waiting for a slice of berry pie. She poured fresh coffee and slid into the seat across from him. "So what's new in your life? The cow giving you grief?"

"No." Jacob looked up, mildly amused. "Cow seems about the same as this morning. Maybe a tad gassy, but then she's a cow."

"Does having to milk twice a day tie you down? Do you mind the responsibility?"

He seemed confused. "I guess not. It's normal. Like shaving. Something was missing when I lacked the need."

"Oh. Good answer."

He reached for her and pressed his lips against hers. "How did it go with your dad? Anything new?"

"Well, he's not sick." She was stalling, but she couldn't help herself. Her life was about to change.

"Then why the long face? You remind me of my cow. Pining for her calf when it's time for weaning."

She bent over his shoulder and leaned in close to give him a provocative look. "You have a knack, husband. Your grandma would say you're *hellse-herisch.*"

"Clairvoyant? That is not one of my talents. Definitely not! I keep my feet firmly planted." He returned her smile as he accepted a slice of pie. "You are the one for making plans."

"Well, maybe not. Seems we have a surprise that I didn't plan on."

He paused with a bite halfway to his mouth. "What has happened? Something has broken for me to fix? The car?"

She slipped her hand across his shoulder and brought her mouth to his. "Nothing broken. Something new."

"You have bought me another shirt? Already I have a dozen and only seven days in which to wear them. I have everything I need. My life is full."

She nibbled on his ear, reluctant to let the moment end. "I think it's about to get fuller." She brought the tester from her pocket and held it out to him. "This says we're going to have a baby."

He turned to face her with a look of stunned surprise that changed to pleasure in the blink of his blue eyes. "A *kind*! A baby? Will wonders never cease?"

"You sound like my mother."

"She would feel like crowing? I am ecstatic with this news. A happy man."

"Even if we don't have money saved for a new house?"

"We have a house. What is wrong with this one? All the family under one roof. That is what gives your father hope. A grandson to run about at his feet. He will teach the little one from his wisdom, the same as with the Amish."

Amanda let out a sigh and glanced across the hall at her father while tears blurred her vision. "What if he never meets his grandchild?"

Jacob scarcely heard. "I will make wooden toys for the kind. I should start tomorrow. Get a head start."

"I think there's time," she teased.

"So you take a few days off to rest? Give the baby a healthy start?"

She laughed. "I doubt your mother coddled herself with each pregnancy. Did your father ever do the dishes so she could rest?"

Jacob blushed at the idea as he helped her carry dishes from the table.

Amanda gave her father the news over bacon and eggs the next morning. His gaze darted to her belly and his face softened with a look of remembrance. "It wasn't that long ago, Amanda, I was so sure you were going to be a girl. I even picked out your name and wrote it on a piece of scrap paper so I could say 'I told you so' later."

She nodded. She had the scrap in her baby book, in his handwriting. "I won't be teaching after June. I'll be home with the baby all next year. And with you," she added.

Her father looked confused. "Me? I'll be busy at the warehouses. There's a lot of work to be done down there. I'll need to get Jacob ready so he can take over in a few years when I retire. But I have plenty of time left for that."

She took a breath. "Dad, do you remember what the doctor told us? Your brain is changing. Not all at once. The changes will be gradual. But we need to live every day to the fullest. We'll have walks and conversations. Jacob can tend to the business. He's already learned so much from you. He'll do a good job so you won't have to worry. Will you let him do this for you? For us?"

Her father stared at the floor for long seconds. His gnarled hands twisted around each other as he grappled with the news. "I heard the doctor." He looked up with tears brimming. "I just figured I'd ignore the man." He swiped at an eye. "I never figured for a time when I wouldn't be here for you, Peanut. Not this way. Not a damned burden like this." He looked up and his eyes were twin pools of torment.

She reached for him. For a moment she was ten again and he was the center of her universe. "Daddy, we're not letting you go. Stay with me. Fight this. Let's live our best lives. Prove the doctors wrong, okay? We know how to fight. We're fighters. So let's go to work, okay?"

Her father grinned. "We got this, Peanut. Let's have us a baby. Don't worry about me. I intend to get to know my grandson. And, by gosh, he'll sure know me."

⌘

Jacob sat with his arms wrapped around her midsection. "I do this now because soon you will be so fat I will be unable to reach around."

She laughed and elbowed him so that he fell back on the bed, laughing. "Are we okay?"

"We are better than okay, liebchen. We have all the gifts Gott intends for us." He winked and his eyes lit his face with impish glee that bathed his golden skin in a flush of passion. His kiss heated her until she remembered nothing but the man beside her. Later, he remembered where he had left off. "Gott gives me a beauty to set my body on fire. And he makes her a good cook. Soon I will look like old Amos Byler with his suspenders barely holding up trousers over his proud belly."

Amanda smiled to hear him talk of happy times

among the Amish. So often his eyes retreated into sadness, even while he tried to keep his thoughts from her. "Is it too soon to think of a name?" she asked. "Do you want to name our baby after someone in your family?"

"I know the English often find out the gender before the baby arrives. Is this what you want?"

"I don't know. Do you?"

He considered. "Maybe not. I like the traditional way—to be surprised. We don't need many clothes for a baby. Amish don't worry so much about blue and pink." He laughed. "Most likely he wears the leftovers that are packed away under the bed after the last one."

"Oh, so it's to be a boy. Is it?"

His face reddened. "Maybe the first. Would that be so bad?"

"Not so long as we don't name him Amos. Or John."

"It is traditional for us to name the child after a grandfather or uncle—a name that has been in the family."

"Is that set in stone? I bought a book of names today. I'm considering Caleb, or Benjamin, or even Jordan. We could call him JR for short."

Jacob's face clouded. "Let's pull in the reins a bit. We don't need a name tonight. Let's remember why Gott made this baby. And how," he teased.

"You're right. There's lots of time to settle the name." She tucked the book in a drawer.

Amanda hid her condition in loose dresses and baggy shirts until she was forced to make an announcement to her students. After that, her classroom watched the baby's progress with awe and no shortage of questions. Her family physician recommended a young obstetrician who was associated with the hospital. She and Jacob made their first visit to an office on the third floor of a medical building that occupied an entire city block. Jacob looked around while a receptionist checked Amanda's ID and logged her insurance information into a computer.

"I have maternity leave, but I have good coverage. Blue Cross," Amanda explained. The receptionist nodded without looking up.

Jacob followed Amanda into an office at the end of a long hallway. He shook the doctor's hand and watched as he scanned his computer and asked a few more questions. While the doctor examined Amanda, Jacob inspected the examining room for somewhere safe to look.

"We wanted to meet you before we make a decision about an OB-GYN," Amanda explained. The doctor nodded. When the fifteen minutes was up, he stood and offered his assurances that the process would go smoothly.

On their way out to the pickup, Jacob slowed to inspect the modern medical building. "Do you have midwives in Oregon?"

"We do. I know what you'll say. That was pretty sterile."

"Ja. Maybe we make an appointment with a woman nurse?"

❧

The nurse-midwife invited them into a cool, pastel office lined with photos of babies she had already delivered. Another wall held images of baby gorillas and lion cubs in the wild. Jacob seemed more comfortable with the midwife, Hafsa. He listened to a recap of successful deliveries while she asked questions of Amanda's health history.

"No surgeries, no STDs, no smoking, no prior drug usage, no risky behavior. Good. We can anticipate a safe and uneventful pregnancy," Hafsa assured her. "God willing, you will be fine."

"When can we get a sonogram?"

Jacob studied the hijab around the woman's head.

"Let's wait a couple of months," she advised. "It will give you both something to look forward to. The waiting can get a bit taxing."

In the next two months, Amanda recalled the midwife's word, *taxing*, while she contended with her classroom of rowdy kids, her father's sometimes erratic emergencies and the mounds of laundry and meals that greeted her when she arrived home from work each day.

She found the solution one day when she met Imelda, the wife of Joaquin, one of their longtime employees. Imelda seemed efficient and had a great laugh. She agreed to work part-time as housekeeper, and to keep an eye on Mr. Miller during the day.

On the day of the sonogram, Amanda waited in the midwife's office until Jacob arrived out of breath, his cargo shorts splattered with mud and a stripe of new farmer's tan in the gap between his shorts and his rubber boots. He wore an Oregon Ducks baseball cap perched on his shaggy hair that made her heart quicken when she saw him looking more like a Gen Z'er on college break rather than a soon-to-be-father.

His face was shiny with exertion, but ablaze with excitement. "Your dad got the big tractor stuck in the creek. We had to tow him out with the flatbed. Hooked ropes to the back of the diesel and barely made it."

"What was he thinking? He's supposed to leave the driving to you from now on."

Jacob shook his head. "He sat there like a kid who had just stolen his dad's car. He didn't say much about it. We let it go. He's up at the house now. Got a bit wet. He's changing his clothes. Imelda is there with him."

"Jacob, do we need to lock up the keys?"

Jacob's eyes widened. "Let's not put the wagon before the horse. Your father built this company. He bought that tractor brand new." He stepped aside as the technician started her prep.

Amanda watched as the technician squeezed gel on her belly and passed the wand across her abdomen with gentle pressure. When the microphone echoed the squishing sound of a tiny beating heart, the screen revealed a tiny embryo in a cocoon, throbbing to the rhythm of a heartbeat. The technician moved to the computer and clicked the mouse several times. She finished and printed out three photos. "Time for the Big Reveal!" She held them enticingly just out of reach. "Do you want to know?"

Amanda hesitated before she admitted, "I do, sort of. But my husband doesn't. We decided to wait."

"Okay, here's the photo. You really can't tell from the images unless you know what you're looking for. I'll put the gender on a paper and seal it in this envelope with the due date. But you should have no concerns. Baby Ruth is healthy and has a good heart. You're going to be very proud parents."

"Baby Ruth, like the baseball player," Jacob joked.

"Like the candy bar," Amanda said. "People think it

was named for the baseball player, but it was really named for the daughter of one of our presidents. Cleveland, I think." She remembered the candy machine they'd passed on their way down the hall. "Great! Now I'm jonesing for a Baby Ruth." She held the envelope containing the nurse's note over her head and pretended to tear it. "Buy me a candy bar," she teased, "or I'll open this."

Jacob grinned. "Nothing doing, liebchen. I know you better than that. But just in case, maybe we lock the envelope in your father's safe."

Amanda held up her hands in mock surrender. "I can be trusted. I'll put in my lingerie drawer. And I'll know if it's been tampered with."

He picked her up and swung her in a circle before setting her down again with a grin. "Not by me. I can be trusted, even if my wife cannot!"

In the parking lot, she unlocked her car and got inside. "We brought separate cars. I'll see you at home."

He leaned inside to brush her lips. "Okay, little mother. But no candy bar on the way home, okay? Fresh spinach and cucumbers only."

At home, her father sat at the table with a cup of coffee while Imelda prepared to leave for the day. "I made Mr. Miller cinnamon rolls. I'm afraid he won't need any supper tonight."

Amanda pulled the lid off the cake saver and frowned. "You ate two, Dad? You know better!"

Imelda picked up her purse and did a quick samba with a mischievous grin. "He tell me, 'This is what life is about. A little fun.' And I agree. You see this when you're older. Nothing wrong with a little sugar in your coffee now and then."

Amanda nodded and reached to give her father a hug. "I'm glad you enjoyed them, Dad." She saw the joy that such a simple treat brought to him. He'd earned the right. For his entire life he'd exercised, eaten well. He'd practiced living intentionally. He'd talked to God every day and attended church each week. He'd forgiven his enemies and made them into friends. And now, in spite of his best efforts, his mind was slowly dying. She smiled. "I'll have one of those rolls, too, if you have one to spare, Dad. They smell delicious."

Chapter Fourteen

Jacob reached for his slide rule with a frown at the textbook on the table in front of him. He scowled as he reached for a stick of chewing gum and popped it into his mouth. "This calculus is a challenge. I enjoy the workout, though. Makes me feel as though I'm not the dunce I feared."

Amanda bent to wrap her arms around his neck. She inhaled the scent of Old Spice and Doublemint gum as she nuzzled him in a lazy, sensual exploration. "You a dunce? You're kidding, right? You're frustrated because you want to make up for lost time."

"True enough. I want to catch up with my pals. I told you they defied their fathers and went on to high school. Finished, too. And one went on to college."

"While you wasted your time!"

Jacob nodded. "One fellow came back for baptism after he graduated. He's a preacher now. A pillar of the Amish community."

"And the other?"

"Left the community and became an accountant.

He stays close. Does work for some of the Amish businesses, but he chose a different path, I guess."

"And you? What is your path?" She watched him fidget with the tools on his desk. He preferred the old-fashioned study aids, like the slide rule and an old calculator he'd found in one of the desk drawers. His latest test paper lay discarded near an open book, marked with an "A."

He gave a self-deprecating chuckle. "Maybe I still think to prove my father wrong. I want to get good grades. I want to pitch fastball on that baseball team I joined. I want to stand in front of my class and receive a diploma. All the Englisch ideas I thought were vain and of the world, and now I want them. Strange, no?"

She stood cradling his back until she ran her hand along his arm and leaned to whisper in his ear. "My shy, modest husband has become a glory hound!" She shifted so that her hair cascaded across his chest. "Really, Jacob, look at what you've accomplished. Dad's workers love you. He knows his business is in good hands."

Jacob abandoned his attempt at study. "That's the trouble, Amanda. I don't know how to figure my path. I have so many choices now. When is enough? When will I know?"

Her heart lurched. "You're not happy here?"

He looked up quickly. "Not that. I like to farm. But I always think of the next step. Maybe a gift shop? More outlets for our products." He hesitated. "I feel like I run too quickly for my own good."

She watched his face tighten with worry. "Maybe one step at a time. Take it slowly?" She caressed his cheeks with her lips and smiled when she felt him swallow.

When he spoke, his words came from deep in his throat. "I have a test tomorrow. Maybe I'm just stroovish."

Pressed against his spine, the baby in her womb fluttered, not hard enough for Jacob to feel it; that surprise would have to wait for another day. "You're not foolish. You're impatient to catch up." She laughed and explained, "I think our baby's restless."

Jacob allowed her to nuzzle his neck. "You make a fine mother. I am foolish to feel discontent." Despite his words, his eyes traced the molding on the ceiling as if it held answers.

Amanda saw the frustration. "Jacob? Put your books away. Let's go to bed."

"Later. I need to finish this. You go up. I'll follow when I am able."

Up. As in upstairs, like his parents' home in Ohio, the two-story with the bedroom where he'd spent his childhood. A shiver of fear ran through her.

Amanda left the door to their room cracked while she struggled to fall asleep. When Jacob slipped into bed, his whisper filled the darkness. "I am sorry to be such a trial. It is still strange, this big world. I try to fit, but I feel small."

She turned from her side and reached to spoon against him. "You are a hero to all of us. Dad's employees and customers. To me, and soon, our baby." In the darkness, she nodded toward her father's bedroom. "My father found a son in you. Don't forget that."

He rolled toward her, his nose buried in her hair so

that his voice was muffled. "I don't forget. I don't know what is wrong with me."

"It's summer harvest time back home for your family. I remember how busy you all were. Maybe you feel like you're letting them down."

"Maybe."

She heard the confusion and felt fear threaten her security. "Jacob, live in the moment. Don't try to span two worlds. You won't be happy in either of them. You're creating a life here—if you want one." She stiffened with momentary irritation and turned to face the other side of the bed. "If you don't, and you'd rather go back home, let me know."

The baby kicked again, harder, as Jacob settled himself so that their bodies weren't touching. His breath expressed in a burst of annoyance. "I should not lay with you in the Biblical way until the baby comes."

Amanda bit her hand to muffle her laughter. "Suit yourself."

❧

At the end of her third trimester, Amanda packed a small overnight case and left it near the bedroom door. One morning, she woke, restless and filled with energy. After she tidied the house, she froze the flats of blackberries and peaches she'd bought on a whim at the farmers' market. With nothing else to occupy her, she mended one of Jacob's shirts. By evening she was exhausted. Her back ached. She barely remembered to apply olive oil to her baby bump. "Look at this. It's not a bump, it's a mountain. I'm having twins and somebody forgot to tell me. Jacob, what if we have twins? You need to make us a second crib, just in case. Like, start tonight?"

Jacob laughed. "Lie down here, little wife, and let me rub your back. You act like a mare when the birth approaches. Anxious and fretful. You will probably foal before long."

"Foal? I'm not a horse."

"Sorry. A fretful wife is new to me. A mare is easier."

Amanda struggled to her feet in time to feel water stream down her legs. "Jacob, it's happening! Call the midwife. Now."

Jacob drove toward the birthing center with a careful eye out for deer. Beside him, Amanda practiced deep breathing and panting like they had practiced in their childbirth classes. Jacob fumbled for a pack of gum and managed to unwrap a stick of gum and pop it in his mouth. "Would you like a piece?"

"Chewing gum? Are you serious?" She moaned as a pain gripped her. "It smells disgusting. I'm suffering. This is payback for every foul, treacherous deed women ever committed. Why don't men give birth?"

Jacob's shaky grin was meant to reassure her. "You'll be fine once we get you in the capable hands of your Muslim wonder woman."

"I should have had this baby at home. I'd be eating Jell-O in my own bed."

The lights of the birthing center appeared in the highlights. Inside the building, the midwife, Hafsa's, cheerful, calm voice interrupted Amanda's rant. "Come, welcome. Let's get your contractions timed so we know where we stand. We will settle you into a room where you will be comfortable. Jacob, could you fetch the blanket from the warmer and see that your darling wife is comfy? Is there anything you need, Amanda? We have time for a nice chat and a bit of tea."

Amanda felt herself calm under Hafsa's reassurances. Jacob draped the blanket over her and she gripped his hand as another pain racked her.

Hafsa beamed approvingly. "This is good. A husband's love and respect is empowering to a mother in this time. Amanda, feel his strength as you decide what you would like him to do for you. A gentle back rub? His hands will let the little one know that he also waits. A perfect set of parents waiting to greet the perfect child. What could be more natural? Amanda, are you comfortable? Would you prefer to sit up and have Jacob rub your feet? You are in charge here. Let your precious Jacob know how we may assist you in this most natural process."

Amanda thought of the doctor she had interviewed at the hospital, his clinical examining room and the sharp, medical tools. She looked around at the rocking chair and throw pillows, the muted fabric—and felt herself relax. Until another pain occurred. "Oops, eeeigh, whoo! That was a doozy."

"Soon now. Trust yourself. Feel your power as a woman doing what is natural to your gender. No fears. Only nature and God's design. Let it flow from your Divine Spirit. Give gratitude for all you are experiencing. No fear, only wonder and gratitude."

With Jacob's help, Amanda panted through the next pain, and the next. With each contraction, she felt as though she rode a porpoise, plowed the wave to the surface and dove again. Minutes passed, but she fought to control herself. Finally, she felt an overwhelming need to push. When another urge consumed her, she gave into the desire.

"This is wonderful, Amanda. Look, the head, the shoulders. And we have a baby boy. Round and perfect, like his mother. Father, can you help me to snip this cord? Perhaps you will want to plant it beneath a tree, to commemorate this day?"

Amanda waited until the midwife handed her a naked bundle. She took her son and admired his ten toes and fingers while Jacob traced his own along the baby's cheek. The little eyes were still puffy and closed, but his little head boasted a thick thatch of black hair and long lashes.

"He is a wonder, this is for sure," Jacob whispered.

Hafsa stood nearby. "Everything is good, Amanda. You have a fine son. You have fulfilled women's purpose with dignity and joy. May Allah be with you all."

Half an hour later, Jacob stood beside her, holding the book of baby names she'd tucked into her overnight bag. "I look at the names you circled. I don't think 'Elena' would work so good. But what do you think about Noah Amann?"

"Noah—he looks like a Noah. Amann sounds like a deviation of my name. I love the two together." She glanced outside into the darkness before she turned to her baby. "So Noah Amann, how do you like your new name?"

۞

The first days at home seemed like a marathon of exhaustion for Amanda. Each duty presented a learning curve that she struggled to master. The baby seemed lethargic at times, fitful and colicky, unable to hold anything down. Jacob struggled with late-night diaper changes, but the baby seemed unable to settle back to sleep. Its high-pitched cry seemed to demand something that defied understanding. Amanda tried nursing, holding, rocking, and singing, but nothing helped.

"Oh, Mom, I wish you were here. You could tell me why I'm such a failure at this." She sobbed helplessly as her son writhed in pain, until, finally, they both dropped into an exhausted sleep.

When she woke, the cycle began again. On the second day, she looked up from her sofa as Jacob staggered into the room. "Jacob, you need sleep if you're going to work. No point in us both suffering. Close the door and get some sleep."

When he complied without an argument, the look of relief on his face was almost comical.

In her obstetrician's office the next morning, Amanda struggled to contain her tears. "Something's not right, Dr. Millard. Noah's hungry, but he doesn't want to nurse. He screams when I touch him. He's rigid sometimes."

The doctor consulted his computer. "It's probably something you're eating. Onions, garlic? Maybe CBD? These cause gas, very painful at times."

She shook her head, offended at the suggestion. "I've read the list. I'm really careful. He just seems lethargic. And sometimes he doesn't seem coordinated, like his muscles are off."

Dr. Millard smiled. "Let's not get ahead of ourselves. I think it's too early for concern. Go home and see what happens in the next few days." He held the baby up. "Noah seems fine now, a smiling, alert baby who lets mom know who's boss. Just relax. I'll have the nurse schedule a home visit with the breast-feeding specialist."

Jacob was waiting when she arrived home, anxious for news. Together, they watched the baby arch his back and stretch, his tiny face wreathed in a faint smile that rocked her core. "Oh, Jacob, look what we have done. He's an angel."

Jacob nodded, mesmerized by his son's perfection. "Gott will get the credit. But I agree. Our Noah is perfect."

The following day, the baby gave a high-pitched cry that refused to ease. She picked him up and felt his body go lax. She was frantic by the time she arrived at the doctor's office.

The doctor listened to its heart and lungs. "No fluid build-up. Let's wait and give a look at the diaper. Maybe it can give us a clue as to what's happening in little Noah's tummy."

Amanda held her screaming son until the nurse came in. "He isn't eating. Just fits and starts."

The nurse nodded, unconcerned. "Let's not overre-act. We've scheduled a breastfeeding expert for later today. Let's see what she recommends." She glanced at the computer screen and gave an over-the-shoulder smile without meeting Amanda's eyes. "Babies outgrow their colic, eventually. And no one ever knows why."

Amanda drove home with a list of suggestions that included baby formula. When her baby cried, she bathed him in tepid water and rolled her hand across his back to express the gas. After an exhausting night, her father knocked on her door with a tray. He'd prepared a mug of herbal tea, a soft-boiled egg, toast and marionberry jam. She opened her dry, sleep-deprived eyes and mustered a smile as he set the tray in front of her and straightened.

"How's about I take the baby and give it a bottle of that formula? Burp him while you get a couple hours sleep. You'll feel like a new woman."

She heard the baby fret with the unfamiliar bottle, followed by the famished sound of a baby slurping. When she awoke, her bedside clock said ten thirty. Filled with panic at the silence, she threw off her blanket and raced to the door. In the next room, her father leaned over the changing table, attempting to change the diaper.

"Thank you, Dad. Best gift ever. I think I'll live." She pressed a kiss on his unshaven cheek and took over.

Chapter Fifteen

manda's phone reminded her that she had an appointment with the midwife for her six-week checkup. She was already late by the time she packed a diaper bag, the consequence of remaining in bed with a nagging feeling of self-pity. Her mother's absence was an endless wound. *No grandma to spoil a grandbaby or even to hold you while I talk to the doctor.* As she stumbled with the straps of the baby seat, she added to her list, *Or take a nap.*

Hafsa finished her examination and replaced her instruments on a tray. "Everything looks good." Her eyes narrowed at Amanda's dull, listless expression. "Perhaps you should plan a celebration, a night out for yourself and your husband. A new father often feels left out and forgotten in the bond that the mother forms with her child. Remember your precious Jacob is now both husband and father in your heart."

Amanda considered the midwife's advice as she drove home and realized it was spot on. Everything was so new, so exhausting. And neither of them were prepared. Jacob loved the baby, but he seemed irritated at its unexplained bouts of colic. He was willing to pick Noah up, and happy to rock him, but he seemed increasingly shy around his own wife, as though she might break if he touched her.

At home, her father volunteered to babysit, and Imelda agreed to help. Amanda's heart thudded in sudden panic as she heard them creating a plan. Her father seemed alert and present; indeed the baby's arrival had snapped him back. She heard the house-keeper's determined optimism and made a flash deci-sion. "Okay, I'll go."

She rummaged through her closet for a pretty pair of heels and a dress that fit her surprisingly full figure. While the baby slept, she showered and washed her hair. Blow dried and curled, her hair was an improve-ment over the messy bun she'd worn for the past week. She added makeup to mask her chronic exhaustion, but by the time she finished, she needed a nap.

She was in the kitchen when Jacob entered, weary from work, his body slumped in silent acquiescence to the prospect of another night sleeping alone. He looked up and saw Amanda dressed for date night, glanced over at the housekeeper smiling from the kitchen, and his face lit with a look of understanding. Without speaking, he dropped his work coat and gloves and took off down the hall, slamming doors a testament to his rush to grab fresh clothes and start the shower. When he emerged a few minutes later he was clad in fresh Wranglers and a long-sleeved shirt, his hair still damp. He took Amanda's hand and led her to the door.

Amanda needed every ounce of willpower to avoid

looking back at her tiny baby or the bottle of breast milk she had placed in the refrigerator.

"Do not worry, Mamacita. We have this," Imelda called from the doorway.

"Where to?"

Amanda could scarcely concentrate for the dread fear in her chest. "I don't know. Surprise me."

Tension heightened the silence between them as Jacob drove into town. He chose a steak and ale house that they had visited before, but tonight it seemed that two strangers retraced their steps. He parked the car and hopped out to hold the door as though they were on a first date. Inside, their first words seemed tentative and strained, until the young waiter fumbled their drinks and dumped his tray on Amanda.

She swabbed herself with her cloth napkin and laughed. "Well *that* breaks the ice! Lucky it's only water."

Jacob's face flushed with the attention they received from other diners. The owner rushed up and offered to comp them for their meal, but Jacob declined. She understood. He wanted to claim the evening as theirs. The young waiter had done them a favor; he'd brought their laughter back from forgotten depths.

They lingered over dinner; her dress was long-dry by the time the check arrived. In the shadow of their booth, Jacob traced along her neck. "You are more beautiful than ever, liebchen."

She felt herself ripening under the intensity of his gaze. Like a rose in the summer sun, she radiated confidence. The words of a poet she'd studied in college reverberated in the moment. *Beauty dwells where doubt and insecurity once lived.* She felt beautiful tonight. The light in Jacob's eyes reminded her of how much they had overcome to get to this place. "We are blessed, husband."

Jacob lifted her fingers to his lip and leaned in to kiss her. "Can we steal another hour? I don't want to give you up yet." She nodded, caught in the intensity of his gaze.

As they drove past the movie complex, she leaned back, lulled by the intimacy in the cab. "I don't want to mess this up."

"Mess what up?"

She hesitated. "The balance. You, Noah, Dad, work. I don't want to turn into one of those mothers who talks about her baby."

"No chance of that. You talk a lot." He grinned. "I do not expect big things. I find blessing in the small things."

"I don't talk a lot."

He laughed. "But I think maybe it's time to move little Noah into his own nursery."

Mention of the baby brought back tension she'd managed to sideline for a few hours. "I wish he would stop crying. I don't remember what a whole night's rest feels like."

He drove along a side road where the river cut the channel with a grove of sycamores, to a sideroad devoid of traffic. Satisfied, he rolled down the windows and cut the motor so they could hear the peepers and frogs that filled the night air. Minutes passed while she rested her head against his and breathed in the peace.

"Do you remember the night at the school back home in Ohio? The forbidden sin of wanting each other?"

She turned to him and heard his ragged breath. "You mean, like this?"

They heard the baby scream before they reached the front door. Inside, Amanda's father paced back and forth, his eyes wild and lost. Imelda was trying to get the baby to drink from the bottle of breastmilk while the baby squirmed with pain. Suddenly his little body went rigid in seizure.

"Call 9-1-1," Amanda screamed. "He needs to get to the hospital." The call was a frustrating series of questions. "I don't know. No, he hasn't been sick. Yes, six weeks old. No, he hasn't been poisoned. Just hurry!"

The wail of the ambulance seemed to stall on the country road while her baby seized in short, violent bursts, his head rolled back, eyes open but unseeing. Suddenly the cries silenced. Amanda felt her son's skin, sweet with the hint of maple syrup. In the next instant the medics rushed in.

One of them sniffed and made a face. "How long has the baby smelled like this?"

Amanda tried to think. "I don't know. Off and on. I thought it was just the way babies smell. Sweet."

She and Jacob stood helplessly as the medic attached a small tube and listened to the tiny lungs. When they loaded her baby onto a gurney, Amanda hyperventilated. Someone handed her a paper bag to breathe into. She grabbed it and tried to climb into the ambulance, but the EMT halted her at the door. "We got this." She stood in the darkness, whimpering uncontrollably until Jacob took her arm and pulled her to his pickup. He ran around to the driver's side and started the engine as the ambulance pulled onto the roadway.

At the ER, the attending physician rushed up to lift the baby from the gurney while a nurse directed them to wait. The doctor nodded to Jacob. "We've called in a metabolic specialist. She should be here any minute. Let's make baby comfortable and see what the tests reveal."

Time stood still while they stood in the hallway watching medical staff hover over the baby's crib. A young woman doctor arrived with a long strip of paper in her hand. "I'm Dr. Washington. We have a very sick little boy here. We've started protocol to reduce the serum branched-chain amino acids that are blocking absorption of his protein. It's a rare complication. Lucky we found it in time."

Amanda's heart fell. "What is it? Will he die?"

"Noah has Maple Syrup Urine Disorder. It's extremely rare among the general population. Typically a Mennonite or Amish disorder."

Amanda forced herself to face her husband. "Amish?"

The doctor nodded. "A disorder we rarely see in Oregon. It's an inherited blood disorder we call MSUD. It was brought to this country by a Mennonite family in the 1800s. If we know of the connection, a standard test is given at the time of birth. Your baby's body hasn't been digesting the proteins. It's been intermittent, so the problem wasn't quickly recognized. Our test shows high levels of leucine and isoleucine in the plasma and

urine. Caused by a branched-out alpha-ketoacid dehy-
drogenase complex in the mitochondrial membrane that
creates a breakdown in the amino acids. It's complex,
but easily treatable if we know to expect it."

Amanda couldn't look at her husband. "Will my
son be all right?"

Dr. Washington glanced down at her paper. When
she looked up, her face was grave. "Your baby is pres-
ently in an induced coma to minimize brain trauma, but
we have every reason to be hopeful. Can you think of a
family connection?"

Amanda caught Jacob's eye and waited for him to
speak. When he didn't, she forced herself to admit their
mistake. "My husband is from an Amish community in
Ohio. We didn't know. How could we?"

The doctor nodded at Jacob. "There's no blame
here. We'll find the answers. Do you recall any family
history that can help your son?"

Jacob shook his head. "Not to speak of. My older
siblings were not affected. Maybe the youngest—I don't
know."

She nodded. "It can hide in families. Even if both
parents carry the gene, twenty-five percent show no
signs. Another fifty percent will show no signs but they
will be gene carriers. Another twenty-five percent will
be affected. Unfortunately, your son is one of these."
She glanced at Jacob. "I would suspect you are a
carrier."

The words echoed in the corridor long after the
doctor excused herself and hurried away. Inside the
room, a team of nurses and doctors had stabilized the
baby with a breathing tube and a tiny heart monitor.
Noah looked like a tiny doll inside the crib. Amanda

wanted to snatch him, and bury her nose in his fine hair and inhale his baby smell. Instead, the odor of maple syrup pervaded the room and she remembered; her baby was allergic—to her.

Jacob waited at her side, his face set in concern. "I didn't know. I'd forgotten that Mamm didn't nurse the youngest like she did the others. Young Levi ate a special formula. Vegetarian foods, not much meat. But we never talked about it much. Maybe among the women, but not to us men." He glanced up, seemingly unfazed by the guilt that crippled her.

"God in Heaven, why not?" She strained to make the words. "Why did you not think to tell me?"

He shrugged. "For the Amish, this is not a problem. They don't pray for Gott to give them a healthy child. They pray to accept the one he gives them."

The sight of her baby lying motionless in the medical crib with its snarl of hoses and tubes caused her stomach to quail. Jacob remained in the background, a shadow figure in the hallway. She saw him and forced herself to turn away.

The next two days were a nightmare. She couldn't consider Jacob's reaction when her own pain was all that she could bear. After a tough night, one of the nurses insisted she allow Jacob to drive her home for a shower and a change of clothes. In the silent house, she made her way to the nursery and collapsed next to the crib. After her eyes emptied, she allowed Jacob to guide her into the steamy shower and soap her shoulders with gentle strokes.

Somewhere between his attempts to brush her tangled wet hair, and manage the blow-dryer, his impersonal touch penetrated her grief. Days of anguish and isolation overwhelmed her need for anger. She reached for his hand. His fingers returned her pressure, and she eased the hairdryer away. Suddenly, he was there, his heartbeat strong against her own. In her ear, his voice sounded broken.

"I can't live like this, Amanda. I need you."

Still raw, she reacted without thinking. "No sex. I'm not ready to forgive you, Jacob. Not yet." She pushed away and moved into the walk-in closet to pull on a fresh pair of pants and a shirt. After twisting her still-damp hair into a messy bun, she found a pair of slip-on shoes and hurried out while Jacob remained on the edge of the bed, his hands cradling his head.

In the living room, her father sat quietly in his chair, his shoulders hunched in misery.

"Dad, this wasn't your fault. You didn't make the baby sick. I did." She slipped to her knees and rocked him until he looked up. "Do you understand, Dad? You didn't make the baby sick." When he nodded, she pressed a kiss on his forehead and rose. "We'll bring Noah home, Dad. I promise."

Jacob drove back to the hospital in silence. Once inside the ICU, he stood beside her, quiet and restrained, his only concession to place a pink cotton blanket on her when she shivered under the air conditioning that was needed to regulate the baby's condition. His face, when she finally allowed herself to notice, was a roadmap of emotions. He'd aged in the past two days, and his eyes bored through her as though he were asking something of her. With a feeling that she was drowning, she turned to focus on the tiny bundle in the crib.

When the nurse left, he finally spoke. "If our baby

dies, I will have killed it. My fault, all of this. I deserve the hate you carry for me."

She half-rose and stumbled back, tried again and claimed the distance that separated them. "I don't hate you. I hate myself. I poisoned our baby every time I took him to my breast. I fed poison into his little body. How could he fight it when I was there, feeding him more. If he dies, I will have killed him."

Jacob placed his arms around her to silence her and rocked her while the baby's monitor matched their muffled sobs. "We will pray harder, together," Jacob whispered. "And when Noah recovers, we will do what needs to be done for our son. Together."

She remained motionless against him. *It's true. Love excuses the churlishness in us. It feeds what isn't there and it excuses what should not be.* "I'm so sorry."

"Shhh. We forgive each other, liebchen."

※

A nurse lowered the crib to check Noah's vitals. Despite the coma, her touch caused him to flail his tiny fist "Baby shows signs of recovery," she murmured before paging Dr. Washington. From a nearby chair, Amanda made a quick phone call to Jacob and counted the minutes until he rushed in, his work clothes covered in sweat. They watched as the baby opened his eyes, first a stirring, then a faint flicker of recognition.

Amanda gasped in relief. "He's tracking me, Jacob. Look! He sees us." With the doctor's approval, she scooped Noah into her arms and felt his tiny fists battering her, despite the tube inserted into his tiny nose. "Oh, you're a fighter, little one." She included

Jacob in her relief. "You got this, baby boy," she whispered. "Daddy and I, we got this." She reached for Jacob's hand. "Pray there's no brain damage," she whispered.

"Gott's will. We accept the gift as it is given, one way or the other," he said.

Chapter Sixteen

❧

Amanda watched the aspen and maple leaves fall outside the hospital room where Noah slept. Her mind recalled a similar day when she stood at the bay window with her mother in her wheelchair.

"Fall's here, Mom. The golden period."

WINTERHEALSSUMMERSCA
RS.

"Yes, if there's anything left to heal. Autumn must be God's favorite season."

GODPLAYSFAVORITES?

"You don't think so?"

READTOMESIRACH

"I forget where it is."

FOLLOWSSOLOMON

"Here it is. I'll just pick something at random.

'Accept whatever is brought upon you, and endure it in sorrow; in changes that humble you be patient. For gold and silver are tested in the fire, and acceptable men in the furnace of humiliation.'"

NICE

"I don't pray as much as you do, Mom."

YOUHAVETEARS. SAMETHIN
G. BOTHCALLTOGOD

She smiled at the recollection, only three years earlier. She had been a girl back then.

Her baby's doctor whisked in the door, and she shifted back to the present. "Dr. Washington, thank God."

"I have good news, I'm happy to say. The cerebral edema has eased. Insulin levels are improved. Kidney function is good. We're removing intubation. Noah will soon be eating on his own."

"My milk?"

The doctor nodded. "Supplemented with a special formula. A metabolic nutritionist will work with you on a plan."

"And Noah's brain?"

"We foresee no long-term effects."

"Thank God!" Without warning, Amanda's tears spread across her baby's downy hair. She breathed in his scent and felt herself releasing the fear of the past four days.

Dr. Washington watched with a sympathetic smile. "I suggest you get in touch with the baby's Amish grandmother. It's good to have tips from another mother who understands MSUD."

Amanda glanced at the pamphlets the nutritionist had handed her. Not the same as a grandmother's advice. "I'll ask my husband. It's complicated," she hedged.

A nurse showed her and Jacob how to take a blood sample from Noah's heel with a lancet, and deposit four drops on a blood collection card. The first time Amanda tried, her hands shook so badly that Jacob took over for her when Noah's piercing cries broke her heart.

But the nurse was firm. "Baby Noah can't leave the hospital until Mama and Daddy can draw the blood. I'll send a supply of lancets, a few cards, and some sticking plaster home with you. You'll place the drops on the card and secure it with the leaves of a heavy book. Leave the wet part out, exposed to the air for four hours until it's good and dry." She paused to make sure they understood. "Then mail it to the address on the label." She glanced at Amanda. "When the baby's older, you'll only need to do it once a month. Unless he catches a cold, or the flu, or has a reaction. Okay?" Amanda nodded. The nurse gave her a sympathetic smile. "In a few years he'll be able to do this on his own."

"A few years? You mean—forever?" Amanda's heart sank as the nurse nodded.

In the days that followed, every sound her son made caused her body to produce milk. A nurse showed her how to express it and measure it to ensure that the baby didn't get too much protein. But he suckled with such frantic hunger that it broke her heart each time she had to tear him away. The nurse made a suggestion. "You might want to dry up your milk and rely only on the special formula.

"I've heard about formula shortages, What if—"

The nurse shrugged. "Probably temporary. He'll need to take the supplement for the rest of his life. Your insurance will pay for it. We don't have to make a decision today."

Amanda shared the news with Jacob when he arrived. "The doctor says I can continue to nurse, but it feels like I'll harm him."

"Suffering is part of life. It is our path."

"Jacob, you sound like your father. I don't want my son to suffer."

"Then you are in for disappointment."

She sucked in a deep breath, and then another, as she considered his words. "Maybe so. But I'll fight like a she-bear to keep him safe."

Jacob rose to stare out of the window at the yellow headlights that inched along the boulevard three stories below. "The Amish believe children with special needs are blessings from Gott, to teach us how to love."

"Sent by God? Jacob, this is *our* fault. Our neglect."

"Why *our* neglect? Every child has his own needs. Our son will not be neglected. He will be accepted and loved. And made to feel a part of our lives. No different from any other child."

"Jacob, you should have mentioned it before."

"It wouldn't have mattered. Our son would still have suffered from this condition."

He kneaded his fingers as his stubborn pride warred with compassion for hers. His arguments did not need to be spoken aloud, so clearly did they resonate. He had the right to his beliefs. Had he stayed in the community, his family would have rejoiced over this grandson. His mother would have asked Atlee Hochstetler to include the birth in his report for the *Budget*. People would drop by with cakes and baked beans while Amanda served coffee and washed spare cups.

Honesty forced him to understand that he had only considered his own comfort when he complained. It didn't matter that he existed on salty deli chicken and cold sandwiches eaten at odd hours, and cafeteria food with the blandness of shoe leather. He had brought this suffering on his family because he had refused to admit to the doctors that such a disease existed in his bloodline. He hesitated, trying to find the words that would bring he and Amanda back together.

"You won't want to hear this, but I wrote your mother." Amanda directed her news to the floor, unable to look at him. "I won't have my baby suffer from our not knowing."

"You expect an answer?"

"She'll write. She has a mother's heart."

"Ja, she does that. But also the Pennsylvania Dutch stubbornness."

Amanda's eyes softened at her baby, asleep in his crib. "I read something today that reminded me of you," she admitted. "'A man keeps the secret of his mother locked in his brain, waiting to spring it on his wife.'"

He gave a quick, surprised snort. "I lock away no secrets, wife. My life is an open book." He moved to her side and hoped that her desire for forgiveness was as great as his own. "The sound of poetry is a joy to hear, and your laughter, even better." He brought his lips down so that his whisper was scarcely discernible. "Wife, let me take you home. Please. Just for tonight."

A nurse entered in time to hear the despair in his voice. She glanced from one to the other. "Go. Get some rest and come back refreshed. I promise I'll be here if baby wakes."

Amanda shook her head, her eyes wide and panicked. "Jacob, I can't. We'll be together soon, but my son needs me right now."

He left the hospital with a heavy weight on his heart, lonelier than he could remember. On his way home he drove past the spot on the river where they had spent happy hours getting to know each other. Without Amanda, the trees and water were merely lovely spots of nature. Without his wife, his family, he was like the ripples churning their way to a vast unknown.

❦

"Jacob, we have a letter from your mother." Amanda stood, unsure whether she should open it, even though the letter was addressed to her. She slipped her letter opener across the flap and read the words aloud while Jacob pretended to be unaffected.

Dear Amanda,

It is a blessing to hear of the arrival of Noah Amann. His health struggles will be a challenge for his parents, but they will make you stronger as you learn what Gott requires of you both. Gott saw fit to give our little Silas, John's oldest, the blood disease, a condition laid on us in our jour-

ney, which we welcome. Others have
suffered as well, including one of Jacob's
brothers, Young Levi, but he is able to work
hard and to contribute to the community in
spite of it.

A clinic was set up among the Amish
and Mennonite brethren to study and treat
this condition. I have included the address
that you might correspond with them. Do not
fear to nurse baby at first, only take care
to limit the amount, as the nurses will
instruct you. Our Silas avoids the excessive
good foods that give the farmer strength.
Milk and cheeses, meat from our pigs, beef
and chickens, eggs, fish, beans, nuts and
peanut butter. His diet is most often
vegetables and fruits with grains such as
rice. And of course the protein supplement
that regulates the blood. Our rich, dark
breads create a problem for him, but our
grocers often carry pastas and breads with
low protein. We keep a kitchen scale to weigh
his food. The clinic has taught me to count
the amount of leucine in the diet in order
that he might remain as healthy as possible
to do Gott's work. Take heart in this matter,
as the Apostle Paul struggled with a thorn
in his own flesh.

Our prayers and thoughts are with your precious baby,
Emma

Amanda handed Jacob the letter and watched as he searched for hidden meaning in his mother's words. When he looked up, his disappointment was so poorly hidden that her heart broke for him. "Jacob, she holds you in her heart even if she doesn't say it."

He nodded, but the gulf of loneliness stretched from his eyes to the farm in Ohio. "Maybe. It doesn't matter. I have written my child's and my wife's names on my heart."

I wish you believed your own words, husband. She moved to his waiting arms, to the familiar scent of Old Spice and evergreens, proof that he had spent the day working in the orchard. She rubbed her cheek against his scratchy wool shirt and felt his hands on the back of her head where her tension had settled. In the silence, his heart thudded against her own, and she closed her eyes to lengthen the moment into a memory for later. He dipped his chin and she felt his breath on her skin, heard his patchy breath rumble deep inside. She swayed to the music on a radio one of the workmen played in the yard, a Spanish tune with a happy guitar. When Jacob straightened, she felt the loss of his warmth as the moment ended.

"And your name is written on mine, Jacob," she murmured.

Chapter Seventeen

Jacob woke to find Amanda rocking the baby in their bed. He felt an instant stab of dismay until he checked it. They were home again in their own bed; satisfaction enough for any man. He lay quietly as the baby drank from a glass bottle filled with the low-protein formula the doctor had prescribed. He broke the silence with a confession. "I am having trouble with one of the workers. I think to let him go."

"What does my father believe?"

He hesitated. "Your father? He thinks the boy is the father. Gets the name confused. The father retired and the boy took his place, but the boy is hard on the equipment and doesn't respect me. Thinks he has it made because his father worked here so many years."

Amanda lifted the baby to her shoulder. Her father grew more confused each day, his agitation increased along with his resentment of Jacob. Only the previous day he had tossed over a shelf of germination trays and spilled planting mix on the floor. His anger flared in spurts, quickly replaced by moods of contriteness or confusion.

"What will you do, Jacob?"

"Nothing yet. But I caught the boy fill the gas trimmer with regular gasoline again. He knows the rule. Just doesn't care. I've had to rebuild the carburetor and change out the O-rings again. Nobody took responsibility for it last time. This time I was lucky to see him with my own eyes. I have no use for a slacker or a liar!" Jacob's irritation woke the baby and he lowered his voice. "Sorry. I make your day harder with my mood. I'll figure something out. But I know this, words won't change that boy. He's spoiled. As useless as a kind in diapers if you ask me."

The inadvertent relapse into his former dialect caused Amanda to look up. Not the first time he had reverted to a place of comfort when he was stressed. She bit off her question and turned her attention to the baby.

He waited a moment until her inattentiveness decided for him. "Best I set off now. Try to get some rest. I get my noon meal in town." He paused to feather the downy fringe of baby hair. "What does the doctor say about our son's health?"

"I have an appointment today for a checkup."

Jacob pressed a kiss on his baby's cheek and walked from the room.

Left alone with her tiny son, Amanda watched him suckle with a sense of wonder. His ruddy cheeks and fly-away, downy hair reminded her of a small bird. His fingers gripped spasmodically with each suck. He sniffled, his nose clogged with mucus that would need to be suctioned when he finished eating. His color was normal, his breathing less troublesome now, but she kept a careful watch for any sign the doctor might need to know.

❦

The pediatrician glanced at the screen and bent to tickle the baby's cheek. "Look at you, Master Noah! Good to see you, young man." He tickled the baby's feet with a cold spatula, tracked his eye movement and performed a half-dozen other tests while Amanda's anxiety grew. When he finished, the doctor entered notes into his computer without meeting her eyes. She waited, scarcely breathing, until he finished typing and raised his head. "Baby is fine. Right on track. He's still weak, of course, but he's alert and gaining weight. I see no indication of any damage. We'll keep an eye on him as he gets older, but there's every reason for optimism." He looked up from the computer. "How's that formula working out?"

"Good. He's started on rice cereal."

"Good. Building his strength. Let's see him again in a month."

On the drive home, Amanda felt as though a giant weight had been lifted. She stopped at Dutch Bros and bought two coffees, one with caramel for Jacob.

At the ranch, Jacob's truck was gone. She saw a new employee clearing weeds around the greenhouses. She waited until he noticed her and cut the power before she approached, juggling the cup carrier in one hand and the baby on her hip. "Hi, I'm Jacob's wife, Amanda. Wanna coffee?"

He glanced down and grinned. "*Si. Gracias.*"

She noticed that he set the trimmer on the ground with its head resting on a rock so the gas wouldn't flood the carburetor before he stood up. She handed him Jacob's cup and shifted so Noah couldn't bat her cup from her hand. "How's it going? Haven't seen you around before."

"I'm Hector. I took my padre's place when he got sick. Now I work full time for Mr. Miller and Mr. Ruth."

She nodded. "I knew your father for a long time. He's well, I hope."

"Si. But he has gone back to Mexico. It's better for him there. He wants to be buried with his people."

She studied his intensity. "Does he plan to die soon?"

"No." He shrugged. "Who knows? But he is ready. He likes to see the landscape of his beginnings. This is what he tells us. The roots of his youth."

"Yes, everyone does, I suppose." She noticed the can of mixed gas he used to fill the weed trimmer. "Tell me, Hector, do you read English?"

He shook his head without meeting her gaze. "Maybe a bit. I don't have much education. I must work from an early age, you know?"

"Yes, I see. Have you explained this to my husband?"

"No señora. I don't take the chance he will think I'm not worthy, fire me."

She considered. "I have some materials. Pamphlets. Maybe after work you can stop by, and I'll help you learn to read English."

"Si señora. I would like that. I like my job here. Anything to do better, yes?" He leaned in toward the baby and teased it with a ribbon from Noah's cap. "Cute *niño*."

On her way to the house, she considered her options. Undermining Jacob wouldn't make points with him, but her teacher's instinct saw an opportunity.

Jacob's truck drove into the yard in the middle of her lesson. Amanda glanced around at the room, with no dinner started and the kitchen counter strewn with a half-dozen ESL pamphlets she'd picked up at the high school. When the door opened, Hector leaped to his feet.

Amanda placed her hand on his to reassure him. "Mr. Ruth appreciates effort. He will be happy to see you learn new skills."

Jacob hesitated at the door, staring at them and two empty coffee containers on the table. Color flooded his cheeks as he tossed the mail down on the counter and looked around the room.

Amanda tried to resume the lesson as though nothing were amiss. "Hector, let's look at the word *gasoline* again. Ethanol or non-ethanol? Can you tell me the difference? What about the color? The smell? What is the symbol? Good. You have it! And you are very mechanical. Like my husband." She hesitated for effect. "I noticed that you handle the equipment with skill."

Hector blushed. "I want to learn to be a mechanic, like my father before he got sick."

She met Jacob's gaze over the table. To his credit, his face blazed with embarrassment. "I'm honored that you've agreed to let me teach you to read," she said. "Maybe we can pick this up again tomorrow after your shift ends?"

When Hector left, Jacob picked up the newspaper

and set it down again. He tried unsuccessfully to maintain his stern countenance, but a smile broke his attempt. "A teacher cannot leave well enough alone. Always trying to meddle." He rose and wrapped her in his arms before meeting her lips. "I would be a university scholar if my teacher was so beautiful as you. Take care you do not make your student confused."

"*Stroovish?*"

He laughed. "Ja."

Carol texted from Ohio.

> Here's a website for Amish blood disorders.

Amanda texted back.

> I have more in common with the Amish than I realized.

> LOL. When are you coming to visit us?

> Not sure. Jacob has a lot on his plate. And there's my dad.

> He worse?

> Some days. Some days he's just my dad again.

> Seize those days.

> Trying.

Amanda spent the baby's nap time Googling everything she could find on MSUD.

"It seems that our lives will have some challenges," she told Jacob at dinner.

He paused between bites of cornbread and honey butter. "If the Lord wills it, the brain will be strong even if the body struggles. The doctor gives us good news."

Her father looked up from his plate. "My body is just fine. It's my memory. Today I got lost. I was standing in a stranger's room."

"Dad, it's your room now. Remember?"

Her father nodded, but he kept his head lowered.

Amanda broke the silence. "Dad, one day at a time. We'll be here for you. You know that, don't you?"

Her dad paused with his fork in the air. "I don't doubt that, honey. I'm just afraid I won't be there for *you*."

She pushed back her chair and rushed to throw her arms around his neck. Biting back tears, she whispered, "Then I'll meet you halfway. How does that sound?"

He nodded and blinked hard. "I don't suppose there's ice cream tonight?"

Amanda held her tears until she and Jacob prepared for bed. "Dad's worse, Jacob. It breaks my heart."

Jacob cupped her head and whispered, "You know, Gott doesn't give you more than you can handle. I know this."

She shrugged off her shirt and jeans and tossed them on the bed. "He fell today. I gathered all the throw rugs and put them in the garage." Jacob's touch penetrated the steel of her guilt. "I had to tape over the light switches and the heater control. He turns them on and off. I caught him cleaning the rollers on my vacuum while it was plugged in." Jacob watched with an inscrutable expression as she pulled her tank top over her head. She noticed the direction of his gaze and smiled. "You're distracting me." She slipped into a nightgown and reached for her hairbrush. "Some days I don't have a father anymore."

"Liebchen, your father built this home with his own hands. For a man, this is powerful. Such blessings he has been given. Do not fret." With a single motion, he eased her onto the bed and ran his hand across her exposed skin. "Enough worry for one day. We have something better to distract us," he teased.

She woke, surprised to see a faint sunrise stream into the room, proof that she'd slept through the night. Jacob rolled over and pinned her leg beneath his. "Give me five minutes more," he whispered. "Then I promise to let you go."

"Five minutes? That long?" She gave him a lingering kiss. She was still in sleep mode when she made her way toward the nursery. "You need to recover your strength, husband. I'll take one for the team."

"The team?" Jacob gave a satisfied chuckle. "Does this mean I'm a Duck or a Beaver?"

"Beaver, definitely! Go OSU! I'm a Corvallis fan." She grabbed a robe and stuffed her arms through the sleeves when she heard a loud noise in the kitchen. She slid around the corner to find her father mopping broken eggs from the floor with a fancy, hand-embroidered dish towel a friend had made as a wedding present.

He looked up and scowled. "Egg box slipped. Accident. Clean it in a monkey jiff."

Amanda felt pressure on her shoulder, Jacob gently warning her against overreacting. She grabbed a handful of paper towels and began to swab the floor. "Monkey jiff!" She laughed. "I haven't heard that in a coon's age."

Her father's laughter blended with her own as he swiped ineffectively at the mess.

Jacob returned with the baby in his arm. "Bob, maybe you give the housekeeper more work hours? She sends her daughter to college and money is scarce in their house. Maybe you could see your way to help her out?"

Amanda met Jacob's amused glance. Better to let her father think it was his decision. Keep him on the offensive—just like football. "Beaver," she whispered to Jacob.

"My mother, she had plenty of sisters to help out. She had my grandmother and now, even her own grand-children. But we're alone, Bob. Amanda has taken on so much. Don't you think Julie would agree?" Jacob held his son with a choir boy's look on his face.

Bob Miller stood at the sink, wiping egg from his hands. "Sounds about right. Maybe ask the gal—Roberta—about extra hours?"

"Sure I will, Dad. Imelda will be glad for the extra work. She can quit her night job at the dry cleaner's."

Amanda glanced outside where the trees were just budding. Spring was around the corner. Her favorite time of the year. In the pasture, Yankee frolicked along the fence line like a colt. She had ridden Jacob's horse once or twice since its arrival, on days when her father was well enough to be left alone, but those days seemed a distant memory. She was afraid to leave him unat-tended now, since the day she found him locked out of the house in the rain, with Noah in his arms.

At bedtime, she fell into bed exhausted. "I'm falling apart. I'm not here for you or the baby. I'm not here for me. I'm somewhere in the clouds, breaking into pieces. I'm so tired!"

Jacob massaged her shoulders, kneading her muscles until she felt like she was floating. When his attention shifted, she brushed his hand away. Love-making would cut into her precious sleep. A trace of mustache tickled her shoulder and filled her with guilt. She cradled her head against his shoulder and whispered, "We need to change something, Jacob."

He murmured his agreement. "What happened to that part-time college student you found for a companion?"

"Dad fired him. Said he wasn't picking up the nursery business fast enough."

"So you are not such a good liar, after all." His chuckle vibrated against her chest.

"Apparently not. But at least we still have Imelda. And us. Dad thinks you're great."

"Yeah, but I'm not the solution, wife. We will need a better plan."

Amanda hesitated. "I'll call Lucy Knowles. Dad will think it's like old times again."

"Old times? You never told me the old times were so hard," he joked. "We are like a circus around here. Nothing is predictable."

Amanda raised her head from the pillow in surprise. "Hey, I know you didn't sign up for this. I'm so sorry."

Jacob shook his head in weariness. "Shhh, go to sleep. We face this tomorrow with fresh heads."

She untangled herself and rolled across the bed to

give herself a chance to fall asleep. The baby coughed and she froze, panicking with fear. From down the hall, the bathroom door opened. Her father began his slow shuffle back to his room and the house was still. She opened her eyes and read the clock on the bedside table. *Midnight*.

The sound of Jacob's soft snores woke her. Before the sun rose, she slipped into her robe and stumbled to the kitchen to start coffee.

Chapter Eighteen

From the highway, a row of truck cabs lined one side of the lot, packed in a diagonal line so close together that their side-view mirrors almost touched. A large sign advertised the truck driving school. A row of white box trailers with the school's logo emblazoned on the side left just enough space for the practice lanes.

Jacob found a parking spot as a bulky motorcycle pulled in beside him, a plastic hula girl bobbling behind the bike's windshield. The bike was ridden by a short, bulked-out man in tight denim jeans and black leather boots with raised heels. In a lightning motion, the rider killed the engine, dropped the kickstand and dismounted. He unstrapped his helmet to reveal a middle-aged Hispanic face with a trim goatee peppered with a tinge of gray. More gray was scattered among his inky black hair.

The guy extended his hand. "How's it going? I'm Chewy Hernandez. The guys here call me Chew

Baca." He grinned. "You can skip the *Star Wars* jokes. I've heard 'em all. You here for the class?"

Jacob nodded and offered his outstretched hand. "Looking to get my Class C."

"Long haul or local?"

Jacob hesitated. "I plan to drive for our family business."

Chewy grinned. "So, local! This means you got no old man making you crazy! Or the wife? That's the drive behind a lot of these dudes...the long-haulers. Money's good, you know? But sometimes the stress at home makes the road sing for them. It's crazy, but I get it, man!" His laugh showed off brilliant white teeth and brown eyes that crinkled at the corners.

Jacob felt his blood heat at the suggestion. "It's not like that. My wife's great. We share our home with her father and he's easy to be around. I need the CDL so I can make deliveries in a pinch." He hesitated. "I need to learn every job, including delivery."

Chewy popped the lid off his luggage case and dropped his helmet inside. After re-locking it, he dropped the keys in his pocket with a grin. "Relax, man! I'm just giving you a hard time. I teach the class. Seen a lot of guys come through here and you look like a guy who likes to be home for supper."

Jacob followed a handful of men and women into the classroom and took a seat while an assistant took roll. He took a copy of the workbook and opened the cover while Chewy began the introduction. "We'll cover the basics—road laws, defensive driving, new legislation, ICC regs, basic maintenance. You'll learn about improper welds, stuff that'll keep you and the public safe out there. This ain't an easy course, but you'll come out a real driver, man. No one fails at this school. We'll stick by you until you have that coveted Class C in your wallet." He favored the room with a grin. "We don't waste your time, man. You'll be on the road in one of those little beauties.

Chewy was already on his bike when Jacob wandered out for noon break. The instructor glanced over and gave him a thumbs-up over the roar of his bike's engine. "Wanna grab lunch?"

"Sure." Jacob glanced at the passenger seat. "Let's take my pickup."

At the burger joint, Chewy waved to the waitress and made his way to a corner table. "Soon as this class is over, I figure to take a break from this lifestyle. I'll hit the road for a few days. Take it up a notch, you know, man!"

"On your bike? Where you headed?"

Chewy grinned. "Hey, man, I know that look! You're thinking, why does this little dude get to have all the fun? And you know what? You'd be right. I'll roll over to Bend, up to Joseph and make a little splash over in Hell's Canyon. Party time!" He waved to someone across the room. "I'll make a loop through Halfway and maybe soak my toes in Joseph Lake. It's a cool place, man. I pay my respects to Chief Joseph at the statue they have down there. Watch the colors change in the forest." He laughed. "A bucket list without the heart attack, man. A win-win."

When the waitress arrived, Jacob ordered a reuben with onion rings. "How long you been riding?"

Chewy laughed. "What you're asking is, 'how you manage to survive on that beast?' I'll tell you what, man, novice riders are buzzard bait! Most accidents happen in the first six months—and within twenty-five miles from home." He gave Jacob a piercing look, his tone serious for once. "True fact, I know because I used to teach motorcycle safety. Biggest reason bikers get hit? Drivers don't see them."

Jacob swiped at a fly on the table. "So why do you do it?"

"Why? Ever race your buddy over a dirt trail when you were a kid? On a perfect spring morning, when the rest of the world's home mowing their lawns?" Chewy laughed when Jacob slowly shook his head. "Hey, man, don't tell me you never had a bicycle. Every kid in the country had one of those!" When Jacob looked down at his hands, Chewy reached for the ketchup and doused the plate of rings the waitress set in front of him. "Every good decision I ever made was on a bike. Nothing better to clear the head." He popped an onion in his mouth. "Unless it's making sweet music between the sheets." He laughed. "Seriously, man! I love to shelter from the rain under an overpass. Go through the rain to see the sun through the clouds. Explore new country without the windshield—smell it, taste it, sometimes even feel it —when I get caught in a hailstorm or take a bee down my neck! Cheat death. That's living for me, man! Especially after driving a big rig most of my life."

Jacob spent the meal laughing at Chewy's stories of a half-dozen different motorcycles he'd owned over the years.

"Fast Betty was my favorite, you know," Chewy admitted. "A Honda 750 Interceptor. Full-on tiger between my legs! So fast I could draw sparks off the foot pegs on a corner."

On their way back into the classroom, he gave Jacob

a good-natured nudge. "Hey, man, take the motorcycle course. You can get a bike endorsement along with your commercial license. Sweet twofer. Then you'll be set, man."

"I'm not sure Amanda would go for that."

Chewy grinned. "Hey, dude...easier to ask forgiveness than permission. Anyway, who wears the pants? Go for it, man!"

❧❧❧

Jacob walked out of the test facility with a temporary license in his wallet and an assurance that the permanent one would be in the mail. He waited at the door for Chewy to break away from the two guys complaining that they'd failed their tests. He was one of the seven who had passed. The other two were making arrangements to retake the class. When the last one cleared out, Jacob waved Amanda over to meet his instructor.

Chewy's eyes lifted in surprise. "Yep, definitely a short hauler." He winked. "Take that lady out and celebrate, man. She's a keeper!"

Later, at the restaurant, Jacob explained the joke to Amanda. "A short hauler means I'll sleep in my own bed every night."

She sipped her drink and smiled. "I'll take that as a compliment."

He raised his glass in a toast. "Right as rain."

Chapter Nineteen

❦

Winter arrived, and with it relief from the wildfires in British Columbia sending plumes of smoke south to pool in the Oregon valleys. Throughout the fall, Amanda kept the doors and windows closed while Noah played on the floor with a set of pinewood blocks that Jacob cut and sanded for him.

"The Willamette Valley's a farmer's dream, for sure." Jacob paused in the middle of a page from a thick textbook he'd purchased at the Oregon State bookstore. Across the room, fire crackled in the huge masonry fireplace and rain sluiced against the bay window. "If this storm holds, I will be one course closer to my business degree. *Hands-on* is what interests me, not all this *talk-talk*. But the people at the college have other ideas. They require a well-rounded scholar, not just a capable one. So I take English. I read Steinbeck, and I think his *Of Mice and Men* is a good story. He understands that happiness is not promised, and that personal trial is expected. Not all of life is a happy ending, ja?"

Amanda looked up from her novel. "Steinbeck wrote from the heart. And the heart has its twists and turns."

Jacob slipped from his seat to the floor at her feet. In the firelight, his face seemed happy as he reached for her hands and studied them. When he broke the silence, his words sounded husky and sincere. "Amanda, I appreciate you. For a wife to bring herself pure to her husband in the marriage bed like you did is a gift. Wife and lover. When a man finds both, he is to be thankful, and I am."

She reached to touch his cheek. "Jacob, you're a poet. You could be a writer instead of growing holly."

"Hmph!" He turned away with a blush.

She felt a familiar stab of guilt at his displeasure. "Jacob, did I say something wrong?"

"No, nothing." He shook his head, but his eyes remained smoky. "I have much time to make up for. Life on the outside has so many choices that I am running all the time. Like the Englisch fellows I used to scorn." He tossed his textbook on the coffee table and turned toward the kitchen. He poured a cup of coffee into a mug and carried it outside to watch the rain from the porch swing.

Amanda glanced at a magazine that had been tucked inside his textbook. *Cycle World*. She followed him outside. "Okay, sweetie, what gives?"

He stared off into the pasture where Yankee stood dripping in the rain. "Stuff is piling up. Responsibilities, you know?" He took a sip of coffee. "It's oftentimes too much for a simple Pennsylvania Dutch boy to grasp. But I'll get the hang of it. I just need some time."

"What can I do to help?"

He looked up, his eyes the dark brooding shade they had when he was troubled. "I was thinking of Tibbs and Rosie Bell, my friends in Wyoming. I promised to bring you to meet them, but life here is so fast paced. No let-up." He shifted his gaze from the horse. "I spent a long winter under their roof, and I need to keep my promise."

"So, road trip?"

Her father stood in the doorway, his face angry and determined. "What's this I hear of a road trip? I'm not going anywhere. You get that idea out of your head right now! You take off like a demented fool, but I'm staying right here."

Jacob ignored his father-in-law. "Snow's light enough, the drive would be easy. We could stay for a week and let the old folks have the joy of seeing—"

"They'll adore Noah! Dad can stay here with Imelda and her family." Amanda grinned. "Let's take my Highlander. It has better tires than that heap you drive."

"Are you down on my truck again? It's a fine vehicle. We should give thanks for our blessings." He kissed her and his eyes cleared. "We could leave on Friday. Can you be ready by then?"

<hr />

A sudden storm followed them along the Columbia River to The Dalles and Spokane. Brief squalls and snow flurries kept the windshield wipers flashing until they reached western Idaho. At the mountains they began to climb into snow country, Noah pounding on the car seat in excitement until Jacob pulled into a snow park. Amanda unfastened his restraints and Noah scrambled from the car. In minutes he had ground snow into his mittens. He squealed with excitement when Jacob began building a snowman. Amanda grabbed her phone and captured the moment.

"Isn't he the sweetest?" Her rhetorical question followed Noah as he clambered over a snowbank.

"And yet you worry that he is so quiet."

"Aren't you?"

"His doctor says he has no need of words. And why should he? He has all he needs." Jacob hesitated before his half-formed snowman. "He'll talk when he has something to say." When Noah returned, laughing, Jacob swooped his son over his shoulder like a sack of potatoes and spun him in a circle. "Stop torturing yourself," he called. "Let the boy breathe."

Amanda snapped photos of the two. "I guess you're right. Boys often don't speak until they're two. I learned that in my early education classes."

Noah pointed at a box of Goldfish and she dug out a handful for him to pitch into the snow for a chirping squirrel, his laughter echoing in the tree canopy.

❧

The Bells waited outside in the late afternoon when Jacob eased the Highlander into the long ranch driveway, two days later. The couple's shiny Chevy 4x4 pickup was parked under a shed, with the factory sticker still attached to the rear window. Jacob pointed it out to Amanda. "They gave me their old one. Tibbs said he wanted his wife to be able to listen to Travis

Tritt on the radio without her hearing aids." He grinned. "You'll like my friends."

Tibbs hobbled toward them with his hand extended while Rosie grinned, clad in a fresh pair of flannel-lined jeans with the cuffs rolled over her worn boots. Beneath her sheepskin vest, her sleeves were bunched up to reveal skinny arms corded from years of outdoor work, and rough hands that she tugged from a thick pair of elk skin gloves. Tibbs was stoved-up and bandy-legged, but long-winded and strong enough to claim Amanda's suitcase for the walk into the house.

Jacob got out of the driver's side and stretched his legs while he breathed the icy crisp air. He grasped Tibbs's hand then engulfed the older man in a hug. "Ah, friend, it is good to see you."

Tibbs cleared his throat and pointed toward the covered porch, where a dilapidated porch swing hung from a rafter. "Come on up and meet the missus. Bring that young man along, too. Mother'll have a time with him, that's for sure."

Amanda emerged from the passenger side to find herself immersed in a bear hug.

"How was your drive?" Tibbs eyed the SUV with its luggage rack and heavy winter tires.

Rosie walked up with her arms outstretched. "This baby of yours is the spittin' image of his papa. Got his eyes."

"Have any trouble remembering your way out here?" Tibbs asked.

"Jacob knows his way around these parts. Stop yer fussing, Pa. Are you folks hungry?"

"We had lunch in Sheridan. I showed Amanda the barstool where I met you."

Amanda followed them inside and found herself answering a hundred innocuous questions. She settled into the small living room with her stocking feet ensconced in sheepskin slippers. After Rosie insisted that she leave the food preparation to her, she sat in front of a blazing fire and laughed at Tibbs's ranch stories as the sun dipped toward the mountains.

"We wondered who the gal was enticed our Jacob away from my delicious home-cooking. Now I see you, it's a wonder he stayed as long as he did." Rosie chuckled as she handed Jacob a plate of homemade chocolate chip cookies and a mug of strong black coffee. "Son, marriage agrees with you. You look a sight better than I remember." She bobbed her head and took a seat across from him to study Jacob close-up.

"Give that little fellow a glass of milk to wash down that cookie, Rosie. He looks thirsty." Tibbs pointed toward the milk pitcher, with a finger that was cracked from the weather and the fingernail half torn off.

Amanda glanced at Jacob before she intercepted the glass. "Thank you, but he'll be up all night if he gets too much liquid." Amanda wasn't ready to explain the dietary restrictions that ruled Noah's life. Time enough for Jacob to broach the subject. "But he might like to play with your dog. He's a big animal lover."

While Jacob chatted with Tibbs, she rolled her suitcase into the small spare room where Jacob had spent a winter. In the corner, Rosie had made a crib for Noah from a pile of blankets and an ironing table folded flat to form a barrier. Amanda pressed her cheek against a hand-stitched quilt with rows of symmetrical stars cut from a dozen different patterns. A museum would hang the quilt proudly, but Rosie had laid it down for the most valuable treasure in her world—a child.

After supper, Tibbs made a bonfire on the leeward side of the yard where an outbuilding sheltered them from the wind. The sun had set, and the purple dusk had given way to a star show. Everyone settled into rickety old chairs hauled from the barn, and Rosie handed out quilts. Tibbs helped Noah roast a marshmallow while a battered coffeepot simmered on the coals. "I'd offer you something stronger, but doctor says I gotta watch my whiskey intake," he explained. "Says we old timers get stuck by the weakest organ we got. Shame to think that might be my gut."

"Yer gut's just fine, old man. It's yer memory might need a purgative," Rosie teased.

When the good-natured laughter died down, Amanda asked, "This place has the character of a homestead. Which of you was born here?"

"Reckon that would be me," Tibbs said. "Met Rosie at the schoolhouse when she was six, and me ten. Rode in my first car that year—an old Model T someone brought in to get themselves to hunting camp. We got rural electrification in 1948. Bought us a brand-new refrigerator from the Sears Roebuck catalog."

"We thought we was up-top after that," Rosie added. "Leastways 'till I caught a look at my first electric reading lamp," Rosie added. "Then I had to have one, too."

"As a kid, it was my job to pump water into the old cistern outside the kitchen door. Sure hated that job. Dang thing run dry faster'n I could keep it filled."

"You kids got it easier now, but we had our own particular brand of blessings. I reckon one balances the other in the Lord's eyes. But we're sure glad you're here." Rosie took a moment to wipe her eyes on her apron.

After a restless night with the whistle of wind and the howl of coyotes, Amanda and Jacob spent the morning wandering the pasture bluffs where the wind twanged off the barbed wire stretched across snow-rotted posts. Across the canyon, a high mountain prairie lay like a rumpled blanket. Fresh snowfall dusted a blanket of stubble on the remains of its dryland wheat harvest. In the distance, a dirt road wound its way from the ranch to town, tracing an ancient Indian trail over washouts from a dozen creek crossings.

Jacob studied the scenery with his eyes closed, his mind recalling the scenery. "I'd forgotten this silence." Amanda helped gather an armful of windfall boughs and deposit them in the dead fire pit while a spray of snow sparkled on the frozen rocks. Afterward, she stepped inside the steamy kitchen to find Rosie happily feeding her son a bowl of oatmeal.

Rosie looked up with an appraising eye. "Solitude got you wishing you was riding to the tumble of hooves?" She continued with a faraway look. "Folks call it unscattering. Nothing but the brush of wind and the pound of hooves. Horses half-wild in their hearts, even if they come to the whistle. Like some men, I suppose."

Amanda glanced around and smiled. "It's beautiful out here."

"It is that. But a passel of work for two old war horses like us. Time we thought about packing it in. Find us a winter spot in Bermuda." Rosie looked up and grinned. "Don't tell Tibbs I said that. He'd run me for the corral."

"Bermuda? Is that where old ranchers winter out?" Amanda helped wipe the oatmeal from her son's face while he swatted her hand away.

"Bermuda? Hawaii? Heck, I'd settle for Quartzsite." Rosie buried her nose in Noah's fly-away hair. "Friend from over in Ten Sleep takes herself down to Palm Springs every winter, visits her grand-daughter."

Amanda glanced around for Jacob, but he was outside with Tibbs. She took a breath. "Would Oregon do?"

"Oregon?" Rosie looked over the top of Noah's head, her eyes smiling. "My goodness, now there's an idea. We could be snowbirds of a sort."

"You could be grandparents of a sort. Jacob would like that."

Rosie glanced over curiously. "That husband of yours still pretending he got no kin?"

"It's...it's complicated."

Rosie nodded. "Family breakup always is, 'til one party or the other's gone and then it don't seem like it was all that complicated." She shook her head and changed the subject. "I'll give a thought to wintering in Oregon next year." Hope kindled in her eyes. "Don't suppose Tibbs would consider flying to Portland. He says flight's unnatural. Funny thing for a man who served in Korea. How'd he get there, walk?"

The talk over supper was about the possibility of locking down the ranch after Christmas. "Still got the cow?" Jacob asked.

"Nah, sold her off. Too much work for the little we used. Keep powdered on hand. And a dozen cans of condensed for the coffee. We make do." To prove his point, Tibbs got a half-filled tin of canned milk from the refrigerator and set it on the table.

"Neighbors watch out for the horses. Only two left now, and half-wild from having the run of the place. They think they're mustangs again. Might as well be. All we see of them is a burst of color every now and again when they chase their tail in the wind." Rosie glanced out the window at the faint blur of color near the ridge. "Perty though."

"We got oceans and cranberry bogs. You could make a fine pie, Rosie," Jacob teased.

"More inclined to express my artistic side. Read a magazine about a beachcomber, makes driftwood thingies that city folks hang in their windows," Rosie joked. "I figure to customize for the rural market. Put me some bells on mine to scare the squirrels."

When the laughter died down, Jacob draped a lazy arm over Rosie's shoulder. "Ride back with us. We can pack you up and be out of here before the next snowfall."

Tibbs's faded blue eyes brightened excitement before he turned away with a scowl. "Tibbs has a little procedure scheduled before we can travel," Rosie quietly explained.

"Procedure?"

"Yeah, I need my hearing aid cleaned out." Tibbs flashed a quick glance at his wife and changed the subject. "How long can we expect to enjoy your company?"

"Jacob has to be back in time for the AG inspection on the fourteenth," Amanda said. "We'll stay as long as we can."

"Well then, no time to waste. I better defrost a pot roast for tomorrow's dinner."

After Rosie pulled the paper-wrapped bundle from the freezer, she led Amanda to a cramped study that smelled of dogs and saddle soap. It was furnished with an ancient, scratched leather recliner and a round oak table that rocked with each step they took across the floor. After brushing aside a stack of well-read newspapers, Rosie sank into the cushions. Her stiff fingers fumbled with a lock before she managed to open a battered steamer trunk that held a collection of filmy dresses and hats. "Brought over on the Oregon Trail in 1865 by my grandmother," she explained. The dresses were lacy white, with tiny waists and sheer bodices stitched with tucks. Rosie held one up and laughed. "I could be buried in one, if I chose."

"Will you?"

She shook her head emphatically. "Land's sake, no. I went to school with Morton Hamshalder, the undertaker. Don't intend he should see me naked after all those years. Won't give him the satisfaction. I'll be cremated, fully dressed, with my pastor's wife standing witness." In spite of herself, Amanda smiled. Rosie rested her hand on a dress she was refolding in a layer of tissue paper. "Tibbs is fixing to die here this winter. Wants the comfort of his own bed and the Holy Words read to him as he passes. Got it straight in his mind." She closed the trunk and straightened. "Life and death, part of the same cycle, you know. Nothing to be feared." The sound of the fire snapping in the fireplace spoke a language that both of them understood, but Rosie continued as though she were speaking to herself. "No words needed, only the touch of a familiar hand when it's his time." She roused herself and noticed Amanda. "We'll speak no more of traveling out your way. I don't want to put hard feelings in Tibbs's head. But it was fun to dream." She held out her hands so Noah could wobble into them.

"Maybe Tibbs will change his mind." Amanda's throat was scratchy with the effect of Rosie's revelation. "We'd be honored if you came."

Rosie searched in her pockets for something to pacify the child squirming to be picked up. "Here, let's get you something to eat. How about some fine Wyoming elk jerky, come from Sheridan? Keep those new little teeth shiny till the Tooth Fairy buys 'em."

Amanda hesitated. "Not for the baby."

Rosie looked surprised. "Elk jerky is the best food known to man. Filled with protein and keeps the teeth pearly white like those singers on TV. I'll send some home with you for the boy."

Amanda sighed and began to explain about the special diet. "He has something called Maple Syrup Urinary Disease. He can't digest protein like we can. It's an inherited condition if the parents carry the gene. His father does." She hesitated a moment before continuing. "I've gotten into the habit of sniffing his breath. Making sure he smells like a little boy, not a pecan pie," she admitted.

Rosie's eyes softened as she stroked Noah's head. "No great harm done. You caught it in time. That's the best a mother can do." She looked up, her eyes lit with reflection from the fire.

"He almost died. He was in a coma because we didn't think to tell the hospital about Jacob's condition. He's the carrier. He and his family."

Rosie looked up. "I sense some anger there."

Amanda stood and began walking toward the kitchen as she shook her head. "Not really. I understand that these things happen. It's inevitable."

"And yet?"

Amanda moved to the sink and began putting the clean dishes from the drainer into the cabinet. The clinking sounded loud in the silent room. When she finished, she stood at the window, looking out at the windswept pasture while the silence between them grew.

Rosie broke the silence. "So, no hard feelings with Jacob. That's good to hear,"

Her chuckle hit a nerve, and Amanda's tears started without warning. "I've carried my anger inside me like poison. I try not to blame him, but it's his fault. He didn't even tell me about it. He says it's no big deal, but it is to me." She dragged a chair from the table and sat down before taking a napkin to wipe her eyes. "I couldn't even look at him while Noah was in the hospital. I was afraid I'd say something that I'd regret."

"So you kept it all locked inside yourself."

Amanda swiped at her eyes and nodded. "I don't have anyone I can trust with this. Nothing that won't come back to bite me, later. My mother and I used to..." She sat mutely, too ashamed to look at Rosie.

Rosie rose and pulled a bottle of whiskey from her closet before she poured a splash into two glasses. She handed one to Amanda. "There's more if you need it."

Amanda sipped hers and shook her head when Rosie offered another. "I'm so afraid that I can hardly breathe sometimes. If anything happens to Noah, I'm afraid I'll hate Jacob for it."

Rosie nodded. "Now we're getting somewhere. It's fear, not blame that's eating at you. They ain't the same, you know. One you control, the other controls you. Hard part is figuring out which is which."

Amanda considered in silence. "I'm afraid I won't have enough time with Noah. Every time I look at him, I see him struggle. He never deserved this."

Rosie slipped her worn, calloused hand over Amanda's and leaned closer so that their foreheads touched. "Don't let regret rob you of your good times. Stay in the moment and pray to beat hell. God sees you're grateful, He'll give you a little more time." Her voice was feather-soft and gentle.

The sound of crashing boots and a slamming door ended the discussion as the men trooped back inside. Rosie shifted and stood, after handing Amanda a handkerchief from her apron pocket. "We better get dinner started."

The men pulled their gloves off and held them over the woodstove, warming themselves while they waited for a cup of coffee. "Jake got himself a couple of muskrats on the trap line. Set another for that coyote been bothering the neighbor's sheep." When Rosie set his coffee in front of him, Tibbs added a spoon of sugar. "Boy stays long enough, we'll make a trapper out of him yet."

"You get them muskrats skinned proper?" Rosie asked.

"Yes ma'am. Skinned and stretched on the boards. Jacob did a good job of it, too." Tibbs said. "Should bring us top dollar. Make up for all the elk he's eaten since he got here."

Jacob snorted. "Hardly."

Amanda watched the way the Bells doted on him. Both of them. He was their shining joy and they wanted this visit to last forever. Tibbs reached to take a carved horse from Noah's outstretched arm, her son's favorite toy, carved by his father.

"For me? Why thank you. I'll put it here in my pocket and save it until I'm hungry. No? Well I can't ride it, now, can I?" Noah nodded. "I can? Well then, I'll name it Little Shucks, and we'll go for a ride in my nice pickup after supper. How does that sound?"

Noah's laughter was infectious. By the time Amanda set the tamale pie casserole on the blue-check-ered oilcloth beside the odd bowls of leftovers and chopped iceberg salad, Tibbs was already buttering a slice of white bread. "Seems like just yesterday, I was shoveling the snow pile, slid off the roof from a late spring blizzard," he said. "Not sure where the time went."

"You got the same amount of daylight as everyone else, old man. Stop your griping, or the Lord'll think you're ready to quit." Rosie kept her head down as though she needed an audience to give her courage to say what had been on her mind awhile.

"Grateful for every single day, I am. Just wish I had a few more stowed in my pocket." Tibbs looked up and grinned when Noah pointed toward his shirt. "Yeah, I got me a horse in my pocket, don't I?" He chuckled. "I might trade it away for something else I need. Call it 'Time.' Hee hee hee."

Later, as Amanda washed the dishes, Jacob walked up and put his arms around her. He nuzzled her and whispered, "Tibbs is failing."

She nodded, conscious of the silence in the other

room. Jacob pressed against her, his warm body a shield against the blustery cold outside and she paused to savor the moment. When she picked up her dishcloth again, the warmth of the room kindled inside her.

By the end of the week, Noah was red-cheeked and plump from Rosie's cobblers and green bean casseroles. He spent his days stomping through the scatter of snow as he fed wisps of hay to the two horses and searched the barn for eggs, even though the hens wintered under the straw.

On their last day, Amanda packed their suitcases with an emptiness she hadn't realized she held. Rosie remained in the kitchen, clanking pans as she stirred up a lemon filling for the crust that baked in the oven. The house smelled of life and activity. In a couple of hours the rooms would be dead except for the snap of the fire and the occasional comments of two old people who didn't pay much attention to the other's musings. Tibbs couldn't hear much, and Rosie had already heard most of what he had to say. Amanda stuffed Noah's pajamas into a corner pocket of her suitcase and zipped the case before Jacob carried it to the car.

Their farewell was bittersweet. Rosie wore her sheepskin coat over her apron. She fussed over Noah who was already strapped into his car seat with the heater running.

"I want to thank you for helping us celebrate Thanksgiving early. It was a fine occasion. We'll remember it in a couple of weeks when everyone else eats their bird." Rosie's voice was an octave lower than usual. She bade her time as she fidgeted with her gloves and pointed to a parchment-wrapped package in the back seat, tied with string. "Packed you a lemon meringue pie for the road. Might think of us when you eat it."

Amanda wrapped her arms around Rosie's slight form and brought her lips to a wind-chaffed cheek. "We won't need pie to remember this week. It's all here." She tapped her breast with a flattened palm and tried to peer through tear-filled eyes. "I wish we didn't have to leave."

"Come again in the summer." Tibbs nodded at Jacob. "We'll put that man of yours to work grading the road. Might be, he'll like it enough to settle his family here. Have a second home out here, just the five of us."

Jacob colored. "We'll take some time off in June and make it back here. Promise. And you're welcome to winter at our place. You might take up clamming. Get yourselves a pair of purple flip-flops."

Amanda listened to the banter, a poor substitute for the emotions hidden behind the smiles. Hearts so heavy that humor was the last resort. She hugged Tibbs and made her way to the passenger side.

Tibbs waved and started toward the barn. He reemerged with a gunny sack in his hand. "I meant to give you this, Jake. It's my son's lariat. Old grass rope, the real stuff. He kept it wrapped up real tight against the weather. He'd want you to have it. Call it a Christmas present. Go on, take it." His eyes followed Jacob's hands as they caressed the stiff, braided coil.

"It's a fine rope. I can hope to do it justice, but I'm no cowboy like your Steve. I am only a plowboy," Jacob said. "But maybe I make you proud."

You already have. Amanda saw the pride the old couple felt for Jacob. Her wave, out the passenger window as the car sped west, was made to a forlorn couple in wind-whipped scarves blindly waving back. It was some time before she could find her voice again.

The trip home seemed quieter. Amanda chattered while Jacob drove in silence, his thoughts distant and private. Her cell phone reception was spotty. In the mountains, a call to Carol was interrupted twice before she gave up. Finally, she cracked open a book while Noah slept in his car seat. She was relieved when they crossed into Oregon and began the long, straight route alongside the Columbia River.

Chapter Twenty

"Peanut? That you?"

"Dad—I missed you!" Amanda leaped from the car and crushed her father in a fierce embrace. He stood on shaky legs, his familiar Miller Wholesale Nursery cap partially askew, but the light of recognition in his eyes included them all.

"I wondered where you were. I thought you'd gone to the fair."

Amanda laughed. "Noah's here. Noah, give your grandpa a hug. Let's go over to the barn to see the horse. Would you like that?"

Her father hesitated. "I want a baked potato for supper. That woman doesn't make them for shit."

"Dad—where did you learn that language? You never talked like that." She looked over to where Imelda's teenage son watched with a chagrined look. She shrugged and crooked her finger at him before turning back to her father. "Did you miss your grandson? Noah's right here. Can you say hello?"

Her father reached out his hands. "Hello again." He

was rewarded with a tight hug. When he released the boy, his eyes were damp. "Who's that man? Is he your driver?"

Her homecoming was shattered by the look of confusion in her father's face. "That's Jacob. He's my husband, remember? He lives here. And he cares for the nursery when you don't feel up to it."

"Wait until your mother sees him. She'll tell him to take off his shoes before he sits on her good sofa."

Amanda concentrated on getting Noah into his jacket so he could play with the children who were shyly waiting. The housekeeper hovered nearby. When they had a moment alone, Amanda whispered, "How did it go, Imelda?"

The housekeeper nodded. "Good. He ate good. Took walks. My boys made sure he didn't get lost when he went to the greenhouses. He spent most of the time in his study with the fireplace. We saw he didn't feed the fire, though. My son Manny was in charge. But your father, he missed you. It was good, the phone calls. He like them very much."

When Imelda's family left for their own house, Amanda set out the meal of refried beans and tortillas she'd left for them. She pierced a small russet potato and set it inside the microwave to cook.

Jacob went straight to the office. He came back before supper with a flushed look on his face.

Amanda noticed. "How did everything go? Any problems?"

Jacob glanced over at his father-in-law and lowered his voice so as not to upset the man. "Business turned to mud while I was gone. If it wasn't one thing, it was another. Shipment numbers are off. One of the trucks is out because the driver got sick. He won't be back for another week. I need to take his load out tonight. I'll leave in a few minutes."

"What can I do to help?"

"You might look to the accounts. Get a second set of eyes on the paperwork." He scowled. "I will think on what is required. Right now I don't have a notion. Modern farming is supposed to make life easier, but it just increases the pace, I tell you, wife."

Amanda watched him pull out a few minutes later, carrying a thermos of coffee. He'd driven all day, in a hurry to get home, and he looked tired. The company phone had rung steadily with one customer who needed product for the Christmas season. With one man down, Jacob would need to work double time to make up the shortfall. She spent a restless night. At two o'clock, she gave up any pretense of sleep and called him on his cell. "How's it going? You still awake?"

"Yeah, almost there. I'll grab a couple winks before I unload and start home. I got a call from one of our customers who thinks his snail infestation is our fault. He put a complaint into the regulators. I must see my way to a solution soon as I get back."

She heard the stress in his voice. "Jacob, are you having second thoughts about all of this?"

He hesitated. "You know me better than that." He took a breath. "But to be truthful, I miss the slow life. Back home, we lived a different pace. I miss that. Here, we just run faster, but we don't get anywhere. How many shirts can a man wear?"

"Ouch." She winced at the reference to the wardrobe she'd bought for him. His wedding coat was in the back of his closet, in a dry cleaner's bag where the moths wouldn't get it. He hadn't worn it since the night their baby almost died. He claimed he preferred to eat at home. He called it *plain cooking*.

In the background, his air brakes hissed as he pulled into a rest stop. "I need to take a minute here."

"Stay safe, sweetheart. I love you so much."

"I love you, too." His voice was calm and slow, like he was ready to fall asleep.

"You are my life, Jacob. Remember that."

"Yeah, a good life. I need to hang up now, liebchen. Keep the bed warm. I'll be home late tonight."

In her free hours, Amanda poured over the company spreadsheets until she understood the process that her father had carried in his head. She spent part of each morning in the office, while Noah played in the corner with his toy tractors, and her father sat in the patio, watching the men hustle in and out of the greenhouses.

When he returned, Jacob brushed off her attempts to share his worries. She heard snatches of gossip, enough to understand that production was down and one or two customers had taken their business to a competitor. After a late-night discussion that grew into an argument, she agreed that they would not discuss business in the bedroom.

❦

Jacob spent the evening in the shop, trying to fix a tractor with a slipped gear. He came to bed tired and still smelling of diesel, even after a hasty shower.

"Rough day? Amanda closed her book and watched

as he skimmed his greasy shirt off and threw it on the floor.

"Good. Same. You know, good. And yours?"

"Good." Amanda took a deep breath. "Carol called. They had rain in Ohio. Same as us."

"Good for the farmer." Jacob sounded preoccupied.

"I bought a new dress. I thought we could have a date night on Friday."

"Friday?" His eyes seemed distant. "Sorry. I need to run into Washington on Friday."

"Okay." Amanda rolled over so that she faced the wall and tried to keep her tone even. "Maybe another night."

After three nights, she decided that silence was easier to manage than the stilted conversation that substituted for an honest relationship.

On Thursday, Jacob stood in the yard with someone who had ridden in on a full-dress Harley. The man straddled his bike and revved the throttle outside the kitchen window. Amanda waited to serve supper until the motorcycle roared off in the direction of town and Jacob started toward the back door.

He took his seat at the end of the table opposite her father and grinned sheepishly. "That was Chewy. He came by to show me his new motorcycle. He says it's pretty sweet—his word. He had it tuned up for a road trip. Plans to run down the Coast Highway to Santa Barbara. Stay over in Carmel." He hesitated. "I've heard that route is pretty nice."

Amanda plunked a bowl of vegetable soup in front of him. "Your friend's off on another road trip? Doesn't he have a family?"

Jacob picked up his spoon and turned it over.

"Chewy claims that duty is a hard master. He learned that the hard way. Now he makes time for pleasure." He shifted and spoke without meeting her eyes. "I didn't agree to go with him. I don't even have a bike. But he told me about a motorcycle shop that has some sweet deals right now. I might drive over to Portland and check it out. Not to buy, but no harm to look, ja?"

"Jacob, motorcycles are dangerous!"

"Safer than my buggy back home. You saw what happens on the roads." He glanced up as he flexed his throttle hand. "Sure, I take my chances. But with a motorcycle I keep up with the traffic. Don't worry. I won't be reckless."

Amanda's hands froze in fear. Her mother had spent a lifetime in a wheelchair. She'd heard of riders paralyzed from a moment's indecision. "You promise? You have a family to consider." She tried another tack to defuse the tension. "What do you know about motorcycles, anyway? You were Amish!"

His laugh sounded forced. "Ja, I know this! But anyway, I used to ride. My English buddy had a motorcycle back home. We took it out all the time and I never got hurt on it."

"Yet."

"Don't fret about this, Amanda. Nothing is settled. I won't buy without first talking to you."

Amanda? He only calls me Amanda when he's mad at me.

The next afternoon, Jacob pulled up with a shiny Suzuki in the back of his pickup, its bed filled with a mass of black tank and shiny chrome. He honked and revved his truck's engine before he hopped out. "Come see what I got."

She slowly wiped Noah's hands of apple slices and Goldfish while Jacob backed the bike down two enormous ramps to the ground. He grinned with a look of pride she'd never seen in him before. He reached over on the seat and pulled out a huge black helmet with a yellow blaze across the side and the name *Shoei* emblazoned across the back. By the time he donned a bulky silver jacket with reflective stripes down the sleeves, he looked like a warrior. She watched as he straddled the bike like a victor in a triumphant battle, clad in brand-new riding denims fitted with padding from the knees to the top of glossy motorcycle boots.

When her legs threatened to collapse, she closed the door behind her and leaned against it as he looked up with a huge grin, clearly anticipating her excitement. From the safety of the door, she managed a weak smile. Beside her, Noah struggled to get free from her hand. Without conscious thought, she released her grip. She watched as he ran to his father with his arms outstretched, demanding to be lifted up.

Jacob's gloved hands gripped a pair of levers on either side of his handlebars like a couple of old friends. He revved the engine and slipped the bike into gear. "Put Noah on front." He indicated the space between his legs. "He'll be fine. I will go slow."

Amanda's face burned with indignation. "He's not even three years old!"

"Come on, Amanda, cut me some slack. Just around the yard. No different than riding a horse." Jacob leaned over to lift his son onto the gas tank himself. When he was satisfied, he eased the bike in a wide arc around the parking lot, making slow figure eights in front of the greenhouses while Noah clapped in delight. When the bike pulled up in front of her and Jacob waited, Amanda tried to lift him off while he screeched in protest.

"Now see what you've done," she grumbled while Noah melted into a temper tantrum at her side.

Jacob twisted the gas lever. The engine revved as he dipped the handlebars and tucked his feet back onto the pegs. With a hail of flying gravel he spun out, overcorrected and nearly laid the bike on its side. He recovered and dabbed his feet on the gravel with a sheepish grin. "Hop on. Imelda can watch Noah. We'll only be gone an hour." He reached behind him to unlock a strap that hung from a seat mount. "Look, I even got you a helmet."

Amanda stared at the globe dangling from his fingers while her insides burned in white-hot terror. She saw her mother in the hospital bed, unable to move. A life ruined. Her own life changed. She folded her arms in a self-protective motion to stop her trembling and whispered, "Jacob, I can't."

He studied her for a moment until his scowl erased the traces of his boyish grin. "I get it. I shouldn't have pushed. Maybe when you see there's nothing to fear."

She shook her head emphatically and backed toward the house, trying to accommodate the shift of the last half-hour. "Promise me you won't ride it on the freeway."

The mesh of gears and the sound of tires on gravel followed her back inside as Jacob rode out of the yard. Inside the house, Noah screamed in protest. His meltdown added to her frustration, but even so, it seemed his anger subsided before her own did. He ran to the window and spent the next hour watching for his father's return while she fumed. Eventually, she tried to distract him with *Sesame Street*, but he refused to leave his perch, even for his favorite television program. Even the offer of sweet potato chips and pickles didn't tempt him to the table. Finally, she joined him at the window.

At dusk, a pair of headlights dipped into the yard and headed toward the bay window. Noah gave a squeal when at the last moment, Jacob braked and the bike came to a stop. He cut the engine and pushed his shield back with a grin capturing his entire face. For a moment he seemed imperious, his eyes closed, his body so totally relaxed that she felt a twinge of envy. Noah pounded on the window until his father looked up and waved. He dismounted and walked around the bike to check that the side stand was on firm ground before he gathered his helmet and walked to the door.

Dinner was strained, with Amanda and her father both silent while Noah enjoyed a rare treat—elk that Rosie Bell had sent along. He made "yum-yum" sounds while Jacob ate with his head down, shoveling his food in an effort to escape the table.

Finally, Amanda broke the silence. "Is it paid for?"

Jacob looked up with a flash of pride. "I filled out a credit app. I need to establish credit, even if the rate is high. I intend to pay it off as soon as I am able. So, yes."

"Shouldn't we have talked about it first?"

He shook his head. "What is the purpose? We do not need to be in accord with everything. My father didn't discuss every purchase with my mother. Sometimes a man does what he thinks is right."

"So it was easier to ask forgiveness than permission?"

"I do not ask forgiveness. I have done nothing

wrong." He pointed to a bowl across the table. "Could you pass the carrots."

The rest of the evening was spent in silence. Amanda read to a freshly bathed Noah until he fell asleep then slipped into her own room and tried to concentrate on her book, with little success. Finally, still fuming, she snapped off the light. When Jacob finally came to bed, she pretended to be asleep.

She slipped from bed at first light in a knot of nerves and irritation and managed to fall back asleep on the sofa until she heard the bedroom door open and Noah pad from the hallway rubbing his eyes. Later, she tiptoed to the closet and donned her Sunday dress without waking Jacob. A pot of freshly brewed coffee failed to dispel the bleakness of her mood until her father entered the kitchen, clearly unaware of the drama in the house. Not the Sunday morning she had imagined, waffles, church, and a drive to the coast. This one promised to be as flat and purposeless as her life at the moment.

When Jacob entered, dressed in his new leathers and a tee shirt, she ignored him and continued to fill the dishwasher from the previous night. He looked around sheepishly, picked up a slice of toast and took a bite. "You look pretty. Where do you go this morning?"

She kept her gaze on the faucet. "I'm taking my son to church. You should try it sometime."

He picked up a slice of bacon. "Sure, one of these days. But I need to seat my new brake pads. Get ready for spring."

"What happens in spring?" She set the frying pan in the sink with more force than was necessary.

"Probably take a road trip to Wenatchee for a

couple of days. Run up and see the apple blossoms. Check out the roads. It'll be fun. Wanna come?"

"Thanks, but no thanks!"

He eyed her over a heap of blackberry jam on his second slice of toast. "Maybe Chewy wants to go."

When she finished getting ready, Amanda hurried to be the first to leave the house. "Lock up, you're the last one out," she called as she snapped her father and son into their seat belts. At church, she sat in a lump of misery—a motorcycle widow among couples with arms touching as they shared a hymnal. She tried to sing, but her mind was distracted with mental arguments intended for Jacob. Her father's voice sounded clear and strong as he joined the choir in an old hymn that he apparently remembered. *He still has some long-term memory. This is a good thing—if I'm counting blessings.* When service ended, she picked up her son from the nursery.

On the way home, Noah begged to stop when they passed the arena where two men on horses coiled their dally ropes while a herd of half-grown calves huddled in an adjacent pen. The man in front of the calf looked familiar. When his partner checked his pigging string, the cowboy rode over and doffed his hat.

"Hi, Amanda. What brings you out?"

She mustered a smile she didn't feel. "Charlie Rivers! Hi. On my way home. Noah wanted to watch. He likes horses."

"His mama used to, too." Charlie winked at her son. "Cute kid." He bent to peer inside the window. "Howdy, Mr. Miller." He straightened and nudged a thumb at Noah. "Where's your daddy?"

Amanda sighed and tried to maintain an even tone.

"Seems he's taken up motorcycling."

Charlie's eyebrows lifted. "Whooee! Well good for him."

"Not you, too! You men are idiots. He'll kill himself and Noah will be an orphan," she snapped before she could stop herself.

Charlie bent to squint through the unrolled window. "Darlin', you ain't his mama. Better give him some rein."

Amanda considered his words. "It's hard, you know? After my mother—"

"He's not *your* mother, either. Cut him some slack." Charlie grinned at Noah who was feeding a Goldfish to the horse. "Your kid here, he'll be just like his old man. Better get used to it." His partner shouted and he whirled his horse toward the corral. "But if he doesn't treat you right, you let me know!"

Amanda watched as he looped his lariat and caught a shorthorn calf. His horse leaned back on the rope while the heeler secured the animal with a quick twist and flung his hands in the air.

"Glory hounds, every one of them," she griped to her father as she started the engine.

"Amanda, give him some rein." Her father repeated Charlie's words.

From across the car, she felt her face heat when she realized he was right. He seldom spoke these days and only when he had something important to say. She offered him a feeble fake-it-till-you-make-it smile. "I'll try, Dad. Promise."

She had tears of relief when Jacob rode in hours later, safe and sound. That night, she listened as he recalled his ride with the enthusiasm of a teenager. "I rode down to Newport and around Yaquina Bay. It's nice over there, with small farms and some silos. I found a couple of side roads that wound back through the trees." He glanced over to share his excitement. "Some nice little houses back in there. I noticed some old dairies and antique farm equipment that looked like an Amishman might have settled there." His face lit up with recalled memory.

His voice is lighter. Maybe he feels peace when he's on the road. She broke off her thought when she realized he was still talking. "The air was clear at the top. Fog in the distance." He laughed again. "You should see it hanging over the horizon."

He continued as though he were talking to himself. *Does he feel alone, too? Even when he's with me?*

"I stopped at a shop and had fish and chips." He turned to consider her for the first time. "What did you do?"

The details of her day seemed dull compared to his. She gave up trying the second time he interrupted with another detail of his trip. When he reached for her, she rose from the sofa and left him to finish his beer.

Jacob woke the next morning with fresh energy. "I will store my bike in the garage for the winter. Make time to build a playhouse for Noah before Christmas. Maybe your dad can lend a hand. He used to be good with tools."

"Yeah, like you're so good at keeping promises," she muttered on her way into the shower.

"What was that you say?"

"You promised you wouldn't buy a motorcycle."

He walked away, scowling.

She made pancakes and bacon in silence while her

men sipped their coffee. Noah picked up a piece of pancake and offered it to his father, who made an exaggerated show of wolfing it down while Noah squealed in delight.

"Noah, eat. Don't play." She ignored her son's partner-in-crime and concentrated on cooking another pancake, glad for the excuse to keep her back to the table.

Jacob took another bite and grinned. "You look nice. Did you try something new with your hair?"

She turned to hunt for maple syrup in the refrigerator to hide the tears that were ridiculously close. When she turned back, Jacob was sharing a piece of bacon with his son. She grabbed it and slapped it onto the table. "Jacob, that's protein!" Noah started to wail as she escaped to the sink to load the dishwasher. Holding back her tears, she managed to wash Noah's hands and reminded her father to do the same. Later, in her bedroom, she burst into tears.

By lunchtime, her anger started to feel heavy. With a heavy heart she assembled a stack of sandwiches and a pot of coffee, placed a note on the table explaining that she had errands, and slipped from the house. Her father was asleep in the recliner. He'd wake and eat his sandwich with Jacob. Maybe the two of them could exchange stories of impossible wives that ended with the phrase, "Am I right?" On her way into town, she dropped Noah off at a friend's for a play date.

Two hours later, she piled grocery bags into her trunk while she rued the fact that her life consisted of either buying food, cooking food or cleaning the kitchen afterward. How three males could eat so much was beyond comprehension: Special diets for Noah, strange requests from her dad, and a husband who could eat half a pork roast at a sitting. His capacity for mashed potatoes was legendary. Her father's sweet tooth for homemade apple tarts and cinnamon donuts kept her house smelling like a bake shop most of the time. Add to that the hours she spent on the floor, playing with Noah, teaching him colors and shapes, reading books, and taking nature walks. *I've fallen down the rabbit hole.*

On her way home, she collected a reluctant Noah from his friend's house—but not without a dramatic scene that left her embarrassed and apologetic to the other mother. "I can't imagine what's come over him, Linda. My son's usually so easy-going."

Linda, the mother of four, laughed. "Classic two-year-old meltdown. It happens. Don't take it personally."

"I think Noah's bored with me. I'm the food police, always taking away the treats he can't have. I try every way I know to get him to drink his supplement while he grits his teeth and refuses. We go through this song and dance. I buy him new sippy cups, grown-up cups, superhero cups, and straws. I chill it, put ice in it, change up the flavors. But he's discovered the power of 'no.' He's ready to be around other kids, and I'm ready to let him, but he has to be careful about what he eats. Terrible twos are no excuse."

"Like it or not, twos give way to the inquisitive threes." Linda laughed. "Or is it the little-man threes!" She hesitated. "Where's your husband? Are you and he...?"

"Oh, heavens no," Amanda lied. "He's just got a lot on his plate these days." She caught herself before she poured out her tale of woe. Nobody needed to listen to a whiny wife. "I think I'm bored, too. I miss teaching."

"Someone said the school needs a fill-in for a third-grade teacher who's going out on maternity leave. Might just be your solution." Linda reached to rescue the lizard the two little boys had managed to capture. "Bring Noah by anytime. We love having him. And I have his dietary needs posted on my refrigerator, so no worries."

Amanda called in an order for pizza from Papa Murphy's before she fastened Noah into his car seat. When she picked it up, Noah held onto his special veggie one in an awed state of silence. Pizza wasn't on their list of approved foods for a MSUD kid. They'd pay for it tomorrow with veggie smoothies and spaghetti squash, but judging from the grin on her kid's face, it would be worth it.

By the time she arrived home her heart felt lighter. Jacob gave her a real kiss and reached for a slice of pepperoni. When it was finished baking, he finished three-fourths of the extra-large pie and looked around for more.

She moved the remainder from his reach. "Jacob, you don't farm with horses anymore. You better watch it, or you'll end up like Amos Byler at your brother's wedding," she snapped.

The mention of his brother brought Jacob's head up. "What does my brother have to do with this? Suddenly you find fault with my looks? Or is it just my behavior? You think I should act like my brother John?"

The accuracy of his accusation brought her head up. "Not at all," she hedged. "I just don't think you should eat the entire pie."

"Then buy a smaller one." He finished off the pie in silence.

By the time she had Noah bathed and asleep, she was still angry. In the bedroom, she made the bed with fresh sheets, wafting the bottom sheet high over her head while Jacob waited for her to finish. That he didn't bother to help nettled her even more. "You're going to have to forgive your brother sometime," she snapped. "You can't go through life being angry at him." *Or your beloved Katie, whom you probably wish you'd married instead of me.* She watched his eyes reflect the angst that filled him when he thought about home.

"Maybe so, wife. But easier saying than doing." He took a corner of the sheet and tucked it over the mattress. "I'm tired and stressed. Every day is filled with noise and responsibility. I have no time to think."

And your wife isn't helping.

His unspoken accusation lodged in her stomach, and she caught her breath.

Jacob looked up from the case he was slipping over his pillow. "No more talk about the motorcycle. Amanda, if I'm to live among the English, then let me be English."

She sucked in her breath and froze. *Maybe this is what he feels when he rides—freedom.* She exhaled and felt her own stress ease. "Why don't you take a motorcycle ride on Sunday? Maybe it'll clear your head."

His expression of joy caught her off-guard. She moved to finish her pillow with a smile that took an effort to sustain. When he reached for her, she went willingly into his arms. It hardly mattered that he fell asleep afterward, she felt sated for the first time in weeks.

Chapter Twenty-One

"Jacob, look what I got in the mail. It's my OST certificate."

"What's that?"

Amanda gulped. "It's my teaching license. I'm now officially licensed to substitute in the classroom. And not a minute too soon. My old principal has a teacher out on medical leave for the next four months. And I'm applying for the job." She stretched her arms against the wooden corral while Noah fed Yankee a handful of hay. Jacob looked up from his curry comb and regarded her with a scowl. "It would be a chance for Noah to try preschool for a few months," she continued. "He's bored at home. And I wouldn't mind talking to an actual adult for a change. And then there's the money—"

Jacob curried the horse in silence. When he looked up, his disappointment painted dark pools in his eyes. "We don't have enough for our needs that you need to work outside the home?" He paused, his hand at his side. "One thing leads to another, lieibchen. Next thing, we'll covet what the neighbors have, and that's a path with no end." He finished with the curry comb and returned it to its hook.

"True. But I'd really enjoy the break." She winced when she heard a trace of a whine in her voice. *Stay strong, girl. Hold your ground.*

"A break from your family? Are we so hard to be around that you need to escape us?" He stood for a moment with his head bowed. "There is enough work in your home to keep you occupied. I crave some real pickles for a change. And sauerkraut from a crock, not a jar. A wife and mother does not need to travel outside the home to fill her day. Your son does not yet speak. He needs a special diet. Your father's time is limited. He needs to be honored. Is this the right time to think only of yourself!"

Amanda's eyes glared with impatience. "Jacob, Dad is still independent. He has duties in the greenhouse that keep him occupied on the weekends. He relies on Imelda as much as me. He's tried out adult respite care, and he likes it. He can go more often. I'll pick him up and deliver him like I do now. We'll be together for breakfast and supper. We can walk. And we'll have evenings, and..." Her voice strained with frustration. "Jacob, I really need this."

Despair thickened his throat until he found it hard to continue. "I have said my piece, liebchen. If your scheme turns sour, then it is not Gott's plan." He straightened and grabbed the bucket of oats, spilling them in his haste to escape.

Amanda followed him outside, careful that her voice didn't carry to Noah, still playing in the paddock. "Jacob, don't be angry at me. It's only a few months."

"Do what you will. I have no time for this. I have a load that needs delivered, yet. The driver has jury duty."

"Will you be back for supper?"

"I don't know when I will return. Late. Don't wait up for me."

Amanda studied him with a feeling of dread. "So this isn't a short haul?"

He shook his head without looking at her.

❧

Amanda followed her father into the bathroom and made sure he brushed his teeth. She checked that his pajamas were on with the fly in front this time. He asked for water and she returned to the kitchen to pour a glass. While the tap ran, she watched through the window for Jacob's truck lights.

In the bedroom, her father sat on the edge of his bed. "Amanda, this is a damned business, this memory of mine. I never wanted to put you through this. I wish I'd gone when your mother did."

She wrapped him in an embrace even as she gave a quick peek out the window again. "No, Daddy. Don't think like that. We'll get through this. Together."

Her father engulfed her in a bear hug, and suddenly she was ten again. "No matter how bad it gets, I'll keep you inside me, Peanut. I won't let go of you. I promise."

She remained in his arms until his muscles went limp and he slumped into the sheets. When she paused at the light switch, he gazed at her with the familiar half-smile that hid his confusion. "Sweet dreams, Daddy. Don't let the bed bugs bite."

He raised up on an elbow, frowning. "Bugs in my bed? Need bug thingie, young lady. Bugs a thousand if you stay them."

She caught his flailing hand when he nearly knocked over the bedside lamp. "No bugs. Only sweet dreams. I'll leave the door open. Okay?"

In the hallway, the nightlight illuminated the nursery and she eased the door open. Noah stood in his youth bed, pulling off his wet pajamas. She changed his clothing and stripped the bed. When he was tucked in again, she made her way to the kitchen and poured herself a glass of wine.

In the wee hours, Jacob slipped in beside her, his arms seeking her and his body spooning hers as though nothing had happened between them. She half-turned and felt his contentment when he reached for her.

At breakfast she set a bowl of oatmeal in front of him and turned to pour his coffee. "I've begun to potty train Noah."

Jacob glanced up and nodded warily. "He seems old enough. Older than my brothers, this is for sure."

She collected Noah's empty cereal bowl and set it in the sink. "I suspect your mother was more efficient than I am. I just want to have options. I'm sure you understand—" She broke off to run water in the sink.

"Maybe so, but I don't marry my mother." Jacob studied her with a thoughtful expression. "So it is still your wish to work outside the house?" When he received no answer, he finished his coffee and walked out the door.

She caught glimpses of him in the yard throughout

the day. At quitting time, when employees began to leave in their vehicles, he charged toward the house, his head down like a bull's. The back door slammed and slammed again. A moment later his motorcycle roared out of the yard. She checked the coat rack and found his jacket was gone, as were his boots and helmet.

When it was time for supper, she sliced her veggie lasagna and set it on the table with her stomach knotted. The evening stretched until it was time for Noah's bedtime. She attempted to keep her tone light as she read to Noah, hoping he wouldn't require a tuck-in from his father. Even her father seemed to sense the strain. He ran through his routine without assistance, even checked the doors to be sure they were locked.

When they were both asleep and Jacob still hadn't arrived, she phoned Carol. "Carol, do you have time to talk?"

"Amanda? What's wrong? Something happen? Geesh. What time is it?"

Amanda glanced at the phone. "What time? Oh my gosh, I'm so sorry. Hey, nothing worth waking you for. We'll talk later. Go back to sleep. I'm so sorry."

"Okay. Right. Later."

By eleven o'clock, she was frantic with worry. Every passing car made her rush to the window and count the number of headlights. None of them was a motorcycle.

Jacob gripped the gas tank with his knees and laid on the throttle so hard he felt the front wheel lift. He eased up and felt the bike recover. *No damage done.* He inched into the roadway and concentrated on the sweeping curves that separated him from town. At a four-way stop, he headed for the hills, where the traffic would be sparse, and the road filled with twists and turns. He increased throttle pressure until fifty horsepower vibrated beneath him, creating an adrenaline rush of speed and a bit of fear. He felt alive as the road dipped through the valley, made a sweeping turn and began to climb. Doug fir, pine and oak flashed by; the smell of huckleberry and yew filled his nose. Two miles passed, and then three, as the hypnotic sweep of the turns lulled him into a stupor and each undulation of the pavement brought fresh release from the emotions binding his gut.

Long shadows appeared, hindering his visibility. From the corner of his eye, fog crept toward and settled in the treetops. His hands felt numb, and he ventured a quick glance down at his gauges. Forty-five degrees. Cold enough that biting air blew up under his jacket. He glanced down again at his gauges, over-steered, and looked up to see the railing of the fog-soaked concrete bridge abutment. Too late, he felt his bike break traction.

Ahead, a slow-moving delivery truck crowded a narrow section of road that led into a sweeping s-curve. He started to pass until a car's horn blasted him for his stupidity. He straightened, shaken by the near miss. Amanda was waiting. The thought of home evoked images of a normal dinner and bedtime stories, even another opportunity to deal with the problems. *Time to slow it down, buddy. Nothing is worth losing your life over.*

He recalled their argument and Amanda's tight, unhappy face when she spoke of her need to take a temporary job. Maybe she felt trapped, like he had tonight. He lifted his hand off the throttle and the bike slowed. In the west, the sun slipped fully behind the horizon, washing his anger with festive streaks of red and yellow. Time to go home.

From the corner of his eye, a huge buck stepped into the roadway. Jacob froze. He weighed the dangers of locking up the brakes against the chance of a collision and made a split-second decision.

He braked hard, pumped, released, and braked again with a counter-steering trick he'd learned in motorcycle safety class. He rocked the bike to the left and prayed the lazy "s" would allow him to swing wide.

He was still praying for a chance when the deer bolted into his path.

In slow motion he felt himself fly through the air, his boots level with his helmet as the blacktop slowly rose to meet him. His last thought, as he dove onto the broken pavement was: *This is going to hurt!*

He blacked out. When he came to, a set of head-lights blinded him.

A voice asked, "Are you hurt, sir?"

❧

Amanda was already in bed when the hospital called.

"Is he okay?" Her ears pounded so hard she could scarcely hear the woman's reply.

"I believe it was a motorcycle accident. I can't give you details. You'll need to talk to his doctor once he gets out of surgery."

She hung up and immediately phoned Imelda, explained the situation, and apologized for the intrusion. When Imelda reassured her that she was on her way, she hung up. She dressed and went into the kitchen to wait.

Imelda arrived, winded and frantic. "Don't worry about your boys. I make sure the little one gets his nutrition. And I stay as long as needed. Just go."

A wall of hospital lights lit the parking lot. Amanda ran to the empty information desk, where a sign directed her to the ER. On her way out of the elevator, she realized she was wearing her slippers. After what seemed like an interminable time, a doctor in rumpled scrubs approached with an inscrutable expression he'd probably learned in medical school. She braced herself for the worst, prayed for the best, and felt her nerves quiver while she blocked out the foremost question on her mind.

"Mrs. Ruth?" When she nodded, the physician introduced himself. "I'm Dr. Anigli. Your husband's had quite a spill. But no permanent damage. He has a broken ankle and some abrasions with significant bruising, but nothing that won't heal." He smiled for the first time. "The nurse will take you to him. He's groggy, but he'll be waking soon."

Amanda followed the nurse down the hall, where the scent of antiseptic brought reminders of her mother. They entered a room where a helmet lay on the floor, its bright stripe ground off by black asphalt. After the nurse checked Jacob's vitals and left, Amanda leaned in and tried to find her husband in the bruised, swollen man in the bed. She glared at the helmet and the plastic bag that contained his gear. She wanted to pummel him for the fear that he'd caused. Instead, she saw his lashes flicker and she burst into tears.

"Jacob!" She laid her head beside him on the pillow and felt his warmth. His leg was elevated, and a machine measured his vitals with a syncopated hum that made her want to cover her ears. She'd lived with the sound for fourteen years, every blip a hammer blow.

For the next hour she watched him sleep with a faint smile on his lips as though he held a secret. His hair was damp from a hasty shampooing, and he smelled of antiseptic soap. Even his hands smelled like her mother's.

She must have dozed off. When she woke, dawn brightened the eastern ridge, and her stomach rumbled. She reached for her purse and felt the mattress shift.

"'Manda? Is that you? I was not sure you would come." Jacob's voice sounded blurry from the anesthetic.

The vulnerability in his eyes caused her to crumble. "Jacob, I'm so sorry we quarreled. It was my fault. I know you're under a lot of stress. I—"

"Shhh. It wasn't your fault. It was mine. I'm the one. Everything in the past. My fault. I failed my duty to you. Let you down. I promise—"

She stilled him with her fingers. "Nothing to forgive." She squeezed her eyes closed and whispered, "I was so scared. Thank you for coming home to us."

"I just needed some quiet."

She managed a weak laugh. "Well, the doctor says you'll get plenty of that!"

Her stomach growled again, and she patted it without conscious thought.

At that moment, an aide arrived with a breakfast tray. She set it on the stand and looked quizzically at the tubes and the elevated leg. "Uh, not sure how you'll manage this. Maybe your wife can help." She lifted the warming lid off a plate of scrambled eggs and bacon. "I'll be back later for the tray."

Jacob winked and pointed to the fork. "You, first. You look to be starved."

The doctor arrived shortly afterward and promised to discharge Jacob in a couple of days. "We need to rule out internal bleeding. You took quite a tumble."

Amanda spent the next two days between his bedside and home. By the time they emerged from the hospital with a packet of care instructions and a pair of crutches, she wanted to crawl into the hospital bed and cover herself with a sheet.

At home, Imelda helped her arrange pillows on the sofa while Amanda lifted the lid on a pot of rich chicken soup and tortillas. "I don't think I've ever smelled anything so good," she admitted. She devoured her bowl in a short minute, not even caring that she slurped from the spoon. Noah finished next and asked for ice cream. She rose to scoop him a bit of sherbert, too weary to deny him.

Imelda frowned from the sink as she washed the last of the dishes. "Mrs. Ruth, you need to take a nap. I hold the fort. That's what your father calls it. He don't like to be babysat, he says."

Amanda made her way into her bedroom. She undressed to her skin, tossed her slippers into the trash and stepped into the shower. She emerged feeling renewed but slightly queasy. When she wrapped a towel around her drippy locks and bent to get the hair dryer from under the sink, something caught her eye. She picked it up and pulled out the box. The label recalled the last time she'd used a pregnancy test. She'd picked up the box the previous week, on a whim, and stuck it under the sink when she came to her senses. This wasn't the time for another baby.

She opened the box and slid the stick out. A few minutes later, with the results blazed across the surface, she tucked the stick back inside the bag and chucked it in the trash. Then she finished drying her hair and dropped into bed.

By the time she emerged from her room, darkness had settled. Jacob was engaged in a groggy game of *Go Fish* with Noah while her father kept score. The aroma of roasted chicken drifted from the kitchen.

"Supper *es* ready," Imelda called. "Get the hands washed. All but you, Mr. Ruth. I bring your plate to you. But once you are better, you will be up and help yourself or you hear it from me!"

Amanda paused at the entry, where the sounds and smells of the kitchen, the snapping fire and Noah "helping" his grandfather to the bathroom brought tears. She walked to the sofa and knelt beside Jacob to brush her hands against his. His eyes telegraphed his desire even before he kissed her. "Amanda, I'm so sorry."

She leaned against him for support while her weariness crumbled in the face of her blessings. "Shush. You didn't ruin anything. You came home to us."

"Gott blesses me. Us."

"Maybe more than you know." She felt her tears through a weak smile.

"What do you say, wife?" He leaned up onto his elbow with a question in his eyes, his sandy blond hair rumpled and adorable. His bottom lip caught beneath his tooth, an unconscious thing he did when he was happy.

She laughed. "Jacob, you're going to be a daddy again."

Jacob studied her while Noah climbed into his new booster chair. "Hear that, *kind*? You get a new baby sister!"

Noah glanced from his mother to his father and laughed. Amanda waited in vain for her son to speak. "He better hurry up or his sister will be talking before he does," she said.

"We Ruths are short on words. We're men of action," Jacob teased. He pulled her into his arms. "Thank you, liebchen. For everything. You are a wonder, this is for sure." He flicked a strand of her hair back and gazed at her with a woozy, painkiller grin. "I am a happy man."

Chapter Twenty-Two

✦❖✦

Amanda spent the morning helping Jacob with his physical therapy and her father with his mobility exercises while Noah read a picture book. Jacob had advanced to a set of crutches, and after he finished exercising, decided to hobble out to the office to check on the business.

She sliced an apple with one ear tuned to the activity in the den. Silence. Too much silence. *The fireplace!* Jacob had convinced her not to keep a fire lit in the afternoons after he discovered her father stuffing an oversized log in, one end burning while the other extended onto the hearth, with smoke filling the room.

She dropped the apple plate and raced down the hall. Her dad sat on the floor across from Noah, each of them engrossed in a set of jumbo Legos. They were erecting a square castle with a turret at one end. Neither spoke, but they seemed to understand each other. Noah's tongue pressed the contour of his cheek as he concentrated on the pieces. Her dad looked excited and alert, expressions she hadn't seen in weeks.

She backed out of the room and leaned against the doorframe, watching. Snack could wait. So could potty breaks. This was a precious moment. Noah picked up the completed house and started toward her. A dozen steps later, the castle cracked and broke into two large pieces. He turned to his grandfather with tears brimming in his eyes. She waited for the downpour, but the tears evaporated into a smile when his grandpa laughed and reached for the broken pieces. Slowly, they fitted each piece back into place. When it was whole again, she carried in a baking sheet from the pantry. "Would you like to put it on here so we can show Daddy?"

Noah took his grandfather's hand and solemnly placed it on the finished castle. "Gran-pe, you." His face creased with a dimple.

"Noah!" The sheet nearly slipped from her fingers. "You spoke."

Her father reached for his grandson and spun him upside-down as Noah giggled and squealed in excitement. "Gran-pe, more." He giggled. "More!" Her father permitted himself to be crushed by small, thrashing arms. Noah spun in a circle, his arms flung out at his side. "Wheee! More!"

She exchanged surprised looks with her father, the two of them in a conspiracy of joy like the old days. Then the moment ended. He picked up a forgotten Lego brick and turned it over to inspect the bottom. She captured the moment, a golden memory that would ride inside her until she was a grandmother herself, her lostness shared with a great-grandchild who loved her more than anyone else in the world.

Over crackers, apple slices and juice, her father placed his gnarled, work-worn hand on the table and drummed his fingers to the rhythm of the CD playing in the background. Noah joined in on a ragtag rendition of the song they'd picked up at the Friends of the Library sale, a song about friends and puppy dogs. The melody was filled with bouncy riffs. The two of them used the table as bongo drums, thumping and laughing.

She joined in, hearing her mother's voice remind her that life needed to be savored.

When it was time for naps, Noah thrust her aside and marched his favorite book across the study. Without checking to see if she objected, he climbed into his grandpa's lap and opened the first page. Amanda had to cover her mouth at the convoluted words that came from two serious, intent readers. When the last page was read, Noah begged to read the book again, but his grandpa had already lost interest.

Both of them were napping when Jacob returned. She waited for him to take a seat before she burst out, "You should have seen them, Jacob! They're interested in the same things. Who would have thought?" She heard her laughter and wondered where it had been hiding.

৩১৩

"Everything's so perfect, Jacob. What am I thinking, going back to work?"

Jacob teased her cheek in a lazy circle with the tip of her hair. "Perfect for how long? I know you, liebchen. If I tell you what I want, you will do the opposite. But you feel trapped. The baby will be here in a few months and then the door will close again."

She hesitated. "This moment is fleeting. Noah and Dad...what I saw today...it's magical."

"No magic in it, wife. It is a gift from Gott." He reached to kiss her.

"You want me to stay home."

He shrugged. "You already know this, for the good it does. But I have given it some thought. Mamm doesn't spend her days with her family. She works for her neighbors. She gives service to others. Many times my father and I took our meals at my grandmother's table and counted ourselves grateful."

"Traitor." Amanda felt the tug of indecision. She had expected Jacob to fight her; instead, he had made the decision harder.

His eyes held a mischievous gleam. "You want me to fit the hobbles on you like a fine mare? I won't do it, wife. You will only resent me later."

The next morning, Imelda surprised her with news that her daughter had been accepted into Lewis and Clark College with a scholarship, while her mother in southern Mexico urgently needed an operation. "I will need a month for personal time. I could freeze some meals ahead if you want. But I am sorry. I will not be here to watch your father, Mrs. Ruth."

What did Jacob say about timing? The answer was right in front of her. "Absolutely," Amanda agreed. "Take all the time you need." *No time to waste.* She served supplement to Noah, scrambled eggs for Jacob and cut up cantaloupe before she called the preschool. The director confirmed that a spot had opened up, after being on a waiting list for the past year and a half.

After breakfast, Noah pulled off his toddler diaper and donned new big-boy underwear for the first time.

When he emerged from the bathroom with a triumphant grin, she wrapped him in a fierce hug. "That deserves a trip to the pirate box." She didn't even flinch when he selected the G.I. Joe action hero that their friends had brought over without checking if war toys were acceptable. Noah made a grab for it and clutched it to his chest with a fierce scowl as if he expected a battle, but Amanda chose not to engage. "I guess you won that round, little guy."

Senior respite care wasn't as easy. Her father's name was still third on the list for a full-time placement. Amanda explained the circumstances without resorting to hyperbole; the administrator sounded like she could sniff out desperation at a mile. Finally, the woman relented. "Look, one of our clients didn't come on Monday or Tuesday. Let me make a call."

Amanda spent the rest of the day waiting.

The phone rang just before supper, with a caller ID that read *Senior Support*. She counted to five before she answered.

The administrator's matter-of-fact tone conveyed no sentimentality. "One of our clients suffered a stroke and won't be coming back. And the lady ahead of you on the list is going to Florida to live with her daughter. The spot is yours if you want it. But you'll need to let me know right now."

Right now? This lady was taking no prisoners. "Y... yes." Amanda glanced into the living room, where her son was knocking block barricades apart with karate chops while his grandpa laughed. She closed her eyes and tried not to feel the weight of selfishness. "We can start immediately."

"Monday will be fine. Bring spare clothing and a personal item your father will relate to."

A blankie? Her father wasn't a child. She gritted her teeth and thanked the woman for her efficiency before she finished the call.

On Monday, she dropped her father off for a trial run. Her job didn't start for two days, but she wanted to work out the kinks—if there were any. She escorted him inside and watched him remove his jacket and take a seat in the chair circle. By the time she was back at her car, another man had entered the facility. From the window, the group batted a giant balloon above their heads, laughter and exercise at the same time. She watched a moment longer before she put the car into gear and drove off.

Noah's drop-off was trickier. He clung to her with ferocity, his body rigid as he squeezed her hand until her ring cut into her finger. She recalled the day her mother returned home from the convalescent center while she watched from the window, scared and uncertain, just like her son this morning. She leaned down, intending to pick him up and swing him reassuringly in her arms, but suddenly his grip eased and he turned, enthralled by an object across the room. A boy ran up to them and pointed at the stuffed orangutan Noah carried everywhere, even to bed. The boy pointed at a huge poster of zoo animals on the wall, and the two boys ran off together.

She waited for his tears, but Noah seemed to make a concerted effort to ignore her. When it was time for her to leave, he accepted her kiss and turned back to the plastic zoo figures he and the other boy had staged in a corner. He was lining up dinosaurs according to size when she slipped out.

A day to herself. She didn't need to meet with the teacher until Wednesday. On a whim, she drove to a nail salon with a sign posted in the window that read *Walk-ins Welcome*. Fortified with a take-out coffee she'd picked up on her way, she thumbed through a magazine while two Vietnamese nail techs massaged the feet of a mother and daughter in adjoining stations. Her throat caught, and she tried to swallow. She and Lydia had come here once while her mother had been at home on her ventilator. Guilt was one of the reasons she'd never returned until today.

One of the nail technicians pointed to an empty station. Amanda slid into the massage chair and dipped her feet into the warm water the girl had drawn. She leaned back and hit the massage mode, recalling the day Lydia had talked her into a pedicure. She'd sat in this same chair. She'd settled on Deep Lavender, her power color at the time. Today she went all out—Bodacious Red. Jacob would be appalled.

Forty minutes later, she left the salon with fiery toes and a renewed sense of calm. After a leisurely lunch of fish tacos with a spicy sriracha sauce—and after a wistful glance at the wine menu, an Arnold Palmer— she drove to the birthing center where she'd delivered Noah. Hafsa, her midwife, greeted her.

"Great news, little mother. Baby is on track."

"You don't think it's ill-advised for me to return to work?"

"Not from my perspective. You have plenty of time before you need to worry about low energy or swollen feet." Hafsa laughed. "Or any of the other pleasures a pregnancy offers. Go. Take the job. Allow this baby its time."

Amanda left the office with a bottle of prenatal vitamins and a lift to her step. She needed this. She had this. With a happy heart, she backtracked to the daycare center to pick up her son, who seemed to have grown up in the few short hours. He chattered like a jaybird all the way out to the car and insisted he fasten his own seat belt. "Manny makes his truck run in the sand. He likes mustard on french fries. Can I try some? He doesn't have a grandpa so I said we could share."

"What does Manny's mama do?"

"I think she makes cookies."

"What does your mama do, Noah?"

"You teach Hector to read at the table. And you make Daddy laugh and you smell good. And Daddy says you can get me a baby sister if I want one."

"That about sums it up, kiddo." Amanda laughed. "Let's go pick up Grandpa."

"Mama...Manny's mama sticks his finger for blood, too. He says I'm a baby. So I won't cry next time, okay?"

She gave him a hug. *Thank you, Jesus.* "Noah, you're such a big boy now. Wait 'til Daddy hears what you did today."

Her dad was less talkative when they made their way to the car. He gazed out the window at the passing farms until they pulled into his driveway. At the sound of equipment, he stared as the driver of a forklift carried a pallet of five-gallon tubs filled with holly to the delivery truck. In a graceful ballet, the driver lifted the pallet onto the forks, shoved it in the delivery truck, backed up and spun around. The whirr of the forklift disappeared into the greenhouse and cut to silence.

Amanda reached for her father's hand. "You miss it, don't you, Dad?"

He nodded, his eyes wistful.

"You built this, Dad. You did all of this. We're so proud and grateful. Noah will have this someday. His grandpa's name will be on the sign, and everyone will remember you. Won't they, Dad?"

He nodded again, but his eyes were uncertain.

Amanda squeezed his hand and felt him return the pressure. She glanced down at his fingernails, no longer darkened and rough from work, cleaner than she'd ever seen them—no longer her father's hands, but still able to move her to tears at their strength. She gave a final squeeze and slipped his seat belt loose.

"Let's go in and get some supper, Dad. Noah wants to show you what he learned today. You want to hear what Noah learned?"

Her father nodded and turned to smile at his grandson, already unbuckled.

Chapter Twenty-Three

❧

Amanda's temporary assignment was at the same school where she had previously taught. On her first day she greeted former students, now fifth and sixth graders, with cell phones and crushes on boys she'd taught to spell. One of the other teachers stopped by to invite her to discuss school politics and office gossip in the staff room, over tuna sandwiches and bad coffee. She listened and nodded, gratified by adult conversation again. She didn't want to be like the kindergarten teacher she'd met at the grocery store who admonished the clerk to "use your inside voice, dear."

"How'd it go?" Jacob's question scarcely waited for her to make it in the door as he rolled into the living room with a cup of coffee to watch the news. She managed to put together a hasty meal of macaroni and cheese, hot dogs, and frozen vegetables. Later, she got Noah bathed and into his pajamas, and her father settled for the night before she had time to sit down.

Jacob shared news of a snail infestation in the newest shipment while she folded clothes on the cleared table.

"What did the doctor say about you working?" Jacob plucked a crisp Braeburn apple from a bowl. "Does he agree a mother shouldn't take chances?" He took a bite. "He foresee any problems?"

Amanda closed her eyes and counted to ten. "*She* says I should get my husband to unload the dishwasher." She stacked plates in the cabinet and reached for more. "We'll be fine when Imelda gets back. This is temporary."

"Ja." Jacob bit off another bite. "My leg hurts tonight. I thank Gott when this craziness is over and I have you home again."

"Jacob, don't make a big deal of this. A lot of modern women work outside the home."

Jacob was silent. "Can we set aside our strife and share a bed together? A husband and a wife have unfinished business when the day is done."

Amanda shut the dishwasher and pulled off her apron. "But tomorrow, you learn to cook."

☙❧

"Your insurance check came for the motorcycle. It paid off the loan, but that's about all. They paid for the helmet that was ruined." Amanda set the envelope next to Jacob's coffee cup. When he read the letter without response, she turned back to the stove.

"Don't give me that look, wife. That deer hit me, plain and simple. Could have happened in a car. Plenty of accidents do."

"Yes they do. Deer hit cars. But they don't send drivers to the hospital."

"Some do." He approached the stove and wrapped his arms around her. "What are we talking about here, liebchen?"

Amanda set a pan on the burner while she considered her answer. "Maybe we can find a hobby to share? I like golf and pickleball. Square dance. Bowl. Hike. Fish. Any of those float your boat? Oh, I like rafting, too."

He scowled. "Your old boyfriend Charlie has some ideas. Maybe I could try bareback riding."

"Men!" She dumped the pot of chili in a bowl and set it on the table beside a vegetable salad. "Dinner's ready. Maybe you could pour the milk?"

Jacob scowled at the milk pitcher without picking it up. "Chewy's ridden his motorcycle for twenty years and he's never had an accident."

"Well good for Chewy. He's also had three wives."

"Ouch." He dipped a finger into the chili and licked it. "Not the same."

"Maybe not, but Chewy's a juvenile delinquent. You're not. The baby will be here in a few months, and she'll need a father with all his limbs."

"Amanda, the bike is no more dangerous than a farmer's buggy. Back home, people drive their whole lives on dangerous roads. Gott's will, what happens. He wants me here with my family."

"Thank God for that." She wiggled out of reach when he eased against her, teasing. "I don't want anything to happen to you." She set a plate of buttered rolls on the table and hesitated. "What if Noah wants a motorcycle when he's sixteen? What will you tell him?"

"I tell him, start with a dirt bike. Take the safety course. Ride alongside me. Learn good habits. Watch for careless drivers. Trust in Gott's plan."

"The Bible tells us—"

"Amanda, don't you be quoting the Bible in this matter. Let us eat in peace and talk about something that brings us joy, not conflict."

After she finished bedtime stories, Amanda slipped into her recliner and elevated her legs. She had assignments to grade before she could go to bed, but she wasn't ready to trade the coziness of the fireside for sleep.

In his chair, Jacob worked on a blueprint for a play structure he planned to build for Noah.

⚜

Amanda tossed a soggy box of fried chicken on the table and started toward the bedroom to change. Her legs ached from standing all day. After eating her lunch in the car between stoplights on the way to her OB-GYN's, the appointment had been a disaster. Hafsa planned to move to Seattle and wouldn't be available. The scales claimed she'd gained six pounds, and her blood sugar was high. The midwife gave her a lecture about gestational diabetes and a list of "no-eat" foods. Dr. Washington, the metabolic physician, was already on the team, ready to test the baby for MSUD.

Jacob wasn't home yet when she returned from school, so she punched in Carol's number while she massaged her ankles and slipped into a pair of pink Crocs. "I feel like Typhoid Mary, waiting to see what we've exposed our baby to," she sobbed. "I can't tell

Jacob because he'll blame my job. He blames everything on it. Even my swollen feet. My toes look like elephant clubs. I'm marked for life."

"Amanda, have you considered a career on stage? You're good at drama!" Carol laughed. "Got anything else?"

"I had to promise to give up my morning mocha lattes. Carol, I'm in caffeine withdrawal. This is serious!"

"Hey, you can do this. I don't know—drink cocoa. Herbal tea. You got this. I know you do. Hey, I gotta run. Sorry I can't talk you off the ledge. Take care."

Amanda closed her phone and lay across the bed, fighting sleep. *Just a few minutes. Can't fall asleep. Gotta finish dinner.* In the hallway, hesitant footsteps halted at her closed door before they moved on. Noah was in the family room. It was probably Jacob, wondering about dinner. Leftover rice in a Pyrex container. Frozen vegetables. Maybe she could get away with a vegan meal for once. "I'll be right there."

The sound of a refrigerator door shutting was the last sound she remembered. It was late when Jacob slipped into bed beside her, smelling of Noah's bubble bath and his arms still damp. He nuzzled her and slid his arms around her.

"Rough night?" she whispered.

He chuckled in her ear. "Who knew it was so hard to wash a small boy's hair without soap in the eye? I think I have lost the respect of my son."

She smiled into her pillow. "Soap happens. He'll get over it." She smelled his earthy male scent on the pillow. "Dad get to bed okay?"

"A good night for him. The kitchen isn't put to

rights, but we ate. When does Imelda return to us?"

"Soon. We can do this, Jacob." He rubbed her back in the small area where he knew she ached. She hesitated, dreading her next sentence. "By the way, I've got state testing next week."

Jacob shifted and ceased rubbing. "What does this mean?"

Amanda sighed. The Oregon Statewide Assessment test period was exhausting. Third grade students were new to the process. Her week would be filled with the same questions from a dozen students, broken pencils, confusion, tears, and panic from nervous over-achievers. "Nothing important. Just work stuff."

He held his breath while the silence grew. She leaned over and kissed him good night.

❦

Amanda was loading a batch of crusty dinner dishes left from the previous night when Jacob walked in. He picked up a crumpled take-out sack and shook it in front of her. "Is this the way other families live? Salty chicken and drippy cabbage slaw from a vendor's sack? This is no proper way." He dropped into his chair and glanced at the clock. "Clearly school is more important than family. When you are here, you mark papers and prepare tests. Is this the way you wish to live?"

Amanda froze at the disappointment in his voice. He had used the word "home" the other night to describe his father's farm. She finished wrapping a tomato sandwich made with the last two slices of special bread and placed it in Noah's lunchbox with a bottle of protein supplement. "Today, I finally got through to a little boy who couldn't understand the STEM assignments. I worked with him and today he made a breakthrough. Jacob, he had tears in his eyes when he told me. Tears!" She watched to see if he understood the import of her announcement.

He poured himself a cup of coffee and glanced down at the mug. "I see how much you love teaching, liebchen. And I am glad for you. Your face glows with contentment when you speak of your classroom." He took a sip and his eyes swept hers. "I understand this. But I just want more. Is this wrong of me?"

She swallowed the nausea that had welled up again, worse in the evenings with this baby. "Fine. I won't go to church on Sunday. That will give us a day with no distractions."

Jacob's look bordered on guilt. "I do not ask this of you, wife, that you give up your church."

"Then come with me. We'll sit together. Get to know other nice people who share our values. Go out to breakfast afterward." Her voice was quaking, but he seemed not to notice.

"Maybe. I will give some thought to your idea. Is there a Mennonite Church around?"

Her heart fell. "There is." *He intends to return to his church and repent of his mistake in marrying me.* Frustration lent strength to her resolve, and she lifted her chin. "I need something from you, Jacob. I need you to step up your game. Maybe barbeque dinner one night a week? Help me out with the dishes? Noah's not *my* son, he's *ours*. You can help put him to bed sometimes." She gave him a look that she hoped would convince him she was serious. "Like you told me one time, if you are to live English, you need to act English."

His look of confusion was almost comical, but it quickly changed to understanding—if not immediate agreement. But she'd said her piece. They could work on the details. If he wanted to be an *Englischer*, he'd better learn the rules.

In the next trimester, the weight of the baby pressed against her when she sat at her desk and her legs ached when she stood. She spent her free period with her head buried in her arms, trying to catch a quick nap. One day, two of the other teachers approached her as she unwrapped her lunch in the faculty lounge. Rachel, the first-grade veteran teacher, held up a small gift while her friend Celia carried a steaming coffee in a take-out cup. "Alms for the forlorn, Amanda. We want you to know we're here for you."

Amanda looked up, fighting tears as Celia added, "We raided the Sunshine Fund. And we'll take over your recess duties so you can put your feet up and rest for a few minutes."

"You can skip the early bird school duty, too. We got that covered."

Amanda gulped and tried to mask the tears that welled up in spite of her efforts.

Rachel thrust the gift at her. "Here, this is for you. You're a super teacher and sometimes you need to hear it. Open it."

Amanda opened the envelope and found a gift certificate from a local restaurant. She cradled the card as if it were a baby. "The Sunshine Fund? I thought we guarded that with our lives! You guys are the best. This means so much. I can't tell you—" She looked up and recognized the empathy behind the smiles. They'd both been in her shoes. She took a deep breath and exhaled.

"I remember why I love this school and you guys. This is amazing."

She spent the rest of the lunch period listening, while fellow teachers argued the merits of the latest round of state-mandated changes. She couldn't wait to get home to set things right with Jacob. *No more take-out chicken,* she promised herself. She glanced at the clock and remembered she needed to finish up the lesson plans for the rest of the week. Cheryl Bentley, the tenured teacher she'd replaced, was due back from her maternity leave in three days.

☙❧

Amanda looked up when the door opened and a sleep-deprived woman entered with a new baby in her arms. "Cheryl, good to see you!"

The teacher gave an embarrassed laugh and looked down at the infant. "My sitter fell through at the last minute. We're dealing with a bit of a sniffle. I hope she's better by Monday." Cheryl made a broad inspection of the classroom that included a mural Amanda had painted for a unit on acorns and native food. A bowl of ground acorns gave evidence of the hours she'd spent to collect and grind the meal before she baked it into bread to serve at open house.

"I can't wait for her to sleep through the night." Cheryl glanced at Amanda's baby bump. "This class-room must be jinxed!"

Amanda reached into the desk drawer. "I got you a little gift. Trust me, you'll need it." She pulled out an envelope.

"A gift certificate for a delivered restaurant meal!"

Cheryl's eyes held a sheen of exhaustion. "This is going to be hard, isn't it?" Her tone sounded a little desperate. "Will you be available if something comes up?"

For the space of five seconds, Amanda considered. But she had made a promise. "I'm sorry, I can't."

She drove to Noah's preschool with a light heart and a cardboard box filled with materials. At the preschool, Noah showed her a new picture he'd painted that included his grandpa and a smiling little pink bundle propped against his leg. Her father was happy to see her when she picked him up. He sat in the passenger seat and described the town's history as they drove through the old part of town.

"You're a walking history book, Dad."

At home again, she hung her empty briefcase in the hall closet and started into the kitchen. When she saw Imelda at the stove, she collapsed into a chair.

Imelda carried a glass of iced tea to the table. "You glad for your last day, eh señora? Time now to prepare for la niña. Mr. Jacob, he will be happy."

Amanda nodded, her eyes closed. "Imelda, you spoil me. That poor teacher has no idea what she's in for."

"Maybe you grade her papers while you rest at home? This is allowed?"

"I'm not sure. Maybe. Teachers should get a medal for what they put up with."

"Life is a struggle, señora. Everyone has their share."

During dinner, Amanda eyed the bottle of pinot noir in front of Jacob while Imelda hovered nearby. "Have a sip, señora. In my country, women drink wine to have strong babies. A little won't hurt." Without waiting for a response, Imelda poured a dram and set it in front of her.

The wine had a soothing effect. She fought sleep while Jacob made sure the doors were locked and the lights shut off. She heard him douse the hall light and close the bedroom door behind him before he glanced over at the lump she made in their bed.

She chuckled. "Remember me?"

He glanced away. "Barely."

"Jacob, I'm not going to apologize."

He grunted. "I'm happy to have my wife back. I missed her."

She made room for him to curl up against her and felt him massage her back. "I missed this."

"Me too. I should be used to you by now. My wife who does as she pleases."

"Is that how you see me?"

"Maybe. Sometimes."

She slipped her arms around him and felt the baby kick against his back. "Jacob, let's not argue anymore."

He sounded gruff in the darkness. "Ja. You are home again, and this is what matters."

Thin ice. Time to change the subject. "Noah loves his preschool. He's an artist like you. Maybe we should buy a video camera. Make some home movies."

He chuckled. "A new hobby? Instead of a motorcycle?"

"I didn't say that. You'll be busy once this baby comes."

He nuzzled her and his breath tickled. "A baby will fit into our lives. Not us into his."

Chapter Twenty-Four

Amanda looked up from her phone and frowned. "Jacob, I waited an hour at the doctor's office today. They were overbooked. The midwife had to fit me in between her other patients. She's new, and I need the doctor's okay for any procedure."

"Yeah, sorry I didn't make the appointment. Something came up."

"You didn't miss much. I spent an hour watching other patients come and go. I hate the word, patient.' I'm not sick, I'm pregnant." She waited until she had his full attention. "Let's have this baby at home." She waved her phone at him. "It says here more mothers are doing it. Especially for second births."

He tossed aside the newspaper, unsure how to respond. "After your worries with Noah?"

"Your mother had all of hers at home. I'm healthy and determined. We'll have this baby tested."

"Hospitals cost dearly on an Amish farmer's

income. It wasn't a choice for us. Our community does not carry insurance."

"You said Amish men deliver their children all by themselves."

"Ja, this is true. But maybe my *daed* would have preferred it otherwise."

"Imelda can help. She delivered babies in Oaxaca."

"You consulted the cook before you ask me?" He scowled. "She has agreed?"

"Not exactly. But we can do this, Jacob."

He dropped onto the sofa next to her and sighed. "I will pray on this. No promises do I make."

Amanda laughed excitedly. "Whatever we decide, it needs to be soon."

"Soon?" He blinked back a look of surprise. "I thought you had another month."

"A month or a week. This baby seems ready."

He stretched to ease his tension and smiled. "So it is decided! We have a baby girl like her mother. Stubborn and determined."

"If we do, what do you think of 'Rae' for a middle name?"

His groan of dismay was a giveaway, despite his forced grin. "What is this strange name I've never heard of? I thought you wanted to honor your mother."

"Yes, Julie Rae. We'll call her Jules." She hesitated. "Unless you really want to name her Emma? Or Sarah? If it's a girl, I mean." She'd given the subject much thought. "I like those, but they sound so..."

"Amish?"

She nodded again. "Rae is old-fashioned."

Her flash of a smile caught his breath. "And if it's a boy, we name him Levi the Lesser!"

"You joke, surely!"

Her fine hair glistened in the noontime light that streamed through the window, making her seem like an angel in the cozy quarters. "We'll find names that aren't so traditional. To mark the new road we take together." He caught her hand and pulled her close. "But we don't name our children after a movie actor or a singer."

"So no Clooney? No Bieber?"

He laughed and caught the scent of nursery shrubs on his wool shirt, proof of his morning's work. Life was good. In the kitchen, Imelda banged pots on the stove. *Chicken enchiladas.* He felt the faint shadow of two days' growth of whiskers as he lowered his lips to hers. "I love you." When the kiss ended, he reluctantly eased himself up. "How about after lunch we let our son ride the horse around the paddock? He thinks he's a cowboy like your boyfriend, Charlie."

"Jacob, you're jealous!" Amanda chucked a pillow at him and laughed when it connected. "I'm a broody hen, keeping an egg warm," she teased. "I feel like one, too."

When Imelda called for them to come to the table, he pulled her up from the sofa and followed her into the kitchen.

At the barn, Amanda took a seat on a hay bale while he showed Noah how to bring the curry comb across the haunch in gentle strokes. When Yankee's hide gleamed, he helped his son clamber on, bareback, while he held the lead rope, watchful for any uneven clumps of native grass that grew in the meadow.

"Wait for me. It's been ages since I—" Amanda's foot caught on a clump of buffalo grass and she lumbered clumsily in an attempt to regain her balance.

"I feel like a beached whale. I should have worn my—"
Suddenly, the ground raced to meet her. She gave a
half-twist, desperate to protect her belly, and sank to
her knees with enough force that she bit her tongue.

Jacob dropped the reins and turned just as her
water broke. The next moment he was by her side,
asking questions without waiting for an answer. "Are
you okay? Do you hurt anywhere? Can you walk?"

She glanced over his shoulder to where their son
stood staring, his eyes huge. Jacob helped her to her feet
and tried to calm his son. "Noah, let's get Mama to the
house. Can you get the gate?" He scooped her into his
arms and started across the field.

"I'm okay. I can walk—"

He strode ahead without permitting her to object.
At the house he managed to get the door opened and
the blankets stripped from the bed before he carefully
deposited her, still clothed, in the shower. "Son, go get
Imelda."

He found a fresh nightgown and helped her to bed.
When the next cramp began, he tried to find ways to
mitigate her pain. Imelda arrived, tugging off her coat
and rolling her sleeves. She returned to the kitchen to
scrub her hands and fill a pan of hot water before she
brushed past Jacob to stroke Amanda's brow. "You been
busy, señora. La niña, she come."

"Apparently so," Amanda panted. "I fell. In the
pasture."

Imelda ran her hands across the belly and gave a
relieved smile. "Maybe you shake the little one loose.
We see." She glanced at Jacob and flapped her hands
impatiently. "Mr. Ruth, you tell us how your people
deliver their babies. Maybe you ease the waiting time."

He nodded, grateful for a task. "Many families have eight, ten children. But no one makes a fuss about it. We don't speak about pregnancy, not even Mamm, but my sister tells me afterward. I remember, once Maam is busy with the household chores and she sends me out to get my father in the field. He comes quick and sends us out to gather eggs. We don't know what's wrong, but after the first few times we catch on, because each time we have a new baby—and a skillet of scrambled eggs for supper. Afterward, Mamm takes a day to rest, but before the birth, she doesn't even trouble Grossmummi. Each time my father is there to catch it."

"Catch it?"

"That's what we call delivering it. Daed catches it. Then Mamm cleans it with baby oil, binds the belly and dresses it. I don't remember ever a sound. Birthing is a woman's chore, same as any other."

Amanda bit back her groan. "If Emma Ruth can deliver her babies with dignity, then I can do the same," she gritted. She pushed herself into a sitting position and focused on a calendar image of Mt. Hood on the wall while a cramp crested and eased. "Ride the wave," she whispered.

Jacob's hands shook as he returned a tight, nervous smile while sweat beaded across his forehead. "You are doing fine, wife."

Another cramp caught, and she bit her lip. Another wave, and another. "Imagine you are on a raft, riding the Willamette River," Imelda whispered.

Jacob rubbed her feet and brought a hot water bottle. Imelda put on a CD of soothing Latin music and danced a mamba with an imaginary partner to take Amanda's mind off her pain. Finally, Imelda said it was time. A moment later Jacob was there, catching it. He lifted the baby for her to see. "A girl."

Imelda showed him how to pat the baby's skin and rub on olive oil. With her help, he secured a disposable diaper and threaded tiny arms into an undershirt. His mother had sent a stack of old-fashioned, hand-stitched flannel kimonos with a drawstring at the bottom to give the baby room to kick. He wrapped the baby tightly in a flannel receiving blanket and stood back to admire his handiwork. "This one has Mamm's dark eyes and long fingers," he marveled as he handed the baby to Amanda. "Julie Rae. How does that sound to you, *kind*?"

Amanda's father appeared at the door, his face a storm of emotions. "Julie," he said when he saw the baby for the first time. "I think I know you. I knew you before."

Jacob lifted Noah up for his first glance. He pressed his finger against his sister's cheek and looked up at his mother. "Is she ours now? Do we have to give her back?"

Jacob grinned. "Gott send her. She will be with us always. Until you are old like Grandpa. Isn't that something?"

Noah nodded hesitantly.

Amanda's eyes filled with a memory of standing at her mother's bed, among strange hospital equipment and tubes. She patted a spot alongside herself and waited until Noah climbed up. "Aren't we lucky that you can already read your picture books, Noah? It'll be a long time before your little sister can do that. She'll need you to show her." She waited for his enthusiastic nod. "Daddy and I got you a new book. It's about a big brother." She reached for it. "We can read it after you finish your supper. Imelda made your favorite, macaroni and margarine. Can you remind Grandpa to wash his hands, too? After supper we'll read it together. Okay?"

Amanda phoned Carol while the others were eating. "Carol, we did it."

"Was it terrible?"

"I channeled an Amish home birth. I was Superwoman. I didn't make a peep."

Carol laughed. "None? You're kidding. Wow. Jacob married a beast. He must be so proud."

"Yeah, he's pretty happy. I'm demanding a refund for the labor room. We'll use the money for the christening."

Carol hesitated. "So you've come to an agreement?"

"On what?"

"OMG—you haven't discussed it yet? The Amish practice Believer's baptism. They don't baptize infants."

"Well my church does. We need to baptize both the kids. I'm sure he'll agree with me."

"Elephant in the room! Don't count on it, Amanda. It's his baby, too." Carol's chuckle sounded harsh on the phone, especially when she added, "Don't say I didn't warn you."

Amanda attributed her flush of irritation to hormones. "We'll work it out."

Carol laughed. "Like the dog? And the old boyfriend? And the motorcycle?"

"Carol, trust me. We'll figure it out." Amanda

laughed. "We don't know the birth weight. We forgot to buy a scale."

"Okay, change of topic. So she's healthy? No MSUD?"

"She's perfect. We'll have her tested tomorrow."

After they hung up, Amanda sat cradling her baby. She was glad her milk wouldn't come in for another day.

The next morning, Jacob drove them to the doctor's so the pediatrician could perform an Apgar test, drop silver nitrate into the baby's eyes and do a blood draw while someone typed up a birth certificate. The nurse handed it to Amanda without meeting her eyes. "Your baby's doing well. But you took a chance with the home delivery. We in the medical profession don't recommend home birthing."

❧

The ringtone of her phone woke her from a late-afternoon nap. She glanced at the caller ID and caught the call on its sixth ring. "Yes?" Her heart was racing.

"Mrs. Ruth, it's Dr. Washington."

When she hung up, Jacob was standing at the door, his face bathed in worry. "Test is negative. Doctor says no complications. We're safe." Relief flooded across his features as she reached to stroke his cheek. "Jacob, Noah's doing fine. We have this."

He rested his chin against her and gave a deep sigh. "A worry off my back. Makes me wonder what is next."

"Next?"

He laughed. "You're right. I must savor this moment. Two healthy kinders. My son and your dad play in the family room. The baby sleeps, safe. You and me with a moment to ourselves. I am a grateful man."

"Will you write your parents?"

Jacob chewed his lip as he considered. "Maybe it is best the news comes from you."

"You'll have to write to them one day."

He shook his head so emphatically that a lock of hair obscured his vision. He needed a haircut; another thing she'd neglected lately. "They don't give a thought to me. Daed against son, brother against brother, the way of things in our community."

"Do you really believe that? A mother is a mother. A father—"

Jacob gave an impatient shrug. "Amanda, let it go." He watched their baby daughter's tiny fingers clench as she slept. "I made a decision and I live with it gladly. So no tears for your husband. He is not an orphan. He is a patriarch now."

Her eyes filled as she watched her baby sleep. "This is true."

A sound from the pasture caused him to jerk his head up. A horse's whinny. He lifted the curtain and saw Yankee with his head down, the lead rope tangled around a front hoof. "I forgot about the horse." He turned and ran down the hallway toward the pasture.

Amanda glanced up to see her father at the doorway.

"Amanda, she looks just like my wife Julie's baby photos. The nose and the forehead, especially." He crept closer with a confused, vacant expression. He touched the baby's lip and smiled. A moment later, the smile dimmed. "Did you know Julie?"

Amanda slipped her hand over his. "Yes, I knew

Julie. She was my mother. She loved us so much." His nod was uncertain as his smile wavered. "Here, Dad, see how soft our baby Julie's skin is? Like our other Julie's."

She placed the baby in his arms and reached for her phone to take a photo for the baby book. "You were so proud when I was born, Dad. You wanted four babies. But there was only me."

"Julie's here." His voice was wistful as he handed the baby back. At the door, he turned to smile. His contentment remained in the room after he padded slowly down the hall.

When Jacob returned from the barn, he dropped a letter on the bed and waited while Amanda read. "Rosie and Tibbs are taking the train out, and plan to stay a month. They ask if there's anything we need from Wyoming." She laughed. "Noah would ask for a pony, but it probably wouldn't fit in their suitcase."

Chapter Twenty-Five

J acob's horn beeped twice. Amanda opened the
door in time to see Tibbs climb out of the back
seat and place his worn Stetson on his head. Rosie
emerged from the passenger side, wearing an
unfamiliar house dress of uncertain vintage that she
clearly had brought out of her closet for the occasion.
She straightened before wrapping Amanda in a fierce
clutch.

"Whew, that driver was a treat. We thought to drive
out in our new pickup, but it's made for high-grade
roads and gully washers. Tibbs has to boost me up ever'
time we make a pit stop. Still, the view from up there is
like we got us a Peterbilt. King of the road, my husband
thinks he is." She took a few stiff steps before she caught
her stride. "Is that the baby? Gimme a look. Oh, my!"

Jacob came up in time to see Rosie take the baby in
her arms, her rough, wind-burned face a mask of
wonder that softened as she rocked the baby. Her
crooning brought Tibbs's head up with a jerk. He
watched intently as his wife returned to a time of young

motherhood. His unguarded expression said he would trade his life to restore that magical time to her again.

A moment later, Rosie looked up and remembered where she was. With an embarrassed chuckle, she returned the baby to Amanda and turned to give Jacob a hug. "You're doing a fine job on these little ones, son. Tibbs always said the offspring will tell the proof of the stud." She looked at Amanda and laughed. "'Course most of the bringing-up and the nurturing is on the mother. No substitute for a good dam!"

Jacob blushed and turned toward the house. "Let's go in. It's cooler inside. We're having a bout of what Amanda calls an Indian summer. She has a room set up for you. Noah will bunk with his grandpa."

"We don't mean to put anybody out."

Jacob grinned. "My boy will think he's camping. He's at preschool, but we'll get you settled and then Amanda can run over and pick him up. He'll want to show you his horse."

Half an hour later, Noah exploded from the classroom with a yelp for Rosie that brought tears to her eyes. He gave her a fierce hug and handed her the painting he'd completed, signed at the bottom with his name.

"My horsey eats flowers, Tibbs. Wanna see?" He handed the sheet of construction paper to Rosie. "For you."

"Why thank you." Rosie tilted the artwork to inspect it from every angle. "My goodness, if this isn't the finest rendering of a pony I've ever seen. I'll have it framed as soon as I'm able."

On the drive home, Amanda watched the two from her rearview mirror. Her son seemed to speak a language that only the two of them understood. When they arrived home again, he slipped his hand into Rosie's and helped her up the sidewalk to the door.

Rosie lingered with little fingers clutched in hers until Noah grew impatient. "We missed you folks something fierce when you left," she said to no one in particular. "House seemed empty. Tibbs, he decided not to die during the winter after all. Didn't want me coming out here without him. Paid a young man to drive us to the station, and we took the Amtrak. Hardly call it a train, considering half of it was bus rides!"

Rosie waved the potato peeler like a flashlight as she shared her travel stories. She wore an apron that swamped her tiny frame, its ruffles fussy atop the faded Wranglers and plaid workshirt she'd changed into as soon as she arrived. She caught Amanda's amused glance and looked down at her worn boots. "What? I need a new wardrobe to impress? Figure you're as close to kin as we got." Jacob came into the kitchen in time to hear this last. He crossed the room to capture Rosie in a bear hug that swept her, feet flying, into the air. "Wahoo! I ain't had such a hug since Tibbs and I started to keep company. You got yourself a man there, Amanda. I hope you know it." She returned peeling with a glow to her cheeks.

"He's a flirt, no argument there."

Jacob's cheeks glowed with embarrassment.

Rosie pointed her peeler in his direction and grinned. "Man outta get used to being appreciated. Good looks is a gift. Makes your wife proud she roped you! Am I right, Amanda?"

"Right as rain, Rosie. I count my blessings every day."

As banter filled the house, Amanda recalled the laughter she and her aunt had shared while her mother listened from her wheelchair. Even when her mother could no longer speak, her face had reflected the joy that Amanda felt this night. Jacob, too. He had clearly missed the bustle and confusion of women chattering among themselves without being conscious of their menfolk. She pulled a bowl of shrimp from the refrigerator and drained the marinade while the aroma of marionberry pie filled the room. Her father's favorite. In the living room, Tibbs was expounding about wild horse hunting in his younger days while her father listened with avid interest. Jacob walked the baby around the kitchen. His smile of contentment filled her heart.

"Jacob, supper's almost ready. I'll take Jules so you can eat."

Jacob's look indicated that he cared little about late suppers. "A mother is the heart of the family. We wait to eat with you."

Amanda sat the baby on her lap when she slid into what had been her mother's place. Jacob was right. Her mother's huge electric wheelchair and her lifeless hands hadn't mattered as much as the fact that she had been there with them at each meal. The heart of the family. She speared a slice of acorn squash with a rush of gratitude.

"Land's sake, but you're a fine cook, Amanda. Tibbs is gnawing like he ain't seen a feedbag since last Sunday. He picks at my fare like a cornfield starling at the end of the day."

"Is that bad?"

"Well, a bird can eat its weight in seed, but it knows

when it's full." Rosie's eyes softened on her husband. "I reckon he's close."

Amanda shook her head in amusement and looked over to see Tibbs grinning. "Tomorrow we'll drive over so Tibbs can see the ocean."

"He can't shut up about that ocean of yours. Wants to see the waves lapping the shores like when he was in the service. Always recalls the Pacific like it was grain fields. He's quiet now, but he's content. And he sure likes your shrimp."

"Let me get a word in edgewise, woman," Tibbs growled.

After the berry pie was divided and the dishes stacked for later, Amanda led Rosie into Noah's temporary bedroom to read him a bedtime story. He insisted that Rosie be the one to read him a book. Rosie glanced at the book about a giant and a caterpillar and tossed it aside. "How's about I tell you a story? About a big grizzly and how it pert near scared my horse to death and me in the process?" Noah nodded and she began. Amanda listened, half-afraid the story would give her son nightmares, but he gripped the covers, his eyes twin saucers in the lamplight as he focused on each gesture and intonation. When she finished, Rosie smoothed the sheets around his neck and shook her head at his request for another story. "One per night, young man. And only if I get another fine picture for my wall."

The next day, Amanda filled her ice chest with food for the trip that would be the highlight of Tibbs's vacation. Tibbs's wonder as he took his first glance at the ocean was worth the drive over. He stood at the base of the Yaquina Head lighthouse and squinted at the placard that explained how it had been erected to keep ships from the rocks on a foggy night. Wind gusseted his head and blew his hat across the grass until Jacob gave chase. They gathered for a photo before they drove back down the hill to tour the museum until Tibbs's legs gave out and he found a bench.

Rosie insisted on a mug in the gift shop. "I'd take a jar of that ocean breeze, but we got enough at home." Farther down the coast, she scooped a bag of sand to take home, along with a piece of driftwood and a half-dozen fist-sized ocean-polished rocks.

Amanda watched her father and Noah playing tag with a length of kelp that they snaked in front of them like a bullwhip. Their laughter pealed in the breeze while she unpacked the picnic basket and set a vegetable tray on an old bedspread that her family kept for such occasions. Jacob and Tibbs waded in the surf with their pants rolled up, for the good it did; by the time they emerged, they were wet to the knees, even the rolled hems.

Everyone waited while Noah drank his supplement before they filled plates with carrot sticks, jicama, squash, avocados, cheese and salami, crackers, and olives.

"Quite a spread. Almost too fine to touch," Rosie protested. "But I'll force myself to the task." She winked. "Top it off with some of that fine chardonnay you packed. Don't say I won't!"

Amanda laughed as she poured. "Jacob, we need to get you a pair of beach shorts and sandals. You can't be an Oregonian without river sandals."

Rosie and her husband exchanged glances. "Those boots a good fit?"

Jacob looked down at his lace-up work boots, confused. "I guess so. Why?"

"'Cause you may need them yet. We got us a damn fine ranch needs a good set of boots to work it." Rosie's glance included Amanda and the baby. "Figured to leave it to you folks when the time comes." She laughed. "Me and Tibbs ain't getting no younger. That's fer sure."

Jacob glanced at Amanda. "We might need to think on this."

Rosie nodded. "Sure you do. Take all the time you need. We figure to stick around a few more years, anyway."

"We'd like to see it go to a young family. Proper values." Tibbs paused with a slice of Edam cheese in his hand. "Seeing you young folks makes us remember the times with our own boy. Good times."

Jacob nodded.

They spent the rest of the day watching locals fill crab nets with chicken thighs and toss them back into the sea. Afterward, they walked on the sand while the rippled current undercut the sand beneath their feet. When their stomachs rumbled with hunger again, they stopped at *Mo's on the Waterfront* for clam chowder, fish and chips, and soft-serve ice cream.

That night, Amanda waited until they were in bed before she broached the subject with Jacob. "Do you want to sell Dad's nursery? Move to Wyoming? Ranch? What is it you want?" she whispered, even though her heart pounded with fear.

Jacob hesitated. "We have a good life here."

"A good life or a forced life? This is your chance to decide what you really want, Jacob. Because I don't think you'll be happy until you do." She turned away, taking slow, even breaths so he couldn't notice her panic.

"This isn't the time. Let's take this one step at a time." He reached to take her in his arms.

A month later, Jacob was already up when the baby woke her for its morning feeding. Rosie was in the kitchen, cooking oatmeal and coffee, judging from the smells already filling the house. She slipped out of bed and tended the baby while she considered her future. She was still deep in thought when she started toward the kitchen.

"Morning, Amanda. Hope you like your eggs hatched," she teased with a wink at Noah. "That's the only way Tibbs'll eat them."

Noah ran past her in the hallway, followed by the horse and buggy his father had carved out of a branch of Oregon white oak. The wheels scraped on the painted wall, leaving a mark. "Noah, on the floor. You know better," she warned.

A door opened, and her father added to the cacophony. "No rules. Licorice?"

Noah backed away, his bottom lip quivering and his horse clutched against his chest.

Amanda leaned to console him. "Grandpa means breakfast. No licorice right now." She rescued her coffee cup from the table and tried to divert Noah. "Your buggy's on the floor, Noah. Better pick it up or a big truck might run over it."

Noah looked around. "Daddy drives a big truck today? I go with him?"

Amanda set Jules in her baby carrier. "Can you watch for Daddy? Do you see his big truck from the window?" It was Imelda's day off. Tibbs and Rosie's train was due at noon. They had offered to take the taxi to the station, but everyone agreed that Noah would be fascinated with the train. He liked all things mechanical —just like his father.

Rosie cleared the table with a curt nod at the fancy dishes. "This linen tablecloth is too fine for ordinary folk. I'm used to oilcloth. Scared I'll drop gravy on it and leave a permanent reminder of my visit."

"No worries. Gravy or no, we won't forget you. It's been so much fun having you here. I can't believe a month has flown by. Seems like you just arrived." Amanda set her empty cup on the sideboard and began making sandwiches for the train ride.

"We probably wore out our welcome by now. But we got real feelings for your little family." Rosie glanced up. "Not my place to say, but it seems there's tension between you two lovebirds, wasn't there when you last visited. Everything alright?"

Amanda rested her knife on the cutting board. "I had a letter from my attorney in Ohio. Aunt Lydia's house is coming vacant. He wants to know if we want to convert it to an Airbnb for tourists visiting the Amish country. It would require some new furniture and kitchenware, but it might be a good idea." She picked up a slice of bread and spread mayonnaise on it. "What do you think?"

"Are you asking me about furniture, or are you asking me if Jacob is unhappy here and maybe one day might go back to his folks?" Rosie fussed with a china coffee cup and waited for Amanda to speak. When the silence built, she set the cup on the table and turned.

"You afraid the pull of that home farm might be too much for your man to resist?"

"No." Amanda flashed a look before she could stop herself. Rosie had nailed it; she *was* afraid. So afraid that she hadn't mentioned the email to Jacob yet. One problem at a time. "His family is tight."

"I thought that boy was shunned. Wouldn't that make a difference to those people?"

Amanda added sliced ham to the bread. "Shunned? I'm not sure. He acts like he can't go back, but he's never actually said why."

Rosie thought for a moment. "I think you should go. And take your father with you. His long-term memory is crackerjack. He might give you stories of his childhood that got lost somewhere along the line. Whatcha got to lose?"

Amanda added salt and pepper to the tomato. "Do you think Jacob would rather raise horses in Wyoming than grow plants here in Oregon?"

"Pshaw! We ain't stupid! We got a couple of great-nephews who would be happy to have the place. But Jacob needs to know he has a choice. He's a rough-broke critter needs to find his home range. Turning us down will require a lot of thought. He needs to come to the sorrowful conclusion that he has to disappoint someone in order to be happy."

Amanda slipped her arms around Rosie and pressed a kiss on her short hair, which still carried the marks of Tibbs's efforts despite Amanda's best efforts to correct it. "Rosie, what would we do without you?"

"Shoot! You sound like this is the long adios. Tibbs 'n me still got some tread on our tires. That lad of yours'll be in high school before we come to that juncture." Rosie sniffed and wiped a speck from her eyelid. "Now let's get those sandwiches wrapped. Train fare is priced to kingdom-come. Better we fill up on your dime." She grinned. "While we're at it. I'll add some of those beefsteak tomatoes your father grows. Be the envy of the dining car, we show up with them."

Amanda placed three tomatoes in a sack, grateful for the change of subject. "You must miss your grass-fed beef. Jacob sure talks about it."

"Steaks? Shoot, I'll take a clam cake and a couple of avocados any time. You folks don't know how good you got it, out here on the edge of the Pacific. Spoiled if you ask me."

Amanda laughed and tossed a half-dozen avocados into the sack with the tomatoes. "Rosie, you make my troubles seem like nothing. I've been sick with worry that Jacob would decide he doesn't like it here."

Rosie glanced around to see who might be listening. "Takes more than knowing how to doctor a horse to be a cowboy. Raising critters in this market takes skill. A man needs to have history, the same way I learned from my father, and he from his. Not even an Amishman could make a go of it without some coaching." Rosie picked up a plate and set it down again. "We saw the writing on the wall the day our son was killed by that drunk driver. It's been all downhill since then. I expect that's why we took to you folks so. It was like God sent us a little family to keep us from despair." She looked up and her eyes were filled with peace. "It worked, too. Now we got us some kids to buy for, come Christmas and birthdays."

Tibbs arrived for coffee and pulled out a chair for her father, both of them arguing good-naturedly about who won their game of checkers. Jacob slipped into his seat and told a joke. After Tibbs led them in a blessing, he reached for a piece of the cinnamon coffee cake that Rosie had risen early to prepare.

"Can we ride train, Daddy?" Noah said. "All of us?"

The flare of surprise in Jacob's eyes lasted only a second, but Amanda understood that he was unsure of their future, just like her. "We're taking Rosie and Tibbs to the train, Noah," she explained. "But we won't ride today. We need to stay home with Daddy because we love him very much."

"Will Daddy ride?"

Amanda made a quick decision. "Maybe soon. Aunt Carol wants us to visit her in Ohio." She paused when she saw Jacob's fork suspended in midair. "Wouldn't you like to see the house where Daddy grew up? You could meet your other grandpa and grandma."

Noah shook his head. "Rosie is my grandma."

"Your other grandma's name is Emma Ruth. She's very kind, and she makes donuts," Amanda explained while Jacob sat shaking his head in disbelief. She tried and failed to catch his eye. "But no more about that. First we need to see Rosie's train."

Jacob waited until Rosie and Tibbs went to their room to collect their luggage. "This is the first I hear about Ohio. You and Carol put your heads together to try to get me to go back and make amends with my family?" He wadded his unused napkin and threw it into the trash. "Your friend Carol needs to put her own house into order before she tries to repair ours."

"I'm sorry I blurted it out like that. It's not Carol's fault. Mr. Wright made the suggestion. I was thinking out loud. I didn't commit to anything."

"Maybe not. But our kinder thinks to take a train to see grandparents who won't welcome them. Noah'll suffer a false promise made by his mother."

"We could do it, Jacob. Rosie thinks we should take Dad and go. We could spend a week with your family and let them meet the kids."

"They will say we are unequally yoked."

"Then join the Mennonite Church. Start attending services."

He shook his head. "Not that easy. The local church here is Reformed. My folks don't accept that."

"But you're not baptized. Maybe there's a way—"

"It's too late. *That* gate's closed." Jacob turned away with anger sparking every word.

Rosie stood at the doorway, listening. "Son, you think you're the only one carrying the burden of regret? Tibbs and me, we railed at our boy for wanting to ride the rodeo instead of settling into the ranch. It got so we was poison to each other—no good words exchanged among us." She slid into a chair and sat with her hands folded like she was praying. "The day he left, he was drinking. So mad he near hit the dog on his way out the lane. Tibbs was standing at the barn, cursing him for the fool we thought he was."

Tibbs slipped up behind his wife and reached for her hand. Amanda felt her father enter and stand at her side, the five of them in the kitchen surrounded by the leftover smells of cinnamon.

Rosie continued. "He left, and we thought we didn't care if he came home again or not." She looked up at last. "And he didn't. The police report blamed the other driver for drunkenness, but it was a miracle our boy wasn't charged. It is us who carried the blame all these years."

"I should have loved my boy for his skill—not cursed him for it." Tibbs's grief carved shallow furrows down a face grown old with sorrow.

"When Jacob turned up at that little café in Sheridan, we seen him as an angel to help us get right with our past." Rosie's lips pursed and her voice hardened. "You need to go home and make this right with your brother, Jacob. Or the burden will destroy you."

Jacob gulped and raised his gaze to Amanda while tears welled on his thick lashes. "I can't."

Chapter Twenty-Six

Amanda gripped her baby in one hand and the diaper bag in the other, maneuvering through the line at the travel center where they had stopped for gas. She needed to change Jules's diaper and maybe get a minute to herself while Jacob took her father and Noah to the men's room.

The rest break included a snack on a picnic table where Noah could run on the grass. Amanda opened the sack of roasted chicken and mojo potatoes she'd purchased at the counter from a fresh-faced teenager with a purple swag in her hair. Not the healthiest lunch, but the best she could find in the middle of nowhere. She'd picked up a bunch of bananas and a bottle of apple juice for Noah, along with a cup of broccoli salad with raisins.

Across the lawn her father wore his favorite Pendleton sweater. From the back he looked younger. The trip so far had perked him up; he rode in the passenger seat next to Jacob, pointing out the rock formations across Wyoming with a wistful look that hinted of road trips he'd planned in his head while her mother lay in bed, unable to move.

They'd had a spirited competition earlier to see who could spot the first herd of antelope and he'd won. He'd found a track of Oregon Trail wagon ruts that cut through the snow-dusted sagebrush and explained how his people had come across on a wagon train, the wife pregnant with the baby that would become Amanda's great-grandmother, twice removed.

"Dad, I never knew that. Why didn't you ever tell me?"

Her father shrugged and turned to look at the scenery. After that, she was careful to let him talk.

Every mile seemed to calm his longing for adventure. He recalled his military service, the early years when he'd taken an old Chevy across the country with two buddies to see about jobs in Chicago. One had stayed. The other two returned to Oregon with a new appreciation for their home state. As the miles passed under a darkening sky, the closeness inside the car seemed to inspire his reminiscences. Amanda sat in the back seat, squeezed between child seats as she recalled her own journey in a rental truck five years earlier when she, too, had returned to her roots and settled down. In the driver's seat, Jacob seemed immersed in his own memories of a hurried trip across the country on a blustery day like today, crouched in the passenger seat of an eighteen-wheeler driven by a kind stranger.

Sometimes the miles passed in silence as the empty land filled the voids in their souls. Other times, they varied their travel with side trips to scenic parks and Native American gift shops. Amanda pointed out the turn-off to the Little Bighorn Battlefield, where the soldiers of the 7th Infantry had made their last stand. "Let's take the detour, Jacob. Dad used to be an authority on the battle. Let's do it for him."

The ghostly feel of the battleground seemed to penetrate her father's consciousness; he stood motionless, the chill wind ruffling his hair and his face frozen as though the spirits were talking to him. In the cemetery, he studied soldier's names on neat markers, one with a prairie grouse sheltered against the headstone. She reached for her camera and snapped a photo of him with his eyes closed. Later, in the museum, he pored over artifacts collected from the battle, fascinated by the guns and empty cartridge containers, a bullet-ridden canteen, and a broken bit. Back in the car, he rode in silence, filled with peace.

༄

Jacob pointed out an Amish farm with neat red barns and orderly fields worked by tractors driven by bearded farmers. "The communities make allowances if it is necessary. Each community makes its own rules," he explained. A few miles further, they passed a farmer driving to town for supplies on his tractor, with his wife beside him and an older son standing on the crossbar. "The fields here are less fertile than those in Ohio. Land is farmed in sections, many miles of corn, so a tractor is required."

"But they are still Amish?" Amanda asked as she turned to watch the tractor grow smaller out the back window.

Jacob smiled. "You English are always worried about the outside appearance. It takes more than one tractor to deter a stubborn Amish family from their path. These are dryland farmers, dependent on rain. In the west, it takes many more acres to support a family. Horses would be impractical. Necessity makes for necessary."

"Thank you, professor," Amanda teased as she gave his shoulder a caress.

Jacob's body responded. He gave a quick glance to make sure his father-in-law was still asleep before he admitted, "I miss you up here beside me. Makes for a long day. Maybe tonight you will rub out my sore neck?"

He glanced over his shoulder into the back seat where Amanda hid her smile behind the baby's cap. "You're just nervous at the prospect of meeting your brother," she teased again.

He had given in at the last minute when they stood with Rosie on the train platform. Rosie was too wise to let him off without a firm promise. He accepted the idea with surprising ease. Now they were headed to Spencerville with a case of *Miller Nursery* shrubs as a gift for the Ruths.

Jacob insisted on driving their SUV, with an enclosed trailer for the essentials of a few weeks' stay, in a partially furnished house with a toddler. Carol and Rennie had already terminated their lease. The new tenants were stuck in a prior lease until the end of June. The house was theirs for three months if they wanted it.

The Indiana roadside seemed to call to Jacob; his neck grew stiff, twisting to see every blade of grass. He joined her father in long conversations about soil, farm methods, and quality of yield while Amanda read to Noah with one ear tuned to the conversation. She lifted

Jules from the car seat on a straight stretch of highway and allowed her to nurse.

"My wife breaks the law?" Jacob teased as he glanced outside for a state trooper.

"What law? We haven't seen a car in ten miles. Besides, who's calling the pan black? You're the rebel in this bunch!"

"Kettle. It's 'calling the kettle black.' Clearly you've never cooked in a good cast-iron kettle. We need to make a trip down south to Lehman's Mercantile when we arrive in Ohio. Get you a proper frying pan from an honest-to-goodness Amish store."

Banter felt good after tense months of brushing past each other and curbing their words. What had Rosie called it, ignoring the elephant in the room? No more elephant. Only the satisfaction of humming tires and laughter, and salty, truck-stop chicken.

"If I learn to cook like your mamm, will you agree to wear suspenders?" she teased.

"Only when I have a gut to match. Doubt you'd relish that look on me."

"No, I love you just the way you are."

Jacob flashed a look through the rearview mirror that made her insides quake. The look suggested that the kids would be asleep early that night. She returned the look with a smile that telegraphed what she was feeling. Peace.

Spencerville was just as she remembered. Jacob drove past the little community park with its naked gazebo, its dormant lawns covered with budding elm trees. She unrolled her window, ignoring the blast of cold air while she savored the scent of caramel corn from an open door.

"Jacob, let's stop."

Jacob pulled around the corner and found a stretch of parking that could accommodate the SUV and cargo trailer. He got out and stretched before he opened the door to release Noah from his car seat. He helped his son into a jacket while Amanda unfastened Jules from her carrier.

Her father climbed out and started toward the park with Noah at his side. They climbed the three steps to stand inside the gazebo. "This is where the band plays Souza tunes on the Fourth of July," he explained. "Ice cream is over there where the table stands. Sack races and other shenanigans over there, by the tree."

"Will you buy me a shenanigan, Grandpa? I think I need one."

"Oh, you don't need me. You get old enough, you'll find enough of those all by yourself." He ruffled his grandson's hair and glanced around the town square. "Let's get us some popcorn. Best in the world, trust me."

In the candy store, Amanda stood back while her father fished a few bills from his wallet and paid for a small sack of Karmelkorn. He offered her a handful as they made their way back onto the sidewalk. Noah filled his hand and took a bite. "This is good, Grandpa. Can we eat this for supper?"

"We'll ask your mother. But I'll show you something that tastes even better. Raw milk from my friend's dairy."

"You have a friend here, Grandpa?"

"Yep. Next door to where I grew up. His name is Levi Ruth."

"Hey, he has the same last name as me. Can we go visit him?"

Her father's look of surprise was priceless, as though he was connecting the dots. together. Still confused, he turned and met her eyes, seeking assurance. She nodded, and he turned back around. "I think we can. He's your other grandpa. Like me," he said.

"Can we go now?"

"I think we better wait until your papa sees him first," Amanda said. "We don't want to spoil the surprise." She opened the door that read, *Clement Wright, Attorney at Law.*

She waited in the reception area for Clem. He emerged from his office, beaming from her to the baby, to Noah, hiding behind her legs. "Well, little lady, you've been busy since I saw you last. Congratulations. A beautiful little family." He chucked Jules under the chin. "She looks like Lydia."

Amanda nodded. "Dad thinks she looks like Mom."

"May I?" He crooked his elbow to secure the baby with an expression that caused her to blink back tears. The moment spoke of an old bachelor's regrets and his love for a woman lost to him through death and disappointment, but for a moment he had triumphed, the master of his dreams. The baby began to fuss. Amanda felt his hands tremble when she took the baby.

"She's a miracle," he murmured.

"We think so."

He bent to Noah's height and solemnly offered his hand. Noah took it and pumped three times, as his father had shown him. Clem cleared his throat. "So you're Noah. I'm pleased to meet you. You seem to be a chap I'd be proud to call my friend. May I do so? After all, we both think you have the best mama in the whole world. Don't we?"

Noah nodded and glanced up, sealing their friendship.

Clem's eyes misted. "I'll drive out and open up the house for you if you want."

Amanda shook her head. "Jacob and I know the way." The storm was gone from his eyes. It would be easier, now that he had held the baby he imagined might have been his and Lydia's. Clasping her keys, she led the way back to the street. On her way out, she glanced down at the sidewalk. "This is where I met Jacob, Dad. Flat on my back in those high-heeled boots you warned me not to wear."

He laughed. "I guess they were good for something after all."

At the car, Jacob was eating an ice cream cone, bundled in his overcoat. After tossing the remainder in the trash, he climbed into the car and waited for everyone to find their seats. The route took them past the schoolhouse. When he reached it, he pulled over and studied the dormant lawn and the trees in their winter bareness.

"This is where your grandpa went to school," her father explained. "I graduated from eighth grade with my friend, Levi Ruth."

"My other grandpa?"

"Yep. We used to play Andy Over and kickball right there on that field. He was stronger than I was, but I was faster."

"Did you wrestle each other?"

"I don't recall we did. But we played tag and raced each other home. He had to start chores, and I had to do my homework."

"Did you ever do chores?"

"Oh my, yes. I helped chop the firewood and feed the pigs, and I helped my father plant the crops we grew on our patch of ground. I hunted squirrels in the woods and sometimes we got a deer and I helped skin it. I helped my mama in the garden with the spading and hoeing. There was always something to do around our place."

"Did you have horses like Daddy?"

"We had a tractor. My father didn't want me riding along the road, so a horse would have spent its time in the pen. Not like the horses across the fence. They work every day. Even Sunday."

"My daddy says that's a sin."

Her father laughed. "I don't think horses read the Bible. Anyway, the buggy horses have to take folks to church."

"Why don't they just drive like us?"

Her father glanced at Jacob. "Why don't you let your daddy explain? He knows a lot about it. Or ask your grandpa when you meet him."

"What should I call him?"

Jacob considered. "You can call him Grossdawdy if you want. That's what his other grandchildren call him."

"I don't want a gross daddy. That would be—gross!"

Jacob reached to give his son a hair tussle. "Wait until you meet him. Maybe the two of you can decide between yourselves."

"What if I call him Granddawdy?"

"I expect he'll like that just fine."

Jacob eased back onto the roadway and Amanda saw her house growing larger as they approached. She watched her father sit up straighter, his eyes scanning ahead to where a huge, dormant tree filled the windshield. She pointed toward it. "See, Noah, there's the swing Grandpa built when he was a boy. It was my favorite place when I lived here."

Jacob flashed her a grin. "She used to sit there so she could wave to me when I drove past."

"Did you wave back?" Noah asked.

Amanda smiled in recollection. "Sometimes. When he was alone. But when his brother was with him, he acted like he didn't see me."

"Why? Didn't he like you, Mama?"

Jacob laughed. "I liked your mama plenty. That was the problem."

When the car came to a stop, Amanda reached for her doorknob. "Let's try out that swing. I think Grandpa would like to push you. But you need to hang on tight."

Her dad frowned as he approached. "Those ropes are frayed. I'll need to replace them before long."

Amanda's heart plummeted. "No, Dad. We'll let Jacob fix the ropes."

Her father stood behind the ropes and began tentatively pushing while Noah squealed with delight. Amanda stood nearby to steady him but his fingers tightened on the rough ropes. He pleaded for more when his grandfather tired of the game and turned to inspect the porch.

"Place looks better than I remember. My sister kept it up, gotta hand it to her." He ran his hands along the old wooden fence as though he recalled its origin while Amanda recalled the broken flowerbeds, the peeling paint and dingy wallpaper, the worn hardwood floors, and the sagging foundation she'd had to contend with. Hearing her father's pride in his childhood home made it worth her efforts. Hers and Jacob's; he'd done most of the work.

"Let's go inside, Dad. See what you remember."

She followed her father into the mudroom where Lydia's apron once hung. She saw the floors, stripped of the old asbestos linoleum, the fresh paint, and the hardwood countertop that Jacob had fitted to replace the rotten one. The house smelled musty and closed-up, but underneath she caught the scent of lemon oil and pine cleaner. Carol had left it spotless for them, but the house was frigid. No one had bothered to start the heater.

Her father stood in the kitchen with his eyes closed, as though recalling hot apple strudel and freshly baked breads from his mother's stove. While she lit the oven and opened the door to help heat the kitchen, he inspected nooks and crannies until he turned toward the dining room, where the hardwood floor gleamed under a dozen coats of polyurethane finish.

He moved into the living room and pointed out a notch on the mantel he'd made with his penknife when he was ten years old. "My mother took a switch to my bare backside for that. I never forgot." He sounded proud and happy, no longer struggling to recall events and names. Details crisp in his mind like they had happened yesterday.

"I wondered about that notch. I'm glad you solved the mystery." Amanda fumbled with the heater control before she followed him up the stairs to the first bedroom.

"This was mine," he told her proudly. "I was the boy and needed less room, even though I was older. My sister needed space for her geegaws. I kept a tidy ship. Most of my things in a trunk my dad helped me build. I had a little desk here. And a twin bed. With a Red Ryder bedspread Mother ordered in the Sears Roebuck catalog. Kept a leather glove and a softball on my bureau so it would be handy. Mother hooked me a rug. Winter mornings could be a shocker on bare feet."

Amanda waited until his recollection faded. "Would you like to sleep in your room while we're here? Mr. Wright had a couple of beds delivered for us. We rented them."

When she pushed the bathroom door open, Jacob's expression told her he remembered his bath in the claw-foot tub, soaking the soot of the barn fire from his over-heated body. She'd washed his sooty clothes in the washing machine downstairs and later carried the dry garments upstairs, her heart thudding.

Next door was the master bedroom, still painted sunny yellow. Surprisingly, it still held Lydia's old bed. Mr. Wright must have held on to it and returned it after Carol and Rennie moved out. She glanced to the window overlooking the Ruth farm and saw Jacob do the same.

"Maybe you want to head on over to your folks' house while I start supper?" she asked.

He shook his head. "Plenty of time for that." He started downstairs to unload the baby crib and bedding from the trailer. She returned to the kitchen to find that he'd already unpacked a box of cooking utensils. She was nursing the baby when he returned with a suitcase. The house had begun to slowly warm, even though most of the heat flowed up the stairs to the bedrooms.

Her father disappeared into the cellar and returned with a dusty mason jar of Lydia's applesauce. His clothes held the dank, musty odor of the enclosed space, but his face beamed with satisfaction. "Different down there than I remember. More solid. New siding," he remarked.

"Jacob did that. He rebuilt it for me. Remember? I wrote you about his work on the place?"

"Jacob lived here?"

"No, I lived here. Jacob worked for me. As a carpenter."

"Did a good job. He rebuild that porch? Never set quite right as I recall."

"Yeah. He did."

"I helped my father build that porch. Never liked the fit. But it looks just fine now."

Her father inspected the porch from every angle. In the dining room, Noah pulled toys from a box while Jacob hauled in their furniture. On his last load, he shut the back door with his toe. The chill had burned off the upstairs, and the lower rooms would be toasty before long.

Bedtime was easier than she expected. Noah insisted on his own room. "Good plan. We'll put your sister in with you." On their way to their own room, she whispered to Jacob, "We need to pick up a toddler gate for the top of the stairs."

"For which one of them? Your dad or your son?"

She nudged him to silence. "Don't even go there."

Dawn brushed the peak of the Ruth barn. Jacob sipped his second cup of coffee while Amanda stirred up a pot of oatmeal, her eyes blurry with fatigue. They'd fought the need to rise before the sun, but they'd given up between the rooster crows and the cows still mooing for their milking. A familiar sound of laughter filtered across the field; the younger Ruth brothers pushing a herd of cows into the barn with their lanterns bobbing in the semi-darkness. Jacob rose from his chair and pressed against her to watch the activity next door from the security of the kitchen. Too late, he realized their forms were backlit in the kitchen light. The older of the two boys turned to stare and Jacob lifted his arm. It was a moment before the boy returned the wave and turned to say something to his brother. They both turned to gawk before they resumed their work.

Jacob frowned. "It won't be long for Daed and Mamm to know we're back."

"Maybe it's better for you to make your presence known. Your mother will be happy to see you."

He shrugged. "Maybe we take a ride to see the neighborhood today. Pick up groceries. Too early in the season for the farm stands, but sauerkraut and rich brown breads can be had. And eggs. There's a mercantile that sells canned beets I used to have a craving for."

Amanda smiled. "Beets and sauerkraut? If you think to eat yourself home again, you'll end up looking like that man you always talk about. Go, meet your brother. Get the thing done. You'll be glad of it afterward."

Jacob turned toward the door where across the field,

his brothers called to the herd. *Flossie, Whippet, Mary, Belle.* He looked eagerly for animals he might remember. *It's only been five years.* He crossed the road and slipped through the fence before taking his place along the left flank. The herd plodded single-file toward the barn. Some of the cows were new, their distinctive black and white pelts like Oreo cookies. Dutch Belted cows. John had made improvements to the herd.

Chapter Twenty-Seven

Jacob grabbed an oil lantern from the barn and swung it in an easy arc as he breathed in the familiar scents of straw, offal, and warm milk. Inside, he hung the lantern on a nearby hook and rolled his sleeves to the elbow.

Down the row, Samuel and Young Levi, his youngest brothers, washed down the last cows' udders with a pungent solution that puckered his nostrils with its familiarity.

John stood with one hand on the generator that powered the milking machines once the boys attached them. When one of the younger boys tittered at his shocked scowl, he abandoned the generator and strode to the end of the barn to grab one of the old-fashioned milking stools. He started on the first cow without acknowledging Jacob, already hand milking a cow, his head braced against the cow's side.

Milk streamed into both of their buckets, a race to see who finished first. John earned the privilege. He stood, took up his stool and moved to the next cow seconds ahead of Jacob. Finally, he spoke. "So, the prodigal returns."

Jacob concentrated on his task while a dozen responses competed in his head. *Don't get bent out of shape. Only a visit. I have a good life now. Married and settled.*

John's voice was muffled by the milk streaming into his bucket. "You take that Englischer to wife?"

Jacob fought his irritation. "She has a name—Amanda. And yes, we got ourselves married, right as rain." He winced at the phrase. Five minutes and he'd already lapsed into his old cadence. He held his tongue and waited.

"You right with Gott?"

"You betcha!" Jacob emptied his bucket, grabbed his stool, and began stripping the next cow, easing into a familiar cadence as he tried to outpace his brother. "How about you? Ya stand before the others and beg their forgiveness?"

His brother swung his bucket around and emptied the contents into the holding tank before moving to the next. His face flooded with suppressed anger. "No concern of yours, Jacob Ruth. You left. Those of us stay fast to the principles are the ones that count. You are a slave to the world now, bruder. Come to our service on Sunday and see if the others don't say the same." When Jacob kicked the stool out and moved to the next cow so quickly that it side stepped, John turned to glare. "Careful you don't be upsetting Bessie there. She and Buleuh, they have their odd ways."

Jacob picked up his bucket and rejoined his younger brothers, who were silent, waiting to hear the argument. "He don't need to be telling me how I should milk! Good ole Bruder John always steers the straight course for the rest of us. It's a wonder he don't be sitting up to the house, feet up and a cup of Mamm's good coffee in his hand while the cows milk themselves."

John scowled over the top of his next cow. "I don't be drinking Mamm's coffee these days. Got me a good wife cooks my morning meal, no sweat."

"Yeah, by the looks of you, she cooks more than just the morning meal. You are packing on the weight." Jacob finished his cow and gave it a pat on its back before moving to the next. John began a moment later. Their younger brothers emptied their buckets into the holding tank, their eyes wide with excitement.

John finished up the last cow and stood, his face shiny with sweat in the chill air as the first rays of sunlight crept over the horizon. "That makes the lot of them. Don't aim to keep you. No double you got that fancy car and all them gizmos ta keep repaired, now you're an outsider. Boys will clean the barn. Samuel's job. He'll get it done before breakfast. Then he's off to school. He's thirteen now. Old enough, he does the haying in the summer. He's taken over your chores and happy to do it."

Jacob shrugged. "Glad you don't miss my help around the place."

John glanced up. "You handled the manure wagon fair enough. And the harvesting. Had a straight arm for pitching hay. My wife does a lot of that now."

Jacob felt his cheeks heat, not all of it from the exertion of milking. "Used to sneak off and pitch baseball with the town boys during rumspringa. Played on a town team. Wore the uniform they provided. Used to hide it under my mattress between games."

"Mamm knew it. So did Daed. They bore their trials with you running around, getting into the wrong gangs. Now it's the younger boys that push their patience."

"Guess you'll be immune from that."

John snorted. "It'll soon be my turn, soon enough. My oldest turns five this year. Time to start him on your chores."

Jacob ignored the jab. "You and your missus getting along?"

John looked up sharply. "You mean after the confession I make?" His face flooded again. "Ja, she is a Godly woman. All is forgiven. I've not strayed."

"And Katie Melvin? She is content?"

"She moved with her family to Kansas. They saw the opportunity to buy a farm over there. I guess she likes her new community pretty good. Never heard." He shouted to the younger boys to release the cows from their headstalls, the command unnecessary for young fellows doing the chore morning and night since they were three years of age, Jacob thought. *So John is as nervous as me.*

When his brother filled a bucket with soapy water and began sloshing the filthy cement, Jacob grabbed a push broom and began pushing water into the drain for something to occupy his hands. "I hated you for a season, bruder."

John paused, his voice low as he bent to tighten a loose hose connection and rinsed the cement. "Your burden, then. Everything worked out for the good."

"Easy for you to say. You sinned against me, bruder.

I came back because I needed to hear you confess to me."

John looked up, anger mottled in his cheeks. "No need. It's over and forgotten."

Jacob threw down the broom, dirty water splayed over his shoes and trousers, as he glared at his brother coolly wrapping the hose around the faucet. "Not by me, bruder. I need to hear the words."

John turned to grab another bucket, his stern words an imitation of their father's. In the shadowed barn, his profile looked tense. "It was you, caused most of the headaches around here," he bellowed with no regard to the frightened cows behind him. "How many times did you apologize to our family? The shame you brought? The whispers and tongue wagging? Daed facing the deacon time and again over your pigheadedness? Seems it's you should ask forgiveness."

"I was ready to eat crow. To do what it took, that morning I stood up! We were to announce the marriage Banns after I made zeugnis. But you took my turn in seeking forgiveness. You are a damned fornicator!" Jacob heard his carefully rehearsed words tossed aside for ones he'd vowed never to say, even if he carried them in his heart.

John's eyes widened. "I saw you leave. So did everyone else. Afterward, some of the men said they expected it. Some thought you had it coming for all your past behavior."

"Wrong! Don't twist the truth to suit yourself, bruder. The words of Cain to Abel! You drove me out, bruder. Not the rest of them. You!"

John sloshed through the run-off water with his broom held like a weapon. When the last blade of straw was swept away, he grabbed the lantern, extinguished the light and turned toward the door without inviting Jacob to follow. From the house, his wife stood on the porch holding a cup of hot coffee and a fresh cinnamon roll, clearly an excuse to see for herself the commotion in the barn. John glanced back at the row of harnesses and the waiting horses before he turned his toes toward his house.

Jacob watched his brother trudge toward the house without a backward glance. The younger boys hesitated before they followed their brother inside. Fury raged inside him, Jacob grabbed the harnesses for the team of Belgians waiting in the paddock, the stiff, heavy leather, the buckles, the rawhide strips familiar reminders of his youth. When he finished, he looked around for something else to do. The smell of new milk offered an excuse. He rolled the heavy cans onto his brother's wagon, the burn of muscle a welcome relief for the anger in his gut. One of the lids slipped, sloshing cream against his leg, the action so familiar that it brought tears. His mind played a slow, rhythmic dance that stretched the minutes with yearning for the life he'd left behind.

With the wagon loaded, he made a final pass through the barn, less from the satisfaction of the place than fear that he might never return. On impulse, he climbed into the wagon and clucked to the horses. They started down the driveway toward the auto fumes and the clang of the railroad crossing. He steadied them with his voice, gratified that their ears twitched at his command.

From the corner of his eye, he saw his brother from the window, his form barely visible in the lantern light. Jacob gave the reins a jerk and turned right onto the roadway toward his wife's old Miller house, where the sunrise painted the walls with cream shadings.

With his anger softened, he pulled up at the gate and saw his son bundled in a hooded jacket. Noah stared with moon-sized eyes. A grin split his face into twin orbs of fascination.

"How did it go?" Amanda snapped the gate shut behind her, her words whispered as though they might carry back to the farm.

"No need." Jacob glanced around. "Where's your dad?"

She cocked her head toward the creek, where her father stood transfixed by something he saw. "He's happy here. He remembers. I think this was a good idea." When he failed to respond, she repeated her question. "How did it go with your brother? I thought I heard shouting."

He kept his gaze over the backs of the restless, stamping horses, afraid to meet her eyes. "Ja, we exchanged a few words. Time they were said. At least I thought so. Him, not so much. He's a deacon now. Feeling the weight."

"A deacon? So soon?"

He glanced around and rubbed his hands together in the chill air. "The co-op sends a milk truck out to pick these up, but I felt the need to load them. Now I have caused him extra work, I need to deliver them."

"He gave you permission?"

He ignored the question, unwilling to admit his hasty decision. "Fetch the boy. He can ride along. It'll be an adventure."

Amanda frowned and shook her head. "Noah isn't dressed for the cold."

"Don't coddle him. He's dressed good enough. Nothing extra is required. Set him up to me." He turned to her and his face tightened. "Might as well fetch your father while you're at it."

Behind him, his younger brothers had turned onto the roadway on their way to school. He had no wish to face them after the morning's tempest. "*Now*, wife. I need to get started or the milk will be soured."

Bob Miller settled in the wagon seat, with Noah in the middle, his heels kicking the bottom of the seat in excitement. Jacob settled a blanket across their laps as Bob leaned over to grin at his grandson. He pointed at the passing boys. "I went to school with these folks. I remember."

Jacob saw the look of pride in his father-in-law's face, glanced at Amanda, and nodded. He started off without his forgotten gloves, half-glad that the burn of leather reins against his palms settled his anger. On the seat beside him, Noah's chatter subsided, and for a mile, the clip-clop of hooves was the only sound, until the road began to fill with commuters on their way to work. A semi pulled alongside. A school bus stopped at the crossing and opened its doors. When the doors closed and the bus rattled off, Noah squirmed with excitement.

He gave his son a playful nudge. "A marvel, huh, son? This was how I went to town when I was a *kind* like you. No cars for me."

Noah's face lit with excitement. "Sell our car and buy horses. Okay, Daddy?"

Jacob reached over to rub the fine blond hair that

escaped his son's wool cap. "We see about that. For now, you just enjoy the ride."

When they arrived at the processing plant, Jacob leaped down. "Stay still, son. I will be right back."

He returned from the office with a scrap of paper that he thrust into his hat before he climbed back up. "Daed's cows produce only 'Grade B' milk," he grumbled to anyone who listened. "The government assigns the Amish this lesser grade. Our milk must be used only for cheese and yogurt. An excuse to pay the farmers less than they deserve." He glanced around at the people coming into work. "But it is my concern no longer."

At the loading ramp, he waited for a young worker with a dolly to help heft the heavy cans.

The ride home was made in silence as they passed fields warming from the frost. At the school, his brothers gawked while their game of kickball went on without them. Amanda ran from the kitchen clad in a light sweater with her camera in hand. She called for them to smile as they rolled past with Noah and his grandfather staring proudly ahead.

John waited at the Ruths' driveway, his arms folded across his chest and his face wreathed in a scowl. It seemed that he intended to block their entry until he moved grudgingly aside to let the team pass.

Jacob climbed down and began unharnessing the team as he had done a thousand times before. Overhead, the windmill stood tall against the sky, its blades whirring in rhythm to his heartbeat. Everything so familiar, and yet nothing the same at all. He turned a shoulder into the first horse and reached for the leather strap to lead it to the field.

John approached from behind to grab the reins from

Jacob. "The day does not end with a simple trip to town. The horses have work to do."

From the house, his wife Lorie appeared with a plate of fresh donuts. "*Willkumm*. Come inside and warm yourselves." Jacob opened his mouth to decline, but his stomach rumbled from the aroma emanating from the plate. "The child requires hot chocolate on such a morning." She bent to inspect Noah's face and rose with a bright smile. "Is this your *sohn*, Bruder Jacob?"

Jacob nodded. "And this is my father-in-law, Bob Miller. From the place down the road."

"*Gut ta meetcha*." She greeted them both with a clear, contented smile, and encouraged her young son Silas, hiding shyly behind her skirts, to make the acquaintance of his cousin. Jacob watched the two boys negotiate which of them would have the first turn with the peddle toy in the yard.

His attention shifted back to his sister-in-law, who clearly harbored none of the stubbornness of his brother. Without thinking, he lapsed into the dialogue of his childhood. "Lorie Ann Kurtz, my brother has got the better bargain in your marriage. He does not deserve you."

"Gott's plan for us, nevertheless." Lorie gave a welcome smile and urged the little boys into the house with her. Jacob followed more slowly when the shock of recognition halted him at the door. Without thinking, he doffed his hat and stomped the dirt from his boots on the worn coir mat his mother had traded egg money for when he was a youngster. He took a step inside, where his mother's plain chairs still hung on pegs, and her huge oak table waited its next meal.

Lorie noticed. "Your mamm has no use of these in the *dawdi haus*. She left them for us to use."

Sunlight filtered through the curtainless windows, topped by plain cloth pull shades. In the kitchen, coffee and cinnamon sugar melded with the scent of crisp-fried sweet dough. For a moment he was three years old again, tasting homemade donuts for the first time, like Noah.

Noah darted a look to his father before he shyly accepted one. "Can I take one for Mama?"

Before Jacob could protest, his sister-in-law waved her hand to include the entire plate. "Of course. We send over a few for her coffee break." She shook her head in a mock warning. "Unless you two gobble them all up first. Do you drink coffee?" When Noah shyly shook his head, she laughed. "Maybe with some cream and sugar, you would not mind so much."

Jacob accepted a cup and a second donut with a wry awareness that he sat at his usual place at the long plank table. Next to him, his father-in-law munched on a cinnamon donut with a look of contentment. "Good times, huh, Bob?" he asked.

Amanda's father glanced around with a dawning light of recognition. "I remember this place. We cut into watermelons on the lawn and afterward, Levi raced me to feed the rinds to the hens. I won because he had to carry the lion's share." Bob shifted as if searching for someone who wasn't there. "I learned to garden from the grandmother, Sarah. She gave me my first tomato seeds."

The door opened in a blast of cold air, and John entered. He scowled, but a warning look from his wife silenced whatever he intended to say. He gave Bob a wry smile. "Ja. You remember right, Mr. Miller. You grew the good tomatoes. Even Grossmummi, she does not have such a way with them as you."

"Plant when the moon is right. That's the trick." Bob grinned. "I made a fine bargain with your granny for some of your fine manure. Aged it out back in my compost pile. Added a few trace minerals from the feed-store and watered from the well." He laughed. "I guess my secret's safe with you." He said, "How's your granny these days? I remember her. She had the sense of five men and the heart of a saint. Good woman."

Lorie looked up from where she was peeling pota-toes for the noon meal. "Sarah lives in Florida now. In a Plain community with her sister. They are active with their relief work."

"And your father?"

"Levi and Emma live in the *dawdi haus* now. You will find him in the garden. Nothing much has changed for them. Maybe the hours. His heart is not so good these days, but his spirit is strong."

Bob had already lost interest and was getting to his feet. Jacob led him to the door. They started down the road with a plate of fresh donuts, a jug of raw milk, and a carved wooden horse for Noah. Jacob caught himself before he thanked Lorie for the coffee and sweets. She would not accept thanks. It was enough that Gott had provided.

At the house, Amanda tended the baby. "How did it go?"

He shook his head and slumped onto the sofa. "Best ask your father. He enjoyed himself. So did Noah. Made himself a friend."

"And your brother?"

"Nothing changed. Same old John."

Amanda paused in her diapering and gave him a hopeful smile. "Your mother would say 'it's early days yet.'"

"Yeah, maybe. And maybe I'm a fool."

Chapter Twenty-Eight

Jacob pushed the curtains aside in the upstairs bedroom to watch his brother hitch the wagon and start into the field with a load of manure. John began pitching it on the ground, the motions so familiar that his fingers twitched, watching.

Amanda handed him the baby while she smoothed the covers of the bed. "You're unsettled today, husband? From the visit yesterday?"

Jacob idly stroked the baby's downy hair. "I'm a stranger in my own land. The visit only proved what I already knew—no going back. John is a stranger to me. I see him for what he is; not a Godly man as he would claim, but stubborn and unyielding. Set in his ways."

Amanda finished the bed and straightened. "Jacob, go and see your mother."

"You think she wants to see me?"

"She should see how happy we are together. It will change her thinking." She picked at a loose thread on the baby's blanket. "Carol's coming over tomorrow. She wants to see the baby."

"Carol? You show the baby to your friend before the grandparents? How is this possible?"

"Jacob? Listen to yourself." She positioned the baby and unbuttoned her shirt. "What would happen if we just dropped by today?"

He considered her question. "Mamm's used to stretching the main meal for visitors. It will be fine." He looked up and grinned. "You planned this, didn't you, wife?"

Amanda transferred the baby without looking up. "We'll just stay for a few minutes. And under no circumstances will we eat there, even if she invites us. Agreed?"

"Agreed. No roast and boiled potatoes. None of Mamm's pickled cucumbers. No moon pies or *schnitzboi*. Your dad will be disappointed. He likes Plain cooking."

"My dad will eat anything. Especially junk food."

Jacob sobered. "He's earned the right. If he wants one, he should have a pop."

"You mean soda. Nobody says 'pop' anymore."

"Wanna make a wager on that?"

She laughed. "If you were a betting man. But I know you better than that."

He pushed off from the bed, pacing the room from door to window and back again. "Mamm finishes with housework by now. It's a good time."

"Let's go then. I'll get Dad and the kids ready while you go sit in the car and honk," she teased.

✦❧✦

"Jacob! *Willkumm, sohn. Gott segen eich*, God bless you." Emma Ruth answered the door with her apron in hand. She smoothed her hair back under her kapp with a nervous gesture, but her welcome was calm and generous. Behind her, the kitchen was infused with the aromas of sausage and sauerkraut, and fresh bread just out of the oven. Jacob entered and stood in stunned stillness.

Poor Jacob. No man is immune to his mother's cooking. Amanda waited while his mother greeted him. No hugs or kisses. Instead, Emma lifted her arms in praise, as though she expected something to fall out of the sky. "Gott has answered my prayers, son. We parted so suddenly that I wasn't sure we would see each other again in this lifetime."

She turned to Amanda with a smile. "Amanda! Jacob's wife...our dear neighbor. And now the mother of his children." She bent to Noah's level and held out her hands. "And the boy. Named after a great man of God, builder of the Ark. May the boy be also a builder of wood. His father will see ta that." She glanced at Jacob. "As he will also guide the child's development." When Noah remained silent, she straightened and approached Amanda. With a practiced motion, she pulled a corner of the blanket back and pressed her lips to the baby's forehead. "Such a blessing, this little girl. What name did you give her? Oh yes, Julie Rae. After your mother. It is good, using the familiar names. Keeps the tradition alive."

"Would you like to hold her?"

Emma cradled the baby without pausing her conversation. "Your father will be in shortly. He has surely noticed the arrival of our visitors. Perhaps he is tied up with a problem in the barn."

"We saw him in the field."

"Ah, yes. Preparing the land for another season. First the spreading of manure, and the working of the earth, a farmer's duty to steward God's promise." Emma turned to Jacob with brimming eyes. Amanda saw the joy. But the conflict was there in the quick words and nervous, one-sided conversation.

"Our son has discovered he has the same last name as you, Emma." Amanda turned to Noah. "Do you know this is your grandmother?" She gave him a gentle nudge, but he remained pressed against her skirt with his fingers in his mouth.

"I fear my strangeness is daunting ta a child. It is often so, that the Plain clothing is noticed, not the person inside." Emma gave a wry smile and turned to her grandson. "Would you like a cookie, Noah?" She was already on her feet before he shyly nodded. In a moment, she was back with the baby in one hand and a towering plate of molasses cookies in the other. She returned with a pitcher of milk still warm from the cow. "I have fresh apple cider and a pie crust cookie for you, Noah. A proper drink for little bodies who must watch their protein consumption."

Amanda relaxed at the concern Emma showed for Noah's restrictions, a relief she rarely enjoyed. Jacob's expression was comical as he savored his mother's cookie, his eyes closed and a milk mustache across his lips. He finished the first and reached for another.

"Would you like ta stay for dinner?" Emma asked.

His hand paused midway. "It's been a bit since I've

tasted honest kraut." He glanced at Amanda, his cheeks blazing. "My wife is a good cook, but—"

The women broke into laughter.

"Careful, son. You will be eating plain meat sandwiches with no mustard. And a just punishment it will be for such an ungrateful husband."

Emma prepared a plate for Noah while she explained about the special foods that could make his diet manageable. "I serve your supplement in my other grandson's favorite cup. It is not too difficult. He accepts that he is different from the others, but this makes him closer to Gott. 'A carrot for every sin,' we say."

"At home in Oregon, we have a big garden. Noah helps me pick vegetables. He likes to choose what goes into his salads. I admit, raisins are his favorite. He puts them in almost everything."

Emma frowned. "He must learn to feed his body, not his taste buds. Often, this is hard for a boy." She cast a fond look at Jacob. "Sometimes even for a grown man."

"I don't want Noah to suffer," Amanda confessed.

Emma glanced over at Jacob. "I'm sure my son has told you our belief about this. Do the best you can for your child, but do not fuss overmuch. The boy won't starve. Gott's bounty is never-ending." She listened as the clock struck the quarter-hour chime. "Time for me to prepare the noon dinner. Your father has eased his workload, but he has yet the farmer's appetite. His belly will be roaring like a lion in a few minutes."

In short order she filled platters with apple and caraway-infused kraut, and new sausages with small potatoes simmered in parsley butter. Thick slices of brown bread and butter filled a small plate in the center of the table, alongside a bowl of steaming, chunky applesauce and a jar of Emma's brown mustard. To Amanda's amazement, she even provided a loaf of low-protein bread from the icebox.

Levi arrived with the dinner gong. He stomped his boots against the mat and entered scowling, with a glance at Jacob as he pulled off his hat and hung it on the rack. He followed with his coat while Emma continued with the meal, her eyes watchful. "So the prodigal returns!" The same words as John had used; they had already discussed his arrival. Jacob's face blazed, but he remained silent. "Missed your mamm's cooking? Or have you come to your senses and decided to return to the fold?"

Amanda darted a quick glance at Jacob, but he was studying his mother's wooden floor, tongue-tied and uncomfortable, his face inflamed in the blush of embarrassment. She shifted the baby in her arms, her appetite as flat as her hopes for the visit.

"Speak up, boy. Don't shame my home with your sinfulness. Own your transgressions, agree to meet with the bishop or take your leave. We are righteous people in this household. No room for fellas who choose the world over the Almighty."

Jacob's glance flickered to his father. He stood and swept Noah up into his arms. "Come, wife. Collect your father. We shake the dust of this place from our sandals."

Amanda snatched her diaper bag from a chair and helped her father from his place at the table. She gave Emma a look of apology and saw her standing with her lips pursed and her face as white as her kapp strings.

The smells of the uneaten dinner followed them down the path until the door shut behind them.

Humiliated and numb, she snapped Jules into her car seat and helped Noah do the same before she slid into the back seat. Her father took his place in the passenger seat. On their way down the dirt drive, she saw someone behind a window shade before they disappeared.

Jacob drove in silence, past their house and the schoolhouse, his eyes fixed on the road. "Your son is hungry," she snapped. The red-painted café on the main street was crowded with diners. "Not here. I don't want to meet anyone I know," she whispered. He nodded and continued on toward the county road.

In Medina, the *Five Guys* burger shop was nearly empty. She relented to Noah's plea for a grilled cheese sandwich. "You can have two bites." *Raising expectations.* She'd pay for that decision for the next month.

"Four bacon cheeseburgers, one grilled cheese, and four waters," she ordered.

Her father frowned. "I want french fries and a soda pop."

"Dad, you can't just eat junk food. It's not good for you—"

"Respect your father, wife. Give him what he wants!"

Amanda turned toward Jacob, his face a blaze of anger. She nodded, too stunned to argue. "And f... french fries," she added.

Jacob claimed a table while she took Noah to the bathroom. Afterward, she found some crackers in a pocket of the diaper bag and handed Noah the entire package. When the food arrived, they ate in silence, but each bite reminded her of the Amish dinner they'd left behind. She ventured a quick peek at Jacob and saw him brooding, his mind miles away. She inched her hand toward his but drew back before their fingers touched. Time for explanations later; this was too big for small solutions.

Afterward, they drove through Medina County, all of them viewing the neat farms from a tourist's seat except, apparently, Jacob. She saw him flinch when an Amish buggy passed and again when a man appeared in a field behind his plow.

In some areas, snow dusted the ground. At a hilly woodlot, a group of children coasted down a small hill on an ancient wooden sled. Noah implored her to let him join them.

"Not today, Noah," she whispered, breaking the terse silence.

"Let the boy have his fun!" From the passenger's seat, her father's tone sounded tired. "There's been enough hatefulness today. Let the boy be."

Jacob helped Noah into his jacket and carried him to the top of a knoll. A young girl and her brother made room on their sled, and his squeals on the slide down the hill brought lightness into the moment. He reached the bottom and immediately begged for another ride. The little girl took his hand and helped him to the top, her little plain dress and braids the twin of another girl playing nearby.

Amish children. A blast of wind threw snow into Amanda's eyes, and she stood hunched in misery, her hair matted and damp in her hood. When chill fingers of icy wind crept through her light jacket, she returned to the car and its heater, where Jules napped.

"When do people become so hard?" Amanda asked Jacob that night when they lay in bed with the lights off.

"You mean my parents? They have hardened their hearts for the strength of their group. It's the only way they can remain among them."

"But the heart can shut off to compromise. I saw it today," she protested.

"A price too steep for me. My father has closed the doors of his heart to all but what he must do. I feel sorry for him."

"And your mother? Did you see her face when we left?" She reached to cradle him. "I saw a side of you I didn't know. I learned a lot about you today, Jacob. I love you so much."

"I learned about myself, too. And there's no chance I'd permit my daughter to grow up in that culture."

"You just decided that?"

In the dark, he swallowed. "It's a hard life. For the women, especially. For them, suffering is a virtue." His breathing slowed as he considered his next words. "My mother was molested by a member of her community. When she was a girl."

Amanda forced herself to remain still. "She told you?"

His silence was torturous. "I heard the man repent of it in zeugnis when I was a child. They made my mother stand up and apologize for enticing him into doing it." His voice lowered to a whisper. "She was only ten when it happened."

"Oh, Jacob!"

"She never told anyone. She just carried it inside

her all those years. He went to prison for doing the same to an English child. When he was released, he stood up to make zeugnis and they blamed her."

Amanda's heart pounded with rage. "That was why your rumspringa...your indecision went on so long? You were angry with your church?"

"Angry. Confused. I watch my mother keep her head down, not meeting his eyes when the man is around. She never forgave him, I know that now. She wanted my father to stand up for her, but he sided with the community's rule."

"Same as he did with John. Against you."

Jacob shifted. "Yeah, that's right."

"This public zeugnis is important to your people?"

"Not *my* people!"

"Shhh, you'll wake the baby."

Outside, a nightbird rustled in the naked trellis. The baby stirred in her cradle, turned, and resumed her soft snores.

"Jacob, I hate seeing you like this."

"Nothing changed today. Not for me, anyway." He crushed her into an embrace, his kisses hungry, his body seeking oblivion.

Later, they lay entwined, and he felt his blood pulse in his ear.

"Maybe we should go home," she whispered.

He lay still, considering. When he was sure of his course, he shook his head slowly in the darkness. "We are here now. Let's visit the area. We won't be coming back. That's for sure." He lay next to her, his heart eased. "I have an errand tomorrow, something I must get for the house. You want to come with me? Your dad might like to see Medina again."

"Not tomorrow. Another time. Today's events really upset Dad. I think he should stay home tomorrow and rest."

"Suit yourself. Let's try to get some sleep. I'll get an early start."

Chapter Twenty-Nine

✦

"Dad, where are you? Noah?" Amanda ran upstairs and flung open the door to her father's bedroom. Empty. She pushed into Noah's bedroom and picked Jules up from her crib before she turned to check her own room. Downstairs, she scanned the living area on her way to the backyard. "Dad, where are you?"

On the way to the creek, fear gave her wings. She stumbled over a root and tightened her hold on the baby as she scanned the overgrowth for signs of a little boy and an old man in his second childhood. At the creek, she halted, fighting the knotweed and hemlock that choked the waterway. No path. Nowhere for two adventurers to make their way to the water. She followed the chokeweed to the edge of her property and turned back toward the house.

The baby fussed, but she didn't lessen her pace. "You'll have to wait, Jules. We need to find Grandpa and brother."

She ran to the garage, jiggled the lock, and returned

to the house for her keys. Jacob had taken the car. She changed the baby, set her into the baby-wrap carrier and tied it over her shoulders before she grabbed a bottle of water. At the roadway, she hesitated. *Right or left?* She considered her choices. "Dad talks a lot about his school days. Maybe he decided to show Noah where he went to school."

Halfway there, a stitch in her side forced her to ease her frantic pace, and she slowed, fighting for air. Suddenly, panic brought a surge of adrenaline when she heard laughter in the schoolyard. *Scholars at play.* As she approached, her young brother-in-law stared at her behind his sunglasses. She waved and was rewarded with a grin and a cool jerk of his index finger, a neat imitation of Clint Eastwood pointing a gun. She recalled other Amish boys make the same gesture.

"Samuel? Have you seen an old man and a boy about four?"

"Mr. Miller and my *bruder's sohn*, Noah?"

She nodded, surprised that he would know them by name. "They're missing. My father is...*stroovich*. He is confused in his head."

Samuel nodded sympathetically. "Maybe they visit the dawdi haus?" He grinned. "Grossmummi, she cooks *wonderful gute*."

Amanda swiveled in the opposite direction, where the silo of the Ruth farm was barely visible, a mile distant. Her heart sank. "Thank you. I'll check."

"Ask Mrs. Stevick if I can go with you. To help," he suggested.

"Mrs. Zook is no longer your teacher?"

He shook his head. "She takes herself down to

Florida to live with other retired teachers. Maybe they will correct each other's penmanship, ja?"

She glanced around, unsure what to do as she adjusted the baby. "I don't wish to disturb her. I must go, but thank you for the offer. You are kind like Jacob."

He hesitated. "Bruder Jacob got himself the bad end. I am not supposed to speak of it, but our older bruder was wrong in his actions."

"John doesn't seem to think so. Jacob wants an apology." She glanced down the road, hoping for a glimpse of her wayward men, but she was disappointed. "I need to go, Samuel. And your father would not be pleased if we showed up at his farm together. I'm so glad I met you again. You were just a boy when I last saw you."

She turned in the direction she had just come, half angry at her earlier decision. She would be at the farm by now, instead of twenty minutes farther down the road. A horse and buggy approached from behind without leaving her much room on the narrow strip of blacktop. At the last minute, she edged to the side and watched the buggy pass, driven by a young man in a black winter hat. A random thought broke the chain of worrisome thoughts in her head: Jacob claimed the Amish men changed to straw hats in early May, at the time of their spring communion service.

"Your daddy's straw hat is worn out, Jules. When we find Grandpa, we must get him a new one. One with a real ribbon hatband, not that nasty old electrical tape he uses to keep the shape. He says it saves money. Isn't Daddy a cheapskate?"

At the midpoint of her journey, she raced back inside her house to check if they had come home, but the house was as silent and strange as when she'd left it.

She downed a glass of water and checked upstairs before she rushed back outside. A car approached from the direction of town. "Please, God, let it be Jacob, back from his errand." A minute later, the car passed, filled with carefree strangers. Beyond the tree swing, the road was empty. The baby squirmed, reminding her that she needed to hurry. "Where's your daddy, Jules? Why isn't he here?"

Her head ached and the baby carrier dug into her shoulders. She cradled her hands beneath the baby to ease the strain on her back, but sweat covered her cheeks, even in the brisk morning. Random thoughts triggered her terror as she raced down the roadway. She clutched Noah's coat that she'd found lying on the sinkboard next to the dirty breakfast dishes. *He'll catch pneumonia without it in this weather*. She glanced back, hoping for a glimpse of Jacob, but the road was empty. By the time she turned into the Ruth driveway and started toward the porch, she was out of air and clutched a stitch in her side.

John emerged from his house, his beefy arms folded over his chest, the rolled sleeves revealing corded muscles as thick as a tire. When he recognized her, his head jerked up and a scowl spread across his face. "It is not a fit day for visiting on foot. What sane mother brings her newborn out in this weather?"

Amanda felt her face heat. She darted a hopeful glance toward the house, in the hope that her sister-in-law might appear, but no such luck. "My father...and my...son are missing," she stuttered. "I thought maybe —"

John hesitated. "I heard a noise in the barn." He

started down the steps at a run. "Get the baby into the house. The wife will see to your needs."

On cue, a pretty young woman opened the door and stood to the side to allow Amanda to enter. "*Willkumm.*" She offered a smile as she closed the door behind them and shooed off her young son, a child about Noah's age who stood next to a little girl about one. "Ach, finally I have a visit with my sister-in-law. You must be freezing. What makes it necessary that you travel out on such a day?"

"My father. My son. Missing. My father suffers from...he isn't well." Amanda struggled to retain her footing as a blast of heat from the woodstove brought on a bout of dizziness. She began shivering uncontrollably. Lorie frowned and took her arm.

"Come, nearer the fire and I get you a cup of coffee. You suffer from the cold and you look worn out." Lorie filled a thick mug with coffee, added a generous dollop of thick cream and set it on the table and reached for the baby. "She is cold, as well. You must feed her quickly."

Amanda fumbled with her buttons and drew the baby to her breast. A moment later, she felt the baby sucking. Tiny hands battered against her and she realized they were blue with cold.

"Not to worry. I will draw a bath. We have her heated in no time." Lorie poured hot water from a pot into a tub and pumped in cold before testing it with her elbow. "Just tepid at first. We don't want her little fingers to throb. Careful." She waited for the baby to finish. When the baby was burped, she fumbled with the zippered jumpsuit and chuckled. "I am clumsy with these newfangled fasteners.

But I can see why they would be a help to a busy mother. And these *Englisch* onesies. Such a convenience!" She lowered the baby into the water, added a squirt of castile soap and began sluicing as she sang a soft, lilting lullaby.

With the baby in safe hands, Amanda walked to the window in time to hear John shout to someone inside the barn, his voice angry and sharp. Suddenly a horse and buggy broke through the partially open doors with a loud crack that sent the horse racing down the driveway toward the road. Amanda scratched furiously at the window as her father rocked from side to side in the buggy, struggling to maintain his balance.

The horse bucked in panic, and John jumped back in time to avoid being crushed. At the last second, he threw an arm up in a desperate attempt to grab the reins, but the horse was already past. "Halt! That horse isn't buggy broke. Rein in, Miller! Sit down!" His warning went unheeded.

Amanda watched in horror as the horse took the gate at an angle. Noah clung to the buggy seat, his eyes wide and terrified. She heard herself mewling as she tried to reach out. "No...no...no."

The buggy pitched and Noah flew through the air, his body suspended. After an interminable period, he landed in a water puddle and lay unmoving, with one leg crumpled at an odd angle.

The horse reared, lifting the buggy off its wheels while her father shifted, trying to balance himself. He started to topple, slowly at first, and faster when the buggy overturned. In slow motion, his body hit the wooden post, his torso wedged pinned between the buggy and the post.

John lunged forward and grabbed the buggy, using

his weight to rock it back on its shattered wheels as he crooned softly to his horse. "*Ruhe*, Prince. Stay calm."

Amanda flung open the door and raced to Noah, fearful of the worst when she saw him lying with his eyes shut and his face white with shock. She eased him from the mud and felt warmth in his little body. "Noah...come back to me, please. Please, God, let him come back."

Noah's eyes opened in a weak smile. "My leg hurts, Mama."

She ran her hand down his right leg and felt the break in his bone, just below his knee. "It's alright, baby. You're going to be fine." She checked his pulse and found it strong and steady. "Mama needs to call an ambulance," she whispered. "Hang on." She heard the 911 operator's soothing voice on her cell phone. "We need an ambulance." She glanced over to where her father lay obscured by the wrecked buggy. "Two. My father's injured, too."

She found a blanket in the wreckage and wrapped it around her son to insulate him from the wet ground, grateful when his hand gripped hers. Levi worked alongside John, slinging splintered buggy parts away to free her father. One of them turned and attempted to shield her, but he was too late. Her father lay still, his eyes open as she had seen him in his last seconds, laughing, triumphant. A thin stream of blood coagulated at the corner of his mouth. The haunted, evasive eyes of the men told her what she feared the most.

She clutched her son, torn by a need to see her father and the terror on her son's face. Images filtered through her: her father's down jacket had torn on a sharp object and goose down wafted over him like a snow flurry. Beneath her, Noah's eyes filled with shock and pain. The horse croaked a strange, eerie sound that sounded like remorse.

A blast of cold caught her, and she shivered, until someone slid a thick, crocheted afghan over her shoulders. Lorie stood behind her with a mug of steaming coffee, but nausea welled over her. She saw pity in Lorie's eyes and knew there was nothing to be done for her father. Noah clung to her, his face racked with pain.

In the distance, a siren blasted from the direction of the schoolhouse. She had a quick vision of Jacob's young brothers in their classroom. Samuel would probably gather his coat and start home on a run.

She placed a call to Jacob's cell as the ambulance approached. When he answered, she had to shout over the sound of the siren. "Something's happened, Jacob. Come home." It was all she could manage.

"Where? Amanda, what's happened?"

"Noah. My father. An accident. Noah's injured. We'll be at the hospital."

"In Medina?"

She double-checked with an EMT and nodded before she realized he couldn't see her. "Yes."

"I'll meet you there." He hesitated. "You have a ride?"

Reality slammed her with the force of a blow. "I'll ride with the ambulance. Lorie will watch the baby. I'm at your brother's. My father—"

"I'll start home. I'll meet you on the way. Be strong. We'll deal with this together."

The EMT stabilized her son while a group of Amish men gathered to watch. A police car arrived with the coroner. Everything seemed hazy, especially when a police officer approached with questions she couldn't answer.

"No problem, ma'am. We'll wait until you're ready."

Emma arrived with mugs of coffee. She stood with Lorie, apart from the emergency workers. Lorie held Jules, who was dressed in strange clothing that probably belonged to one of her own children.

Emma slipped her arm around Amanda. "Do not worry about the baby. We take good care of the little one." She handed Amanda a mason jar filled with warm soup. "For you and Jacob while you wait for the surgery. Take it. This will be a long day for you both."

Amanda pressed a quick kiss on her daughter's cheek and crawled into the back of the ambulance. Her vision seemed hazy. As the ambulance glided past the wreckage and turned into the traffic, she caught a glimpse of a black bag over her father's body. Regret caught in her chest until she struggled to breathe. *I haven't said goodbye!* One of the EMTs handed her a sack and advised her to breathe into it with her head below her knees. "Your son's stable, ma'am. Take this time to settle yourself. We'll be there in a few minutes."

The double doors of the ER swung wide. Fighting panic, Amanda followed the gurney inside. Her arms felt empty without her baby. Everything seemed surreal, especially Noah, lying so still and brave. She pressed her hands over her lips to quell her misgivings about leaving Jules with a total stranger, even if she was a relative. She signed papers before Noah disappeared into the operating room accompanied by a young Asian doctor. In the next second, she looked up to see Jacob running toward her, his arms wide to catch her as she collapsed.

"What happened?" Jacob's face was ruddy with shock. His clear blue eyes shone with an intensity that frightened her. When she tried to explain, he interrupted to demand, "Why was your father driving John's buggy? With our son?"

She shook her head to loosen the confusion of the past hour. "I couldn't find them. I took the baby and searched. I thought maybe he'd followed the creek. Or went to the schoolhouse." She looked up, seeking Jacob's understanding. "You know how he's slipped back into his childhood."

"But why the buggy? I doubt he's ever hitched one up before."

She started to argue. Felt responsible for her father, even his memory. His poor judgment. "He said something while the horse was leaving the barn. He called Noah, 'Levi.' He must have been confused and thought he was a kid again. Getting into mischief with his best friend, Levi Ruth. It's all that makes sense."

Jacob slumped, cradling his head in his hands. "Gott in Heaven, why?"

Amanda sat huddled in a pool of misery while waves of incrimination pummeled her from every side. It was her fault that her father hadn't gone to Medina with Jacob that morning; hers for choosing the wrong direction. Her fault that she was inside Lorie's house, warm and comfortable instead of inside the barn where she could have stopped the buggy. Jacob reached for her hand, but she pulled away with such force that he flinched. Afterward, she kept her head lowered to hide the tears sluicing down her face.

"Amanda? Liebchen?" He pulled her close, and she recalled the night they watched the moon at the beach in Oregon. She eased into his arms and felt the warmth of his body beneath his jacket. "Not your fault. None of this. Our son will yet recover from his adventure. As for your father, well, he made a mistake because of his illness. He would never have meant to hurt his family, would he?"

She shook her head. "He didn't know what he was doing. I'm not angry with Dad." She reached for his handkerchief and sobbed, "But, Jacob, I would give anything to just go back to this morning. Anything."

"Gott doesn't make such bargains," Jacob whispered. "I know this." She looked up, startled at the pain in his voice. "Your father left us on his own terms, wife. In good times. Noah will remember sitting in the buggy, watching his grandfather be a young man again. Is that so bad?"

She shook her head. "Dad hated that his mind was slipping. He wanted to be remembered for his prime. You know?" She tried to continue, but a lump in her throat made speech impossible.

"We will honor his memory, wife. He was a good man."

She heard the sincerity in Jacob's voice, but her heart seemed devoid of feeling, as though she were wandering in a mist. "I can't get my head around that he's gone. I miss him so much." She hesitated when another couple entered the surgery area and took seats. Her stomach rumbled, and she reached into her purse and found the glass jar still warm. "Your mother's soup," she said. "She told me to make sure you had some."

Jacob grinned and unscrewed the lid. "Food is her answer to every woe."

The surgery doors opened, and the surgeon appeared, his face wreathed in a smile. "Good news. A simple fracture of the tibia. Your son will be off his feet for a while, but children are resilient. He'll recover pretty fast."

Chapter Thirty

"**D**ad asked to be cremated. He wanted to be buried next to Mom at St. Paul's Cemetery back home. That's where he belongs." Amanda sat on the stoop, listening to the creek in the fading light of a long day. "I'll honor his wishes." She hesitated a moment before she continued. "He was the best father. A special man." She turned to rest her cheek against Jacob's. "I miss him so much my heart aches."

"He was happy to be here. To close the circle of his life, you know? In this childhood home, he was a boy again, filled with mischief." Jacob's words settled the vacant part of her heart, and she forced a smile, biting back tears.

"His final act of rebellion."

"Daed said he looked so fierce and happy," Jacob said.

She smiled. "He came out of that barn like a four-teen-year-old sneaking out for a joyride with Levi. He was fearless. Noah, too. They were off to conquer legions." She shifted to relieve the pressure of the cement steps as a songbird returned to its nest in the wisteria overhead. A thought interrupted her musing, and she turned. "You paid your brother for the buggy, right? And the fence?"

Jacob shook his head. "Daed said we're square. He has the money from my buggy. One of the others brought him a newly milled post for the gate. It is not our people's way to profit from a loss such as this. No money will change hands over the matter."

Our people. She heard the slip and swallowed. At the Ruth farm men had already pounded in a new post to replace the broken one. The cows were returning to the field after the evening milking, and Jacob's family was inside at their supper. "In my world, someone would sue."

"No lawsuit. Gott's will this happened. Forgive and give comfort to the grieving."

"Your family has cooked us so many meals this week."

"Ja." Jacob seemed distracted. "Seems we were meant to have our kraut and wursts after all."

Amanda gave him a crooked smile. "Dad felt so bad for the way your family treated you that day."

He shrugged. "It was what it was."

"We talked about it later. The night before he died." She hesitated as the scene replayed itself in her head. "He was so clear-headed and alert. Serious. He told me something I never knew. He said, 'I've been down that road too, Peanut. I held it against my father that he wasn't the man I needed him to be.'"

Jacob considered her words, his eyes dusky and thoughtful. "That's why he never came home again?"

She nodded. "And when he finally did, he regressed back into childhood."

Behind them, in the living room, Noah stirred in his bed. Upstairs, Jules woke and began fussing. Amanda stood and shook out her skirt. "Time for me to return to the land of the living."

When she met his eye, Jacob watched her with an unfathomable look. "Liebchen, you grieve as you see fit."

She paused with her hand on the screen door handle. "You mean that?"

"You know I do." He squinted, waiting to hear what she might be hiding behind her question. "I know you, liebchen. You will do this in your own manner."

She released her hold on the door and slumped against the screen. "I heard you on the phone. You told someone we'd return home. Was it Dad's lawyer?"

"Yep. Tax stuff. Insurance stuff. I need to reassure the employees they're going to be okay."

"When?"

He considered. "We need to start home day after tomorrow. Any problem with that?"

She took a deep breath and slowly released it. "What if I stay behind for another month? With the kids?"

"Alone?"

She held her hand up to ward off his protest. "Wait, hear me out. My best friend's here. And your mother. And Lorie. And your brothers. The kids need to know their family. And I need to discover who my dad was. I want to spend time seeing things through his eyes." She glanced up at Jacob's expression, serious and thoughtful, and her heart soared with hope. "I'm not ready to say goodbye to my father yet."

Jacob slowly nodded. "Noah will need to stay off his feet for a few weeks. You think you can manage?"

"I have Carol. I'll find a meal delivery service."

Jacob laughed. "Good luck with that. You will maybe eat a lot of pizza."

Amanda laughed. "Your mother won't let her grandkids starve."

"The women in my family are good people. I'll miss you guys." Jacob rose and followed her inside.

"One month. We'll go home as soon as Noah can travel." She laughed. "Go. Pack. I'll book you a round-trip ticket. That way you'll have to return."

Jacob's eyes burned with intensity as he reached for her. "You think I would not return? This is nothing to tease about. You are my world."

❦

From the driver's seat of her SUV, Amanda pointed to the plane taxiing down the runway. "Wave to your daddy, Noah. He's going home to make sure Yankee eats his hay. He'll call you tomorrow night."

"Will Daddy die like Grandpa?"

Amanda slammed her eyes shut and swallowed. "Grandpa will watch over Daddy. And we can say a prayer for both of them tonight. Deal?"

"Deal."

They watched until the plane disappeared before starting home. "Aunt Carol's coming over. She's bringing egg rolls. Your favorite."

"I want Grandma's schnitzen pie."

"No pie tonight. We have applesauce."

"Applesauce is for babies. I want schnitzen pie."

"Sorry, bud. Not your turn to choose." She kept her voice light. *The Amish have it easy. They eat what's on the table. Easy-peasy.* "Come on, Noah, let's go back to our house."

"Can I ride in Grandpa's swing?"

"Absolutely. He fixed the ropes for you. He wanted you to be safe." Amanda eased the car into traffic and checked her rearview mirror. "One day you'll be a hero, like your grandpa was to me. And you'll have grandchildren who love you, too."

"Does Grossmummi love me?"

Amanda tried to hide her smile. "I don't know. Why don't you ask her?"

"She won't tell me." His eyes lit with mischief. "I know what. I'll ask her to make me a pie."

At the stoplight, she reached to contain a curl that had escaped Noah's crop of curls. His hair was so different from his father's, but his heart was Jacob's, through and through. *He's the best of us.* "That's a great idea," she said.

In her new, forward-facing car seat, Jules was looking around with such intensity that Amanda was loath to disturb her. *She'll be like my mother, thoughtful and wise.* When the light changed, she pulled into the traffic and started home. Silence rode in the back seat, a rare opportunity to reflect. Even if their family wasn't perfect, they had a lifetime to get it right.

A Look At Book Three:

PROMISE OF FAMILY

FALL INTO A STORY OF HEALING AND REDEMPTION IN THIS CAPTIVATING AMISH ROMANCE

Following an unfortunate accident, Jacob Ruth returns home to Oregon—leaving Amanda Miller stranded in Ohio with her new in-laws. Resolute in her mission to reconcile Jacob's family issues, Amanda tries to build bridges with their Amish roots, but instead finds solace helping Jacob's shunned sister reveal a crushing secret.

Witnessing the profound impact of the Amish rules of shunning and banishment, Amanda insists on Jacob's return to Ohio. But when tragedy strikes, the question of whether Jacob's family will ever be whole again instills fear into their hearts.

As Jacob and Amanda embark on a whirlwind journey full of deep connections and transformative lifestyles, they must learn to embrace all that life has to offer...including the unexpected promise of a new family.

Uncovering hard truths, can Jacob and Amanda accept the idea that family might not match the picture they originally had in mind?

AVAILABLE FEBRUARY 2024

About the Author

A fifth-generation Californian, Anne Schroeder's love of the West was fueled by stories of bandits and hangings, her great-grandfather and his neighbors working together to blast the Norwegian Grade in Southern California out of solid rock, Indian caves, and women who made their own way. She worked her way through Cal Poly University with a variety of odd jobs that included waitressing at a truck stop cafe in Cholame—near the spot where James Dean died.

She recently served as President of Women Writing the West, and her short stories and essays have appeared in print and online magazines. She has also been awarded several Will Rogers Medallion Awards and LAURA Short Fiction Literary Awards for western and inspirational fiction.

Anne lives in Southern Oregon with her husband, dogs, and free-range chickens where she volunteers regularly for the St. Vincent de Paul soup kitchen.